The Seven Daughters of Dupree

Nikesha Elise Williams

SIMON &
SCHUSTER

London · New York · Amsterdam/Antwerp · Sydney/Melbourne · Toronto · New Delhi

First published in the United States by Scout Press,
an imprint of Simon & Schuster LLC, 2026

First published in Great Britain by Simon & Schuster UK Ltd, 2026

1 3 5 7 9 10 8 6 4 2

Simon & Schuster UK Ltd, 1st Floor
222 Gray's Inn Road, London WC1X 8HB

Simon & Schuster Australia, Sydney
Simon & Schuster India, New Delhi

www.simonandschuster.co.uk
www.simonandschuster.com.au
www.simonandschuster.co.in

The authorised representative in the EEA is Simon & Schuster Netherlands BV,
Herculesplein 96, 3584 AA Utrecht, Netherlands. info@simonandschuster.nl

Simon & Schuster strongly believes in freedom of expression and stands against
censorship in all its forms. For more information, visit BooksBelong.com

A CIP catalogue record for this book is available from the British Library

Hardback ISBN: 978-1-3985-3426-1
eBook ISBN: 978-1-3985-3428-5
Audio ISBN: 978-1-3985-3430-8

Printed and Bound in the UK using 100% Renewable Electricity
at CPI Group (UK) Ltd

MIX
Paper | Supporting
responsible forestry
FSC® C013604

The
Seven
Daughters
of
Dupree

For Annelise and Mylen, me,
Mommy (Jacqueline) and Grandma (Rilla Mae),
Ida and Wrilla and Sarah,
may we forever reign.

I go forth along, and stand as ten thousand.

—Maya Angelou, "Our Grandmothers"

Prologue

They cut off her head because she ran. But who could know? Certainly not Tati. She was looking for her daddy. Her mama, Nadia, wouldn't tell her. Gladys, her mimi, wouldn't tell her either. So she searched for him. She didn't know to search for anyone else. It wasn't like there was a burial or body; no coffin, no cemetery. But in a way she found her. In fact, she found them all, including her daddy. In the kitchen table whisperings and the basement murmurings where her mother used a hot comb to press out her hair every Saturday night.

Part 1

Questions

1.

The noxious scent of burnt hair and relaxer coldcocked Tati with a closed fist, singeing her nose hairs, as she made her way into the basement. A yellow neon sign that read NADIA'S NUBIAN SALON hung on the wall of the landing, led the way for customers who entered through the back door. Not that Mimi ever came that way. She insisted on coming through the front. As soon as she crossed the threshold, her eyes roamed as her gloved hands swiped across furniture that was neither dusted nor polished, and her feet traversed the floor that wasn't mopped. For the unwashed dishes in the sink, she shook her head and kissed her teeth.

Behind the heavy basement door, Mary J. Blige's *My Life* album provided the soundtrack for the Sunday-morning appointment. Nadia sang along in her own version of praise and worship. She didn't abide no gospel, and since all the R&B stations got holy from seven to noon, Nadia was her own DJ, despite Mimi's misgivings. The elder woman never said anything. The only indication of her displeasure was the turned corners of her lips, which made her face look as if she were sucking on something sour. She knew that if she wanted to get her hair done, music was Nadia's nonnegotiable, especially Mary. It was Nadia's third copy of the CD. She had played the other two out so much they skipped. At least that's what she said, but Tati knew dropping hair grease, spritz, and holding spray on the discs didn't help the scratches none either.

Tati retrieved the broom hidden behind the sliding gray door that separated the laundry room from the rest of the salon and swept the perimeter. She moved between the two washbowls along the right wall and the three dryers on the left before she treaded through the middle, where Mimi was enthroned in the client chair. The curling iron hissed in Nadia's hand. All of her Soft Sheen and Dudley's products along with rollers, curlers, and irons of different widths were in arm's reach on shelves that butted up against the basement wall below a second flickering, yellow NADIA'S NUBIAN SALON sign.

"Tati, stop standing there like a dazed deer and help me," Nadia snapped.

"Whatchu want me to do?"

"Damnit, Tati, *help*. Finish sweeping. Clean out the washbowl. Pick up Mimi's towel that fell to the ground and put it in the basket. I know your eyes good 'cause we just got 'em checked. You need to put 'em to use and earn your keep after all the money I'm spending on you for your lil' birthday."

"Nadia, that's not right," Mimi said.

"Whatchu mean that's not right?" Nadia asked exasperated. "Yesterday we did the movies and dinner at the Cheesecake Factory with Toya and Desirée on top of shopping at the Water Tower Place. *And* she sprung her class trip on me at the last minute. Shit, I had to give her a postdated check. She lucky I don't make her lil' ass go get a work permit to bag groceries at Jewel's. Earning her keep is the least she could do. Ain't that what you told me when I was little?"

"I told you a lot of thangs when you was little. It don't mean I was right."

"It worked for me. I turned out all right."

"And we want Tati to be better than all right!"

Mimi turned in her seat and glared at Nadia, who only rolled her eyes and clicked the curlers. A direction and a threat. *Turn around before you get burned.* Mimi huffed then faced forward.

"Tati, where is Desirée anyway?" Nadia asked.

"Upstairs sleeping."

"She spent the night?" Mimi asked.

"First time since we were five," Tati answered excitedly.

"And she still sleep while you workin' wit' ya mama?"

Tati shrugged. Desirée had been her best friend for years, and she'd never known her to be a morning person. She was always late and they were bussed to school. The mornings Desirée didn't miss the bus completely, the driver waited on the corner at Sixty-Fifth and Green for her to come out. Sometimes the driver would even go around the block and pull up to Desirée's front door—after Tati had pointed it out—and beep the horn to encourage her to hurry up. Sometimes she made it, sometimes she didn't. When Nadia had yelled up the stairs for Tati to come help, Desirée didn't move and Tati didn't make her. She secretly hoped she could get through Mimi's appointment with Desirée being none the wiser.

Mimi asked, "Tati, how old you is now?"

"Fourteen," she answered.

"Your mama told me you got your first monthly yesterday."

"Dang, Ma!"

"Ain't no secrets in this house," Nadia said.

"Oh yeah, there are, but that's what you get for ruttin' 'round with a married man."

"It wasn't just me ruttin'," Nadia responded through clenched teeth.

Tati was so focused on her mother's pursed mouth, Nadia's tell that she wanted to smoke, she didn't realize she'd lost her grip on the broom until it clanged on the lacquered copper of the concrete floor, unnerving them both.

"What the hell you doin'?" Nadia yelled.

"It dropped on accident."

"You wouldn't have no accidents if you wasn't listening so damn hard."

"She wouldn't have to sneak and listen if you would just tell the girl what she wanna know," Mimi said.

"He ain't here and ain't ever been here," Nadia said. "Ain't I enough?"

It was a refrain Tati heard often: *Ain't I enough?* One Nadia usually said when she was pressed about the identity of Tati's father. The subject came up once a week when Mimi got her hair done before church.

"Why you always do this?" Nadia asked, clicking and turning the curlers against Mimi's hair.

"Do what?"

"Mention that girl daddy. He ain't been around since I told him I was pregnant."

"Because you didn't try hard enough to make him take care of his responsibilities."

"What was I supposed to do, huh? Go around asking random strangers if they knew where he went?"

"Oh, so that's what you call friends now? Strangers?" Mimi hmphed and crossed her arms.

"Don't start," Nadia warned. "Toya and I are in a good place."

"What y'all talkin' about?" Desirée asked, entering the basement.

"Nothin'," Nadia said quickly.

"Just about how fast y'all growing up," Mimi answered. "Becoming young women. Able to have babies."

"Mama, ain't neither one of them thinkin' 'bout havin' no babies. They don't even have boyfriends."

"You don't know what they got. They could be invitin' trouble with lil' snot-faced boys, and you and your friend would be none the wiser."

"That's the same thing you said when I got my period. Carried on for days to anybody who rang the phone, unless it was a bill collector, about how I was sure to bring babies out of wedlock—"

"And you did, didn't you?" Mimi turned around and glared at Nadia. "I rest my case."

"Keep it up and you'll have to find somebody else to do your hair before church on Sundays."

Nadia's threat, empty and devoid of emotion, was all she had. The only leverage over her own mother she could hoist with a wave of her hand and a gesture toward the door. But Mimi didn't move. Tati shook her head and sighed, exasperated, as she walked across the room toward the burgundy futon to take a seat beside Desirée. Never one to let an insolent child go unchecked, Mimi glared at her, demanded to know what she had the nerve to be huffing for.

Nadia intervened. "Tati, chill out. When I'm done, your mimi will be on her way, and then we'll go to breakfast to continue celebrating your birthday. Focus on that and let the rest slide off you like bullshit on ice."

Now it was Mimi's turn to huff, but whatever she wanted to say, she swallowed all the way down to her feet. Patent leather shoes tapped her thoughts on the metal bar of the burgundy chair, ripping wide the run in her pantyhose. Mary sang as Nadia clicked the curlers, which smoked and sizzled against the blue grease. Mimi didn't flinch. She didn't give Nadia the satisfaction.

"You done," Nadia said, snatching the cape from around her neck.

"Thank you, daughter."

"Mm-hmm."

"So it's just the three of y'all going to breakfast?" Mimi asked.

"No, Toya's on her way," Nadia answered.

"Ooh wee! I knew my ears were burning in the car for a reason," Toya Grant said, coming through the back door. "The first thing I hear coming inside is my name; I must be about to win me some money."

Toya's bright laughter and feet slapping across the floor added to the din as Nadia cleared her station and Mimi pushed herself up from the client chair and grabbed her purse from the futon beside Tati.

Straightening her body, she asked, "What y'all doing after breakfast?"

"Dang, Mama, you nosy," Nadia jeered. "Ain't you gon' be late for church or something?"

Tati and Desirée erupted into a fit of giggles on the futon, Tati louder than her friend because she knew her mother's assessment of her grandmother to be true. Mimi liked to know too much, especially when she thought someone, namely her family, was intentionally hiding something from her. She also loved to be right. It was a dangerous combination. One that led her to embarrass and humiliate. An act she relished and wrapped in scripture as justification.

"'Pride goeth before destruction, and a haughty spirit before a fall,'" she'd say.

Tati knew the proverb well. During spring break, when Nadia left her with Mimi while she went to Atlanta for a picnic, Mimi had made her write lines. She'd copied that verse one hundred times from the old Bible with the smooth worn cover, loose spine, and frayed golden edges that had names crossed out and rewritten inside the front. Her offense that day: dancing with her headphones on in front of Mimi's full-length oval bedroom mirror with the initials EGD etched in the frame. She usually wasn't so reckless as to do something she knew Mimi would have a conniption over. But between her reflection in the mirror and the bass line beating heavy in her ears, something had come over her. Her movements were free and rhythmic, as if she didn't have control over her own body. Sitting on the futon with Desirée and now Toya, Tati was relieved to finally see Mimi get back all the ire she dished out.

"So, you gon' answer my question, or y'all gon' keep on laughin' like somethin' funny?" Mimi demanded.

"We're going back downtown to take the girls by Union Station so they can see it before their trip to DC."

"That fancy school they go to is puttin' them on the train?"

"Seeing as how *we, the parents*, are paying for it, they for damn sure ain't flyin'," Toya said.

"Yeah, Mama, didn't you come to Chicago on the train?"

"Me and your daddy came up in the segregation car at the old Central Station. That's where Eugene worked as a Pullman porter before they built Union Station. I'll be sure to see Tati off when it's time ya hear."

"That's not necessary," Nadia said.

"It is for me," Mimi said, her voice lower as if she were talking to herself. "I have to see that Tati's experience gon' be different from mine."

"What was your experience?" Tati asked.

"Don't worry about it, baby. It's not for you to know. Everything don't need to be remembered."

"What I know is y'all need to go get dressed," Toya said. "Nadia, I don't know why you had me come over here this damn early and y'all ain't even ready to walk out the door."

"Have you met you?" Nadia chuckled. "You always late."

"I still didn't need two hours' advance notice, and we just going to the Pancake House in Hyde Park."

"If you would learn to be on time, you wouldn't need that much notice," Mimi muttered.

"Mama, don't start," Nadia admonished.

"It's all right, Nadia," Toya said. "Your mama always likes starting shit with me."

"I didn't *start* anything," Mimi said. "Just made a suggestion. But, you know, some folks take advice. Some folks don't. Some folks take care of their kids. Some folks don't."

"Mama, go to church," Nadia said sharply. "We don't need you carryin' on like this."

"Nadia, your mama been carrying on like this since we was comin' up," Toya said. "The calendar changes. She don't. And in the end you always take her side."

"If you don't like it, ain't none of y'all got to be friends, the girls included," Mimi sneered. "You can learn to stay with your own kind and your own line."

"That's enough."

Nadia's clenched-teeth yell sent Toya and Mimi to their respective sparring corners. The bomb, always set to five seconds between them, was defused for now. Tati and Desirée, aware of the nice-nasty arguments that sometimes flared between their mothers, shook their heads as they sat on the futon. They had learned years ago to stop asking, *What's wrong?* and *Why y'all always mad at each other?* Questions that got them evil eyes from all adults present and a swift rebuke to *Stay out of grown folks' business.* But just because they stopped asking didn't mean they stopped wondering. They swallowed the discomfort and pretended they didn't see the sour faces.

"Desi, I brought you something," Toya said.

She reached inside her purse and handed Desirée a new disposable camera.

"Ooh, thank you," Desirée gushed. "I finished the roll on the one I brought while we were out last night."

"I figured as much," Toya said with a smile.

It was Desirée's dream to be a photographer. She had hundreds of pictures of random people from all over her neighborhood in Englewood. Once she opened the plastic packaging, she aimed the viewfinder first at Tati, then Toya and Nadia, and finally at Mimi, who continued to linger in the basement. Click. Flash. Click. Flash.

"Girl, stop taking pictures of me!" Mimi yelped, throwing her hands in front of her face. "I ain't one of your little friends."

"I got it now." Desirée giggled.

Toya and Nadia laughed as well, the ice thawing between them, if only for the moment.

"I told you to go to church." Nadia continued laughing.

"I'm going. Just tell me one thing. Is either one of y'all chaperoning the girls on this trip?"

Toya and Nadia looked at each other and then blankly at Mimi.

"Mm-hmm," she huffed, readjusting her purse from her shoulder to across her body. "I don't know why I thought the womenfolk would take care of their daughters better than they do. In my day, my mama and daddy wouldn't've let me go so far away by myself without their personal supervision," she said, voice rising with the lie no one could detect.

"Well, it ain't your day anymore, is it?" Toya muttered.

"Mama, we doing the best we can, but we're single mothers."

"And whose fault is that?" Mimi glared from Toya to Nadia. "It's just a sin and a shame. The both of you. Just a sin and a shame."

Neither Tati nor Desirée made eye contact with their mothers, even though they heard the insult loud and clear. One that warped Toya's and Nadia's faces with frowns and fatigue.

"Walk your mimi out," Nadia commanded.

Tati pushed herself up from the futon and followed Mimi upstairs, stopping by the cold fireplace in the living room just before the door.

"Give me some sugar," Mimi said, pulling Tati into a hug. She whispered, "I'ma come see you off on the train, but you got to remember to be careful, you hear."

"I'ma be with my school," Tati said. "Nothing's going to happen."

"I'm not saying it will. I'm just sayin' be careful."

"What was it like for you on the train with Papa Eugene?" Tati asked.

Mimi paused. One hand on the door, the other at her side, the surly and saturnine woman from the basement was gone. Instead, her entire face became a kaleidoscope of clouds. Her blue-rimmed eyes never left from their fixed position. Entranced, Mimi didn't move her mouth or further crease the wrinkles in her face. She barely breathed. She stared past Tati through the hallway, as if it were the corridors of the train station she once traversed. As if it would impart a knowledge about her own arrival years before Tati was born.

"Mimi," Tati repeated gently. "What was it like for you coming on the train with Papa Eugene?"

"It was the longest . . . hardest ride of my life."

Tati nodded as Mimi opened the door to leave. Before she crossed the threshold she warned Tati about growing up too fast.

"I'm not a little girl anymore."

"No, sugah, but you'll always be a little girl to me. I remember when you was born. A blessing in a burden."

Tati chewed the inside of her cheek.

"You was the cutest little chocolate baby, with these big old eyes, like the moon." Another cloud passed over her face; thoughts unknown.

"I love you," Mimi said. "Happy birthday."

Tati didn't respond. Teeth in cheeks, heat beneath her skin, and stings in her eyes, she closed the door behind her grandmother and took the stairs to her room two by two as feelings about her unknown parentage bubbled to the surface. She didn't want to go back to the basement. Didn't want to face Toya and Nadia or even Desirée with the slightest glint of tears in her eyes. Where her friend had photos, she had words. Tati pulled her new monogrammed journal from between her mattress and box spring, flopped across the twin frame, and wrote.

Dear Daddy,

    I'm 14 now
    Legs brown

Same for my hair and eyes
Mimi say she worried 'cause my hips round
It don't matter
Ain't no boys calling
Phone don't ring
My line don't sing
I just pose in the mirror
Mama say I'm looking for the wrong kind of attention
But I just be looking at the symmetry of my face
Trying to see yours, but hers I can't erase
Oh, I forgot to mention
I think I wanna pierce my nose
But mama would have a fit
I suppose
And I can't do something drastic like that
Can't alter my appearance until you get back
Or until we meet
At least
I just wanted to let you know
What to be on the lookout for
Your little girl
Maybe a bit bigger
Chocolate like you, I think
When mama's drunk she cuss me and say I got your mahogany
*   brown*
Just thought you'd want to know what I look like now

Love Tati
March 26, 1995

P.S. Today's my birthday!

2.

Emma never had a birthday. Born an orphan, she had only Evangeline to rely on for raising. Evangeline being the root-working woman she was, didn't believe in celebrating births and deaths on the same day. Especially when they were linked. It wasn't until Emma was nearing her ninth year that she even realized she should have been keeping up with her age. That it was something for her to keep up with, let alone celebrate. The confirmation of her newly piqued curiosity came in a series of events.

It started when Zephaniah Foster Dupree was in transition. His wife dead the year before and his two sons killed in the Battle of Mobile Bay, he had no one but his former property, who stayed on sharecropping to see him through to the other side. Well, them and Evangeline. She stayed on the land, but she never worked it. Not enslaved. Not free. She was the cook, but her real business was birthing babies and closing eyes. Called on to care and comfort whenever folks, white or colored, were crossing paths between the living and the dead.

When it was Zephaniah Foster's time, she remained by his bedside with Emma, her assistant, beside her. Emma did the fetching Evangeline no longer could, gathering the roots, herbs, and flowers as directed. From her basket of white willow bark and devil's claw spiced with turmeric, ginger, and a little lavender, Evangeline made up the tea to relieve his pain. She had expected the potion to put him to sleep, but instead he remained awake. Fully lucid and in a talkative mood.

"When this is all over, it's you who's gon' get all I got left," he said.

Evangeline nodded in response. With his time so near, she knew not to put too much stock in anything he said, if she ever did. White men were good for saying one thing and doing another. Even facing death, they'd lie themselves to heaven, telling tall tales to the Lord. She listened, passing time by pushing a needle through an embroidery patch, humming her lips and rocking her back to disrupt the silence of bodies ceasing to function.

He continued, "You know Evangeline did more to keep me rich than I ever did."

Zephaniah Foster directed his attention toward Emma. He didn't call her to his bedside for fear of seeing a mixed reflection that would surely haunt him on his way to death's door. Instead, he talked at her while she sat idle on the floor at the foot of the bed.

"Everybody would have died if it wasn't for your mammy. I kept 'em bred and she kept 'em fed. When the yellow fever spread through the quarters, I thought I was going to lose it all. The niggers and the harvest. But Evangeline got us through. Healed them all one by one. Wasn't down longer than a week or two before we were back up and running. Anything I needed her to do, she did. Even when she didn't want to . . . like how you was born. I've never forgotten that. After all these years, I got no choice but to finally make it right."

That evening, when it was just Emma and Evangeline in the quarter shack, Emma asked, "What Mr. Dupree mean when he said you didn't want to do something when I was born?"

"Chile, don't concern yourself with the fool talk of a dead man," Evangeline dismissed. "He got to get all his words out before he go in the ground."

Emma wanted to mind her ma'am. Had planned to, really, had

not Zephaniah Foster died in the night. Between the sorry gathering for the funeral and no one else to read the last will and testament to besides those who worked the land, Evangeline was some surprised when it came to pass that he had told the truth.

"As for the matter of my estate, all land parcels and property structures, I, Zephaniah Foster Dupree, of sound mind and body, do leave all my worldly possessions to Evangeline and daughter Emma."

The Land's End town attorney, a man by the name of Watkins, stumbled over the words as he read them. His forehead damp beneath the curved brim of his top hat, he removed it to wipe his brow as he read the words again and again. More to himself than anyone else, because who could believe a white man had left his house, his land, his money, clothes, and jewels, to a colored, let alone a colored *woman*. It was scandalous if it was true. Begged the question, what kind of hoodoo had she worked on him to make him so benevolent in death when he had been anything but kind in life? But the gift was given on account of one condition being fulfilled.

"Emma must attend school to learn the facts and figuring of an enterprise such as this."

Watkins, so besotted by the words he'd read, kept murmuring to himself. But the matter was settled. The will final. Since it was written in Zephaniah Foster's own hand, and with no living relatives to contest its validity, Watkins folded the papers, placed them back in the Bible he'd retrieved them from, and handed it all over to Evangeline—will, Bible, and keys.

He had barely galloped his horse across the boundary line of the Dupree farm before Evangeline gave her first order to the families working the land in freedom as they had enslaved. "Take what you want and tear the house and that tree down," she said, nodding toward the large oak standing proud between the stables and the shacks where they lived. "I'ma continue minding my business, and y'all can mind your'n."

The next day, obedient to a dead man's wishes, Evangeline sent Emma to the freedmen's school, lest she be haunted by a restless soul on the other side. It was inside the school, a quarter shack on an abandoned farm nearby, where Emma's curiosity was piqued and she was left with another question. Upon introducing herself and where she came from, the teacher asked if she knew her birthday. Emma stared blankly at the brown woman, whose hard vowels and clipped speech belied her Northern-born upbringing. The teacher tried again. Asked if she had any idea how old she might be. It was a question Emma had never heard before. What did she know about age?

Of course she returned to Evangeline for an answer. One the old woman was reluctant to give.

"Why the teacher need to know that?" she asked.

"To put me with my right group," Emma answered.

"Ain't like they ever seen you befo'. Why cain't they just put you with the new chillun? You don't know nothing 'bout no book learning."

"But do you know how old I am, or my birthday, or when I was born?" Emma persisted.

"I suspect it's in the record books I pulled out of the big house, but I can't 'cipher them letters and numbers."

The answer was satisfactory. Enough to keep Emma from questioning even more. She didn't know that on the occasion of her birth Evangeline had kept an excellent record of her own. One she would never forget. Evangeline recognized the coming of Emma's day of return with the change of the seasons from winter to spring. The encroaching of longer days and shorter nights always brought with it a thickness in the atmosphere. More than humidity, there was a heaviness hanging. Lurking. The kind of environment where the wet heat grips and you either grow or you rot. And even that is a kind of growth in itself. Especially for a secret. The rot spreads and metastasizes over everything in its path until the malignant cannot be deciphered from the healthy, the good from the bad, the help from the harm. Untold mysteries thrive in such an underbelly. They threaten to consume all who try to contain them. Evangeline could always feel it creeping like moss or a vine. It was waiting to greet her, to remind her of what happened before and what was still to come.

That's why Evangeline welcomed Emma's third inquiry all on her own. Too full with the untold threatening to burst, it happened on Census Day. Evangeline had heard about the assistant marshals going from house to house, taking record of all the families. They'd started on the other side of the sliver of land that had been cordoned off by white contractors driving colored inmates for the railroad to come. When a marshal finally reached the Dupree place, Evangeline stood outside the quarter shack with Emma and readily gave him the information he asked for.

Name: Evangeline Dupree.

Race: Colored.

Age: Unknown.

Occupation: Midwife.

Husband: Henry Dupree. Deceased.

"Ma'am, you was married?" Emma asked.

"We jumped de broom when he couldn't stud no mo'," Evangeline began. "But the consumption got him couple years before you came along. Was the only one I couldn't save. Truth be told, my Henry was so stubborn, he ain't wannna be saved."

Emma chuckled with Evangeline. The census taker, peeved and impatient, cleared his throat and spat a brown, slimy wad of tobacco-tinged phlegm near their feet. They both shuffled over to avoid the mucus sitting atop the dusty road. While Emma stared at the ground, Evangeline met the man's icy gaze with her own cold glare, both incensed by the other's insolence. He continued:

Children: None.

"Then who is this gal here beside you?" the census taker asked.

"She mine, but she ain't *mine*. Cain't you tell? She in the world by herself. You can record her as such."

"We don't record children without they parents."

"Well, you gon' have to for this one," Evangeline said, looking down toward Emma. "I'll tell you what you need to know and you can write it down just like you did for me."

The marshal, instructed to make as little show of authority as possible, disagreed in silence and wrote the information as Evangeline gave it.

Name: Emma Dupree.

Race: Mulatto.

Age:

Emma looked expectantly for Evangeline's answer. Never taking her eyes away from the marshal, she said, "She was born the same year the war started."

"Eighteen and sixty-one," he said.

Emma did the quick figuring in her head and exclaimed, "I'm nine, ma'am. I'm nine years old."

"Yes, you is. Now hush."

Occupation:

Husband:

Children:

"Is there a place where she can put her parents?" Evangeline asked.

"I guess she can write it down where it says children. The gov'ment'll figure it out."

~~Children~~ Parents:

Emma looked to Evangeline. Evangeline to the marshal. She said, "For her pa, write Zephaniah Foster Dupree."

"Old Master Dupree was my pa?" Emma asked.

"Who else could it be?"

Evangeline shifted her weight from foot to foot on the rickety porch where she stood as the marshal dipped his pen in ink and wrote the name as he'd been told. When he finished forming the final letters, he and Emma turned expectantly, but Evangeline had gone silent. Eyes closed, mouth shut in a line, she neither looked nor spoke, though she could feel Emma's eyes imploring her to give up the ghosts.

The marshal sighed with edged impatience. "What's the ma's name? I knows you know it."

"I knows it. But you don't need it." Evangeline stepped off the porch and marched past the marshal toward the farm storehouse. "C'mon, Emma. I gots work to do."

Emma scampered behind her, leaving the marshal as bewildered as she. Evangeline figured an age and a pa would have to be enough for one day. It was more knowledge than Emma had ever had about herself her whole life, but now that she'd been fed she was insatiable. Hungry for what Evangeline swallowed. Greedy, she peppered her with questions.

"Did you know my *real* ma'am?"

"What was she like?"

"What did she look like?"

"Was she big like you?"

"Light like me?"

"Wait, did you deliver me from her like you do the other women's babies?"

It was the last question Evangeline silently prayed Emma wouldn't think to ask. The girl had been assisting her with births for the last couple years. She was training her up in roots and wombs and knowing when to pluck at their peak both herbs and babies. She'd told herself as she watched the marshal make his way to their door that she'd tell Emma the truth. The whole bloody, sordid affair. But now that the time had come, she wasn't sure if she could handle it, never mind Emma.

"Ma'am, did you birth me too?" Emma asked again.

Evangeline stole a glance at the girl, who had eyes wide as the moon. Though she wasn't dark like the cosmos her mama came from, she held her features all the same. Eyes, lips, dimples, and twitching ears. Everything else was Zephaniah Foster Dupree. Evangeline studied Emma—the innocent and the evil resting in one face—and made her choice.

"Ma'am?" Emma asked again.

"I birthed you," Evangeline said. "'Twas the same day yo' real mammy died."

"Oh." Emma paused. Relief and confusion washed over her at once, her delight short-lived much like her own mother's life. Evangeline didn't know how old she was when she died. Only that she was young, just a few years into her tide. Fecund and nubile enough to carry and birth, but much too young to die.

Evangeline turned the only words she had to describe that day over in her mouth. She folded them between her lips, teeth, and tongue, like she would later do to her chewing tobacco. Only this she had to be careful how she spit. Wouldn't be no tin can to catch it but a person. Emma. The daughter.

"What was her name?" Emma asked quietly.

Another question Evangeline hadn't expected. She was ready to answer what happened and why. She was even ready to answer for her role, forced at the lash of Zephaniah Foster Dupree as she was. She was not prepared to color in the details. The defining features that make a person whole. Amongst them being a name. To speak of the dead in anything but reverence and remembrance of who they were when they were alive was to curse them on the other side. Evangeline didn't know enough about Emma's ma'am's beginnings to tell her about the end *and* give her name. That she could not do. She could not call forth a spirit and not have pleasant things to say. Names were sacred. She wouldn't risk tarnishing the pure with the profane.

Instead, she hedged her attempt at honesty. She said, "The name we called her wasn't her real one. You know, your ma'am came from across the water. Old Master Dupree named her before she got here."

"Well, what did he call her?"

"That's enough." Evangeline heaved a sigh. "You don't need to know everything today."

Satisfied with what she had, Emma returned to school bubbling with information for her teacher and few friends who hadn't been snatched away to prepare for harvest. Giddy at the chance to confirm she was nine years old, she had forgotten to ask after her birthday, or even what season she was born, because she knew Evangeline didn't keep up with no calendar. She could call Christmas and New Year's and sometimes Easter but not much else. She followed the seasons. Planting season. Growing season. Harvest season. Resting season. It was generally the same for the women as it was for the land, with her busiest time for births being in the late summer and early fall, before rest was necessitated on account of the healing body and a demanding new babe.

"When you go home, ask your ma'am about the time when you was born, and whenever it is, we'll be sure to celebrate your birthday," the teacher instructed.

Emma did as she was told. Ran all the way home with her lunch pail, her primary reader, her math ledger, and the Bible passed to her from Zephaniah Foster Dupree. She was breathless and eager when she arrived to an empty quarter shack. Dizzy with her own discomposure, she tried to focus on the lesson she was to complete for the next day—writing the names of her family in her Bible—but she was too riled up with her own rapacious need to know. When she heard what she thought might be Evangeline's steps coming up the road, she ran out the door to greet her. Several times it was nothing but the wind whispering, making her think she heard mud mushing, or twigs breaking under what should've been the woman's weight. It wasn't, but Emma answered the conspicuous calls until finally it was.

Lugging her bag of tools and tinctures, Evangeline walked side to side, weighed down by her bag on one side and a sudden grief on the other. If Emma noticed the sadness, she didn't care. What child concerns themselves with the murky emotions of an adult? She fired into the tale of her day, showing off the names she had written in her Bible once they were inside. Evangeline followed Emma's finger as she pointed across the neat handwriting as the girl read, "'Emma Dupree and Zephaniah Foster Dupree.'" She pointed to the blank line and looked at Evangeline expectantly.

"This for my ma'am. My real ma'am." Emma's voice trembled. "Can you tell me her name?"

"I told you it weren't her real name, so why write it down? You don't wanna lie in God's word, do you?"

Emma shook her head no, found her pencil, and filled in the blank anyway.

"What's that say there?" Evangeline asked.

"That's your name," Emma answered. "You like my ma'am. The onliest one I know."

Evangeline snatched the pencil from Emma's hand, turned the Bible toward her, and furiously scratched out the place where Emma had written her name.

"I just told you don't lie in God's word, and you do it anyway."

"I gotta have something to show my teacher tomorrow," Emma protested.

"No, you don't," Evangeline shouted. "Not everybody gotta ma'am. Not everybody gotta pa. Be glad you got someone here looking after you in the first place."

"Well, can you at least tell me around what season is my birthday? Ms. Jacoby said we can celebrate whenever it come 'round."

"Why would you want to do a thing like that?" Evangeline asked.

"She say it's what you do on birthdays. Celebrate."

"What them white people do."

"Do you know when it is?" Emma asked softly.

"Planting season," Evangeline answered. "You was early. Three days after the equal day and the equal night. But we ain't celebrating. Not in this house. I told you, yo' ma'am died the day you was born. What's there to celebrate about that?"

Even with a few of the answers she craved, Emma had been dashed just the same. In the light left inside the shack, she looked up at Evangeline, resolute in her decision, with her hands hugged to her hips, her flat nose blown wide across her face, and the sturdy posture of planted feet. The white apron covering her shirt and skirt were spackled with fresh blood. Emma examined her, from the rolled sleeves to the hat askew on her head.

She asked, "Ma'am . . . did the birth not go okay?"

Evangeline humphed. She reached for the table and chair her Henry had whittled himself and collapsed under her own weight. She looked down at the floor she and Emma covered with boards from the big house. Shoulders rounded, head hanging, sadness wore her like a wet winter coat. Sopping and heavy.

"It went something like your'n," Evangeline said with a slow, gravid tongue. "The baby's here. The ma'am on the other side."

Evangeline lifted her head enough to see Emma's hands covering her eyes as her fingers pulled at the edges of her hair. The image was too much for Evangeline to process. Too identical to what had happened before. Springing from her chair, she snatched Emma by her bent arms and yanked her from where she stood.

"Get yo' hands outta yo' head," she said, tongue moving lightning fast. "You keep up with all these questions about your ma'am, and you may end up just like her. Freedom only been a few seasons. They might fight another war and take it away."

Arms held down by Evangeline's grip, Emma couldn't move to

hide the tears that welled, pooled, and fell down her face. Evangeline continued unmoved. She had seen worse. She said, "You wanna celebrate like them white people? You go'n right ahead. But not here. Not all birthdays is worth the trouble, let alone the memory."

3.

May 1953

For Gladys Dupree, it wasn't a birthday she wanted to forget but something else entirely. Long before she was Tati's mimi, or Nadia's mother, Gladys remembered how they came with hot pans in hand, crooked smiles and curious eyes. Heads on swivel trying to catch a peek, a glance, at who they'd heard about and wished they knew. It's a peculiar position, for sure, to hear but not know. Knowing, grounded in fact, is altogether different from hearing. With hearing, words could be lost, messages devoid of meaning. Implications could be treated as incontrovertible fact and fact as merely fiction. Perhaps this is the reason most people only hear. Few ever really know, and only one knows all. But trying to be in that number, though impossible, provides the fun of the hunt.

The hearers sidled up to Ruby and shook hands with Sampson, all saying the same thing. "We heard . . ." It was enough to drive Sampson to drink. He too had heard and still didn't know. The wall of silence between him and the Dupree women was thick. He may have wanted to marry Ruby Ann Dupree and have her take his last name, Benjamin, but they never got around to it, what with Gladys, and the farm and all. She would always be a Dupree woman. Her allegiance belonged to her mothers and the secrets they kept amongst themselves.

Still, talk had reached him as it had everyone else in Land's End. Everyone save for Eugene. An out-of-towner already, and that didn't account for his professional travel, he was stuck at the foot of the steps of the new house, where Ms. Mattie from church had come to call, ignorant as the day is long.

"We heard what happened," Ms. Mattie said, standing on the front porch.

Ruby and Sampson remained seated on the long wooden bench with the high back as Mattie's words, nearly whispered, arrived to their ears, loud as the church bell piercing the air with the weight of what was left unsaid.

Gladys heard her too. She shouted, "Good afternoon!"

Her voice filled the void of dead space before Ms. Mattie could say more. The deaconess turned her pillbox hat–covered head toward the interruption of what she hoped would become a gathering of information. Gladys and Eugene stood in front of the porch over-looking the fork in the road, arm in arm, affection apparent if only for appearances.

"Good day to you, Ms. Ruby, Mr. Sampson, Ms. Mattie." Eugene tipped his hat.

"How do?" Ruby answered.

"Blessed and highly favored, how 'bout yourselves?"

"Boy, when the last time you stepped foot inside the house of the Lord to even be on his blessin' list?" Ms. Mattie's face crunched into a scowl.

"To tell the truth, it's been a while, but I've passed enough churches back and forth on the train to know the Lord heard at least one of my prayers."

"Oh yeah, what's that?" Ms. Mattie asked.

"He saw fit to bless me with a wife." Eugene squeezed Gladys's arm against his body as his smile spread across his face. "I came to ask y'all proper, but she told me yes when I disembarked at the depot."

It had only taken a week of wearing spit-laced herb pastes—

pokeweed, yarrow, and the like—beneath a bundle of bandages for the gash on Gladys's face to close. She took it as a fortuitous sign since it was just in time for Eugene to arrive. An omen of sound judgment to give herself over to his advances. When she stood waiting at the depot, her healed face half-hidden beneath a new hat, it was her first test to see if he could tell something was off, that she was different. He couldn't. Not like Ms. Mattie, who grunted an *mm-hmm* and shoved the pie in her white-gloved hands toward Ruby and Sampson. "I'll leave this here and be on my way," she said.

Ruby caught the pie Ms. Mattie released like it was still hot from the oven and burning through to her skin. Relieved of its heft, Ms. Mattie slip-slapped her palms one against the other and ambled down the three stairs. The humidity-worn wood sagged in the middle under the strain of her weight. Back on solid ground, standing right in front of Gladys and Eugene, Ms. Mattie dusted the front of her white skirt suit and adjusted the matching hat.

She said, "The other deaconesses and I are praying for you, Gladys. But congratulations on the engagement. I think this is a fine time for you to get married. A fine time. Don't you, Ruby?"

"It was right kind of you to bring over this pie and well-wishes for our girl," Ruby said. "Give the other mothers our regards."

Ms. Mattie nodded her head and marched back the way she came: toward the church for choir rehearsal, her stop at the Duprees' a well-devised scheme to know more than what she'd heard through town chatter.

"Take this inside, would you?" Ruby passed the pie to Sampson.

He looked down at the condolence confection and tried to see its flaky, sugary goodness as compassion and not cruelty. Grace instead of gossip. Looking up at Gladys and Eugene still standing at the foot of the steps, he shook his head, got up from the bench, and went inside the floppy screen door. It slammed behind him, its clang the shame he wished he could voice. But all he had to show for his suffering was food. The pie from the deaconesses. A whole roasted hog from the deacons. Money and macaroni and cheese from the pastor and first lady. Potato salad and collard greens from the mother board. A pound cake from the presiding elder. Green beans and perloo rice from the ushers. His kitchen was a kaleidoscope of cuisine and culinary delights he had no appetite to indulge. One by one, two by two, or even in threes and groups bigger than that, the entirety of the congregation of St. Joseph's had come to call on the Dupree house.

"Did you tell everyone else before me?" Eugene asked. "They hardly seem surprised."

"Perhaps I spilled the beans a little," Gladys answered.

The glee in her voice was a sound she didn't recognize. It wasn't of herself but who she'd become, who she'd transformed into, in six days' time.

"Well, since it's out now, I guess we getting married," Eugene said. He threaded his fingers through Gladys's and raised their hands high above his head, drunk on happy. "Mr. Sampson, why don't you bring that pie back outside and celebrate with us," he yelled toward the door.

"Yeah, Daddy, c'mon out," Gladys encouraged.

Overwhelmed in his own unknowing and the activity of his imagination, Sampson fluttered his lips until he was out of breath and slammed the heavy door of the house he'd built with his own two hands.

Eugene looked from Gladys to Ruby. Hands clasped over the paunch of her belly, she chuckled a bit before explaining away her would-be husband's abrupt departure. "Don't mind him. He can't stand to let go his only girl. Whatchu got in your hand there?" Ruby motioned at the heavy bag still tucked beneath Eugene's arm.

"Just some copies of *The Defender* for you," Eugene said. "I wrapped them in sheets, and it's a good thing I did. The deputy down at the depot was trying to search me for contraband."

"Which deputy?" Ruby asked.

"Stringer," Gladys said through closed teeth.

Ruby looked up and eyed her daughter. "He didn't give you no trouble, did he?"

"He made a threat. Said we been lynched for less, but I know how to handle his kind," Eugene answered.

"They let us go," Gladys added.

"Who is 'they'?" Ruby asked.

"JB was there too," Gladys answered, referring to the deputy's son.

Ruby, stone-faced, looked to Eugene and waved her hand, motioning for the bag. He stepped up on the porch, set the biggest case he carried at Ruby's feet, and then rejoined Gladys.

Fingers entwined, she squeezed his hand and let her head rest on his shoulder as her body rolled with relief. She had survived. Twice.

"We're getting married," Gladys said to herself.

"Yes, we are, cher."

"How soon?" Ruby asked.

"Next time you come back on the train. Yes?" Gladys asked Eugene.

"What my wife wants, my wife gets," Eugene said, his smile big and bright.

"Well then go'n in the back and tell your grandmama and Mama Em the news," Ruby said. "That oughta perk them up."

Dutifully, they did as directed and walked around to the house in the back. They kept to the brick facade of the new house instead of skirting by the fence and the patch of dirt where nothing grew. They pretended not to notice the stream of cars headed toward Ms. Teena's or the smell of fried fish wafting through the air. No matter, though. Soon enough, everyone from the Dupree house on down to the church would know Saturday night at Ms. Teena's had begun. From the smell, to the sound, to the looks of the packed dirt parking field, evidence would abound that the weekend was in full swing.

But it was still early yet. Early enough for Jubi and Emma to be sitting on their own front porch, which faced the back of Ruby and Sampson's home. Like Ruby, they too were dressed in all white, from the wraps on their heads to the long skirts draping their ankles. They'd been wearing their healing clothes since Gladys staggered home from the fields. Jubi snapped beans, and Emma sat still, her wrinkled fingers clasped tightly around an inheritance left by her George: a hand-carved cane.

Between them, on either side of the door frame, the threshold marked with a line of salt, sat a bowl of water and a bucket of what looked like ash but was really goofer dust. A libation for the lost ones and a weapon against the wicked meant to suffocate ill intentions before they got a foothold to form. Emma and Jubi guarded their entryway, protective over whose energy, living or dead, was allowed inside. As Eugene guided Gladys closer to her kindred, the old woman's hand stopped him before her aged voice said, "Don't come any closer."

"Just came to call on you to tell you the news," Eugene said.

"And what's that?" Jubi asked.

"We're getting married," Eugene answered, ebullient.

Jubi dropped the beans in her hand and set her bowl to the side. She never let her gaze linger long away from Eugene's face. Assessing, determining, she finally said, "Y'all make a fine couple. Don't they, Mama?"

"They'll do," Emma said.

Her blue-rimmed, nearly blind eyes never left from their fixed position. She stared off into the space between the two houses. Entranced, Emma didn't move her mouth or further crease the wrinkles in her face. She barely breathed. She studied the ripples of the water bowl as if she could read them. As if they imparted a knowing hearers would beg to be privy to.

"Gladys, go inside and get you something to drink," Emma said.

Releasing Eugene's hand, she asked, "You want something? Lemonade? Tea, maybe?"

"What's in this house is for you."

"What she means is that all the food and drink is back by Ruby and Sampson," Jubi clarified.

"I said what I meant, Jubilee. Gladys, go'n in the house."

Eugene had no choice in the matter. Standing before the women, sweating in his uniform under a sun that was far from setting, he waited for Gladys to reemerge.

"So, whereabouts you from again?" Jubi asked. "Louisiana way, right?"

"Yes, ma'am. Assumption Parish."

"So, how'd you take interest in our Gladys?"

"Well, ma'am, after this became my permanent route with Pullman last year, I decided to make sure I knew my way around since I'd spend a day or two down here before we headed back north. That's when I met Gladys."

And that was almost the truth. Eugene didn't so much as meet Gladys as he saw Gladys and devised a scheme to run into her. He had been at Ms. Teena's one Saturday after the train came in, taking a piss between the cars parked in the field, when he saw her emerge from the big brick house with a basket. Corn liquor–covered eyes watched as she pulled sheets from the line and disappeared back inside. To Eugene it was as if the home had swallowed her whole, Jonah in the belly of the whale, only she wasn't spit up in three days' time.

He waited around to see if she would come back out. Maybe come 'round the other side of the fence, where he could buy her a drink and dance her across the ground until her ankles were dirty and musky sweat gathered between her breasts, but it wasn't to be. Back on the train Monday morning, he asked his partner, Dewey, as they loaded bags into the carriage about the sight he'd seen. Irreverent in his words, he asked as much to try to make her acquaintance as to confirm she wasn't an apparition.

Dewey said, "Them Duprees don't hang around over there. Only amongst their own and at the church on Sunday."

Two weeks later, when he was back in Land's End, Eugene skipped the raucous night at Ms. Teena's for the conservative quiet of St. Joseph's on Sunday morning. That is until the choir started singing, the musicians started playing, and bodies started moving, so full with the Holy Ghost Eugene could hardly tell the difference between what was happening to the worshippers around him and what happened in the juke. The only noticeable difference was the family in the front pew giving their bodies over to God to ride with abandon. Amongst them was the woman he knew would become his wife, though then, he didn't even know her name.

"You drank it all?" Emma asked as Gladys appeared in the doorway.

"Yes'm," she answered.

Eugene stared at Gladys in her black dress and hat, sandwiched between the women in white. He said, "Cher, we gon' have to get you a nice dress before the wedding. Let me take you into town and you can pick something out."

"Won't be no need of that," Jubi said.

"Ma'am?" Eugene questioned.

"She got a nice white dress inside she can wear."

"I do?" Gladys asked.

"You will," Emma said.

The holes in the conversation didn't bother Eugene. Dewey had told him the Duprees were different, standoffish and arrogant. "They think real high of themselves and real low of the rest of us," he'd said. But Gladys hadn't been that way with him. She'd been easy to talk to, eager even.

The shift he should've sensed, he didn't. The change happening inside his woman, he couldn't name. He was unaware that Gladys's retreat behind the wooden walls of the women in white was more than just a barrier to entry but a blockade he would always be forbidden access to. Who she was inside and who she became outside were altogether different from the girl he got to know every other Sunday during his weeks in Land's End. Perhaps if he'd been on the Sunday last, there would've been no need for the secrecy. The twoness. But he wasn't. And so it was.

"How you feelin'?" Jubi asked.

"Good as ever," Gladys answered, with a smile Eugene didn't know was forced.

"Anything?" Emma asked.

"No, ma'am."

"Eugene, where you staying while you here?" Jubi asked.

"I usually stay at the boardinghouse close to the depot."

Jubi tsked. "Well, that's no good now. You engaged to my grand-baby and planning a wedding. That makes you family. Why don't you go on up to the house and see if Ruby and Sampson can't find room for you. Gladys can sleep back here by us, so there ain't no more talk than what needs to be."

"That's a fine invitation," Eugene said. "Just hope Ms. Ruby and Mr. Sampson don't mind."

"They won't mind," Emma said.

"They won't mind at all," Jubi reassured. "Go'n back up there, get you something to eat, and take a rest. You family now. It's as good a time as any to start treating you accordingly."

"Thank you kindly. I'll see you for supper, cher?"

"She'll be 'round," Emma said.

Gladys watched as Eugene made his way through the dirt patch around to the front of the new house.

"You need to get back in the water," Emma said, once he was out of sight.

"And take your hair down, wash it, and leave it alone to dry," Jubi added.

"It's enough crisscrossed out here without you inviting evil to live on your head."

"Yes'm" was all Gladys could say in response. Standing between them, she removed her hat and took the tail end of her braid captive in her hands. She unraveled Ruby's work until her hair fell in waves dusting her shoulders as it tickled her back.

"Much better," Jubi said. "I'll get your water ready."

She scooped up a pinch of the ash mixture before she stood from the chair. Throwing it over her shoulder, Jubi pushed past Gladys into the dim inside.

"Shouldn't be long now," Emma said, staring into the distance. "Shouldn't be long at all."

"You sure?" Gladys asked. "I should be—"

"These things take time," Emma said. She shifted the cane to hold Gladys's hand.

"I don't have much time left."

"You got plenty more ahead of you than behind you. Won't be no trouble for you today. Tomorrow either."

Gladys nodded. It was all she could do. Belief didn't belong to her yet. The reassurances of others was all she owned. One hand on her belly, the other squeezing Mama Em, she looked down at her body, wishing she could see beneath fabric, beneath skin, to bone and blood, but she didn't have that gift. She didn't know how to read waves or manipulate the dust. The call of her kindred muted, she looked down to Emma, sitting in the chair.

The old woman squeezed her hand as she stared beyond. "Won't be no trouble at all."

In a way, Emma was right. Trouble didn't find Gladys that day. Or the days and weeks after. It wasn't until after her wedding and wedding night, when she was packed and dressed in her Sunday best to board the train with Eugene for Chicago, that trouble found her. But even in the grip of its agony it was more like relief. Deep-sighing, long-exhaling, back-stretching, neck-cracking relief. If Gladys had to pinpoint the moment of her undoing, it would have been on the platform at the station in Land's End. Standing beside her mothers, Ruby, Jubi, and Emma, who had all come to see her off, she felt a flutter.

Standing out in the sun, the covered part of the platform reserved for white folk, the flutter rolled up and down her body at once. Reverberating in its wave, Gladys undulated with the tide, her mind momentarily bereft of thought. Emma was the one who noticed. She poked over on her cane, white fabric flowing in the breeze, and placed a hand on Gladys's back. She steadied her great-granddaughter and advised her to breathe.

"This is just the beginning," Emma said. "You gon' have to hang on for your own self when you gone."

"Yes'm," Gladys answered.

She didn't have time to unravel Emma's riddles while she waited for Eugene to finish loading the other passengers' bags beneath the carriage. Only when those moth wings evolved into long reedy fingers, extended its hand, and closed its fist did Gladys dwell on the old woman's words.

You gon' have to hang on for your own self when you gone.

They'd been playing on a loop since the stop in Meridian. An hour past Memphis and the words muted in her mind as she concentrated to keep from expelling her horror. She was rooted to her seat. The ghostly nubs of her knuckles could push nails through drywall from the way she gripped the rails beneath her window. Teeth ground against each other, filed down to blunt terrain, left her mouth chalky dry.

"How you doing, cher?" Eugene asked.

Gladys shook her head and yawned. "I'm okay. Go'n back to work and stop worrying with me."

"It's my job to worry about you. You're my wife."

"No, your *job* is to worry about your passengers." She added a smile, small, because she couldn't both banter and bear down.

Eugene eyed her with tiny lids closed to near slits. He said, "I'll come back to check on you after I make this next set of rounds."

If he noticed the color that had drained from her features, he didn't say. In the low light, she hoped he didn't see. That he wouldn't wonder what was happening beyond the facade. Though she never asked, Gladys was sure Eugene knew enough about womenkind to know that if trouble occurred it was bound to show. Laying her head against the closed window, she breathed in through her nose and out with her mouth. The scent of fried chicken, dinner packed by the other passengers, lingered around her as she loosened her hold on the rails.

Her toes bumped up against her luggage as she tried to make herself as comfortable as possible. Her dreams formed the face of her father, Sampson, his cinnamon skin furrowed in grooves like the symmetrical rows of soybeans grown on the farm when cotton had drained the dirt of its life. The lines had set in stiff and stony since the day he wasn't allowed to darken the doorstep of the old house.

Instead, Sampson hid behind old copies of the *Chicago Defender* Eugene had brought, reading the stories as if they were new. As if he didn't know how they ended. In his chair, paper in front of his face, hard hands gripping the printed pulp, the leather formed around him like parentheses. When Gladys said her final goodbye, a mousy muffle no one but a daddy could decipher, all Sampson could do was turn the page. Though her face barely registered for him, the moment was burned into Gladys's memory and found its way into her dreams.

While asleep, she remembered who she'd been, and who she'd shed in order to become something she didn't recognize. A woman, all sharp angles and set mouth, sad eyes and small smiles that didn't connect. Iron words and a steel heart created a cage around the softness she sloughed off as life leached from her loins on the train ride north. The car cradled her crib-like and rocked away every inch of who she'd been in Land's End. When Gladys opened her eyes, Sampson was gone from her mind for good.

"C'mon, cher. We're here."

Eugene shook Gladys's arm like a baby rattle. She shifted in her seat. "Can I use the bathroom and clean up a little bit before I get off?" she asked.

Eugene looked around. His excitement urged him to say no. He wanted to show off the woman he'd brought back as his wife to the guys who called him crazy for keeping up a long courtship when, as they put it, "It's plenty of Southern-bred gals already here. No need for you to go catch a fresh one."

"City take over too quick," Eugene had reasoned. "The gal I got be sweet like sun-cured tea and cast-iron-cooked corn bread."

He was betting Gladys would keep the ways of her mothers longer than the ladies he'd been known to keep company with over the course of the cold winters.

"I just wanna freshen up, change my dress." She sensed his reticence. "I'd hate to step off the train in a big city still looking like old Land's End."

"Go'n 'head, cher." Eugene smiled. "Make sure you put a coat on too. The cold up here is like nothing you've ever felt. I'll be waiting by the door to help you down proper."

In the bathroom, barely big enough to turn around in, Gladys shed all that was left of her last weeks in Land's End. Blouse, skirt, silk slip, pantyhose, and undergarments were swapped with replacements, the old tied and tucked into a ball in the corner of her suitcase. She washed with the water that trickled from the tiny sink and re-dressed.

Gladys chanced a look in the circular mirror about the size of a steerage porthole. Her hair, neatly wound and pinned at the back of her head, gave full view of her face. She searched it for any sign of difference. A physical designation that she'd been stolen from, discarded, and put back together again. She looked for cracks like what would've shown on a shattered porcelain vase. But there was nothing, thanks to the quick work of the women who refused to suffer injury and gave no mind to labels like "survivor," "victim," or "victor."

At the bottom of the metal steps, Eugene stood with his hat in hand, waiting. When Gladys appeared in the entryway, he bowed at the waist.

"Madame." He offered his hand.

She took it and wished she had on dainty lace gloves to match his manners, like the ones she'd seen Jubi make out of the Sears, Roebuck catalog. Gloves or no gloves, she held his hand with her pinching fingers as he took her suitcase.

"Welcome to Chicago, cher."

They made their way through the grand concourse and past the ticket counters until they were outside surrounded by buildings taller than she'd ever seen. Eugene hailed a jitney from downtown to Forty-Seventh Street. Inside the car-turned-cab, Gladys listened to the men go back and forth about women and sports and the recent weather as she mustered the concentration to ride out the waves rolling through her body. The driver didn't help her none. He cut in front of buses, trucks, and cars as if he were playing a game only he knew the rules to. There was no order to his maneuvering, just sharp whips in and out of lanes. Gladys gripped what she could as she breathed in through her nose and out through her mouth. There was no way over, under, or out. Her only choice was through.

From the car to Forty-Seventh and King Drive, where masses of people loitered the corners as much to see as be seen, to the cramped basement kitchenette two blocks away, the commotion inside Gladys's body forced her through.

"Where is the bathroom?" she asked.

"On the other side of the beaverboard, cher. We may have lucked up this week. Don't seem like nobody else renting the other rooms in here. We might have the whole place to ourselves, and right in the heart of Bronzeville."

His eyes held a mischievous gleam Gladys couldn't meet. She clip-clopped her way to the facility and closed the door behind her. Leaned against the hard wood, Gladys slid down to the cold tile floor and lay with her belly on the ground, the cool a friend to the skin of her cheek. Curled in a ball, she remained unmoving as what had become familiar on the train returned. When she managed to pull herself up, it was only to strip down.

Standing in front of the sink in her slip and brassiere, Gladys washed her hands and stared in the mirror. She was still looking for difference, the markers of her misfortune, but all she saw was herself. The face she'd always had, skin the color it had always been, long hair pulled back and wrapped around itself in a neat and unmoving position. It was the closest she'd get to the braid Ruby gave her after her bath. The one Jubi wished she didn't have and Emma called evil. Staring at herself in the mirror, she tried to find the evil done to her, something like the mark of the beast Pastor Erickson talked about when he delivered a fiery scripture from Revelation, but there was nothing. No mark, no brand, no bruise, no streak, smudge, nick, or scar. Just her face and two sets of dirty clothes that could easily come clean in the wash.

Hadn't they already?

The rap of knuckles on the closed door shook Gladys away from her searching.

"Can I come in?" Eugene asked.

The knob on the unlocked door turned before she could answer.

"You all right in here, cher?"

Eugene looked first at Gladys's face then scanned her clothes-less body, covered only in silk chemise and lace. He stood with one foot over the threshold. No longer in his uniform coat and hat, he'd changed into a brown pair of slacks and white T-shirt, attached suspenders draping his thighs.

"You need me to call the doctor?"

"It's over now."

"What happened, cher?"

"You wanna look at me when you ask me again or you want me to keep pretending like you ain't heard?"

"I'm asking you, Gladys. I'm asking you."

"Who told you?"

"Dewey said some things. Some folks on the train, Black *and* white, gave me them pitying looks. You know the ones."

She did know. It was the look Ms. Mattie had the day she dropped off the pie. It was the look all of Land's End had, whether she saw it personally or not. She felt the familiar faces turn against her. Wide mouths crooked with contempt and big eyes colored with compunction even if their noses tipped slightly toward heaven, haughty with how the Dupree women had fallen again. What Ruby had outrun had caught up with Gladys.

She nodded. He knew.

"Word gets 'round," Eugene said.

"Then it's no need of me recounting what happened. You know enough."

"Why ain't you tell me what was going on, cher?"

"Wasn't for you to know."

"Who told you that?"

"Mama and them. They didn't even tell my daddy."

"And you think he don't know?"

Eugene stepped fully into the bathroom, closed the door behind him, and leaned against it. There was nowhere left for the secret to go. Nowhere for the unsaid to run but into him.

Still hunched over the sink, staring at the one crease across her forehead, Gladys answered. "I didn't say he didn't know. I said he wasn't told. Everything don't need to be voiced. Everything don't need to grow wings, ride the air, and visit folk you don't know with stories they got no stake in."

"I got more stake in your story than anybody else does. We married now."

"I know."

"Your troubles are my troubles."

"Ain't no more trouble."

Eugene moved toward her, closed the distance between them. He opened his arms and gave her a choice. She had to make up her own mind about what she wanted. Which family she belonged to. The Dupree women on the farm or the husband she'd moved one thousand miles to be with. It wasn't no use being in the same city, the same house, if it was a thousand miles' worth of words unsaid between them. He knew all about unions built on bricks with secrets on the other side. Just because the lies faced the ground didn't mean they descended into the depths. A little shallow digging always wrenched them loose. What's kept quiet is always looking for any reason to get loud.

Gladys sighed, let go of the sink, and stepped back. In Eugene's embrace, she allowed what she knew and what he'd heard to be absorbed into him. She didn't tell and he didn't push but pressed together the power of the whispered, the pitied, became a solute in solvent. The salty, the acidic, and even the sweet turned tasteless if there was enough water to drown it.

"You know, cher," Eugene began, hands pulling loose the pins in her hair. "We can start again."

Looking up to see both of their countenances in the mirror, Gladys nodded ever so slightly as her hair, loosed from its hold, waved around her face. She agreed on one condition: to go to school and become a nurse like she'd planned all along. He nodded his yes against her ear as his hands grabbed hold of her strands and crossed them one by one at the nape of her neck until he'd formed a loose braid. When he finished, he draped it across the front of her left shoulder. Gladys reached her hand to meet his as she sank further into him until only the wall held them up. Only the wall heard what was said. In the small, cramped space, the weight of their bodies weighed down what wanted to fly and suffocated what sought to be known. Even the moth wings stilled, and the long fingers retracted. Gladys looked at their reflection, the hair he'd braided a symbol of their union. They were entwined. The crease that had crossed her was gone. Dissolved.

4.

What Eugene did for Gladys, only one other Dupree woman before Nadia knew how. Nadia, while the first to make a living out of the enterprise of doing hair, wasn't the first to heal in that way with her hands. There was, of course, the one no one knew about. The one whose legend lived in one-line rumors too horrific to be believed. And then there was the one Nadia would never remember meeting.

July 1934

RUBY WAS SEVENTEEN WHEN SHE FIRST PUT HER HANDS IN HER hair to do more than just gather it together at the nape of her neck or pin it in place in an elaborate creation piled atop her head. It was about the same time she met Sampson.

On a day in town, on the other side of the tracks, Ruby ran errands for Jubi and Emma like she'd been doing since she was a young girl. Mostly she carried things back from Danube General Store. Fabric, eggs, milk, sugar, rice. Items the women needed that they did not or could not grow on the farm. It was on one of these treks when Ruby saw a figure she thought she recognized. Years had passed since she'd seen his face the color of a cinnamon stick with deep-set eyes, a ballpoint nose, and heavy lips like the back end of a loaf of bread.

Ruby had to dig down to her earliest memories for a name. It still hadn't come to her by the time he stood before her, trying to pull from his own bank of remembrances. They spoke friendly, smiles and nods, before they entered the back door of the store one at a time. But speaking to people because it was custom and holding conversation because you knew them were two altogether different aspects of communication.

Inside the store, Ruby approached the far end of the counter. Away from the front door. Away from where Logan Danube and his niece Delilah Grace were helping a line of other customers. All she needed was flour and salt. *That is until they tell me they need something else*, Ruby thought to herself. *I already been in here twice today. I'm sure they're sick of me.*

The strange young man she thought she knew stood behind her. They waited for the Saturday-afternoon activity to calm. He studied her form. The black of her skin, the drumming of her fingers against the sides of her dress-covered legs.

"Is it always this slow?" he asked.

As soon as the other line dwindled to the last person, someone else came in, keeping them from getting any service. The long wait inside Danube's was part of the errand running. Logan had to be in an especially good mood to tear himself away from helping his white patrons. Growing up in the store, Delilah learned to do the same.

"On a Saturday afternoon it is," Ruby answered. "You either come as soon as they open or wait."

"Couldn't come no earlier. Been stuck in church all morning."

"You here for Ms. Claudette's homegoing?"

"Yes." He shook his head. "She was my grandmother."

"Your grandmother," Ruby muttered. She turned around fully to look into his face. "You seem familiar."

"You do too."

"Ruby." She extended her hand.

A smile spread across his face, elongating his thick lips and ac-
centuating the faint mustache above them that she hadn't noticed
before.

"Sampson," he said.

Recognition danced in her eyes as she tried to keep herself from
squealing. "I thought I knew you! How've you been? Where've you
been? Seemed like one day we were playing in the fields and the next
day you were gone."

"It did happen like that. My momma and daddy moved us to
Mobile."

"Ooh, big city livin'. How's that?"

"It's all I know really. Don't remember much else."

"That mean you forgot about us down here in Land's End?"

"I didn't forget you," Sampson said.

Heat rushed Ruby's body. So much so that Sampson detected
the slightest color change in her skin. It started in the palms of her
hands where she held on to the basket. Her tight grip on the handle
turned her skin red. He found that same red in a barely there under-
tone beneath her cheeks and again on the back of her neck.

Most people didn't take the time to notice the gradients of color
in dark complexions. One look at Ruby and the few folks in Land's
End formed one of two opinions, neither of them true. Their assumptions about the origins of her birth were steeped in scorn and
derision. Amongst themselves they called her skin a stain, an abomi-
nation, and attributed it to a curse. And in a way it was, but it wasn't
like her hue needed to be broken. It was more of a reminder of the
history no one knew.

Well, that's not entirely true. There was at least one person who
knew. One person, maybe two, who could give Ruby all the answers
she was looking for to the questions she was too afraid to ask. Enough
backhands to the face and open-hand slaps to the head quelled curiosity. She didn't let her mind linger on the stories that started any-

time she stepped outside her door. She told herself the buzz of voices didn't bother her and the whispers weren't about her. She tricked herself into believing the hushed tones and stolen glances were for her protection. A badge of honor she should be proud of instead of tail tucked in shame.

Being seen from Sampson's point of view was the kindest compliment she'd received in her life. His eyes told her that while he might not have remembered much else about their sleepy sea town, he'd held on to what was important. A seed of herself planted into him.

"What do you want, gal?"

Startled, Ruby turned around to face the voice. Logan Danube had finally come down to their side of the counter. His blue eyes blazed like the base of a fire. She averted her gaze to where his forearms rested on the countertop. With his striped shirtsleeves pushed to the elbows, she noticed the hairs on his arms stood up.

"Flour and salt," she said.

"How much?" Logan demanded.

"A few pounds of each. They didn't say. Just told me to come get it."

"You've been in here already today." Logan's statement sounded more like a question.

"Yes, sir."

Logan turned away before her final *r* rolled. Ruby waited, overcome with insecurity, stuck between two men, Logan in front of her and Sampson behind her. She didn't like being sandwiched between eyes that roamed, hands that reached, voices that startled, and noses that sniffed out her fear. Switching the grip of her basket to just one hand, Ruby let the other adjust the collar and lapels on the front of her dress. She pulled and smoothed, trying to invite more air around her neck. Anything to settle the acrobat doing a trapeze act inside her body.

"Hey, boy, what do you want?" Delilah Grace asked Sampson.

Though Sampson was five years older than fifteen-year-old Delilah Grace, she spat out the words with the venom and viciousness of a woman well on in years. One who had come through the war planning for a victorious life of leisure where she ruled and reigned and not one in which she had to work to earn her keep. The bitterness of her timbre was acrid. A reminder that hate was inherited. It didn't belong to you by birthright, but was instead passed down by mother, father, and then some.

In Land's End, everyone on this side of the tracks had some version of the hard heart. Their contempt for colored folks unabashed and unashamed. Ruby knew that those still around from Emma's generation and older had a very different plan for the future. One in which they won the war and held fast to their ways, their land, and most importantly their property.

In the interest of returning to the natural order of things once the Union ended its aggression, the owners in Land's End had all agreed to continue buying and building in the business of bodies. They never respected the 1808 ban. How could anyone other than planters, drivers, and their women know what was needed to manage the most important exports of their time—the moral tariffs, if you will. They continued to import. Under the cover of night, ships built to look narrow but held hundreds of people streamed up and down the bay. Even the blockade didn't suspend activity. When the bay was all stopped up by blue-pants-wearing patsies who never had any dealings with niggers, the Gulf was fair game. That's how Land's End became. Where the land ends, bondage begins.

Only history hadn't prevailed the way planting families, including the original Duprees, had predicted. Surrounded and forced to surrender to the Union, former property walked free, walked away, and some walked north. Made other homes beneath colder suns. Entire cities and towns all their own separated by an acknowledged dividing line, sometimes invisible, sometimes tangible like on the other side of the tracks.

The heavy anger and tinged condescension coloring Delilah Grace's voice told of the tales she'd been infected with since the occasion of her birth. A replica of the indoctrination that'd been first used to radicalize her mother and uncle who wrapped his warped feelings in the packaging of Ruby's flour and salt and sent her on her way, after she pushed over her pennies, of course. Logan didn't charge her extra like he did the rest who came through the back door of the store. It was the least he could do on account of who she was.

Outside, Ruby breathed easy. The last of the errand items retrieved, she'd begun her walk back across the tracks when she felt she was not alone.

"You wasn't gon' wait for me?" Sampson hollered, a few paces behind her.

"Didn't know I was supposed to," Ruby said. "Just because we going the same way don't mean we going the same place."

Sampson closed the distance between them. In his hand he held a pastry wrapped in a napkin. He offered some to Ruby, who looked first from the gift in his hand to his face and back again before shaking her head no.

"That's all you went in there to buy?" she asked, eyeing him quizzically.

"I hadn't planned on buying anything at all."

"Then why did you?"

"I was following you."

At this, Sampson lowered his head to hide his smile, but it was too late. He'd already told on himself. Like Ruby, he felt the familiar even if he couldn't call her name at first. Walking back across the tracks, he was sure he'd never forget it again.

"You still following me?" Ruby asked.

"I'm heading back to the repast," Sampson said. "I left to get some air. Too many people talkin' about dyin'. It's like they long for it. Me, myself, I like life. It ain't everything, but it's what we got. And only one chance at that."

Ruby nodded as she closed in on the fields of the farm. Sampson lingered at the fork, and so did she. He finished his treat as she held on to her basket. Neither spoke. What do you say to a friend you haven't seen in ten years or more? The first boy you'd ever known? One whose family worked for yours? They stood in their awkwardness, not wanting to walk away but knowing they should. At least Ruby did.

She asked, "Y'all heading back to Mobile in the morning?"

"I don't think so," Sampson said. "Mama said she still gotta clean out Granny's house with her brothers and sisters, so I expect we'll be here a little longer."

"You going to church in the morning?"

"If we are, I surely don't have a choice in the matter. Mama'll have my hide I tell her I ain't got time for the Lord."

"Then maybe I'll see you there."

"Maybe so," Sampson said. "Maybe so."

Back home, Ruby brought the basket to the wooden table, where Jubi would sift the flour for worms. Aside from the table and the hearth used for both cooking and warmth, there wasn't much else. Two rooms were in the back, additions to the original quarter shack thanks to a long-departed Papa George. But they were for sleeping, and she knew everybody was still awake.

"It's about time you came in the house," Jubi said, emerging from the back. "Standing in all that sun, no hat on your head, and you got the nerve to be talking to a man almost as dark as you."

"He wasn't no real man, Mama. Only three years older than me. That's Sampson. Ms. Claudette's grandson, remember?"

"Everything and everybody don't need to be remembered," Jubi muttered.

The utterance gave Ruby pause. Made her wonder who and what

her mother was talking about. She knew it didn't all have to do with Sampson and his family from the way her eyes closed and the breath in her chest became more pronounced, but she dare not ask.

Jubi sighed. "You get what I asked you for?"

"It's right here." Ruby motioned to the basket on the table.

"Well, go'n head get out the way so I can work. Gotta get these biscuits made to go with the jam we preserved."

"What for?"

"With so many people in town for the service, they gon' be wanting to continue in the fellowship hall tomorrow. Somebody gotta make the food."

Ruby raised an eyebrow. "*You* going to the fellowship hall tomorrow?"

"No indeed!" Jubi glared. "But you are."

She bumped past Ruby as she rounded the table, intentionally shoving her shoulder and stepping on her foot. Taking the hint for her disregard, Ruby excused herself. In her own room, with just the sunlight pouring in from the window, she sat on the floor at the foot of the bed with a broken comb in her lap. She stared at her reflection in the old mirror with the initials EGD carved in the wood. She assumed it was for Mama Em and Papa George, but she never asked. She'd been living in the same house all her life and was no closer to understanding its mysteries or unlocking the secrets of its other inhabitants.

Ruby shrugged and studied herself in the mirror. Her skin, closer to Sampson's than it would ever be to Jubi's or Emma's, was still darker than that of anyone else she knew. She wondered where it came from. *Who did it come from?* It was a question she'd asked herself since the first time she was admonished for running around like a little tar baby, blackening up with no regard for her own mother's feelings.

"You just outside flaunting yourself and taunting me like I didn't try to make our lives better," Jubi had sneered when she was only eight years old.

Anger and sadness colored Jubi sallow and left her soul sorry; in a perpetual state of apology for not being able to escape what lived in her too. It would be the curse of her coupling that reversed the trend that started with Emma. Light skin, light hair, light eyes.

Not for Ruby. Dark. Black as night. Eyes obsidian. Hair unruly. The only saving grace was its length. She unwound the locks pinned to the top of her head and let them fall to her shoulders. Using the end edge of the comb with patches of missing teeth, she parted her hair in sections. Normally, she only did this to oil her scalp with a vial of potion Emma made up for her from the herbs in the garden, but something had come over her. Ruby let her hands lead. They parted and sectioned, secured and lifted, crossed and bound as she began to braid. First one side and then the other, until her hair trailed down her back in two neat rows.

When she was done, Ruby set the comb to the side and looked at herself with new eyes. As if she was seeing someone other than herself. Another girl of seventeen. Or maybe she had never seen herself this way before. Fully Ruby and not an off-brand image of the mothers she could never mirror. With Jubi and Emma, her family connection was always in question. The way she looked now, with her braids, it didn't matter who claimed her. She knew she belonged to someone else entirely.

"Ruby Ann, come in here and help me with the fire," Jubi said, stepping into the doorway.

Looking over her shoulder, Ruby reveled as Jubi gazed at her until disgust crawled across her face and derision turned down the corners of her mouth. Jubi swallowed. Her face cleared.

"You just can't help yourself, can you?" she asked. "Doing things you ain't got no business doing just to hurt me."

"Whatchu mean, Mama?" Ruby asked, but Jubi didn't hear. She

was trapped in her own tirade. Inserting Ruby into questions she'd been asking herself for years. Substituting her daughter for the ones she couldn't talk to. The ones she couldn't get answers or second chances from. Scratchy voice husky and deep, eyes heavy and dry, Jubi's features wore wretchedness as she continued her screed.

"I tried to give you more than this, but you just didn't want it. Never did, I guess. It's a shame *you* were the baby who lived."

Ruby wanted to ask again what she meant, but she was hanging on to the other girl in the mirror so hard she didn't have room to hold the past *and* the present at the same time. She'd listened to her mama go off on her enough times to know to just let her be. Eventually, she'd shake her head, replace her face, and go on back to being Jubi. Emma's Jubilee.

Jubi sighed. "Where'd you learn to do that?"

Ruby didn't know how to explain the possession. How her fingers instinctively knew what to do. She turned back. The girl in the mirror gave her the answer.

"I don't know." Ruby shrugged. "Something just come over me, I guess."

5.

Nadia's decision to do hair was a touch more deliberate than Ruby's. She didn't just learn to braid by the spirit of possession. She was trained in the ways of tresses, a graduate of Debbie's School of Beauty Culture. She attended years after she dropped out of the University of Illinois Chicago, about the same time she'd met, dated, and broke up with Tati's daddy.

It was early in the morning of a new day when Nadia woke up at his home, which buttressed a park on Ninety-Ninth and Princeton. It was where they connected and convened to congress without acknowledging that when they left it was to go to the places they truly called home. Where mail came addressed in their names and the people who said they loved them were waiting for them to make a timely and consistent appearance.

She stood in front of the large picture window at the front of the house that overlooked a dewy jungle gym and sagging swings. Gladys's voice nagged her.

If you ain't gon' make the money like them white folks, then you need to find something else for yourself to do.

Staring out the window, Nadia had only one answer so far: *Not this.*

As a twenty-five-year-old college dropout still living with her parents and kid brothers, Nadia worked as a cashier at the Carson's department store in Evergreen Plaza. When she'd first started there four years ago, she'd told herself it was just so she could make enough money to reenroll in school and finish the last year of her finance degree, before going to business school, and then eventually working downtown at the Chicago Stock Exchange. She'd always been good at math and excelled in her high school economics classes, a fact that garnered her attention from her AP teacher, who'd done some day-trading in New York before moving to the Midwest.

But her ticket to trading had been derailed after her first semester at UIC, when Gladys demanded she take classes around Gladys's nursing schedule. She was going back to the day shift after years of working nights, and Nadia needed to step up and help out around the house. Her new responsibilities required picking up four-year-old Terry from day care and being home when nine-year-old Bryan got off the bus from school. At the time she'd had a used Pinto, but driving downtown early in the morning and trying to make it back in the afternoon to be with her brothers was too much on the car with all its other problems. Nadia was resigned to taking the bus and train downtown to class and driving only on the weekends as the inconsistent transit schedule didn't align with her new responsibilities.

She started taking night classes, once Gladys got home from work, which was fine until the year she began taking courses specifically for her major and her troubles staying awake left her with gaps in instruction, assignments she couldn't complete, and midterms and finals she did not pass. She had no choice. It was either fail out and let her 3.6 GPA take a hit or withdraw and let her transcripts remain intact.

She promised herself she would get back. Her only bills were the maintenance on her car. One that gave out two years prior. She'd been saving ever since, but minimum wage minus state and federal taxes and social security didn't leave her with much. Not enough for UIC, which she'd have to pay in full, out of pocket, as she'd already used her one chance for financial aid. She thought about taking a loan, but Gladys made clear she for damn sure wasn't cosigning for it.

She'd now been out of college longer than she'd attended. Her first semester walking the blocks of the downtown campus, when her only responsibility had been her books, was a dream she didn't want to remember. A time when she'd smiled easily and laughed loudly. A carefree Black girl unbound and unburdened if there ever was one. Now, beaten down by life and her mother's demands, all she had to offer were the same sour and surly expressions Gladys gave her.

She pulled away from the window and the ache of her own abandoned plans and padded through the empty house. There wasn't a lick of furniture in the living room. No sofa, no love seat, not even a futon. The kitchen wasn't much better. It was more decorative than functional. A card table and two metal folding chairs from a nearby church with the letters AME spray painted on the backs served as the dining area, formal, informal, and otherwise. Nadia passed by the manila envelope that lay on the card table on her way to the bedroom. Divorce papers his wife had him served with weeks ago. Though he tried to hide them, she knew what they were. And what's more, he knew that she knew.

They were evidence that his life was changing. No longer could he pretend he was giving her space, taking a break, or still working things out together but apart. They were parting. He just hadn't accepted it yet, as evidenced by the lack of homely touches. Furniture would admit defeat. His house was that of a man in limbo. One who hadn't expected to be in the three-bedroom rental as long as he had. His denial was best of friends with Nadia's own delusion that fucking a married man before his divorce was final made some kind of relationship.

"What are you doing up?" He rolled over on the bed.

"Thinking," she answered as she climbed atop the mattress supported by a squeaky metal frame. Similar to the rest of the sparely furnished house, the mere thought of attaching a headboard and footboard had not occurred to him, let alone investing in an entire bedroom set.

"About what?"

"Something Mama said."

He grunted. "What's that?"

"She asked me what I'm doing with my life."

"What did you say?"

"Didn't have an answer. Hadn't thought about it in a long time. When I was in school I had a plan. Now . . . I'm just working."

"You could always come up with a new plan."

He was right. But the ease with which he suggested she adapt, adjust to the land mines life had thrown in front of her, made her ache even more. She was giving up a dream, and that deserved to be mourned. Nadia rolled away. He didn't push for more. It was another reminder that they were living a fantasy masquerading as reality. At least when they had pretended to be *just friends* they had honest conversations, challenged one another in ways lovers rarely did. Like with all couples, real, imagined, or somewhere in between, sex clouded communication. Made what was once clear, hazy.

He rolled toward her and nuzzled her chin. His hands explored all that he had already conquered. Atop the hard, springy mattress they made a knot of their bodies. Hands and mouths found new and old connections to wring out every last drop of pleasure. It was more denial. A placeholder for pain. Nadia's body a convenient receptacle as long as she was willing to participate.

"You wanna get breakfast?" he asked when they finished.

"Nah," Nadia demurred. "I need to go home and change before work."

"You know, you could leave some things here."

"Why?" she demanded. "To play house with you? You barely leave your *own* clothes here."

The suggestion incensed Nadia to no end. She swung her feet to the side of the bed and walked to the bathroom. They showered separately. Nadia first, then him. They dressed in the clothes of the night before, his dark suit and her yellow mini dress with the bouffant sleeves giving way more than what the morning required. Creatures of the dark, they squinted in the bright of the day as they scrambled into the tinted interior of his ruby-red Cutlass Supreme.

It wasn't until they were around the corner from her house, where she lived with her mother, father, and brothers, that the silence between them broke.

"You comin' back tonight?" he asked.

"Maybe," she answered, gathering her purse.

He slowed the car to a stop in front of her door. He never pulled over to the curb, never parked. There was no need to pretend his time was languorous. That he didn't have somewhere else he needed to be. Another house, a home, that held a wife and two children of his own.

Nadia opened the door. He grabbed her arm. "See you tonight?" His pager vibrated against his hip. She shrugged out of his grasp and rolled her eyes. Not that he witnessed her indignation. His eyes stared at the tiny rectangular screen of the beeper filled with familiarity.

"Bye."

"Tonight?" He looked at her briefly.

"Maybe."

She slammed the door and he sped away. It wasn't lost on her that the site of their first indiscretion was inside his car. High off a funk concert, they conscripted one another into selfish service that rendered them mute save for the guttural grunts and soul-shattering screams emitted under the cover of night. Even then, they were moving in opposite directions.

INSIDE THE HOUSE, THE SMELL OF BACON, EGGS, GRITS, AND BLACK coffee hit Nadia at the door. She heard dishwater running, pots and pans clanging, and her brothers, Bryan and Terry, playing a game of hot hands while Gladys played referee. Eugene muttered his occasional *Listen to ya mama, now* as Nadia stepped into the kitchen.

"Well, good morning to you too," Eugene said. He sipped his coffee and read the paper. "You want some?"

"I—"

"I, nothin'," Gladys interrupted. "Go take a shower and wash yo' behind before you even think about sittin' down at my breakfast table with last night's funk on you."

"Ooooh," Terry instigated.

"Mornin', Mama," Nadia muttered.

"Gotcha," Bryan shouted triumphantly, with a stinging slap of Terry's hand.

"Stop," Terry whined. "I wasn't ready."

"Pay attention, then."

"Y'all cut it out," Gladys reprimanded.

Nadia shook her head as she passed her siblings on the way down to her basement apartment. It was all fun and games until one wrong move turned hot hands into slap-boxing and Terry was in tears because Bryan, five years his senior, had hit him too hard. She smirked to herself. Someone was always bound to get hurt in a game where there were no rules. At the time, she didn't have sense enough to hope it wasn't her.

Nadia soaked her hair beneath the hot water spraying from the showerhead. An impromptu decision to wash and condition her strands, which smelled of sweat, sex, and his cigarettes. She luxuriated in the act as she massaged shampoo down to her scalp. It was as if four hands and twenty fingers went to work at once before she combed the conditioner from roots to ends. *If I miss breakfast, I miss breakfast,* she thought to herself. She didn't rush her washing. It was a ritual she'd learned to enjoy since she started doing her own hair when she was a teenager. Where Gladys could just use setting lotion and the scrunch of her hands to form curls, Nadia had to employ more effort. Gladys was never the hair-combing kind of mama. It wasn't a skill Ruby passed down. Emma and Jubi wouldn't allow it. Not that Nadia knew that. She'd never even heard their names. Nor was there a lasting memory of when she did. Her attention to her hair came from the relentless teasing she endured in school when the styles Gladys had pulled, tucked, and pinned inevitably fell apart, leaving her length springy, shrunken, and all over her head.

As she got older, she got better. Especially once she dropped out of college and Gladys cut her off, save for the roof over her head. Nadia only messed up once. She left the relaxer in too long and cut too much, leaving scabby scalp burns and a lopsided style. That was all it took, after Gladys offered her a smirking condolence of "It'll grow back," for her to realize that was not a satisfactory solution to accidentally bushwhacking her crown. Now she clipped her own ends, relaxed her new growth smooth every eight weeks, and even played around with color. She knew she was good when she got compliments on her style and questions of "Who did your hair?" from other Black women waiting at the bus stop. Smiling when she answered "I did" was the only point of pride in her life.

Nadia wrapped a towel turban-style around her head and another around her body when she finished in the small bathroom Eugene had built just for her: stand-up shower, toilet, and face bowl. Even in its efficiency, it was still a luxury. In no rush to return upstairs, Nadia relished in moisturizing her skin as she tried to come up with an answer to the question Gladys was sure to ask. *What are you doing with your life?*

When she emerged from her sanctuary, hair pulled into a hasty bun, Bryan and Terry were still tag-teaming the dishes. Eugene re-mained in his spot while Gladys sat in her corner against the wall where the rotary phone was mounted, a Jackie Collins paperback in front of her.

"Anything left?" Nadia asked.

"I left a plate warming for you on the stove," Eugene said.

"Thank you, Daddy."

"I guess he the only one in here worth thanking, huh?" Gladys muttered, without looking up.

Nadia sighed. "Thank you for breakfast, Mama."

Gladys humphed and turned the page.

Nadia was using both the fork and a strip of bacon to scoop grits and eggs into her mouth when Gladys closed her book. She felt her mother's eyes before her mouth gave the fire that blazed their words.

"You know," she began, "if you keep on out there doing what you doing, something gon' get done."

"Gladys, let the girl eat in peace, please."

"Eugene, you need to stop taking up for her when you know she in the wrong."

"In the wrong about what, Mama?" Nadia dropped her fork and met Gladys's glare.

Nadia was her mother twenty years prior, only without the gnaw-ing toddler at her knees. Now in a housecoat and glasses, staring that same child in the face, the contempt she seemed to always have for her was discernible in the creased line scowl that contorted her face.

"You know what you doin'," Gladys said.

"I'm livin' my life. Havin' fun. I ain't hurtin' nobody."

The lie sounded good in the moment, but its sweetness turned bitter in the air. Her wavering voice helped Gladys seize upon her suspicion. "You don't know who you hurtin'," she pounced. "If it ain't nobody else, you still hurtin' yourself."

"How, Mama? Tell me how?"

"When the last time you even looked into going back to school, let alone talked to us about it, huh?"

"That requires more money than I've got saved up. And you already made clear that y'all wasn't helping."

Gladys sucked her teeth, irritated by the reminder of her own faults. She charged on, "Instead of blaming everybody else, you need to figure out what you gon' do with your life, and it better be more than runnin' behind some man."

"You ran behind Daddy."

Terry dropped a knife to the ground. It pinged against the tiled floor. Running water in the sink where Bryan rinsed soapy dishes seemed to roar like a waterfall. The rustle of Eugene's newspaper added to the din. He folded the pages together and cleared his throat.

"Nadia," he began, "I think what your mama is trying to say is that we don't want to see you wanderin' 'round here aimless, settling for any old thing when you better than that." He sipped his coffee. "That goes for the job and the man."

"Eugene, she ain't hearin' you. She ain't tryin' to hear you. We been sayin' the same thing for weeks."

"I'll figure it out."

"When?" Gladys yelled.

"Hold up," Nadia said, raising a hand. "When I tried to move in with Toya damn near—"

"Watch your mouth when you talking to your mama," Eugene said.

"Sorry, Daddy." Nadia began again. "When I tried to move in with Toya two years ago, you begged me not to go. Told me you needed help with Bryan and Terry, when helping you with them is why I got so overwhelmed and had to drop out in the first place."

"But what you been doin' since?" Gladys demanded.

"Trying to figure out what I wanna do, since what I *was* working for died. *You* killed it."

"Delays are not denials."

Nadia humphed as the self-righteous tone Gladys used to make the church announcements took over her voice. She counted inhales and exhales, waiting for Gladys to rail, even though she ignored Nadia's excuse as if parenting someone else's children weren't a valid complaint.

"You wanna blame me for your failing out of school because you helped out with your brothers? That ain't nothing but your own choices. I went to school, got my degrees, *and* held down my job at the hospital with three children. You ain't had none."

"You did that because you had *me!*"

"So I guess I'm to blame for you not doing nothing else with your life since then? Bryan fifteen now. Terry ten. They watch themselves. And what you doin'? Nothin'?"

"Workin'?"

"But what you workin' for?"

"To get the hell up outta here," Nadia muttered.

"All right now, that's enough," Eugene admonished.

His even-keeled intervention silenced everyone. Standing up from the breakfast table, he smoothed his hands over his pajama pants and white T-shirt and tucked the paper beneath his arm.

"Y'all do this every weekend, and I'm sick of it," he said. "Now, both of you ain't right. And both of you ain't wrong. Nadia, you either want to be here or you don't."

"Your wife either wants me to stay or she wants me to leave."

"Gladys, she's right. You can't have it both ways."

Gladys didn't respond. Instead, she burrowed her eyes into his face, wishing they were daggers, arrows, anything sharp to make him feel her anger, but she did not sharpen her tongue and wield her verbal sword. In his presence, she allowed him the last word. Eugene poured himself another cup of coffee and carried it, the paper, and himself through the kitchen and up the front stairs. Gladys waited until she no longer heard his feet shuffling above their heads before returning her attention back to Nadia.

She softened. "Maybe I don't say it right, but you can do a whole lot more than you doing. Don't you want that for yourself?"

"Of course I do. I'm just trying to figure it out."

"Well, what you got so far?"

Nadia could never explain why she answered, "I don't know, maybe going to hair school." But it felt right in the moment. The dull ache in her belly she felt that morning with Roman seemed to disappear. She went with it, adding, "I always get compliments and people asking me if I do hair."

Gladys slapped the table with both hands, incensed.

"Hair school? Really?!" she yelled.

It was an insult and injury if Gladys had ever heard one. There was only one person in her life she knew could do something with hair, and she had no control of her. Quiet as it was kept, those who thought they did had no control over her either. But even though Ruby learned to braid by the spirit, she had no designs to make a life of beauty culture. She, like the women before her, was trained in the ways of agrarian society. She ran the farm like Jubi, like Emma, like Evangeline. The first one to discover the talent hidden in the hands of this particular line of Dupree women. The first one to witness the consequences of what could come of such talent if allowed to flourish.

Gladys didn't know the story. Not all of it. It was whispered in the old house between women who cast a cold eye anytime Ruby set hands to her head. What Nadia wanted to cultivate, they called wicked. The talent she wanted to train was rumored evil. It was bad enough her mama's soul had been captured by sin, but for her daughter, she wouldn't have it. Gladys paced the peninsula of the kitchen table, hands on hips, blowing air, trying to find the words of reason and not the superstitions of the departed.

Through clenched teeth, she said, "You can't do no better than doing hair."

"This is why I don't tell you nothing!" Nadia flailed in her seat. "When I do it's always an issue. Dropping out. Working at the Plaza. You want me to figure it out, but you only want me to do it on your terms and your way."

"That's not it at all. *At all.* You ain't never said nothing about doing no hair. Never in your life have you ever talked about you wanna do hair. That sound like some dumb idea that just floated to the top of your mind while you was in the shower."

"Or maybe God put it there," Nadia sneered.

"Then, chile, if it's your God-given purpose, then go'n 'head, get to it, be the best at it, and get the hell outta my house while you doing it. You wanna play with the Lord, you best remember the wages of sin is death."

"Mama, I'ma be doing hair, not killing nobody."

"Whatever you doing, it won't be here."

"No problem," Nadia said, standing from the table. "I'll enroll as soon as classes start."

She walked her plate to the trash can against the back wall and scraped the half-eaten food into the garbage. When she handed it over to Terry and Bryan at the sink, neither of them looked her in the face. It was only when she placed the plate in the sudsy water did Terry chance a glance.

"You really leaving?" he asked, bottom lip quivering.

"I can't stay here," Nadia said.

"She sure can't," Gladys added.

Spite dripped from her tone like venom from a snake's fangs as she returned to her novel. Later she'd sit in that same spot, the Bible in place of *The Bitch.*

6.

Tati tried not to fidget too much inside the graduation hall. The eyes from her family beamed on her as she waited in line to cross the stage and receive her diploma. She spotted Nadia, Mimi, her uncles, and their wives sitting at one of the white-linen-covered round tables that dotted the perimeter of the room as soon as she marched in at the beginning of the ceremony. Also at the table were Toya and Desirée's little brother, Felix.

"Tatiana Washington," Mrs. Harrington called from the stage.

In addition to being the history teacher, she was also one of the administrators at the Central City High School seventh- and eighth-grade academic center. She waited with a wide smile as Tati ascended the roll-away staircase to accept the fake diploma scroll tied with a ribbon.

"Congratulations, grad," Mrs. Harrington said off mic in her raspy voice.

They shook hands, and Tati looked up and smiled in time to see Nadia snapping pictures with her disposable camera. A camcorder was glued between her uncle Bryan's hands and covered one of his eyes as he captured every moment for posterity. Tati shook her head as she descended the stairs back to her seat. It was rare to have her whole family together outside of a holiday. It almost made up for who was missing from her table. Though her uncles were great stand-ins, she still wished she had a daddy there rooting for her too.

She couldn't help but believe she was missing out on something. Even if she didn't let herself dwell on the grand absence from her life, her young cousins believed it for her. Last Christmas, Brandon, her uncle Bryan's four-year-old son, asked the same question she'd been asking for years.

"Tati, where's your daddy?"

Sitting around Mimi's dinner table, no one answered his inquiry just as no one had answered her the first time she'd had the nerve to ask the same. The question hung in the air surrounded by uncomfortable silence, like when you smell a fart that carries the stench of hard-boiled eggs somebody forgot about two weeks after Easter. Though everyone was sitting at her table for graduation, Tati couldn't help but feel like that stench still clung to her and Nadia. They were supportive because she was without something, someone, they deemed necessary, not in spite of it. As if they believed broken homes rubbed off and daddylessness was contagious.

"Would everyone please stand," Mrs. Harrington said from the stage. "Ladies and gentlemen, I present to you the Central City High School eighth-grade academic center graduating class of 1995. Students, you may now turn your tassels."

Music resounded through the hall as cheers erupted from students and the tables of family and friends. Tati sidestepped her way out of her row bypassing some friends she'd gone to elementary school with and others she met the year prior when she started seventh grade at Central City. By the time Tati reached the table, Desirée was already there with Felix in her arms. Though he was too big to hold, he animated under the attention as he pawed her body to snatch the cap off of her head.

"Come on, Tati, let's take a picture," Nadia said. "We been waitin' on you. Desi, you and Toya get in the picture too."

"Ooh, you must be in a good mood today," Toya said, a smile crossing her lips.

Toya and Nadia huddled behind Tati, Desirée, and Felix, who refused to be put down, while Bryan traded his camcorder for the disposable cameras that were handed to him from everyone who wanted to capture the image.

"Now just family," Mimi said. "I wanna take a picture with my grandbaby before we have to go'n 'head and get up outta here. I know they don't want this many negroes in they establishment after the sun go down."

"Mama, relax," Nadia chided. "Ain't nobody finna kick us out. Black folks are allowed south of the Jeffery Manor, you know."

"You can come up here in all these 100s if you want to, but I remember a time when we wasn't allowed over here."

"You also remember a time when you wasn't supposed to be on the North Side either, but that don't stop you from shopping on Michigan Avenue, now, does it? Things change."

Mimi humphed. "Not that damn much, they don't. C'mon here. Family only."

The emphasis in Mimi's voice was followed by a hard stare at Toya, Desirée, and Felix as she waited for them to step away. Tati looked from her friend to their mothers, all their expressions pained smiles everyone else pretended they didn't see. Emboldened by being the center of the celebration, Tati spoke up. "Desi and Miss Grant and Felix are family."

Nadia's long exhale was unmistakable, but she didn't take up for Tati. She never had a chance to.

"Not all skinfolk is kinfolk," Mimi said. "But since your friend like taking pictures so much, I'm sure she won't mind taking ours. Go'n 'head, y'all, hand the lil' girl your cameras."

"Oh, hell nah," Toya snapped. "I'll do it."

She stepped in front of Desirée and collected the cameras from Nadia, Bryan, and Terry. And snapped several rounds as they all said, "Cheese."

"Hold on, we got one more," Toya said, switching to her own camera. "Desi, go'n 'head get in there."

"This is family only," Mimi emphasized.

"And this one is my camera," Toya said, waving it in the air.

Desirée rushed to stand beside Tati, squeezing between her and Mimi. Felix on her hip did the work of further separating the old woman from her granddaughter. Once Desirée was situated, Toya kneeled on the floor beneath everyone, set the five-second timer on the spin dial, and held the camera up high and at an angle.

"Say, 'You go, grads,'" she yelled.

Everyone's voice repeated the cheerful phrase right before the camera flash except Mimi's. Her dour expression, captured in the photo, only deepened further, wrinkling her face as everyone else extended their congratulations. Tati and Desirée shifted from foot to foot as they thanked them all.

"Y'all goin' to high school now," Bryan said.

"Get your pennies ready; they 'bout to be fresh meat," Terry added.

"Now why would you say such a thing like that," Mimi snapped. "Don't be puttin' no fast tail labels on Tati because that's the kinda women you like to chase."

"Yo, your grandmother is wild," Desirée whispered through a giggle.

"Tell me something you don't know," Tati said, trying to stifle her own laughter. "You heard how she came at yo' mama crazy."

"That's all right, I fixed her," Toya said, butting into the conversation. "Half the pictures I took, my finger is over your grandmother so you won't even see her."

"Now you know you wrong," Nadia said, joining in.

"No, your mother is the one who's in the wrong and you know it."

Nadia shrugged her shoulders, letting Toya have the last word as she caught Mimi's glare shift from them to Terry's wife, Chloe, who sported a hot-pink pencil dress and bolero to match his Now and Later taffy-colored Stacy Adams suit. Mimi's eyes pierced like throwing knives. Tati snickered.

I guess it is better to talk about people you don't like in front of their face.

Not that anyone had ever told Tati directly, but she'd overheard enough conversations to know Mimi's disdain for Toya was nothing compared to her feelings on her sons' marriages. Bryan and Lorraine had been together the longest, and she was no closer to getting on Mimi's good side than Chloe, who'd married Terry within the last year. She'd had a baby within the last year too. A few months after the wedding, which only gave Mimi more fuel for her disdain.

"She knew what she was doing, trapping my baby," she'd complained on more than one occasion.

Nadia cleared her throat.

"I think Tati will be just fine going into her ninth-grade year," Lorraine said.

Ever the diplomat, she took Mimi's insults in stride. Perhaps because she took satisfaction in knowing Mimi liked her better than Chloe. In reality, she only tolerated her more. Lorraine and Bryan had been together since they were in college at U of I down in Urbana. While Mimi complained about him coming back from school with a wife, she didn't take it too far because they both returned with two degrees a piece. Bryan taught high school math at Hyde Park, and Lorraine was a psychologist with her own private practice downtown. It was more than could be said of Chloe, who didn't have a job and had no prospects of getting one, let alone a degree to aid in her search.

"Congratulations," Chloe said. "We're so proud of you. Both of you." She nodded toward Desirée.

Chloe shoved a sealed envelope toward Tati, grabbed her purse from the back of her chair, and slung its gold chain strap across her body. Yanking Terry's hand, she apologized for their abrupt departure. "We need to get back to the baby," she said.

"Okay." Tati blinked. "Kiss Alexis for me. Maybe I can babysit her sometime."

"That won't be necessary," Mimi said. "You got a job working right there in your mama shop. Let your aunty and uncle figure out their own affairs with their family."

"C'mon, Desi, we gotta go," Toya said. "You know you're leaving to be with your dad for the summer tomorrow, and you ain't nowhere near packed."

"Hmph." The sound came loudly from Nadia. "How's *he* doing?"

"Hell if I know," Toya said, her voice sharp. "It ain't like we talk much."

"I wonder why," Nadia muttered.

"You already know why," Toya shot back. "But we don't need to get into that here. Desi, tell Tati bye."

"I'll check you later," Desirée said, adjusting Felix as she sidled away.

"Send me a postcard. And some pictures," Tati said behind them.

"I will." Desirée turned around. "I promise."

"Cross your heart and hope to die?"

"Kiss this promise to the sky."

They kissed their peace fingers and raised them high toward heaven. Grins shined from both of their faces before Desirée turned around to rejoin Toya, who never looked back at Nadia and her family. As close as Toya and Nadia had been before, those old times were long past, and neither of them had word the first as to say why. Theirs was a friendship that fizzled, rekindled only because of the closeness of their daughters. An intentional closeness, yes, orchestrated by their mothers, but one that would see them live vicariously through Tati and Desirée than have them pick up where they left off. The lies and disagreements between them wouldn't allow it.

"Hey, Tati, congratulations," Terry said. "I gotta go."

He walked toward the doors of the graduation hall, back rounded, a picture of pity, to where Chloe, angry and offended, had been waiting for him to catch up. Tati waved three fingers at them as they pushed through the heavy double doors.

At least nobody had a real fight.

Of all her family members, Tati's favorites were Terry and Chloe. She preferred to be around them more than anyone else. As the youngest, Terry was closer in age to Tati than he was to Nadia or Bryan. He treated her more like a kid sister than a niece. He also had no problem going against Mimi. Nadia and Bryan often reminisced on how he got away with more than they ever did without punishment or even verbal chastisement. Mimi blamed his notions to follow his impulses on herself for the lack of discipline she'd exerted over him in his youth. It's the reason, she believed, he ended up marrying Chloe in the first place. She was a former dancer for the Bulls, a job, if you could even call it that, conditioned upon youth and beauty—ephemeral qualifications that inevitably faded like day into night, summer into fall.

"That was a piss-poor excuse for leaving Tati's graduation ceremony," Mimi said, her eyes focused on the door where Terry and Chloe had made their exit.

"It's not like you can blame them, the way you started up with Chloe," Nadia said.

Bryan sighed. "Here we go."

Lorraine punched his arm, and Bryan sat down. When her eyes connected with Tati, who'd observed the exchange, she raised a finger to her lips. She hadn't meant for anyone to see her physically admonish Bryan in public. Though Tati was grateful to see some of her fire. Most times Lorraine played small. She didn't talk too much, she didn't disagree, and she barely had an opinion when everyone was together. Tati had asked her once why she always sat around and listened. A question to which Lorraine smirked and replied, "We have two ears, two eyes, and one mouth for a reason. It's enough people in this family who stir the pot. I don't need to be one of them."

While Tati wasn't completely sure about all of what she meant, she knew shade when she heard it. After that comment, she respected Lorraine a little more. She may have dressed forgettably in muted colors, small heels, and basic jewelry like pearl studs, but Tati knew she had spunk, whether she chose to exercise it or not.

" . . . All I'm sayin' and all I said is he don't have to be puttin' no labels on our Tati about what kind of woman she gon' be, because that's what he like," Mimi continued. "Chloe may be his wife, but I don't have to like it."

"We all know you don't," Nadia said.

"But you should at least respect it," Bryan added.

"Respect. You wanna talk about respect?" Mimi raised an eyebrow. "Terry and that thang he call his wife walked out on Tati's graduation ceremony. Now *that's* disrespectful."

It's over, Tati thought.

Bryan said the same. "And you ain't make it no better either, Mama," he added.

"At all!" Nadia emphasized. "Not with them and definitely not with Toya and Desi."

Mimi rolled her eyes in response as Bryan brought his hands to his temples and massaged the sides of his head. He said, "We're gonna go too. Congratulations, Tati."

"Now, you don't have to do that," Mimi protested.

Everyone knew Bryan was her favorite. The only one she appeased. The only one she would sometimes defer to. Her first boy. The son she fawned over as a baby, passed off to Nadia when he became a restless toddler, and then tried to guide as an adolescent and teen into a career she thought respectable. She was still trying to guide him now as all parents try to direct their children no matter how far they get up in age. Whenever Mimi saw Bryan, she'd find a way to ask if he was thinking about making the switch from teacher to administrator. She wanted him to be a principal, maybe even a superintendent.

Bryan never said that was what he wanted for himself. Other than marrying Lorraine and speaking his mind unmuzzled, he'd never done anything to make Mimi say a foul word against him. Not that she would since he looked so much like Eugene, the only man, the only person really, Mimi had ever held her tongue in front of. Bryan also never gave her a reason to become the subject of her ire. He never talked out of turn, least not when she could overhear. Like Lorraine, he didn't stir too many pots. Compared to Mimi's other children, Bryan was the least problematic.

Tati watched as Mimi's face twisted into a frown. It was as if she couldn't bear the sight of watching her son walk away. While Terry's departure had induced anger, watching Bryan leave was downright distressing. Mimi picked imaginary lint from her clothes as Bryan led Lorraine out of the graduation hall. Her tongue rolled around her mouth and poked at her cheeks for words, but she didn't have the language to express her anguish.

She shook her head and muttered to herself, "After all I went through just to get them here, they could at least be grateful."

Neither Nadia nor Tati knew what she meant. And in the moment they didn't have the presence of mind to ask. But even if they had answered the call and asked the questions, "What do you mean? What did you go through?" it's not like Gladys could have said. Yes, she'd had difficulty carrying her last two pregnancies. Her boys. But she had carried them. Delivered them. The same couldn't be said for the women before her. Not for Ruby, not for Jubi, and certainly not for Emma.

7.

Like all children forbidden to do something they believed important, Emma promised herself that as soon as she had a family and a
baby of her own she would celebrate all of the birthdays she could. It
just so happened that George Dupree wanted the same things. He
came off Zephaniah Foster's plantation too, but by way of Virginia.
He and his ma'am were sold south a few years before the war by the
mistress, who wouldn't stand to suffer looking at a little pickaninny
who nearly carried her own children's complexions, not to mention
their features. That she sold mother and child together may have
seemed merciful but was really only a temporary fix for her own
insecurity.

In Land's End, George and his ma'am stayed on the Dupree
farm after it was deeded to Evangeline and Emma with no designs
to return. Therefore, it was inside the schoolhouse on the abandoned
farm where he and Emma first struck up a friendship. That they
married years later and tried for a family of their own brought Evangeline, ever surly and set in her ways, an effervescent joy. She spent
her days humming and rocking as she worked. Her sturdy body
lumbered around with song; a permanent smile spread across her
thick face nearly erased the creases of the life she'd lived.

Nearly.

Until the blood.

In the day, George, a woodworker by trade, built and banged

around the quarter shack, adding rooms and spaces for them to spread into. In the night, he and Emma tried with enthusiastic effort, verve and vigor, to bring forth a little one. And their work was rewarded. Initially. Evangeline knew each time they had been successful. She read the signs of Emma's body. The outbreak of bumps on her face that first signaled the shift. When they cleared, a glow radiated from her smooth skin. But it was always before she would begin walking around with her fingers laced together over her belly that the pains would start. The cramping Emma described as being pulled apart organ by organ. As if something inside her demanded to be set free. Released. If it started in the day, she'd moan through the night, and in the morning the blood.

The first time, Evangeline, rarely one to show affection to her ward, held her close, brushed her fine hair smooth, and told her she and George could try again. "These things happen," she said. "Nobody knows why."

The second time, Evangeline said the same.

But when it happened a third time in the same year, the shiver of cool up her back told her something unnatural was amiss. Instead of taking the bloody bedsheets and nightdress away for a thorough washing, Evangeline smeared the sticky wet refuse above the door frame George had built.

"What are you doing?" Emma asked.

She had gotten used to some of Evangeline's ways from learning her own self, but this was new. Evangeline was possessed. As if a spirit, not of herself, took hold of her body and controlled her limbs. Mind set to sleep, Evangeline only pantomimed the required actions. When she finished the door frame, it looked as if it had been painted red and the color was peeling. The sheets were light pink instead of deep, rusty iron.

In a breathless voice, she said, "You need to give her an offering."

"Who?" Emma asked.

But Evangeline was gone, carrying the sheets and nightdress outside for the wash. At least that's what Emma thought until she smelled the smoke. George came inside and asked, "Why she setting our bed things on fire?"

"She said we need to give an offering," Emma said.

"To who?"

Emma shrugged.

When Evangeline came back inside, she carried two pots with her: one filled with fresh water, the other filled with black dirt from the field and in it a small green shoot.

She said, "You got to have balance. Make her feel welcome and let her know you wants to be fertile like this here soil. You wants to grow full like this here orchid gon' do. You always want to be specific when you dealing with the wants and ways of them people on the other side."

"Who from the other side?" Emma asked.

"Your ma'am," Evangeline answered unblinking. "She here. Coming for all the things that belong to her. Including yo' chillun."

"Who's here?" George asked.

"You ain't tell him, did ya?"

"Tell me what?"

Evangeline humphed. "Dat's between you and yo' wife. Just don't be meddling with my bidness, if'n you don't want the blood to come again. Leave it be and let it work."

When Evangeline plodded out of the room, Emma faced an unsettled George with more questions than she had answers. What she knew of her own ma'am was limited. Only given the details Evangeline wanted her to have and even those were more warning than worthy virtues. She looked at him from where she sat in the stripped bed in a new nightdress and inhaled his woody scent. He worked in what used to be the stables. The horses long sold off, George had made it his workshop just like Evangeline had converted the old, detached kitchen from the big house into a storehouse where she and Emma ran the farm.

Emma sighed. Wondered how she was going to start the story. Staring away from George, she turned to look in the mirror he'd made for her. Tall, oval, and adjustable. He'd even carved their initials into the wood.

"You know how I only use a comb on my hair and never my fingers to pick through the knots?" Emma asked.

"I reckon."

"It's because of my ma'am. My real ma'am. Mama Evangeline, she took care of me. She raised me. She the only ma'am I know, but I didn't come from her."

"So what happened to your real ma'am? She was sold?"

"Mama Evangeline say she died the day I was born. I heard her talkin' about it to Ms. Claudette in the storehouse one day when I was comin' in from school and they was going on and on about how to tell me the truth."

Emma closed her eyes as she thought back to that day. One of the rare times she'd seen her ma'am hospitable with someone else. She didn't know that while Evangeline had been friendly with everyone who came off Zephaniah Foster Dupree's plantation, that all changed when Emma was born. Since then theirs had been a lonely life lacking laughter other than their own, and now George, who could only add but so much to their pitiful chorus. Emma learned from Evangeline to stay with your own kind, never having any friends outside of the Dupree line.

"What happened?" he asked.

His eyes jumped from Emma to the blood-smeared door frame and back again. But Emma didn't answer. She shook her head, unwilling to give voice to what she'd heard. Credence to conjecture. Like Evangeline, she had her own superstitions. Just as some things weren't meant to be celebrated, she believed some things weren't meant to be repeated. Some things weren't meant to be remembered.

"She felt me near," Emma said. "She turned her head to the corner where I was hiding and ordered me in to help. We never did talk about it, but she knows I know something."

"Something enough to think it's your ma'am taking our babies from your body from the other side?"

Emma nodded.

George, with only half a story and none of the details, could only follow the lead of the women he'd made family. It was under the protection Evangeline built from blood that he and Emma found themselves in the family way for a fourth time, though none of them acknowledged it until Emma's belly swelled in her sixth or seventh month. They'd held their breath waiting for the pain, the blood, waiting for the life to be snatched away, but it grew. Like the orchid sitting in the door frame, Emma's body changed, curved, and bloomed full.

"You carryin' low," Evangeline remarked, one day when she felt it safe. "You know that means it's a girl."

"You think so?" Emma asked, from where she stood chopping vegetables for the stew they were preparing.

"I knows so," Evangeline said. "Girls got to be closer to the earth. Fertile begets fertile. Conjured by the hands of God, we come from the soil, fashioned complete in the mud. That's why we's known to create thangs out of nothing. To make a way outta no way."

"I thought it was 'cause men always like to rule over us. Can't get no lower than a woman. Even if'n you is colored."

"It's some truth to that too."

Emma nodded in time as Evangeline hummed. She didn't tell George Evangeline's new myth about their baby or even her own projected regrets. Some things you have to keep to yourself and just wait and see what comes to pass. Whether it was a boy or girl, the three of them were all just tickled that for the first time Emma had made it to the point where she had a right to complain. Her back ached and her feet hurt, swollen as they were. Everything George made with his hands was uncomfortable. She craved soft instead of sturdy.

Seeing Emma evolve from afraid to joyfully crotchety, persnickety even, about every little detail set a stillness in Evangeline's stomach. Something akin to peace but not quite. She tended to the altars she erected in honor of Emma's real ma'am, watering the orchid every week from the leftover in the offering pot beside it before refilling it fresh. The orchid opened and blossomed, and so did Emma. But Evangeline left nothing to chance. In her own room, she had George build her a small table. She covered it with a white cloth that had four inches of lace she'd sewn herself, draping the floor. A candle burned in the evening; a bowl full of fresh water never went empty or stale. A mason jar always held flowers picked from the verdant garden in front of the expanded quarter shack where Evangeline grew her herbs, plants, and little pops of color for something pretty to behold. And there was always a plate of corn bread and sweet potato pone reminiscent of her favorites Evangeline stole away for the short time she was on the plantation. The entire installation as well as the threshold of every doorway was surrounded by a circle or line of salt for protection and healing, purity and breath. Both Emma and her ma'am were well-fed and tended to. What all the lingering long for. Someone to care. Someone to remember.

When the day came for Emma to push even it was bewitching. In the hour between dusk and nightfall, Emma's labor began. George demanded he be in the room instead of outside. Not used to men meddling in women's work, Evangeline used him as her assistant to fetch water, sheets, towels, and whatever else she hollered for while she sat watch between Emma's legs. Back straight as an ironing board on her little three-legged stool, she kept time between labor pangs waiting for the water, but the bag never broke. Even when the contractions intensified and quickened, no preface flowed from Emma's body to announce the baby's arrival.

Evangeline had never birthed a baby dry. She'd have missed the transition had it not been for Emma's own warning.

"It's time," she gritted through bared teeth and fists balled in sheets.

Having assisted in enough births of her own, Emma read her own signs while Evangeline sat momentarily stupefied. It was Emma's first push, uncoached and unassisted, that brought the baby into view. Crowning at the gates of life, Evangeline hollered for George as she arranged the water and towels. She massaged Emma's opening with her fingers to let the baby pass through.

"It's a girl," Evangeline said.

Veiled en caul, the baby didn't cry, and Evangeline didn't force her. There was no urgency to pound her back or clear her lungs. She let the baby float in the bowl of water until the cord connecting her and Emma stopped pulsing. Only then did she usher her into the world from the peace of the other side.

"You gotta name?" Evangeline asked, when she finally presented the swaddled baby girl to the parents.

"Jubilee," George said.

"We have been set free," Emma echoed.

She looked between the high-yellow girl in her arms and the tall orchid she thought swayed in the still air. After latching the baby to her bosom, Emma focused on the altar of offering in the doorway and mouthed *Thank you* to the dancing shadows.

"It worked," Emma said. "She's gone."

Evangeline followed Emma's gaze and saw the shadows playing around the orchid. She smiled, knowing Emma had the sight. Most women did upon giving birth, whether they felt a hand wrapped in their own, a breeze by the leg, a pool of light above their head, or something else entirely unuttered. Birthing is rooted in feeling and emotion, timing and tension. It is reflex. Base-level instincts of creation, entirely ineffable. Some say God is in the room. Others the heavenly hosts. And who can deny those accounts when the women are the ones in balance between Earth and the other side, the body rendered a portal?

Evangeline nodded, knowing she'd have to wait and see if Emma's discernment stayed. If her sight developed depth of vision. The kind of clairvoyance Evangeline was endowed with without ever having birthed any living babes of her own, though she and Henry had tried mightily, led her to look past the orchid and beyond the shadows. She read the ripples troubling the water.

"We'll see" was all she could muster.

Though she wanted to agree with Emma, to say, *Yes, she's gone,* optimism wasn't her specialty. Especially when she knew the girl's hardheaded ma'am, even in spirit, wasn't going that easily. The baby girl was a gift, wrapped as she was. They'd be fools to expect another. But you don't say that to young folk cradling their baby, less than an hour old, and trying to get her to coo.

It would be a long time before Evangeline said, and Emma accepted, what they both would grow to learn to be true: spirit was stingy, selfish, and stubborn as the days.

ALMOST A FULL YEAR PASSED BEFORE EMMA AND GEORGE GOT the itch to try again with intention. They kept a pot of water beside the main entrance of the quarter shack—which was now more home with George's additions—and in the door frames of each bedroom. Flowers and greenery were abundant inside and out. Orchids and sunflowers, ferns and ficus waved from the garden, the newly added front porch, the living area that was the only room in the original quarter shack, as well as in George and Emma's doorway and on Evangeline's altar. But there was no blood. Not fresh anyway. The last smear had been for Jubilee. Whatever was left was barely recognizable. A thought that crossed both Emma's and Evangeline's minds but neither of them said out loud. How could they go to the trouble of building and tending their altars, spreading salt, and presenting offerings if they didn't believe?

As it would happen, Emma got big in the summertime. She didn't say anything at first. Didn't let on that her and George's routine practice had provided possibility. She kept on in her work of the farm, keeping track of the seed lent, the crops harvested, and who was owed what for their labor and service. But the heat got the best of her. In the storehouse one August afternoon, Emma keeled over from where she sat on her stool and landed on the hard ground.

"Somebody run get George and Evangeline," hollered one of the men in line.

A woman behind him set to running the land yelling, "Emma fell. Emma fell," as loud and obnoxiously as she could.

It was a voice that carried both concern and exuberance, and not the kind created when anxiety attacks and makes you nervous. Though felled and trying hard to focus on keeping all her feeling, especially about her belly, Emma heard the unmistakable sound of glee. With a glance toward those once waiting in her line, she detected mischief alight in their eyes. Something akin to delight. She'd heard tell that some of the folk minding crops and renting space on the Dupree women's land didn't feel right about their landlord being a colored woman. Even if they did pay fair. What they wanted was what Emma had. A chance to own. Not rent. While their grumbles never reached her personally, she knew they talked, passing judgment all the same. Their jealousy left them bitter as unripened vine fruit, a taste memory stored in the mouth, always available for quick recall.

With Emma on the floor, knees balled into her belly, the bitterness turned sweet as some thought to themselves, *Serves her right.*

Don't nothing come for free. By the time Evangeline and George reached her, the shock of her fall had worn off.

"Are you hurt?" George asked.

"I don't think so, but . . ." Emma let her eyes do the talking. She didn't want to let on to the crowd that had now gathered in the storehouse that it was more than herself who could have been hurt. They didn't need her business, and she didn't need their ill intent. Emma didn't want any of their antagonism or hostility to dissuade her purported beliefs. Like Evangeline said, "Spirits fill the shift. Dey knows when your heart ain't in it and it's only your head making you go through the motions."

"Let's get you to the house," Evangeline said, helping George hoist Emma from the ground. "You can lay in the bed beside Jubilee. She still napping anyhow."

"What happened?" George asked, sweeping her full body into his arms.

"I'm not quite sure," Emma began. "One moment I was helping Abe figure how much more he needed to make a decent profit and the next I was on the ground."

"It's the heat," Evangeline said beside them. "Neither one of you need to be out here in it. Y'all ain't built for field work. Ain't got the color or even the disposition to handle it."

"I don't know what you talking about. I does right fine in the workshop," George retorted.

Evangeline grunted and kept on toward the house. Inside, George laid Emma beside Jubilee. He asked, "You sure you all right? Don't need nothing?"

"I'm fine. Mama Evangeline here. She'll take care of me. Won't you, ma'am?"

"I got her," Evangeline said.

They waited until George had cleared the doorway and they

heard the front door rake against the wood of the porch and close with a clang. Clearing her throat, Evangeline spoke first.

"How far along are you?"

"Only a few months. Two, maybe three moons."

"You feel any wetness between your legs?"

"No. Was there any on the ground after y'all picked me up?"

"No."

Their sighs filled the room heavy with the hot air of what wasn't spoken. The fears they refused to give voice to. On the one hand there was relief. No blood. But on the other, a little could've gone a long way. A few drops of fresh wet smeared above the door could have bolstered the protection they were building around them. Would've signaled to the spirit ma'am that they hadn't forgotten gifts required sacrifice. Soul for a soul.

Despite the lack of injury and the missing blood, Emma and Evangeline continued not acknowledging the present growth beneath Emma's dresses and gowns. That is until they couldn't hide it any longer. While George may not have had gifts, he was still astute. Forever a student, he noticed the curve carving itself from Emma's belly. He also noticed the demeanor of the Dupree women. Careful. Not fawning.

One evening, in the living area, where they were preparing for dinner, a jug of water in his hand, George asked, "So it's a girl or a boy this time?"

Emma didn't have an answer. Evangeline only tsked.

She said, "Her belly stuck in the middle, like the baby deciding what it want to be."

Now, neither of them would tell you that it was George with his acknowledgment out loud of what was happening that set the pain in motion only a week later, but it was all they had to go on. They had been tending the altars, even without the blood, convincing themselves of their own belief. There should have been no reason for her to feel ignored. But the knots formed and felt to Emma much like labor. With the baby too early to live, she spent a week in bed with her legs vertical trying to keep whatever she was having in, but it was no use. Between the fatigue and the misfortune of it all, the knots tightened, the cramping worsened, the pulsing intensified, and her cervix opened, breaking water and delivering a baby boy who refused to breathe.

No matter how Evangeline pounded his back or thumped his chest, cleaned out his nostrils or tried to make him choke up any fluid he may have swallowed, he did not cough. He did not wail. Eyes closed, he belonged to the other side.

"He was too early," Evangeline said.

"I had a boy?"

Emma's voice was light and airy, disoriented as she was. Her body, processing, released let-down milk to feed none.

Evangeline saw the circular stains at the nipples of Emma's dressing gown, and it was enough to flood her eyes with tears she didn't want to fall. Choking back her own cries, she asked, "You wanna hold him? See him?"

"What for?" Emma asked.

"To remember."

"I'd rather remember when he was alive, a flutter in my belly, than see him now, knowing it weren't even real."

Evangeline nodded with intimate understanding. Unlike Emma's, her body had been a complete failure. One that could create babies, nine in fact, but never carry to term. It's what Zephaniah Foster said made her the perfect mammy. With no babies of her own to feed, she had nothing but milk tinged with grief to give. She nursed the naked young until their teeth buds dropped and they could swallow gruel. Now she felt mush pooling in her own mouth as she held on to another dead thing. Dead baby. Baby boy.

"I'll bring him to George to build him something nice."

"Where's my Jubilee?" Emma asked.

"In the workshop."

"Send her to me. The milk for her now."

WITH HIS OWN HANDS, GEORGE BUILT HIS SON A COFFIN TOO FINE for the ground. It was the first of three. All babies. All boys. Though it was the third boy that did them in. Unlike the first two, born without breath in their bodies or life in their lungs, the last one had the nerve to live. Though early, about the time between the seventh and eighth month, he pushed into the world an arm and an elbow in the air, with feet and legs running from the womb. To be so small, his fight was big. Eyes open, screams piercing and loud. There was no need to pound his back or reach fingers down his throat to clear his airway. He did that all on his own. When Evangeline placed him in Emma's arms, she named him immediately. Jeremiah Christopher Dupree.

George, anxious and outside with four-year-old Jubilee, was drawn into the room by his own son's cries.

His own son's cries.

Just the thought, the reality of what he was witnessing, made him weep. Too prepared he was to build something beautiful whose only purpose was decay. To be feasted on by the land. He set Jubilee down at the door marked with salt between the bowls of water and pots of flowers when he saw Emma holding a bundle with a smile spread across her face.

"Come meet your son," she said.

They were the sun and George a planet trapped by their gravitational pull. He didn't remember walking over to their side, but he was there. He didn't remember the sleep he lost for the five days and nights Jeremiah cried with all his might, but he was there. On the floor, in the bed, around the house, his presence steady and willing. Anchored as he was by the boy he'd longed for. The one he'd dreamed about so vividly he awoke achingly empty knowing it wasn't real. Until he was. For five days and five nights he was there. Until the crying stopped and he wasn't.

It happened in the night. After he'd been nursed to solid sleep. Emma, radiant but exhausted, turned over and drifted with him. The sleep enveloped the whole house. Jubilee with Evangeline in one room. George, Emma, and Jeremiah in the other. Everyone slept until morning. Emma didn't even arise when her milk dropped three times in the night. It wasn't until she opened her eyes to see Jubilee playing in the shadows of the doorway, smearing the salt lines, that she registered her engorged breasts and reached out to nurse Jeremiah.

But he was gone.

Already on the other side.

Skin cool to his mother's touch.

She didn't accept what she felt. Instead, Emma lifted his heavy body to her teats and tried to feed him anyway. She offered one and then the other. Her nipples leaked milk over her fingers as she jostled her dead baby, trying to get him to latch to her aching breasts.

"My brother's over here, Mama," Jubilee said, from where she played.

"Nooooo," she moaned.

Emma looked to her daughter in the doorway. The flowers wilted. The water still. Jubilee played amid it all, unaware she was dancing with death. That's when Emma chanced a look at Jeremiah's face. It wasn't the closed eyes that told her he was gone. Or his lips, turned on their own into an undertaker smile. It was the cool. The lack of heat. The chill that seemed to shift from his graying flesh to her own body. It pulled up her back like a fingernail tracing from the base of her spine to the middle of her neck.

Emma screamed before life could be choked from her too. Her lips trembled as she repeated, "No no no no no no no no no no no." Snot ran and eyes hemorrhaged tears as her voice cracked. Broke. Reached a pitch to shatter glass as her heart had been shattered. She pierced the veil of silence that had befallen the house in the sleep and forced everyone awake with her wails, including George. Her low moans and fevered howls pinched George through skin and muscle to bone. He fell to the floor, startled as he was from his slumber. Evangeline even sprang into the room despite the girth of her build and the tendency of her ankles . . . and knees to ache in the morning.

"What is it, chile?" Evangeline asked.

"He's gone," Emma shrieked.

Those were the only words Evangeline and George could make out between her cries. Wet heavy sobs that began in her gut, gurgled up her throat, and fell out of her mouth without any control. The sound mothers make when they lose their young is distinct and distinguishable from any other on Earth. A cry greater than grief, wider than mourning, and deeper than distress. Animalistic is the sound of a mother bereft after losing a cub. Whether the child is five days or fifty years, children aren't supposed to go before their parents. A trip to the other side was supposed to be a path paved by elders. Not babies who'd barely learned to blink.

Clutching her son, screaming and crying, Emma didn't know when Evangeline removed Jeremiah from her arms or when George retreated with Jubilee to his workshop to build his best yet for his boy. Racked as she was, she drank what Evangeline gave her, praying with some other part of herself that the tea would take her too.

Emma stayed in bed under clouds of unconsciousness as Evangeline cleaned the blood smears from the door frames and dismantled the altar she had built in her bedroom. The flowers and their pots, the bowls sans water, the table, its plates of food, and its lace cover—she set it all ablaze. As the fire consumed, Evangeline watched the flames rocking back and forth on her feet and nodding her head in conversation with no one and someone all the same.

In three days' time, when Jeremiah should've been a little more than a week old, Emma came from under, coaxed out by another one of Evangeline's teas. Dressed in all white, from her silky hair tucked in a turban to the dress Evangeline made her wear, she lumbered outside to the yard, where George, still in his work coveralls, had dug a hole and placed their boy beside his brothers.

Restless, Jubilee wanted to run, but Evangeline held fast to her wiggly frame. None of them had words to say. No eulogy or benediction, calls to Christ or remarks to wield repentance. All they had were themselves. All they could hold on to were themselves. George, unmoored, drifted, a planet without a star. A galaxy without a universe. Wearied and depleted, he was unknown even unto himself. They all were. That's how vast the heaviness hung. Standing in front of two tiny white crosses and another hole in the ground, Emma stepped forward and grabbed a handful of dirt from the mound piled beside George.

She tossed it onto the pristine pine box, murmuring, "Your ma'am'll see you on the other side."

Emma made her way home beneath the blue, cloudless sky. The sun above mocked as she swayed across the ground that still reeked of smoke from the fire where their dreams were scorched, their future selves incinerated. Sensing her girl's need, Evangeline released Jubilee to run while George was left with his shovel to bury their boy. Side by side the women walked to the house where they'd been forged. Babe and ma'am. Ward and guardian. Almost mother and daughter.

Breaking through the quiet of the day, Evangeline said, "It's best y'all be satisfied with what you got."

Emma remained mum.

"A girl is good. One is all you gon' get. All she'll allow."

"Why is my ma'am doing this?" Emma asked. "Why she keep takin' my boys and keeping 'em for herself?"

"It ain't about what she takin' or what she keepin'. It's what she didn't get to have."

"What's that?"

"You."

Emma stopped and held on to Evangeline to be still with her too. She looked at the woman who raised her; worry, weary, and grief etched in her face, Evangeline appeared even older than her years. Emma searched her for what she didn't say. What she'd heard tell to be true.

Evangeline continued, "She couldn't have you, so now only her girls can have her."

"You saying I'm cursed? Me? My Jubilee? All our girls to come?"

"What's a curse but a christening by another name?"

Evangeline heaved her sigh. She'd already lost so much. Her own babies. Her husband. Emma's real ma'am. Friends. She was already set apart because of the work she did enslaved and the work she inherited free. Now with Emma losing babies there was even more reason for the Black folk of Land's End, the ones who came up in the same quarters with her, to steer clear. Those who remembered, those who were there, those who had known Emma's ma'am—however briefly—knew some version of what they'd witnessed years past was back and possessing the present. They knew the same as Evangeline. Back rounded, chest concave, she walked away, leaving Emma with what she'd learned from the fire. The blackened ground of the burnt offering belied the answers to questions asked of the dead. Its whimpers and whispers were stolen by the wind to be enshrined in the earth, where the brothers were buried by their father.

By the time George finished filling the third hole in as many years and placing the tiny cross to forever mark the memory, he was awash in a mess of muck and mire. His body and clothes were covered in dirt, shellacked to his skin by his own sweat and tears. Headed home, he longed for a cleansing but was barred from entering his own bedroom door. It was his memory that kept him at bay. All he could hear were Emma's screams. Shrieks that pierced the dawn of a new day, woke him from sleep, and greeted him with grief. All he saw was his daughter, the girl named Jubilee, dancing in the doorway with the salty shadows, the broken blessings of the altar burdens before them. He couldn't go in the room where they'd slept, Jeremiah between him and Emma. He was well divorced from accepting that he'd never have, let alone hold, another son. Prevented even from building in his workshop, George moved his space outside. Tore down the walls and roof so he couldn't be haunted by the baby ghosts whose dead eyes shot their souls into the beams of his barn.

But it was of no use. He remembered.

The wound closed over time, sure, but the crosses in the yard and the burnt earth where grass no longer grew were a reminder. Emma asked George to hide them. Make their loss less conspicuous. So he built her a fence, incorporating the crosses into the design so that you couldn't tell where in the length of the open barrier the memorial began. That is, to the untrained eye. Before he hid the resting places from his wife, George etched a notch in the gnarled wood of the original crosses to mark the remains of his dead baby boys.

In their own way, sometimes one more than the other, they remembered.

When Jubilee ran off . . . they remembered.

When George tried to swing his ax for the last time . . . he remembered.

When Jubi, neé Jubilee, was forced back across the tracks . . . she remembered.

And when some young ones came a-calling, an enterprising man and his wife, asking Emma to buy the land to the left of the main lot for a new venture that would get them out of farming, Emma was all too eager to give them what they asked for. It was only her, Jubilee, and baby Ruby then. But she remembered.

With Ms. Teena's sitting far back from the road and the wide-open space between its door and the fence post used for parking, Emma had no use for looking over to the left. Didn't need to see the ground where her babies were buried being defiled with drunk piss and debauchery.

Losing children, three snuffed out before they could even be considered, was a kind of pain Emma wore every day. She knew it well. She had gotten used to the cold spot in the bed; it had been there ever since Jeremiah. In life she learned that all you love you lose. Everything ends up on the other side.

8.

"You know Tati went to her first homecoming dance last night," Nadia said.

Laid across the basement futon, hair still wrapped in her scarf, wearing leggings and a Roxanne Shanté T-shirt, Nadia initiated the line of conversation for the morning's session with Mimi. Tati stood behind the client chair in an undershirt, sweatpants, and socks, ready to take Nadia's place for the morning. A spur-of-the-moment decision Nadia made as Tati left with Desirée for the dance.

"Why don't you do Mimi's hair tomorrow," Nadia had suggested. "Especially since you did so good with your own."

Tati's bangs and ponytail had been curled under, the hair she'd left hanging in the back flipped up. Her face shimmered with eye shadow that accentuated the depth created by eyeliner and mascara. On her lips she had worn liner and gloss. Nadia had taken one look at Tati's made-up face and shuddered internally as if her blood temperature had dropped three degrees.

"What was that about?" Desirée had asked.

"I don't know. She on one tonight."

"She wanna make sure you don't have no kind of fun."

But fun wasn't Nadia's concern. She had looked in the face of her former self and was determined to keep history from repeating. So she shook Tati awake though she'd only been asleep a few hours and told her to get up and get ready for Mimi.

Tati had trudged to the basement. Her perfect style from the night before was smashed and flattened to the sides of her face. She figured she'd fix it when Mimi left; she just had to make it through the morning. Her *Miss Thang* CD pulsed from the stereo as they each staked their positions for whatever side of the shit that was to be stirred in their direction. They were one against one against one. No teams. No alliances. Every girl/woman for herself.

"So, where was the dance?" Mimi asked.

"At the Hyatt on Wacker," Nadia answered.

"They had a hotel party for a bunch of high school kids."

"It wasn't like that," Tati blurted.

"Then what was it like?" Nadia asked. "Tell us."

A grin revealed itself across Nadia's face as she sat up on the futon and crossed her legs. Tati's empty stomach dropped three feet to her ankles as she watched her mother's grin dissolve into a smirk that played across her lips as delight danced in her eyes. Tati was caught. Hook in her gut, line protruding from her mouth. Everything Nadia had wanted to ask the night before when she noticed Tati came home wearing Xavier's jacket was being asked, with Mimi presiding as mistress of ceremonies.

But Tati delayed answering. Instead, she sang louder as she scratched flakes of holding spray from Mimi's spritz-laden hair and remembered how perspiration had beaded on her scalp when she danced with Xavier—a boy she'd known since second grade.

Inside the downtown hotel ballroom where the Central City High School homecoming dance was held, Tati and Xavier traded lyrics from one song until the DJ faded Skee-Lo for Groove Theory. The switch from rap to R&B was enough to embolden the friends who'd known each other since they were snaggletoothed to maybe becoming something more.

Xavier grabbed Tati's hand, turned her around, and palmed her hips the same way he palmed a basketball. She wound her body into his as his hands fingered the hem of her red pleated tennis skirt. Her head against his chest, she relinquished control as his chin nuzzled the inside of her neck. On the dance floor, amid throngs of couples and groups of friends, they sang along with Amel Larrieux. The chorus and ad-libs. Every word and sound. All the *ooh*s and *I want you too*s.

"So, you gon' really tell me what you want?" Xavier whispered in her ear.

Before Tati could answer, the DJ's voice—loud and obnoxious—cut through the crowd to announce the beginning of his slow-jam set. He encouraged everyone to couple up as if they hadn't done so already as a Boyz II Men ballad oozed through the speakers. Xavier turned Tati around to face him. Her arms around his neck, his hands at her waist, they swayed to the song, forehead to forehead. She lifted her lashes to peek at him through her bangs, and what she saw startled. His eyes, wide open, brown and imploring with soft attention. She saw the warmth that resided there.

Tati simmered under the heat of his gaze. Her body pulsed as she closed the slim distance between them and laid her head on his shoulder. His muscles widened to envelop her as he wrapped both arms around her back and cocooned her into his sweet and spicy scent. A shiver sizzled down her spine.

He felt it. "You cold?" Xavier asked, taking off his jacket.

He wrapped it around Tati's shoulders before she could answer as the duet between Subway and 702 urged them to play a game of their own. And they did, taking turns looking at each other when one had closed their eyes lost to the moment and the music. The song changed to Blackstreet's "Before I Let You Go," and they continued dancing their bodies hugged up against one another. Xavier fingered the ends of her hair. Tati admired the one dimple in his right cheek and the cubic zirconia studs that twinkled from his ears.

"Tati, if you gon' be down here with ya mama doin' hair, you gotta learn how to keep up conversation," Mimi said, interrupting her reverie.

Tati rolled her eyes. "You ready for your wash?"

Tati turned the water on, further delaying any answer she was expected to give. She tested the temperature before spraying Mimi's head, making sure to splash her ear a little with water so that any sound was garbled.

"Watch that water, girl," Mimi admonished.

"Sorry," Tati mumbled.

"So, tell me some more. Did you dance with anybody?"

Tati recognized Mimi's tone. It was sweet and enticing, like the open red mouth of a Venus flytrap, ready for someone to trip her triggers so she could swallow their simple asses whole.

She answered through gritted teeth, "Friends."

"I know she danced with her friend Xavier last night," Nadia offered.

"Who is Xavier?" Mimi's voice piqued with curiosity.

"Just a friend," Tati answered.

"Is that why you came home wearing his jacket?" Nadia asked.

"I was cold."

"How you cold if you was dancin' all night?" Mimi asked.

Tati increased the pressure of the water and rinsed out the conditioner. She didn't answer. There was no need to. It wasn't as if Nadia or Mimi were really looking for answers. Tati knew they had their interrogation duet planned just like the police. Two against one. Both of them bad cops. She understood why Mimi hadn't questioned why she was doing her hair this morning instead of Nadia. She already knew.

Mama set me up.

"Back in my day when a boy let you wear his jacket, that meant he was sweet on a gal," Mimi said. "Though in my day . . . parents didn't let they kids start courtin' until they was eighteen."

"Is that why you came to Chicago carrying a baby at eighteen?" Nadia asked.

"You don't know what you think you know," Mimi snapped, lifting her dripping head from the washbowl. "And what I was when I came to be with Eugene ain't none of your concern."

Tati looked to Nadia as she slathered cholesterol into Mimi's hair. The way she sat square on the futon, head bowed, clasped hands to her forehead looked as if she were praying for forgiveness. For what she had done or was about to do, Tati wasn't sure. She placed a conditioning cap on Mimi's head and tapped her shoulder. "You can go sit under the dryer now."

Nadia looked up. "You know, it ain't my concern that you was pregnant at eighteen," she began. "But it seems pretty hypocritical to me for you to be so hard on me and Tati when you didn't even do what you been telling us to do."

"Nadia, you ever think that because of the life I've lived I was tryin' to do better by you and your daughter?"

"I was good and grown when I had Tati," Nadia said.

"Grown and alone because you was borrowin' what you couldn't keep," Mimi said, peeking from under the dryer.

"You live and you learn." Nadia shrugged.

"Exactly," Mimi said. "I've lived. I've learned. And I was trying to learn you, but I most certainly am gon' learn Tati."

As Mimi and Nadia grimaced at each other from their respective corners, Tati busied herself with organizing. She put the shampoo and conditioner bottles back on the shelves where they belonged and sorted the rollers and end papers she would use to set Mimi's hair. Every Sunday she insisted on a roller set, even though the curling iron would've been faster. Mimi insisted that a wet set was the only way her hair held a curl. But that wasn't completely true. She had the texture of her grandmothers: wavy roots and limp ends. It never held a curl. Wasn't meant to. But Mimi forced the issue anyway, just like she forced everything else.

"So, Tati, finish telling me about the dance," Mimi coaxed.

"Ain't nothin' to tell."

"Well, who else did you dance with besides that one boy?"

"Desirée."

"Mm-hmm." Nadia and Mimi snickered together.

"I'm sure you didn't slow dance with her, now, did you?" Mimi surmised. "You do anything more than dance?"

"He kissed me."

"You kiss him back?" Nadia asked.

"What does that even mean?"

"Just what it sound like," Mimi snapped. "Don't be gettin' smart witcha mama."

Tati shrugged her shoulders and sighed as she tried to hold on to the moment when she and Xavier kissed. It had been the last song of the night. After an evening of East and West Coast hip-hop, reggae, and Chicago house, the DJ concluded with an R&B quartet from Charlotte, North Carolina.

The unmistakable downbeat followed by the lullaby-like strings of Jodeci's "Freek'n You" had crooned through the speakers. Students roared in approval as girls wound their hips around so their backs were to their partners' fronts, hands rested on waists or below, and bodies rolled together. If ever there was a time for a chaperone to come into the dance with a ruler and pull students apart, that was it. But the three sets of double doors to the darkened ballroom never opened.

Undulating with the sea of bodies on the dance floor, Tati had tried to mimic the masses, but Xavier had held her still, pulled her closer. Forehead to forehead, nose to nose, Tati nearly sat on his upper thigh. They made their own circle. And for a moment, in her mind, they were alone and flying above the crowd like on the Navy Pier Ferris wheel. With her eyes closed, dancing with Xavier was as close to what she imagined it was to be suspended in air. Until she was kissed by clouds. Xavier's lips, soft and pillowy, met her own in a surprise that forced her to open her eyes. He stared right back at her, his forehead never moving from where it pressed against her bangs.

He smiled, said, "I've been wanting to do that for years."

Tati's return smile would have turned into easy laughter had Xavier not kissed her again as the song moved into the bridge. Students around them sang along with DeVante Swing until the song faded and the lights came up.

"Thanks for the dance," Tati whispered as she pulled away from Xavier.

"That's all?" he asked.

"I'll see you around."

She pulled farther away, but Xavier's fingertips lingered against her own for a moment longer. "See you, Tati," he said, when he finally let her go.

Not eight hours later, she was losing the feeling of his lips and fingers against her own as she leaned against the table where the curling irons and stove were set up, cold and wanting, much like her mother and grandmother. Nadia and Mimi reminded Tati of a proverb she'd had to write a response to in English class. There is no honor amongst thieves. Between the two of them, there was neither honor nor respect.

"We waitin' for an answer, Tatiana," Nadia demanded.

"I just said he kissed me. It's not like I can reject it."

"You can do more than you think," Mimi said. "You got the power until you give it away."

"We not there yet," Nadia interjected.

But Nadia lied. They were. When Tati had come in after the dance, she had found Nadia in the backyard leaned against the frame of the house in gray sweatpants, a ratty old T-shirt that covered her bare chest, and a peacock-printed scarf tied down over her freshly pressed and wrapped hair. A cigarette glowed between the fingers of her right hand, and a bottle of beer rested on the ground beside her. The shop radio played the *Boomerang* soundtrack from the raised screen of the window.

"Can I try?" Tati had asked once she settled beside Nadia. Her eyes bounced between the bottle and the glowing cigarette.

"Try what? You start smokin', you gon' fuck up your lungs, and you can kiss all that runnin' and track shit goodbye."

"Okay."

"You wanna sip of beer?"

"Can I?"

"G'on head. I'd rather you do it with me than sneak and drink. Here."

Nadia had handed over the bottle and watched as Tati took a short sip and then a longer one. When Tati gave the bottle back, Nadia took a long swig of her own as Toni Braxton sang in the background about how love should've been enough to bring a man home. Either tipsy on the chug of beer, or high from her kiss, Tati asked, "Is it good?"

"Is what good?"

"Sex?"

"What the hell happened at the dance?" Nadia had exclaimed. "This the last time I let you drink with me."

"Nothing happened. I just wanna know. Is it?"

"Sometimes it is. Most times it ain't worth the heartache. And all men come with some kind of heartache and you, as a woman, have to decide what you will and you won't do about it."

"Whatchu mean?"

Nadia puffed the last of her cigarette and then stamped it beneath a slipper-covered foot. She sighed. "Women do a lot of shit for men," she said, words harder than her face. "Sometimes it's love. Sometimes it's lust. Sometimes it's a little bit of both."

Nadia had been replaying the conversation in her mind for hours, but she wouldn't tell her mother about it. There were some things she agreed that Gladys didn't need to know. But Mimi railed on anyway.

"You don't know where you at," she snapped. "If you did, you wouldn't have been on the phone with me late in the evenin', talkin' 'bout how you don't know what to do with Tati growin' up so fast." She mimicked Nadia's panic-stricken voice. "'She doin' her own hair, wearin' makeup. She don't think about the future or what she wanna be in life. I don't know what to do.' Well, I do!" Mimi said, coming out of character.

She pushed the dryer off her head and marched back over to the washbowl. "Tati, c'mon wash this out. It's conditioned deeply enough."

"This was a mistake." Nadia hugged her knees and rocked back and forth on the futon. "I never should've called you last night."

"Especially not when you was drunk," Mimi said.

Nadia pushed herself off the couch and made her way out of the basement. Knowing her mother was going to smoke, Tati turned on cool water and rinsed Mimi's hair. She took her time pulling her fingers through to remove the coating that softened the strands. If only there were a conditioner for the heart. A substance that made malleable the pugnacious and resistant. Tati sighed. She wrapped Mimi's hair in a towel and tied it turban-style.

"You can go sit in the chair," she said.

Tati adjusted Mimi's seat for her height and went to work dividing sections and then parts for her to create a grid of rollers that would help Mimi's hair fall the way she liked. Monica sang to them while she worked about what she wanted to make right. Tati rolled her eyes at the lyrics. Neither Mimi nor Nadia was interested in making things right. They were more concerned with proving each other wrong. Both of them more alike than they'd be willing to admit.

"You doing a good job, Tati," Mimi said.

"Thank you."

"You know," she continued, "you got to understand that me and your mama just want the best for you. Want you to make something of yourself. You know what you wanna be when you grow up? You ain't got long."

"I like writing," Tati answered.

"That's nice that's what you like to do, but it don't mean nothing unless it can pay some bills and put a roof over your head."

Tati had heard the conversation before. Even Toya had droned on about what jobs would or wouldn't pay for rent, light, water, gas, and groceries as she drove Tati and Desirée to the dance.

And she would know. Working at Commonwealth Edison all these years, Toya had heard every sob story there was from folks who came into the 87th Street branch, where she worked in the call center, on disconnection day. She was adamant that pictures and poetry wouldn't pay nobody's bills. Let alone those of two Black girls from the South Side. Who'd ever heard of such careers for kids with no money but the few dollars their mamas eked away by robbing Peter and Paul to pay themselves. If there was one thing Tati knew, and was tired of hearing, nobody was going to pay her for pretty words about her missing daddy.

"What I'm trying to say to you, Tati," Gladys started again, "is that we want you to learn from our mistakes."

"Are you saying me and Mama are mistakes?"

It was a question she would never have asked on a normal day. She would have saved the inquiry for her notebook and come to her own poetic conclusion from the insults Nadia and Mimi had hurled at each other. But this wasn't a normal day. Tati had to take hold of the opportunities as they presented themselves. Liberties Mimi hadn't expected. She didn't answer right away. An omission that signaled Nadia was her mistake as much as Tati was Nadia's. Despite all the cycles and generational curses Mimi was inclined to curing at church, Tati recognized they had only continued. Theirs was a family born broken, not for the breaking.

Mimi exhaled. "Tati, being with boys and having babies before you're ready is a needless responsibility."

"It was *just* a kiss," Tati emphasized.

"This time." She turned around to face her granddaughter. "You understand what I'm tellin' you?"

"Yeah. Don't get pregnant. Don't worry, I don't plan on it."

"We never plan on these things happenin'. Just ask me or your mama."

"Ask me what?" Nadia said, her voice echoing as she reentered the basement.

"Am I a mistake?" Tati asked. "Mimi said I need to learn from y'all's mistakes about getting pregnant."

"Really, Mama!" Nadia stepped into the light of the salon. "I walk out for ten minutes and this is what you tell my child."

"Tati, come 'round here," Mimi demanded.

Tati dropped the roller and end paper she held and walked to face Mimi, who held out her hands. Tati studied the wrinkles and blue veins that coursed across the tops. A gold wedding band shined brightly against her sallow skin as if it had been recently polished. Tati stared at the bony fingers and manicured nails reaching toward her and stepped back. She wiped her hair-wet hands against her thighs as Mimi put her own back in her lap.

"You were never a mistake," she said. "You were a blessing."

"A blessing in a burden, right?" Tati repeated. "That's what you said."

"When did you tell her that?" Nadia growled.

"I said no such a thing."

"You did!" Tati shrieked.

"Tati, I'm sorry—"

"Don't be sorry now," Nadia snapped. "You probably said it right to her face because you say it all the time. You just don't know when to leave well enough alone. Tati, you are not a mistake."

Nadia turned toward Tati, her face a weathered stone, wrinkled and creased with the worries she never allowed her daughter to witness. She repeated, "You are not a mistake. You are love. My love. Always have been. Always will be. I just want you to be prepared for this world you goin' into in all the ways you need to be. You keep your head in books and your journal so much, I worry you got the book smarts and not the street smarts and common sense you need."

"That's why you set me up to do Mimi hair this morning?"

"Yes. But *this* was a mistake. *You* are not."

"You say that now, but don't act like your decision to keep Tati was all rainbows and roses," Mimi interjected. "You struggled. Hell, I struggled, and me and Eugene was married."

Nadia shook her head and sighed, repeated to herself, "You just don't know when to leave well enough alone."

Sorrow hugged her words. Spoken in despondence, it was normally Nadia's go-to shutdown response. A shield of protection, like a layer of Vaseline, or long johns against the cold. But there was nothing to shield Tati. Nothing Nadia could bulwark between her daughter and her mother except herself.

She yelled, "Mama, you so quick to tell my story. You don't even tell your own. You and Daddy was married when you had me, but I wasn't the first."

"Watch it, Nadia," Mimi said, her voice cold as venom. "I keep tellin' you, you don't know what you think you know."

"Well, that's what Daddy told me before he died."

"Eugene always did take up for you."

"The same way you always take up for Bryan and Terry—"

"You don't know what it took to have them!"

"Whatever it was, they were your blessings. I was your burden, the same as you said about Tati."

"The only burden was that girl's daddy."

Spit flew from Mimi's mouth as the shock of her caustic words was absorbed by silence. The CD, not set to repeat, spun 'round and 'round in the player. Its whirring, like a metronome, marked the minutes as they passed. No one spoke. No one moved. Tati and Nadia remained standing while Mimi sat back in the burgundy client chair. The scowl on her face converted to content. She was the clever teacher who'd outwitted the rowdy class. An iron-fisted matriarch against her unappreciative children. Though she wouldn't have been so satisfied had she known they were all cut from the same curse, just a different generation. The eternally marked heirs of an unoriginal sin.

"What is his name?" Tati asked.

Her own tone was foreign to her ears as she begged the question tugging at her heartstrings, completely dispossessed from the brain that knew better. Absent all manner of her common sense, she asked again, more forcefully, "What is his name?"

The volume of her voice surprised. Louder and louder, Tati repeated her question until she felt anger rise and heat sting. Blood boiled beneath her skin. Fingers damp with setting lotion clenched and punched the sides of her thighs. Lashes fluttered, tears watered—more than stings—as she reached a scream.

"What is his name!"

The sound bounced around the concrete walls and hidden heating vents. Tati had come undone. Years of questions, of writings, of poems, journal entries, and dreams of a faceless man at the head of the table, had led to this. Nadia wrapped Tati in her arms. Her silk scarf smashed against Tati's raw hair as sobs shook both of their bodies. Pressed against one another, their tears bled and dripped in tandem. Tati turned and caught a glimpse of Mimi's face. Haughty in the high chair, she looked down at them both as her half-rolled head dripped dry, her eyes as barren as the Sahara at high noon.

"Roman," she said evenly. "Your daddy's name is Roman Brown."

"Really, Mama!" Nadia shrieked. She held Tati closer and spoke over her head. "You had to do this today?"

"It's about time she know. You for damn sure wasn't gon' tell her."

"She don't need him," Nadia cried. "We don't need him. I'm enough."

"No!" Mimi bellowed. "*You* didn't need him. But *she* does."

"*He* didn't want her. *I'm enough.*"

Nadia was like a CD with a deep scratch. She couldn't move forward. She couldn't move backward. She was stuck in time in a one-sided, one-phrase conversation Mimi couldn't break through. They'd stopped talking at Tati, even though she was still pressed to Nadia's chest, feeling every one of her *I'm enough*s as they rumbled from her gut. Tati didn't move from Nadia's embrace. Despite the tingle in her feet and her notion to run, she didn't step away from Nadia's care. Her show of affection. She lingered in the attention she longed for taking for herself, the same as Nadia took from Mimi. Exacted pound of flesh after pound of flesh, but it couldn't trump Mimi's hand of spades. The sharpened weapons of her verbal comeuppances stabbed through the body and cut to the bone. The marrow of their inner selves spilled all over the copper concrete floor.

Racked with the dry heaves that come after full-body wails, Nadia released Tati and shuffled toward the futon. She collapsed on the worn cushions and covered her streaked face with her arms. But there was nowhere for her to hide. Nowhere for her to render herself invisible from Mimi's masterful gaze. She sat in the big chair, her face as clear as a conscience before death. She wore neither guilt nor apology, just the stern countenance of someone who believed they were in the right. Who'd done what she thought needed to be done.

"Tati, you think you can finish Mimi's hair before she go to church?" Nadia croaked.

"Yeah." Tati trudged back behind the chair. "But if you get a roller set, you gon' be late."

"You can blow-dry it and do it with the iron," Mimi said.

Tati cleared Nadia's station of the rollers, end papers, and setting lotion and instead plugged in the electric curling iron and flat iron, not bothering with the hair stove or hot comb for Mimi's roots. She blow-dried and shaped it then went to work parting, greasing, flat-ironing, and curling section after section. Tati developed a rhythm and a pattern as she moved. Her hands flipped the irons and combs in time with the whirring Monica CD and their breath. Nadia's was heavy while Mimi's came in spurts as she winced, groaned, and grunted from the oil stinging her scalp, but she didn't flinch or say "ow," no matter how much Tati wanted her to hurt.

"You done," Tati said. She pulled one last rake through Mimi's hair with the feather comb, then removed her cape and necktie.

Mimi stood and dusted herself off. "Walk me to the door."

"I'll walk you." Nadia sat up from the futon. Red eyes, puffy cheeks, and hoarse voice, she waved Tati on her way. "Go'n chill out. You did enough for today."

Tati headed toward the stairs. Nadia called behind her. "I'll be outside if you wanna talk."

She didn't want to talk. In her room, she covered her head with her pillow, craving the dark she was made out to be. A stain on both Nadia's and Mimi's lives. Despite her muffled screams, her tears didn't come. It wasn't her sadness to hold. Her cup was erected with fury at Nadia's crocodile tears and shrieks of "I'm enough," as if it made up for a life's worth of lies. She had subsisted on a diet of dishonesty and disinterest and now Nadia had the audacity to offer her sustenance. As if Tati didn't remember everything and everyone being fed before her: the house, the clients, the business.

The front door slammed and then the back. Nadia had retreated to her sanctuary. *She has her thing. I have mine.* Tati reached for her notebook. Pen in hand, she wrote.

Dear Roman,

> *I finally know your name.*
> *Now all that's left to know is, "Am I your shame?"*
> *Or*
> *Am I your shame too?*
> *Seem like I already shamed mama.*
> *What about you?*
> *I fulfilled the prophecy Mimi had for her life*
> *Guess she should've followed her Bible's advice*
> *Something 'bout not speaking death . . .*
> *But ain't I life?*
> *Ain't I a miracle, a blessing,*
> *All the glory worth Sunday dressing?*
> *Seem to me like I would be cause to rejoice*
> *But I'm the reason neither me nor mama got a real voice*
> *We be Mimi's fears*
> *The embodiment of her tears*
> *The sins she shout for forgiveness*
> *Transgressions that don't seek repentance*
> *We ain't never been penitent*
> *Or contrite*
> *But I guess like she say*
> *Us two wrongs don't make her right*
> *So, I write*
> *And mama sing*
> *And we never, ever let our eyes know that broken hearts make*
>   *them sting.*

Love Tati

Part 2

Answers

9.

When Nadia met Roman, it was at the insistence of Toya and Lou. Unlike Nadia, Toya had dated hard from the time they were sixteen and still in high school. Her dating pool had only widened as they'd gotten older. From high school football stars to college students she met at parties from schools she didn't attend, to colleagues and co-workers, Toya's love life had been a revolving door of the many, the tragic, and the always unfaithful. That was until Lou, a CPA she met in line at the Marshall Field's café downtown. He had coffee, a croissant, and, by the end of his meal, a slip of paper with Toya's name and number that read, *Call me.*

He did, and then Toya called Nadia and invited her out to the bar at Seventy-Fifth and St. Lawrence after Lou suggested Toya bring a friend for his friend.

"Is he single?" Nadia had asked while they were in line.

"Not exactly," Toya hedged before they were waved through the door.

While Toya and Lou danced, Nadia nursed a beer at the bar, knowing she was there to play babysitter to the brokenhearted.

"You want me to start a tab?" the bartender asked in a raspy voice.

Nadia shook her head no. "This the only drink I'm buying tonight."

"Is that right?"

The voice belonged to Roman. Nadia assessed him the same way he had given her ripped acid-washed black jeans, red fishnets, and bodysuit the once-over outside, where he worked the door beside the bouncer, deciding who would get in and who wouldn't. His dark skin peeked from the open buttons of his silk shirt along with a gold chain atop a pile of coiled chest hair. A beeper was hooked to the hip of his starched and creased mustard-colored slacks.

"If I gotta keep you company all night while you whine about your woman, then you buyin' everything else," Nadia answered.

"I don't whine, darlin'. Let me get another round," he said to the bartender.

"What you havin', Bishop?"

"Whiskey neat?"

"Why'd she call you Bishop?" Nadia asked once the barkeep had walked away.

"Because that's my name." He extended his hand. "Roman Bishop Brown. Pleased to make your acquaintance."

Nadia rolled her eyes. "Don't you have to get back to work?" She nodded toward the door, where the burly bouncer held the line.

"He got it," Roman answered.

"What do you do, anyway?" Nadia asked.

"I curate experiences. I create ambience and atmosphere. I make people want what they think they deserve, and then I make them wait for it. I'm a master of delayed gratification."

"Women don't like waiting for what belongs to them."

"Is that right?" He searched himself with his hands until he pulled his beeper from his waist and stared at the number. Recognition followed by a grimace. Instead of excusing himself to make the call, he shoved the pager back on his belt loop and pulled a pack of cigarettes from his pocket.

"What's her name?" Nadia asked.

"Deborah."

"Want one," Roman offered.

"No, thank you."

"I'm trying to quit," he said, tapping out the square.

"Sounds like Deborah's doing to me."

"Why is that?"

"Because women always doing shit to make the men in their lives live longer while cutting down on their own life expectancy. Sacrifice kills."

"Is that right?"

Nadia repeated his catchphrase in a mocking tone then took a swig from her bottle. "So, what happened with Deborah?"

"We're going through a rough patch?"

"You cheated?"

"Not yet."

That night, Toya's only instruction had been to "keep him company." And at first that was all Nadia did. He offered her a ride home. She declined. He offered to take her out. She declined. He asked if they could be friends. She hesitated. Though she wanted no part of an involved man, she figured it couldn't hurt to have another friend. At least that's what she told herself. As friends, they browsed the aisles of Woodson Library admiring the Vivian G. Harsh research collection. He offered her a ride home after. She accepted. On the way he said he had no plans for her outside of friendship. He liked her, found her refreshing. It was the reminder Nadia needed to remember that to Roman she was not a person but a thing. A mint for bad breath. A cold glass of water on an overly warm day. He sought neither company nor friendship but a distraction. A deflection from Deborah's demands.

As friends they marveled at the exhibits of the Shedd Aquarium. Their bodies drew nearer to each other as they moved from glass case to glass case, intrigued by fish they couldn't name and lizards they cared less about. As friends, they had lunch at Giordano's and critiqued the stew-like sauce and extra cheesiness of the heavy pies until his pager buzzed, *911*. He returned Deborah's call and that's when Nadia found out that she wasn't a wayward girlfriend but a reasonably exigent wife. She decided then she didn't need any more friends, until Toya called with tickets to a concert.

May 1980

NADIA STOOD BESIDE TOYA AND LOU BENEATH THE TWINKLING lights of the smoky club with live sounds of funk filling their souls. She waited for Roman to finish his official promotion duties for the Chaka Khan concert, hoping he'd join her at the front of the stage. She knew he could never belong to her, even though when they'd met he'd presented himself as just within reach. And as always, it's the things a millimeter outside our actual grasp we try to hold on to the hardest. For Nadia, a married man was at the top of that list. So, despite her better judgment, she stood in the crowd of close-knit bodies bumping up against one another, waiting for him to notice her.

The club was tipsy with anticipation. When the bassist freestyled his way into the opening pulls of "Tell Me Something Good," the crowd roared.

"Chicago, are you ready to get down with the Queen of Funk tonight?" Roman's voice was deep and smooth as well-aged cognac. When the audience answered with shouts and cheers, he teased them more. "Is that right?" His baritone dragged out the words, gave them melody and rhythm, until they were more notes than syllables.

Nadia rolled her eyes at his performance. Pissed at herself for still being interested, for wondering if she was still on his mind because he had been on hers. She knew that there was no reason to act as if she were an ant burned beneath the magnifying glass of his gaze. And yet like a bee to a flower she was attracted, only she didn't know she was the one in danger of being stung.

Roman walked offstage, and Chaka emerged with big hair and a toothy grin decked in a black catsuit and red thigh-high boots. She strutted, sizing up the crowd before she came center, grabbed the mic, and launched into the crowd-pleasing favorite from her time with Rufus.

The singing was infectious, the energy in the club inebriating. Nadia gave herself over to the music, dipping low and swinging her hips to make sure she hit all four corners. Chaka sang them through hit after hit from "You Got the Love" and "Do You Love What You Feel" before she introduced the lead track from her new album, *Naughty*. But it wasn't until "Clouds" turned into "Get Ready, Get Set" that Nadia felt Roman's hands around her waist.

"You having a good time?" he asked.

Nadia danced and sang without answering. He continued, "I was hoping I would see you tonight."

His damp lips tickled her ear. She stepped forward out of his loose embrace and continued rocking to the slowed groove of the music, but he stepped with her. Sang with her. Their voices blended with the rest of the eager club-goers, nearly outsinging Chaka until she slowed the mood more with "Papillon." The opening strings of the song led lovers for the night to face each other. Arms wrapped around backs and waists, hands groped behinds, and noses nuzzled into necks dabbed with cologne for such a time as this.

Roman pulled her first by her waist and then her hands. His body urged Nadia to turn around and face him. To slow dance and grind against him. And she did. Perhaps this was her first mistake. Allowing her mind to convince her that what she was doing was not wrong. That their dance was innocent. That he was not expected to be anywhere else. With someone else. It was one amongst many delusions that kept her from recognizing she was falling for another woman's husband.

Then "Papillon" turned into "Sweet Thing," and he pulled her closer. They sang along together. To each other. And it was then she saw that he had slipped into delusion too. That he believed the moment they were having would last longer than the dance. They sang to each other, line by line, as if it were an actual conversation.

He said, "I like the way you sing."

"Is that right?" she asked.

It was then, when smiles crept across both of their faces and teeth pierced his lips as if another row of stage lights had illuminated the club, that they entered waters where delusions were drowned by force. While Nadia basked in the glow of his adoration, she forgot he was a star who didn't shine for her. When Chaka ad-libbed her way out of "Sweet Thing" and into the dizzying disco opening of "I'm Every Woman," Nadia's decision was made. When the concert ended and Chaka had strutted offstage, it didn't take her long to agree to Toya's suggestion that Roman take her home.

"Let me make sure everything is good here, and then we'll be able to go," he said.

The fantasy was over. The curated experience had ended. Nadia sat at the bar and watched as everyone who had contributed to the atmosphere of ambiance wiped away the facade like the women would wash off their makeup. The band broke down their instruments, the bartender washed glasses, and a custodian swept, mopped, and buffed the gray concrete floor until it shined. In the empty warehouse of a club, its fluorescent lights screaming from the ceiling, Nadia was reminded of the emptiness she held inside. And maybe that's what emboldened her further. The knowing that without a dream or purpose she was a shell of her former self waiting for a shell of a man she hoped was in a shell of a marriage. Their large and pristine exteriors easily overcompensated for the emptiness they hid from each other.

"You ready to go?" he asked.

Nadia hopped down from the barstool and let him lead the way into the cool night air. A shiver sizzled down her spine.

He felt it. "You cold?" Roman asked, taking off his jacket. He wrapped it around Nadia's shoulders before she could answer.

Thankful, she pushed her arms through the sleeves and snuggled closer beside him as she walked, tight-thighed and wobbly, drunk on pheromones.

A train rumbled overhead as he opened her door. It interrupted the deadly quiet of the street, which had magnified every sound. She heard every heartbeat and breath until he turned the ignition and the engine growled to life. Roman eased the car into the street sans traffic and made his way from the North Loop to the South Side. Somewhere along the Dan Ryan, overwhelmed by their silence, he asked her how she'd been.

"Good. Working," she answered.

Nadia bobbed her head along to the low volume of the car radio. The lyrics were undeterminable; only the mood of the music was intelligible, slow, whining, and needy. Everything she felt in the drone of a song. As they zoomed past the projects, she returned his question.

"Getting divorced," he answered sharply.

Nadia choked down the sharp gasp of air that threatened to erupt from her lungs. She didn't want to respond to his provocation, her earlier hopes come true. Eyes trained out the window, she counted the staggered lines separating the lanes of traffic.

He cleared his throat. "Did you hear what I said?"

"Hmm," Nadia purred.

"I said I'm getting divorced."

"Good for you." She answered his reflection in the window.

"I said I'm getting divorced," he repeated, more forcefully.

Nadia snapped her head toward him. "*Getting* divorced is not divorced," she emphasized, "just like *separated* is not divorced. You're still in the same place you were last time I saw you."

Her high began to dissolve. He sighed. Shrugged. "For what it's worth. She asked for it. The divorce."

Nadia watched as his mouth folded over the word as if it were dipped in gall. His tongue disgusted by the taste of the verb.

"That have anything to do with me?" she asked. She didn't want to know the truth. But she wanted to know that she mattered. That he cared. As if the only reason a woman divorced a man was because of another woman.

He hesitated. "Not entirely."

"Then explain," she demanded. "Entirely!"

He began his story with Nadia storming out of the Hyde Park pizzeria while they were on what was supposed to be a lunch between friends.

"Her pages were to let me know my son had fallen and broken his arm skateboarding," he said, looking out the windshield. "I dropped you off and headed home, but by that time they were already at the hospital. That's when she said she realized they didn't need me."

Nadia turned to him and saw the words in the hold of his jaw that he wouldn't say out loud. Least not in front of her. *I still need them.* The unspoken confession fueled the energy flowing between them. His broken spirit preyed with the vicious appetite of a vampire upon her needy heart. It was why he had asked Lou to ask Toya to seek her out. She was a match meant to ease his angst. Never did he believe he too would be a salve for her sadness. As he exited the highway at Ninety-Fifth and Stony, the weight of his revelation added to the intensity of the night, the dance, the duet.

Nadia asked, "Do you want the divorce?"

"I want a lot of things," he said. "That doesn't mean I can have them."

It was then she knew that he sensed what she did and didn't want to do. If she would have him he'd oblige but long for his wife. Nadia sucked her teeth. She disliked the taste of the truth she'd always asked of him.

"Stop right here," she said.

He pulled over beneath a tree on her parents' block where it dead-ended at the CTA training facility. They were shielded from the honey glow of the streetlights. He cut the engine and let the car settle.

Her hand on the gearshift, his hand atop hers, their fingers found one another. Aside from the dance that brought them mouth to chin to nose, this was the closest they'd been. No longer were they transfixed by shining lights and a powerful singing voice. They were sober.

Nadia broke the silence first. "Why did you tell me that?" she asked.

He shrugged. "You asked me what was going on with me. I told you."

"Bullshit! You could've said anything. You chose to tell me she filed for divorce."

"Because it's what's happening in my life."

"Because it's what you wanted me to know."

"So what if I did?"

"What do you want me to do with that information? It doesn't change anything."

"It changes everything."

"Why, because you want it too?"

"No, because it's what *she* wants. We've been doing this dance long before I met you. Long before I—"

"Before what? Before you were intrigued enough to leave because you found me—refreshing."

"Nadia," he called. The sound of her name in his voice seduced and repulsed her. "It's not like that."

Her emotions warred within her. Nadia snatched her hand from beneath his and popped her own lock. "This was a mistake."

"Nadia, wait."

"I'll walk from here."

She opened the door. He reached for her. Grabbed her shoulder. Pulled her back.

"What!" she yelled.

He didn't respond. Instead, he tugged her chin toward his face, the kiss a foregone conclusion. Their noses bumped, lips met, mouths moved, and tongues touched. The parts of her she'd forgotten existed, he resuscitated, ravenous. Their bodies moved with the carnal knowledge of what came next. Seat reclined. Belts removed. Nadia climbed over the gearshift. They crudely maneuvered around clothes to allow contact. Uninhibited. Unhindered. He pumped. She bounced. They made music together off-key and in harmony, just as they had in the club—all a cappella until they reached a crescendoed climax.

The rushed orgasms shivered through them as realization set in. Nadia swung her legs, hips, and ass back into her seat, where she wriggled her black jeans up her thighs. One glance at him and she caught the tail end of satisfaction dissipating into disgust. It was done. The affair. The one he hadn't had. Until now.

He cranked the car and drove the half block to her parents' house as she fastened her bra, her buttons, and finally her belt. Belly bubbling with instant regret, she didn't look at him as she got out of the car. Idling in the middle of the street, one foot on the brake, the other on the clutch, his posture insisted on her departure. Their opera had gone from bel canto to seria. The beauty of the act erased by the tragedy of the actors.

It wasn't until she had reached her bedroom in the basement that she turned on a light. The lamp on the nightstand illuminated what she didn't want to see. Her reflection in the full-length mirror that leaned against the wall just outside the bathroom showed her mussed hair and disheveled clothing, engulfed by his jacket she hadn't bothered to take off.

June 1980

NADIA TOLD HERSELF IT WOULD ONLY BE ONE TIME, BUT GOOD dick is hard to come by when you're starved of affection and living at home with your parents. Even if it had been mediocre, she was going back for more. A month into what was not a real relationship, Nadia fully abandoned the idea of going back to school, finishing her finance degree, and working at the Chicago Stock Exchange. Instead, she settled on the excited utterance that escaped her mouth in the middle of the argument with Gladys. She would be a beautician. No. She would be a licensed cosmetologist. No. She would be a small business owner.

Armored with her own ego, she left Gladys, Eugene, and her brothers behind with a bag of her belongings and took the bus to Toya's apartment on Eighty-Third and Crandon. Though her building was in the middle of the block, Nadia had a clear view of all the cars parked on the street, including Roman's gleaming Cutlass. She hurried toward Toya's door and found Roman and Lou sitting on the stoop.

"Hey, Nadia," Lou said.

"Hey," she answered. Roman didn't look up from the cigarette in his hands. In black jogging tights layered with running shorts and a fitted white T-shirt, he was foreign to Nadia. She knew him at night. The haggard man who sat on her best friend's porch with his legs spread wide and his elbows on his knees was a stranger.

He didn't see her raised eyebrows and twisted lips, which opened and closed as she started and stopped herself from asking the questions that ran through her mind. *What's going on? What are you doing here? What happened?* Finally, she managed, "You get my page?"

"Yeah."

"Were you going to hit me back?"

"You called Toya. She said you were on your way over here. Wasn't no need."

Unsure, Nadia moved toward the wrought-iron fence that separated them. Roman stood. Met her in the middle. "Let's take a ride," he said.

"I need to talk to Toya."

"*We* need to talk. I'll bring you back."

Roman slapped Lou's hand and clapped him on the back before moving toward Nadia on the other side of the gate. He pushed his way through and marched to his car. He didn't look back to see if she was behind him. He didn't open her door. He got in and waited for her to do the same.

They were on 57, heading back toward his neighborhood, where they'd begun their day, before he even fixed his mouth to speak, but nothing came out. Tired of the silence, Nadia asked, "What did you want to talk about?"

"Just got some stuff going on."

"Like what?"

He opened his mouth as he turned the corner, but only silence escaped. His eyes narrowed as he parallel parked in front of his door, a space he could have driven into and still had his wheels comfortably against the curb. He stalled like a caged bird facing an open door. Roman was ready to take flight but fearful he'd forgotten how to fly.

"C'mon," he said, unlocking the door.

Nadia followed, injured prey unaware of the circling shark. Up the steps, through the door, she waited for him to turn around, gnash his teeth, and take a bite out of what Gladys had left that hadn't already been ground down by words, masticated by chastisement, and regurgitated into a self-righteous mound of uncertainty. But he didn't speak.

In the kitchen, Roman gathered the stack of papers and the manila envelope they were served in and dropped them in the metal trash can against the wall. Nadia's stomach flip-flopped. She knew whatever Roman had to say had to do with Deborah.

"You want some water? Coffee?" he stalled.

"I'm good," she said, standing in the doorway.

He pulled out a chair. "You wanna sit down?"

"I'm good."

He took the church chair and searched himself until he found his pack of cigarettes and lighter. He tapped a square loose and lit it just as quickly.

"You're smoking inside!"

She couldn't hide the incredulity from her voice. In all the time she'd known him, he hadn't smoked in his car or in his house. But there's a first time for everything.

He asked, "You sure you don't want anything?"

"I'll take a cigarette," Nadia said.

Surprise registered on his face, but he didn't state the obvious. *You don't smoke.* Instead, he handed Nadia what she asked for and flicked the lighter. She came over to him and retrieved the same solace he sought. After a drag and a teary-eyed cough, she retreated back to her corner.

"Anything else?" he asked.

"Stop stalling," she said. "You said we needed to talk. Talk."

"There's no easy way to say this."

Nadia sighed. If she had to face serrated teeth, she chose to die with dignity. "You and your wife are getting back together."

"Yeah."

"Good for you."

"Nadia . . . don't be like that."

"I'm not *being* like anything."

"It's not like that."

"It's not like what?" she asked. "You and your wife are getting back together. Good for you two. You could've told me that while you were sitting on the stoop at Toya's. You ain't have to drive me all the way out here to drop this bomb."

"Nadia, just let me explain," Roman protested. "I mean, we *were* getting a divorce, but—"

"But what, Roman? You told me you were getting divorced just to get in my pants?"

"No. We were getting a divorce, but then she—"

"Deborah," Nadia yelled. "She has a name."

"Deborah." He grimaced, as if just the taste would erode what was left of him. "She found out that . . . that . . . she's pregnant."

The word exploded around Nadia.

Pregnant.

It's the kind of word that obliterated whatever delusion she convinced herself into believing inside his rental house just blocks from his marital bed in Beverly. Truth is, Roman had never been hers. Only at night, on weekends, when they could pretend, but not in the day. Not when Deborah's pages rang from his hip and he went running. Nadia was the one he found refreshing. The one he cared for. Deborah was the one he loved. The mother of his two, soon to be three, children.

"Nadia," he said quietly. "Say something."

"I ain't got shit to say." Anger fueled the flush that spread across her golden skin, shading her natural hue with the red of rage.

"I'm . . . I'm . . ." he stuttered.

She held up her hand to stop the apology.

"What you got to be sorry for?" she asked, her voice gaining volume. "I'm the stupid one. I'm the one out here fuckin' around wit' a married man knowin' you wasn't over your wife."

"Nadia."

"Save it, Roman. When you told me she filed, I told you then getting divorced ain't divorced just like being separated ain't divorced, and apparently y'all been together the whole time, working shit out, or whatever the hell you do over there all day."

"Why are you mad? It's not like I planned for this."

"I'm not mad at you. I'm mad at myself. Of course you didn't plan for this. Men never do."

"Nadia—"

"We good. I'm gone."

She headed toward the door, but Roman was at her back before she could reach the handle.

"Where are you going?" he asked.

"Does it matter?"

"If you're going back to Toya's or your mom's, I can take you."

"The bus will get me there just fine."

"Nadia, please, don't be like that."

"How you want me to be?" She whirled around. "You wanted me to be nice when I met you. To care about your feelings and shit. You wanted to be friends. When your wife was gon' drop your ass, you wanted to be more than friends. And now that you knocked her up and y'all getting back together—for the sake of the baby, I'm sure—you want me to do what? Not be mad and volunteer to babysit? Fuck outta here."

"I didn't mean for this to happen," he emphasized.

She turned the handle and opened the door. He pushed it closed again.

"Stop. Please!" He grabbed her shoulder. "You mean more than that to me."

"Evidently, I don't. Let me go."

Again, she opened the door, and this time he didn't stop her. He watched as she stomped down the steps and down the block toward the bus stop, neither of them knowing that their lives were already forever connected.

10.

Nadia wasn't the first Dupree woman to fall for a man she shouldn't have. And she wasn't the first to suffer the consequences because of it.

Jubilee thought all babies came out like little red rats. At least all the ones she'd ever seen born by Emma and Evangeline. Even the dark ones looked red when they came out covered in human cottage cheese. Jubi expected the same when she finally was able to deliver her own, but it was not to be so. Ruby was born black as night, and she wasn't even a second old. Jubi didn't have to look at the tips of her ears, elbows, or nail beds to see what color she'd be. She was black like burnt bitter coffee. Too black for Jubi. And definitely too black for her father, Logan Jefferson Danube III.

"How did this happen? What am I going to do?" Jubi shrieked from the bed, where Emma was still cleaning her up. "Mama, what am I going to do?"

Emma looked up at Jubi. "You talking to me now?"

"Mama, what am I going to do?" she shrieked again.

"You tell him the truth."

"I can't do that. I'll lose everything. Everything I worked hard for. I was careful about it all."

"All except this," Emma said.

Wringing out blood-soaked towels, Emma stared at the daughter she once knew. Though they favored each other from their coloring, they were nothing alike. Emma had stayed on her side of the tracks with George. Jubi had chosen a different life. A life she could no longer keep. The baby stretching and turning in her arms reaching for milk she still hadn't provided made sure of that.

"You need to feed the baby," Emma said.

She pulled the top sheet covering Jubi's body, exposing her long pale legs and blood-soaked gown.

"I can't feed this baby. Help it live? I can't lose everything for her."

The sheet fell from Emma's hands to the ground. She turned around to face Jubi, looking for the girl she'd raised. The one who'd tried walking the line between two sides until one became more advantageous than the other. Until she had to choose between her family and the handsome young man she'd met.

The Danubes weren't native to Land's End. They'd made their money in Birmingham between the mining and the railroad. A venture that brought them south to lay the last of the tracks where the land ended at the water. The termination point of one of the new lines connecting the country by hitch or stitch. Their newness kept them in the dark about the history of the Duprees, and their whiteness kept them on their side of the tracks, where they opened a general store to serve the community they adopted as their own, without ever considering there was a need to ask, question, or wonder whether someone who looked the same as them was really one of them. If you could assume whiteness with ease, was it not meant to be?

Jubi had gone to great lengths to supplant her former identity with the one Logan assumed of her and she asserted for herself. Their life was a happy one. Filled with all the finer things she'd never have had on the farm. Even in their ownership they'd still had to work. Once they'd begun running the farm, Evangeline, Emma, and Jubi had all taken to the fields, to show they thought themselves no better than anyone else, and picked as much and as hard as any hand even though their name was on the deed. That was in addition to being on call for the whole of the town on both sides of the tracks delivering babies in the dead of night, in the middle of winter, or against the backdrop of a burning sun. Logan had offered her a way out. She'd taken it, and now this baby wanted to drag her back.

Looking down at the girl she'd taken to calling Ruby once she made it past her fourth month, Jubi laughed. A crazed cackle erupted from her lips and filled the room with a curdling sound. It set into Emma's bones. Reminded her of a scream she once heard but couldn't place.

"You're right!" Jubi exclaimed in her delirium. "I was careful about everything except this. Eight years we've been trying for this baby. I even built the altar and spread the salt like you said hoping she'd be the apple of our eyes. And here she is, the spawn of the devil himself."

Jubi laid the squirming girl in the middle of the bed, satisfied in her conclusion that in all her scheming, in all her careful planning, she'd never planned for this. Maybe because despite all her attendances at births she'd never seen a situation like her own. A couple like her and Logan. An equation with exponential outliers to disrupt the final outcome and make it wholly unpredictable. On her side of the tracks, or the other, she was used to seeing exact copies. Duplicates, of the couples who called forth life from the very substance of themselves. For her and Logan, she'd never considered the possibility of permutation, or worse yet, an aberration. She'd never planned for her baby to be such an anomaly that it'd upend her life before it was even an hour old.

But that's the thing about babies. Nothing about them could be planned for. Not their arrival. Whether they'd be a boy or girl. If they lived or died. If the mother would even make it through the delivery or keel over on the other side. And generally, those were the only concerns. The only ones Emma had ever had to consider in all her years of working as a midwife after taking over from Evangeline. But Jubi presented an altogether different set of conditions. She was trying to control color from head to toe. She thought because she and Logan were so close in complexion that naturally their baby would be as bright as them. Pale skin that would need protection from the sun. Eyes that changed over the years from green to gray to hazel. Hair like corn silk that held nary curl, kink, nor coil. Jubi thought that because she was the same as her mother and father, even though George was a shade or three darker, more yellow than pale, that she and Logan would most definitely have a baby who could pass. This baby, she didn't expect. It had never entered her imagination that something so black could come out of somebody almost white.

Whiteness, she believed, was not only color, because some people had olive undertones, like the swarthy Greeks and Italians she'd seen working for Logan's family in Birmingham. It wasn't just class, because admittedly some of them were poorer than the colored folk on the other side of the tracks. It was more affectation and flair. An attitude of ownership. That you were owed shit. The world. The day. The night. The people. The bodies. The labor. The land. And, of course, the money. If you could have the audacity to believe yourself appointed above all, delude yourself into believing that you were victim, yet posed as the victor while still demanding more tokens and tributes to affirm and establish the position you created for yourself, were you not white? After all she'd done, was she not white?

"Jubilee, you need to feed the baby," Emma said sternly.

"Don't call me that."

"It's what I named you."

"But it's not who I am. My name is Jubi now. Jubi Etienne Danube."

That was who she'd been for the sixteen years she and Logan had known each other. It began when he stumbled into her in the summer of 1901 on her way to the back door of the general store. Logan apologized by offering his arm for her to walk with him through the front.

"You're not from around here, are you?" she had asked him suspiciously.

"My family's had business in the area for years, but I was raised in Birmingham. I'm down here now because my father wants me to take over the railroad business and my mother is sick of the city, so overrun with coons."

His casual language let her know he couldn't tell she was colored. What should have made her wary and distrusting instead made her curious. She played pretend. What loyalty did she have for people in a city she didn't know? He presented her with the possibility of another life through an open door, and she took it and all he offered when she stepped across the threshold. Her mind was opened to what else she could have if she didn't correct people when they were wrong. Who's to say they were wrong in the first place? The only reason she was called colored was because they called themselves white. She figured then that if she didn't differentiate herself, she could mix and blend and cross back and forth as she pleased.

Over that summer Logan and Jubi became acquainted. He regaled her with tales about the iron city and how his family first got into railroad work after the war in an effort to rebuild the South. Their enterprise into coal mining soon followed when they learned there were grand profits to be had without enduring the dirtiness of the work thanks to the practice of convict leasing. Jubi didn't flinch as he easily discussed how his family reenslaved Black people under the guise of punishment for crimes of vagrancy, loitering, or unemployment. She couldn't stop playing pretend mid-game because the rules no longer agreed with her constitution. She smiled and laughed as she thought she was supposed to. When Logan asked after Jubi's whereabouts and her own relative newness to town, she did the only thing she could think of: she lied—told him she was Cajun, her family originally from a bayou border town between Louisiana and Mississippi.

"Only thing on the border there is the river," Logan had joked.

"It was a swampy place," she'd told him.

Whenever she came into the store, he always offered to walk her home, but she declined. Instead, she'd leave out the front and then walk in circles and squares on the side of town she rarely had need to venture into until she thought it safe to make her way back across the tracks to the farm. She believed then that she absolutely could continue to play pretend as long as it stayed on the other side of Land's End. And who on that side of the tracks would say different? Sure, there were some who kept quiet out of both loyalty and pity for Emma. But it was really fear that kept mouths closed and secrets inside. Who would dare speak a word out of turn against a white woman? Whatever Jubilee was up to, they figured it wasn't worth getting lynched over a lie.

Though at that time the possibility of what could be was short-lived. By the fall, Jubi returned to school at Alabama A&M in Huntsville and Logan headed back to Birmingham, where he was already betrothed to another, with a fancy wedding planned a year later. Only after he returned to Land's End in 1908 did her plan fully move into motion. At twenty-six, she was a college graduate in a place where most only finished high school. Too educated and too saditty for the men around her, Jubi was intrigued upon learning of Logan's return.

It's destined, she thought.

She made sure she visited the general store. Of course, they reconnected. Logan revealed his first wife had died in childbirth and he couldn't bear to stay in the city. She too killed off her invented family. Told him she was all alone in the world with only a little inheritance to keep her afloat. She even rented at a white rooming house run by a woman who also lacked a long history of Land's End to keep up the ruse and allow Logan to finally walk her to what he thought was her home. Their courtship after that was quick, connected by what Logan thought was grief when it was truly Jubi's greed, her lust for his life, which she glimpsed the first time she walked through the front door on his arm. They married at the courthouse without him ever meeting her people. When she was finally introduced to his family—after the wedding—they didn't question her story either, who she was or where she was from, the kind of interrogation that evaluates wealth and assigns worth in determining deservingness of the Danube name. After all Logan had lost, they didn't have the heart to try and sully his find. In fact, his sister Adeline, who lived in Land's End with her husband and two daughters, was so happy to see Logan happy, she didn't suspect Jubi to be anything or anyone other than who she said she was, even though their house help knew better.

Like Emma knew better.

Like Logan was about to find out.

His footsteps pounded toward the door. Quick and insistent, it was the pace of a man who'd waited too long to meet the son he'd sired. Logan didn't believe what Jubi said: that after all this time, all these years, all the miscarriages and stillbirths that'd nearly killed her, all he would end up with was a girl—a daughter who looked nothing like him, unlike the dead baby boys who were his spitting image, especially in complexion.

Jubi hadn't believed in the curse either. That Dupree women could carry only girls. She hadn't believed her own mother when she detailed her struggles to carry a baby, all the lengths to which Evangeline had gone every time Emma had gotten pregnant, let alone the late-night murmurings about her brothers.

Jubi didn't believe in most of the stories, especially not of her grandmother. She didn't believe a woman she'd never met, one who was long dead—dismembered at that—had that much power over her body. She refused to allow the stories to color her perspective or change her mind. That is, until Logan stood knocking outside their door while a black-ass baby girl she'd named Ruby lay in the middle of the bed screaming for milk Jubi withheld.

"Is he here?" Logan peeked through the door.

"She is, sir." Emma stepped in front of him to block his view.

"So it is a girl? I didn't believe Jubi for one minute when she kept referring to my son as a she and calling her Ruby. I just knew we were having a Robert. I was fine to keep the *R* name, but I just knew we were finally having my boy. We'd been waiting for so long. Even let her waste good salt all around the doors and erect a hoodoo altar to bring our dreams to reality."

Logan's mouth fumbled over the word *hoodoo*, as if it were foreign to him. As if venerating ancestors was so far outside the realm of worship he had to turn up his nose at what he considered primitive. Who were the angels and saints if not ancestors who'd found favor on the other side?

Tucking her true thoughts, Emma answered, "I understand, *sir*." She emphasized the handle she put on his name. Deference she hated to show, and didn't need to. Unearned respect she rarely gave. But in this situation, between her passing daughter, white husband, and black grandbaby, she knew she was going to need more than deference, more than respect to make it out alive.

"Let me see her," Logan demanded. "I bet she looks just like Jubi."

"She looks like her family, that's for sure," Emma said. "But Jubi needs to feed the baby to get her settled, don't you, Jubil—"

"Yes, I do, Emma."

Jubi snatched the baby from where she'd laid her in the middle of the bed and brought her to her breast. She said, "And you need to finish tending to me. Logan, please, let me get cleaned up, and then I'll bring her to you. It won't be long now."

"I just want to peek at her face, and then I'll go and leave you ladies to it."

He was insistent. A petulant child trapped in the body of a grown man. Never used to being denied, told no, not even by his own parents. Logan Danube had inherited his fortune by digging in his heels and refusing reason. Once he had his mind made up, there was no persuading him. No coaxing him to choose differently. See differently. Think differently.

Standing a foot above Emma as it was, he rose up on his feet to try to get a glimpse of the baby wrapped tight in the dirty sheet and held close to Jubi's breast. This close clutch would have delayed the inevitable a bit longer had the baby not had a mind and mission of her own. Even latched to the teat, she continued to kick and stretch, exercising the limbs that had been cramped in the womb forty weeks. It was another characteristic about her daughter Jubi recognized as different from all other babies she'd ever seen. Most stayed balled up, knees tucked into their chest for the first month of life. But not hers. No, Ruby kept trying to make room. And it was in one of these fits of the legs and arms that Logan didn't have to peek or sneak around the midwife he'd called to his home to deliver what he'd thought would be a son. He was able to see clear as day the pedaling legs and punching arms. Legs and arms that were infinitely more shades darker than he'd ever be. A baby that would never turn red and burn because it was protected by skin the color that had never run in the likes of his family.

"Unwrap the baby," Logan demanded.

With gritted teeth and steely eyes, his voice hardened from the impatient charm it once held.

Emma said, "She's gotta eat, sir, and I have to clean up your wife. We'll bring her to you once she's settled back down. I reckon it won't be long."

"I said, unwrap the baby."

"Sir—"

"Unwrap the baby."

Logan pushed past Emma and closed the gap between himself and the bed where Jubi sat up, clutching the squirming baby to her breast. If she could have suffocated the girl in the fatty folds of her own mammary glands, she would have. But Ruby kept kicking, kept squirming, kept turning for air, for food, for the freedom to look upon her father's aghast face.

"I don't know what kind of shit you two are trying to pull in here, but somebody better start talking and tell me why this girl looks like she's from some dirty nigger on the other side of the tracks."

"I, I, I, I," Jubi stammered, trying to create a coherent sentence. To issue a satisfactory alibi. One that neither suggested she wasn't who he assumed she'd been, nor, worse yet, that she'd had an affair on the other side of Land's End and had tried to pass the baby off as his.

"There's an old rootwork woman across the tracks," Jubi began. "I, I, I went to see her after our . . . after our . . . after our last loss. I asked her for her help. I, I, I think she put a hex on me."

Jubi looked up at Logan to see if he believed her lie. His hardened jaw and unmoving eyes suggested he didn't.

He asked, "What's her name? Who'd you see?"

"Evangeline."

Emma inhaled sharply. Logan reached into his pocket and, quick as a flash, brandished his switchblade. Pressing it to Jubi's neck, he said, "Try again. I know Evangeline's dead. She was the midwife before this one here."

Logan yanked the baby from Jubi's arms and held her upside down by a foot. Stronger than she had the age to be, Ruby kicked and screamed, trying to right her own self in the white man's hand.

He sneered, "I'll cut her limb from limb, head from body, if you don't tell me whose baby this is."

"She's ours!" Jubi screamed. Voice scratchy and hoarse, body trembling, tears leaking, she repeated, "She's ours. She's ours. She's ours."

From behind, Emma approached, and reached for the baby. "She's mine, sir," she said tentatively. "Both of 'em. Ruby is my granddaughter. Jubilee, here, my daughter."

"Jubilee?" Logan groused. "It sounds like a nigger name if I ever heard one."

"That's Jubilee Dupree, my daughter," Emma said. "This baby belongs to you and Jubilee. I reckon she take after my own mammy. Evangeline, she raised me, she told me my mammy was killed before she'd even passed her afterbirth."

"Looks like history will repeat itself tonight," Logan said, pointing the blade at the baby in Emma's arms.

With a free hand, Emma touched his shoulder. Gently, she said, "Let me take 'em back. You can say they both died during the birth. Nobody'll question a man in mourning. It's still late yet. The sun ain't even up. No one has to know."

Logan looked from Jubi's trembling frame, sitting up in the bloody bed, to Emma cradling the black baby that'd finally settled in the older woman's arms. Bending beside Jubi, blade nearly drawing blood from her cheek, he whispered, "Get your black ass out of my house right now, and don't you ever let me even hear of you walking around on this side of the tracks."

Wrapping the soiled sheets around her dirty white dressing gown, Jubi inched herself off the bed and away from Logan's wrath. She sidestepped the bowl of water filled with the refuse from the inside of her body and shuffled beside Emma. Head hanging, body aching from being ripped wide open, she led the way out of the house Logan had built for them and she'd decorated according to her taste. Past the mantel with their wedding portrait and the piano where they had entertained guests, Jubi scooted past the life she'd made from her imagination, leaving a filmy trail of blood behind her.

If anybody was awake or paying attention that night, they would have been able to follow the blood from Logan Danube's door, across the tracks, to the Dupree farm on the other side of Land's End. They would have known that the woman who passed for white by calling herself the Cajun, Jubi Etienne, was really Jubilee Dupree.

But Emma was right. No one on Logan's side of town was awake. They would never know the wife and child he said he lost in delivery after years of trying to conceive were just across the tracks, alive and well. The folks on his side pitied his misfortune. Especially since it had happened before. Which is why Logan had been all too agreeable to the cover-up. He knew how to fake the pain of losing a wife and child. He'd already lived it once. Men offered sympathy in what they believed to be his second bout of grief. Women pushed their daughters before him to help him in his time of need. They would never know.

Across the tracks, however, was an altogether different story. Amongst the many who rose before dawn to prepare for the day, they saw Jubilee, Emma, and the baby, shadows coming from a mile away. Under the moonlit sky they made out the old woman's frame wrapped in white, carrying a bundle that looked like a baby, and then the thing behind her shuffling along, body falling lower and lower as if it had a wish to see the other side.

Those awake saw Jubilee's return, and those who weren't lied and said they did. They said that by the end of the journey Jubi was crawling on her hands and knees to the door of the old house where she'd been born. They said she was so bloody and dirty that it was the one time in her life she resembled her daughter: both black as night. And most of it was true. Jubi was bloody and dirty. And though she didn't crawl to the door, she did collapse once she'd reached it. The blood seeping out of her every step of the way from the house she'd made to the home that was hers had made her dizzy and weak. She fell because she was unable to walk, to take another step.

Face down in the dusty doorway, she lay there awhile as Emma tended to the still-hungry baby inside. Those who saw her shook their heads. Others muttered, "Serves her right." Jubi couldn't blame them. In fact, she agreed with them. She knew some deceptions deserved the dirt.

11.

At seventeen, Ruby wore her color proud, braided hair too, despite Jubi's disdain. Out of spite she didn't own any hats. Every time Jubi had given her one, she had lost it. Sometimes it was an accident. Most times it was on purpose.

What did she need a hat for? She didn't burn in the sun. Her skin didn't need protecting. Not the same way Jubi safeguarded her own. It was for that reason Jubi had told Ruby she didn't go farther than the mailbox or the fence post. The reason Ruby had to do all her bidding in town and, once she was old enough to factor and figure, take over the running of the farm. Never did she say it was because she lived under Logan's threat of death. She told Ruby she no more liked the day-to-day running of the farm than she tolerated the sun. She found both inconvenient and wholly unnecessary.

"Why would God make something so oppressive and call it good?"

Jubi had ranted the question on more than one occasion. She'd said it just that morning, when Ruby and Emma had left for church, their arms loaded with food for the fellowship hall. Ruby carried the biscuits. Emma followed with the jars of jam. It was then she said something about the two braids trailing down her granddaughter's back.

"When'd you do that?" Emma asked.

"Yesterday when I came back from the general store," Ruby answered. "Do you like it?"

"Who taught you how to braid to the scalp?"

"Nobody," Ruby answered. "I was sitting in front the mirror, took my hair down, and did it. I taught myself."

"Mm-hmm." Emma nodded. Quiet and pensive, she watched the girl move about, wanting to see for herself what had come over her.

In the middle of Sunday service, Emma, overwhelmed by what she thought was the meddling of her own mother reaching into Ruby from the other side, raised a finger and tipped out. She went home and set a bowl of water by the door to welcome and guide the spirit. But she was on her way back to the church house when she remembered what Evangeline had taught her. "For every good spirit dey's a bad one. Make sure you have balance when you working."

Now, as she stood beside Ruby, serving St. Joseph's members supper, Emma still hadn't thought of a good balance to the water she'd set for welcome. She was racking her brain as she spooned out preserves, which didn't always land on the plate, when the boy approached. Sampson stopped in front of Ruby first.

"Would you like a biscuit?" she asked.

"Yes, please."

Ruby handed over the roll with the golden crispy edges and the fluffy center. Sampson reached to take it from her hand instead of letting her set it on his plate. Their fingers grazed. A shock ran through them both. Emma felt it too.

She said, "Ruby Ann, take over my station."

"You all right?" Ruby asked.

If Emma heard her, she didn't let on. Instead, she handed over her spoon dripping with blackberry jam, removed the apron covering her clothes, and walked away dazed, chasing after something that wasn't concerned with her yet.

Back in the line, Sampson looked at Ruby and said, "I like your hair."

Heat swam beneath her skin. The kind that changed everyone's color but hers unless you knew where to look.

Sampson knew where to look. He said, "When you finish, you wanna get out of here?"

"My mama and grandmama would have my hide if they heard tongues wagging about me running around outside with you."

"They're not here, though. Your grandmama just left."

"Maybe so, but it's still women watching."

"Well, when you finish serving, you leave first like you headed home. And after a while, I'll leave. We'll meet at the tracks and then go somewhere together."

Ruby nodded as one of the deacons waiting in line behind Sampson cleared his throat.

"Say yes?" he pleaded.

Ruby nodded, picked up another biscuit, and set it on his plate. He walked away thankful for the two pieces of bread he'd received to sop up the thick preserves. He ate the preserves slow, then licked his fingers, one by one, of the sticky and sweet refuse all the while looking at Ruby, who avoided his gaze. She passed out biscuits and spooned jam until all of St. Joseph's was fed and she was scraping the bottom of the jar with a spoon trying to taste a little sweet for herself.

She hadn't had much in life. Jubi gave her scorn, Emma silent contemplation. That's how she'd made it into the fields all those years ago to run around with Sampson until the day he just stopped showing up. No warning. Just gone. She learned then that the things you like and the people you love have no obligation to like you back. To love you back. If they indulge you at all, count it joy.

That's why when Ruby walked away from the serving tables and slipped out of the fellowship hall she had no designs to go home. She was tired of being made to feel that folks only suffered her presence. Jubi especially. As early in the afternoon as it was, she knew

Jubi wouldn't dare set foot outside with the sun high. Ruby wasn't sure what Emma would do, but she took a chance and walked to the tracks in her Sunday dress and shoes. Her braided hair swung across her back as the sun warmed her scalp showing through the parts.

Sampson met her shortly thereafter. She saw him coming in his suit pants, shirt, and tie. The latter he took off and shoved in his pocket. When he reached her, she noticed he'd unbuttoned the top two notches of his shirt.

She said, "Boys are lucky. They can loosen their buttons, roll up their sleeves, take off their clothes even, and nobody bats an eye. Us girls can't so much as have a run in our stockings without crazy assumptions being made about our character."

"Do you care?" he asked.

"I learned long ago not to think too highly of other people's opinions. They always let you down."

"Not always," Sampson said.

"Why did you want to meet here?" Ruby asked.

"So we could walk over to the Gulf together."

"What for?"

"Just something to do."

She studied his face, looking to see if he too wore a mask like her mother. One that taunted. She was looking for any sign to send her home to the women she knew, even if she knew very little. Ruby was unsure of whether she wanted to learn someone else who might find her refreshing in the high heat of the day, but a poor salve for the soul by the time it ended. But she had no warning against it. No worries. No foreboding or misgivings. She tried to channel Emma by looking off down the empty tracks. The old woman was always staring in the distance, entranced by something no one else saw. Looking for someone no one else could name.

"You can see the beginnings and endings of the world if you wait long enough," Emma had said to her when she was a girl.

Ruby waited, trying to see the past in the present. In a flash, there it was. Rather, there she was. The girl in the mirror, who looked so much like herself, running across the tracks. Ruby turned toward Sampson. Wanted to know if he could see. But there was nothing to belie vision. He blinked and reached for her shoulder. There it was again. The shock, electric energy between them. The same tingle she'd felt in her fingertips she now tasted on her tongue. Seeing the girl, seeing herself running free, Ruby trusted it. She trusted it all.

"Let's go," she said.

They walked with their shoes in hand once they reached the water's edge. The blue-green sea lapped their ankles, dampening the hems of Ruby's dress and Sampson's cuffed pants. Side by side, feet leaving tracks in the sand, they enjoyed the quiet of the midafternoon, when the folk from Land's End, on both sides of the tracks, were tucked away in their respective church fellowship halls, eating their fill of food and catching up on the week's gossip. So consumed were they with spreading the goings-on of this one's nephew, and that one's cousin, and the stories that inspired exclamations of "Oh, Sister, I've been meaning to tell you . . . ," no one had time to wonder on the whereabouts of Ruby and Sampson.

They made mention of Emma's disappearance in passing. Though no one wondered about Jubi. She hadn't set foot in a church house on their side of the tracks in more than two decades and no longer sparked the fevered whispers she once had. As for her daughter, who would whisper about her? Who knew to? Who knew that at the very moment they were picking apart the homegoing and repast of Sampson's grandmother Claudette, that Ruby would be shoulder to shoulder with him, sleeves nearly touching, longing for what she hadn't known she desired?

"We not gon' get in trouble walking on this here beach?" Sampson asked. "I know everybody in town still in church, but it ain't like white folk don't get possessive about us strolling their land."

"This part doesn't belong to them," Ruby said.

Both of Sampson's eyebrows raised two inches from where they rested, unsure of her meaning. She threw her head back and gave a good-natured guffaw, relishing what she would tell him next.

"This part of the beach belongs to us," she said. "Mama Em bought it with the earnings from the farm."

"Y'all must be doing real good in this Depression to buy a whole beach."

"We do all right," Ruby demurred. "Boll weevil be damned."

"How far down does the land go?"

"Those trees further up yonder. The one that looks like a knotty elbow coming out of the sand."

Sampson looked toward the trees and then behind him to where they first stepped on the sand emerging from a high thicket of brush and dunes. It seemed to expand by the second as he looked between landmarks. He had no idea how many acres they covered. He had no idea people like him could call such a thing their own. A two-hundred-acre farm and a piece of property on the water was almost too much for him to believe.

Approaching the tree line, he asked, "How she get ahold of something like this?"

"I don't know. The farm always been ours. It's where all of us were born. Me, Mama, and Mama Em. The beach, well, that's a different story. Mama Em say, 'Green is green when you hungry and lean.' That's how she got this here. Her money spend the same as anybody else's. Who cares if it came from us if it put food on their table. She didn't go into the particulars, but I know that much."

Sampson looked out at the expanse of ocean and saw all he wanted for himself. Land, water, space, and a lady beside him. At the edge of the property line, he left the path they'd been walking and started toward the knotty tree. He climbed the elbow first and then turned back toward Ruby.

"Take my hand," he said.

Ruby looked up at the long and bending bark-covered limbs toward the lush canopy of green leaves that could shade them from the sun and being seen. Not that anyone else was out, but she had to make sure. She didn't want to be the latest tale in a jabbering mouth running back across the tracks. Though no one ever said anything to her directly, she saw their looks when she left the house. Those mirthful glances from a joke in which she was never allowed to laugh. Whatever the case, she'd had enough of talk around her to openly invite chatter.

But her heart beat for the both of them.

Quick and fast, she felt that feeling. Ruby glanced toward the water where a dazzling light flashed against the shimmering sea. She trusted her intuition and took Sampson's hand. One touch and she decided right then it was enough. He lifted her up to the sturdy knot on the first limb. She savored the moment: the feel of his slightly calloused fingertips, the musky, sea-tinged smell coming from his skin, even the sweet taste of his breath as he blew air from his nose. It was all so much. The girl and now this. Ruby knew she'd be a fool to say no. To shrink away when she was hungry for more. She took every touch Sampson gave, tender and delicate, gruff and gripping, as they climbed higher and higher until their heads were shrouded in the canopy and their feet dangled above the sand.

Ruby surrendered to her senses, unaware and unashamed of the feelings that grew out of touching and came with consequences, or choices, depending upon the perspective. She turned her face toward his and leaned in close, praying he'd lean back. When he did, their foreheads touched and their eyelashes rested on cheeks as their mouths met in the middle. She couldn't believe she was the kind of girl to go off cavorting and canoodling, kissing and caressing with a strange man she only really knew as a boy. But who knew what kind of girl she was? A girl untouched and never kissed, not even by her own mama. She was kept at arm's length, as if her color would infect, spread from body to body with a brush, a peck, or a tender press of fingertips. Ruby knew she was a hindrance to her mother's way of living, whether Jubi said it or not.

It's no wonder that after that Sunday afternoon, she sought after Sampson every day he was in Land's End. When her morning chores were finished and she was of no more use on the farm, she followed the road beyond the fork to the shacks and shanty homes away from Jubi and Emma. But she couldn't just arrive at Ms. Claudette's, walk up to the front door of the two-room house, and call on Sampson. That would trigger too much talk, too much wonderment for her behavior to continue. Instead, she had to arrive under the auspices of errands. Needing something, bringing something, even if it was just eggs from the henhouse or her able hands.

"My mama and Mama Em told me to come on down the road and check on you to see how y'all doing with gathering Ms. Claudette's things," Ruby lied.

She lied and lied about her leaving and her visits with butterscotch smiles and adolescent earnestness she hadn't lost despite her bigger age. There was never the consideration that she wasn't telling the truth. A girl like Ruby, as dark as she was, what did she have to lie about? And Sampson was no better. A few years older, smug and smelling himself, he concealed their secret. Too eager on his own to run off and swim in her at the base of the knotty tree, tangling the blanket they'd brought in sand-covered limbs.

Their love was physical. All lust. Heavy breathing, dewy eyes, and wrinkled clothes. Ruby's appetite for Sampson was insatiable. She craved him on her constantly. It was not enough to be near; they had to touch, be enveloped, one beneath the other. One within the other. When they met, it was thrust and throttle, a syncopated hum that escalated to rhythmic harmony before exploding into muffled shouting. Just because no one was at the beach didn't mean they needed to hear. Tending crops, though harvest season was still months off, kept folk from their side of the tracks busy from can't see to can't see. No one had time to miss a daughter who did no field work and a man spending borrowed time.

It was always assumed Sampson would return to Mobile once the work of closing down the life Ms. Claudette had lived was complete. He never said as much to Ruby. He assumed she knew. The weeks went by. He enjoyed her company, her body, the shape of her face, the curve of her back, the vastness of her skin. Looking at her, he saw starshine and moonglow, the beginnings and endings of creation in the crevices she unclothed.

One particular afternoon, Sampson ran his hand alongside Ruby's body. He traced her calves to thighs, thighs to hips, hips to arms, and arms to neck.

He said, "I'm going to miss this when I'm gone."

The word was two hundred pounds of burlap-wrapped cotton on Ruby's chest. "Gone." She wanted to snap her body around and face him. She wanted to scream, *Whatchu mean?* But she did nothing of the sort. She had no right.

Finding air through the load, she asked, "You going back to Mobile?"

"It's time," Sampson said. "I done prolonged my trip as long as my family could tolerate. Everyone else been gone but me. I had been staying here for—"

"You don't need to say what you don't mean."

"I wasn't," he said. "I like you, Ruby, but I'm twenty years old. I gotta get a job. I ain't a Dupree with a farm, field hands, and a whole beach. I live in the real world."

"And you saying I don't?"

Ruby sat up, blanket clutched close and shoulders rounded. Anger pushed out her sadness. She didn't need his excuses any more than she needed him to explain her life when she was the one living it. He didn't know what it was to go your whole life hungry, unable to name the pain inside. To live in such a way where food no longer nourished, heat no longer warmed, and money didn't matter. What she was starved for wasn't provision. Of provision she had plenty. But she could no more impress upon Sampson about why her need was more important than he could convince her of his.

Ruby shook sand from her clothes and shoes. She put on the dress of the girl she had been before Sampson had asked her to take his hand. The clothes still fit, even if the body inside was different. For her body tingled with his touch. It throbbed with the sensation wrongfully removed from within. But it was over. He was going home. It was high time she did the same.

They departed together, each lost in their own thoughts. Hands at their sides, they walked back the way they came. Through one side of Land's End to the other. Across the tracks and down the road, Sampson arrived at Ms. Claudette's house first. It was empty now. The belongings given away or discarded. He started to find some last words, but Ruby never stopped. She didn't linger to say an awkward goodbye or a lying *See you later*. She knew that she wouldn't and that because of his needs he absolutely couldn't. So she kept walking, stride straight, back stiff, her own hands touching nothing but herself until she made it to the house sitting in front of the fork and had no choice but to go inside.

On the floor in front of her mirror, a potion of oil beside her and the broken comb in her hand, Ruby parted out sections and shook loose the sand. Her fingers moved on their own; she had no need to look. If the girl was there, she didn't want to see. She'd trusted her and been let down. Led on. It was too much to remember the magic of it all. The fortuitous happenstance that had been four weeks on the Black beach. Now all she had to show for it were sandy hair, a hollow body, and itchy drawls.

Ruby shifted in her discomfort, knowing she should have heated some water for a bath and washed her hair, but she worried about what they would say. Emma and Jubi were somewhere around finishing up the work of the farm, even if they hadn't yet come in the house. Odd behavior inspired odd questions. But for Emma there was nothing more odd than seeing Ruby inside her room, face down with her fingers in her hair, and a girl who looked liked her laughing and dancing in the mirror.

"She's still here."

Emma's voice cut through all manner of Ruby's emotions. She dropped her fingers from the braid she was constructing and let her long hair fall in heavy layers like a weeping willow tree. Ruby turned to Emma, who just nodded toward the girl in the mirror. Looking back, Ruby saw only herself.

"What's going on in here?" Jubi asked, coming to stand in the doorway.

Emma walked off. She found who she'd been looking for. Mother and daughter left mother and daughter alone.

Ruby went back to crisscrossing her strands until she reached the end. She didn't even look up when she switched to the other side.

Jubi sneered. "You not satisfied unless you bringing somebody else down with you? First me, then Mama, and now that boy."

Ruby didn't answer, didn't even look up to watch Jubi walk away. Head down, fingers braiding, she grieved for all she'd lost. Not understanding who she'd found. What she'd been given. It took her a long time to recognize the signs. It wasn't until everything was swollen, breasts, feet, hands, and belly, that she had an inkling that she was big with Sampson's baby.

At first, she thought the tenderness in her chest came from lifting bags of grain and pushing the wheelbarrow around the farm. But the sensitivity didn't subside when the harvest was complete. And the shooting pains that sent daggers through the bottoms of her feet didn't dissipate, no matter how long she sat down for a rest. Her hands tingled always, whether she opened and closed them, or flexed and relaxed her fists. Now, her stomach was an altogether different matter. She didn't understand how the distention worked. One day she needed to let out the tops of all her dresses, the next day the bottom, until they hung away from her in an oblong shape.

That winter, Jubi had seen enough of Ruby in her ill-fitting dresses. She'd been waiting for the girl to come clean, to admit what she'd been up to, but she never did. She was also waiting for the blood. For Dupree women, there was always blood. Buckets of crimson, because the little boy babies never did live.

After six months with no blood, Jubi finally confronted Ruby. They were all sitting in front of the fire. Emma, in her rocker, stared off into the flames. Jubi sat in an opposite chair with sewing in her hand. Ruby was on the floor between them, feet stretched toward the hearth, stress tingles tapping through her toes and fingertips.

"You might wanna write him a letter and let him know you're with child."

Ruby snapped her head toward Jubi, who never lost a stitch.

"I told you you wasn't gon' be satisfied until you brought somebody else down in the pits with you. Well, here we are."

"Jubilee, that's enough, now."

Emma's voice rang strong and clear. Studying the fire as if she were trying to decipher code, she said, "What's done is done now. Ruby Ann taking up with Claudette's grandson ain't so far and away different from what you did, now is it, Jubilee?"

"What I did was try to give myself a better life. It was bad enough I carried the curse. Then when it was all over, when I finally thought I had my miracle, I had something other than myself."

"That's what happens when you run from who you are."

"And who am I, Mama?" Jubi asked. "Who are you? It's not like you know much in the first place. You said Evangeline took all she knew to the grave."

"Not all. I know some things. She living in this girl here, I can tell you that much."

"Makes sense, as dark as she is. She would be the one to carry her color."

"Ruby Ann, pay your mama no mind. But you do need to do as she say and let him know."

"Tell him it's a girl," Jubi added.

"How I'm s'posed to tell him?" Ruby asked softly. "It ain't like we had this planned."

"Babies ain't nothing to be planned for," Emma said.

"Married or not," Jubi added. "Babies come when babies come."

"And in this here family, our girls get here on they own time and of they own mind. No matter how many boys she has to sacrifice for the girls to get here first."

"Who's sacrificing what?" Ruby asked.

Emma didn't answer. She stared at the fire and watched the flames dance. Legs and feet lifted from the ground and hands spread, arms akimbo, in the air. She watched her with joy before she recounted the pain. In a gravelly voice, Emma told the story of how she was born, the day of her own mama's murder. Evangeline and the curse, the boys before and after Jubilee.

"And the same thing happened to me," Jubi said softly.

"Between you and my daddy? Who was he?" Ruby asked, taking hold of the opportunity to get answers to questions she'd long stopped asking as it presented itself. A liberty Jubi nor Emma expected.

Jubi looked to Emma. Emma looked to the girl in the fire. There were only two choices before them and neither included *that* particular truth. Jubi resorted to what she did best and made up a story on the spot.

"Your daddy was in the war but got injured right after he deployed. He came home when I was still big with you, in his uniform and everything. White folks ain't like how proud he was standing all pressed and sharp, brass medals gleaming, injury be damned. Especially the sheriff. Your daddy took a billy to the back. Was arrested and charged with loitering, vagrancy, and for not having a job even though they all knew he worked with us on the farm. He got sent up on a chain gang out Birmingham or Huntsville way. I never knew for certain. Never heard from him since."

Overcome with the details, Ruby didn't have the presence of mind to ask after his name, which was Jubi's aim; to let a tragedy, one that was true in detail but not to the family, settle into Ruby to keep her inquisitive spirit quiet.

Emma shook her head at the fire too disgusted to contradict Jubi's tall tales, but Ruby looked at her mother anew. If only for a moment.

She'd never heard Jubi sound so fragile. As if she remembered the instant she was broken. Usually all sharp edges and gall, Jubi too stared at the fire, looking to see if what Emma saw was true. A curse come back to life, taking over Ruby's body. Despite their differences and all their bickering in this moment, they were of one accord. Agreed in the ways of women with experience.

Ruby asked, "Is it going to happen to me?"

Jubi turned and narrowed her eyes. Clouds colored her face as her hair was backlit in a halo from hell. "You gotta girl on the first try. Be satisfied. We cain't carry no boys. Ain't got no use for 'em."

12.

By the time Nadia needed to tell Roman that he'd left her with life, it was decades after the Dupree women had stopped conversing about the curse. Evangeline, Emma, and Jubi were gone, and Ruby and Gladys believed it to have been broken, for Gladys *did* have two boys. The fact of those two miracles, minor complications notwithstanding, led them to believe that she had been merciful on account of what Gladys suffered. Though they had stopped conversing about that as well. In any case, Nadia had no reference point for the extremity of what she was feeling. All she knew was that nausea washed over her when she opened a tub of no-lye relaxer.

She was in class on the West Side, working on Mrs. Johnson, her test client. With gloved hands, she smeared the cool white cream on the older woman's new growth and kitchen, working her way from back to front, all while taking shallow breaths from her mouth. When she passed the rattail comb through to ensure for even distribution, Nadia had to close her mouth to keep the excess saliva and bile from bubbling out.

"C'mon, let's get you washed out," she said to Mrs. Johnson. "I can't let this set too long or you'll burn."

"I been gettin' my hair permed longer than you been alive. I know when it's right." Mrs. Johnson stared through the mirror. Her dark brown pupils girded by a thin blue circle were unmoved.

Nadia backed away from the rising scent of chemicals. She said, "Okay, I'ma trust you."

"You mean I'm trustin' you." A satisfied smile spread across the woman's rust-colored face spackled with freckles. She said, "Your skin sure is pretty. What kinda makeup you got on? Fashion Fair?"

Nadia smiled but shook her head no. "Well, you sure are glowing," Mrs. Johnson continued.

Nadia smiled again and thanked her for the compliment. When Mrs. Johnson indicated she was ready, Nadia had to stand as far away from the washbowl as she possibly could while still being able to rinse out the relaxer and give the woman a thorough washing and conditioning. After she finished and passed her off to another group of students working on styling, Nadia rushed through cleaning up her station, which reeked with chemicals. The unease in her belly waved through her body and threatened to erupt on land.

It only grew worse when she left the school and boarded the first bus that would carry her back to the South Side. She was beat. Every week for the past four months Nadia's education consisted of three days of instruction, two days of practical application in the beauty lab, followed by an all-day Saturday affair split between the women's cashier station and the salon at Carson's in Ford City. Her plan to become a beautician—no, a licensed cosmetologist—no, a small business owner—was in action. She wanted to sleep, but nausea forced her in and out of consciousness, catching rest by the coattails as her only means of slumber.

After three bus rides and an aggravating walk where she baked in her all-black uniform, Nadia collapsed on the couch overlooking the picture window in Toya's first-floor apartment. She understood why crime was high in neighborhoods away from the lake. Suffering beneath the sun all day made any number of slights and insults that much more acute, inviting immediate response, fist or trigger finger.

"Nadia, that you?" Toya called from her bedroom.

"Yeah," she yelled back. "Why? Lou on his way over?"

"In a little bit."

Toya walked into the living room sporting light denim daisy dukes and a yellow crop top. She looked out over the neighborhood, where kids zoomed up and down the block on legs, bikes, scooters, skates, and skateboards. It was the beginning of the school year, where homework was minimal enough to allow kids uninterrupted hours outside before the streetlights came on and their mothers yelled for them to get their asses in the house.

Nadia moaned from the couch. Toya looked at her spread across the cushions, her book bag and purse still attached to her arms, and asked, "What's wrong witchu?"

"Tired." Nadia sniffed the air.

"You don't look tired witcha face all glowin' and shit."

"That's what the last lady in my chair said to me." She sniffed again.

"Was it an old lady?"

"Yeah. Why you ask?"

"Because you know old ladies don't hold no cut cards. If she gave you a compliment, then you know it's true."

"I guess." Nadia smacked her lips. "She asked me if I was wearing Fashion Fair."

"I'm telling you. You look good. All sun-kissed and what not."

"If you say so." Nadia sniffed and tasted the air around her again. "What the hell is that smell?"

"It's my perfume. You don't like it?"

"Smells like spoiled milk covered by dead roses."

"Well, damn. Let me get the hell away from you. You tired and irritable."

"I'm not irritable."

"If you say so. For a second, I thought you was pregnant."

Nadia jolted up on the couch as another wave rolled through her body, her stomach a tide of unseen rip currents at Lake Michigan's deepest depths. Instinctively, she cupped her hand in front of her nose and mouth. Nothing came up.

"I can't be pregnant," she said.

"You can't be pregnant, or you don't *want* to be pregnant?" Toya sat on the navy leather love seat opposite her.

"Both," Nadia answered. "I definitely don't want to be pregnant. And I can't be pregnant because I haven't had sex."

"Not recently."

"What the hell is that supposed to mean?"

"You know exactly what the hell it means! When's the last time you had a period?"

"I don't know. Last month?"

"You sure?"

Shit.

Nadia recounted the last three months. The last time she saw Roman. Arguing with Gladys. Enrolling in school. Transferring to the Ford City store. Taking the bus out to the West Side or up to Cicero. In none of those remembrances did she recall the flow of blood from her body.

"Shit," she said aloud.

"Mm-hmm," Toya humphed. "Are your titties tender too?"

Nadia pressed a hand to her chest and tried not to wince from the sore feeling. The swelling was apparent in her bras, which cut across the fatty tissue leaving the outline of a muffin top beneath all of her shirts. She began to understand why she hadn't been able to sleep on her stomach and spent half the night flipping from side to side.

Toya sat beside her. "So, are you pregnant?"

She calculated days, weeks, and months. Went over her symptoms again and again. The only confirmation missing was Gladys calling to tell her she'd dreamed of fish. But they weren't speaking, so she would never know. Covering her face with her arms, Nadia wailed, "I don't know."

"You need to get a pregnancy test," Toya said. "They got 'em up the block at the corner store. You want me to get it for you?"

Nadia nodded. Without another word, Toya got up from the couch, picked up her shoes and purse, and walked out the door.

Nadia laid against the leather, as her mind went in reverse to the last time she was with Roman. *Was I already pregnant then?* She tallied different dates. Tried to count the number of times they were together skin to skin without any barriers of protection. *Deborah . . . She's pregnant.* His voice came rushing back from the revelation at the kitchen card table. Followed by her own. *Even if I am, I don't have to keep it.*

Fixed on a way out, Nadia sat up on the sofa and waited for Toya to return. Looking out the window at the kids still playing on the block, she remembered when Bryan and Terry were babies. How Gladys fussed over them as if they would break. She'd put her ear to their lips and noses to make sure they were still breathing, and she always had to touch their bodies to make sure they were warm. She barely let Nadia come near them until well after they'd turned one. Playing with them then was fun. When she only pretended they were hers.

Gladys had carried Bryan while she was in night school for nursing. *Couldn't I do the same?* she wondered. The thought surprised her as she vacillated between escape and acceptance. Her divergent trains of thought ran parallel.

Can't I do both?

Do I even want kids?

His kid?

Outside the window, Nadia noticed parents pockmarked throughout the block. A grandmother who sat in an old chair watched from one end of the street to the other. A father cut grass for himself and his neighbor. A mother used a water hose to manually hydrate her hydrangeas even though their blooming season was coming to an end. Toya maneuvered past them all as she pushed through her gate. When she finally got inside the apartment, she shoved the brown paper bag toward Nadia's face.

"Go," she commanded.

Nadia trudged to the bathroom at the back of the apartment like it was her last walk. She took the test and prayed for a negative result. Outside, she heard the door open and close as she flushed. Heavy feet walked the hard wood followed by a deep voice, kissing, and silence.

"Hold on," Toya said. "I gotta check on Nadia before we leave."

She hurried to the bathroom and knocked on the door. Nadia let her in.

"Soooo?" Her eyes bounced from side to side as she rebounded on her heels. Nadia pointed to the top of the medicine cabinet. Toya reached for the stick and then grabbed the box for instructions on how to read the test.

"Congratulations!" she said gently.

"I'm not pregnant?" Nadia asked expectantly.

Toya bit her bottom lip. "I'm sorry."

Nadia's face fell, her body a ripple of reaction at the realization that she was pregnant with a married man's baby.

"I hope you have a girl," Toya said.

"Who says I'm having anything!"

"Are you serious?" They stared each other down.

"Don't tell Lou."

"Nadia!"

"Don't. Tell. Lou. Not until I tell Roman. I have to figure out what I'm gonna do."

"Fine," Toya agreed begrudgingly. "We gettin' ready to go out, but you need to page your boy."

Nadia promised she would as Toya and Lou left her to lament. In the silence of the bathroom, she scrubbed the skin on the backs and palms of her hands, trying to wash off what was never there. Not dirt. Not guilt. Not shame. She had never felt wrong in the moments with Roman, as if she'd taken something that wasn't hers. She'd fucked and slept without remorse. They hadn't discussed the deep, the future or past. Only the moment.

Bile rose, and Nadia spat in the sink. A buckshotted spray she rinsed down the drain. Her mouth was coated with a bitter after-taste, like fermented fruit left too long in the sun. She emerged from the bathroom and grabbed Toya's pink phone from the wall. Entangling herself in the long cord, she dialed the number she knew by heart and waited for the familiar voice. His baritone was arresting. If her baby hadn't already sent her stomach somersaulting, it surely would have leapt at the sound. Nadia held herself as she waited to speak, moisture inconspicuously gathering between her thighs. Reaction visceral. Not cerebral.

Voice steady and even, she introduced herself as if they were strangers. *Uh*s and *um*s peppered her speech. Potholes on pavement, her request was broken apart into barely intelligible pieces. Only at the end did she manage an unbroken phrase.

"Please, call me back."

She cradled the phone in the crook of her neck before she hung up and dialed again. At the beep she blurted, "I'm at Toya's," then hung up. Only to dial again to say that she'd left him Toya's phone number.

"Call me back. Please," she pleaded.

She hung up. The apartment was silent. There weren't even the sounds from outside anymore. Hovering mothers and grandmothers had gone inside behind children disappointed by the day's end. Fathers, for the houses that had fathers, parked their cars, beeped their alarms twice to ensure they were locked, and went inside. The streetlights were on. Nadia lay back on the sofa still in her uniform, the remnants of no-lye relaxer in her nose. She fell asleep with one arm draped across her future.

The scent of coffee filled the confined space in the morning. Nadia awoke ready to retch. She pushed off the sofa, yawned and stretched, and headed toward the bathroom. Toya was in the kitchen. The loosely tied sash of her purple robe barely hid her nakedness.

"You want some?" she asked.

Nadia shook her head no as she rushed into the bathroom and dry heaved into the toilet. There in the trash beside the sink and toilet was the pregnancy test with its positive pink lines. She retched again. When Nadia finished, she stepped out to see Toya leaning against the sink. A steaming cup of tea sat in front of an empty chair at her small round table. The white wood and matching chairs had an ornate design along the legs and backs. Nadia stared at them, avoiding Toya's gaze.

"You talk to him?"

"Paged him a few times. He hasn't hit me back."

Toya stared at Nadia as she lifted the mug and sipped her tea. Her eyes begged, *Let me tell Lou*, but Nadia shook her head.

"I had to move the evidence when we came home last night so he wouldn't see."

"Thank you," Nadia mumbled.

"Get better at keeping secrets." Toya pushed away from the sink with two cups of coffee in hand and went into her bedroom. The door slammed behind her.

For the next five mornings they met in the in-between. Nadia coming out of the bathroom. Toya emerging from her bedroom. The kitchen was Switzerland. They stared out the window until their eyes would find one another, and Nadia would shake her head no. Toya wanted her to be reasonable. Nadia wanted Roman to answer her pleas of please on his own.

Day six.

Toya made coffee, huffy in her disgust. Nadia sat with her elbows on the table. Her arms covered her face, hands steepled in pliant supplication.

"Tell him," she said, with her head bowed.

Toya whirled around. Nadia lowered her arms. "Tell him. But don't tell him." She sighed, defeated. "Tell Lou to have Roman call me."

Toya nodded.

"Don't tell him about the baby."

"I won't," she said, her voice light with relief. She hurried back to Lou on the other side of the door to carry a message that had already been delivered.

Day seven.

In Switzerland, Toya arrived with news from the other side.

"He said meet him at the library before it closes."

Nadia nodded. "I'll be there after class."

BACK WHERE THEY BEGAN, NADIA BROWSED THE ROWS OF WOODson as she waited for Roman to arrive. She could see from the second-floor windows the moment he entered. Navy pants, a black silk shirt, his short Afro—patted into place—shiny with sheen. His stride was strong and impatient as he breezed into the library looking around for wherever she may have been. By the time he spotted her, she was on the stairs, returning to the first floor in the middle of the fiction section. She offered a small smile. Cleared her throat.

"You wanted to see me?" he asked, forgoing pleasantries.

"Hello to you too," she said, stomach aflutter.

"What is it?"

His jaws worked overtime, chomping gum to sticky mush. Across his forehead, a five-paragraph essay on the tensions caused by women were written in his wrinkles. His face was rigid and sclerotic. It held none of the easy, smiling charm of the experience curator who had willed his way into Nadia's life. No, this was a man in penitent purgatory, trying hard to walk the straight and narrow path back to Deborah.

Nadia swallowed her urge to spit. "I wanted to talk to you. No . . ." She stopped. "I *need* to talk to you."

"The time to talk was before you walked out my door. I haven't heard from you since then. Why you blowing me up now?"

"So you have gotten my messages."

"I got 'em."

"Why didn't you call me back?"

"I hadn't gotten around to it. I'm still getting settled . . ."

At home. Nadia heard what he didn't say regarding Deborah. His pregnant wife. And their two children.

"How's your son?" she asked. "He should be getting his cast off soon."

"Nadia, I know you didn't drag me all the way over here to ask me about my son's cast. What. Do. You. Want?"

"How's Deborah's pregnancy going?"

"I'm gone." Roman turned and walked to the door.

"Wait!"

"What?" He whirled around.

"I *need* to talk to you."

"Then talk."

"Come here."

He didn't move.

"How've you been?" she asked.

"Nadia, stop bullshitting. It's not your style. Never was."

"Damn! Can't I just ease into it? This is not easy for me."

"I never knew you to ease into anything."

"Did you ever really know me?"

"There she is," Roman said. "Now what is it? I gotta go."

Fuck it. "Fine." She sighed. "The reason I've been trying to get in touch with you is because I'm pregnant."

"Is that right?"

His favorite line, which at one time had felt so familiar, was acerbic and biting. Gone was the playfulness from when they used to engage. Instead, there was a sharpened bitterness that cut through calcified cartilage.

"Yeah, that's right," she said, finding some strength.

He paused a moment and looked her over. Her flushed skin and black uniform. The grip of her hands on her book bag. His gaze lingered on the midsection of her body.

"So what." He shrugged. "What's that got to do with me?"

"Don't play me. You know this has everything to do with you."

"If you say so."

Roman turned again toward the entrance of the library. Betwixt the aisles and between the tables, he didn't stop until Nadia lunged for his shoulder as he damn near goose-stepped across the parking lot toward his Cutlass.

"That's all you got to say to me?" she demanded, holding him back.

He shrugged her off. Turned around. "What else you want me to say? Your pregnancy. Your problem. I ain't seen you in months. I don't know where you been or who you been wit'."

"So it's like that now."

"I'm married."

"You've got to be fucking kidding me."

"My wife is pregnant."

"I can't believe this shit."

"I already got two kids."

"You wasn't talking this noise when you were laid up with me."

"C'mon, Nadia, you know what it was."

Arms folded across her chest, her foot tapped the cadence of her anger as her stomach flipped front to back.

"So what you sayin'?" she asked.

"I'm saying your pregnancy don't have shit to do with me," he sneered. "I mean, like, for real, can you even afford a baby right now? You don't even have your own place."

She nodded in understanding. His life came first. Deborah's pregnancy trumped anything she would ever have to say. He hocked the gum in his mouth across the parking lot and reached into his pants pocket for his pack of cigarettes. As he lit his square, Nadia flipped the book bag on her back around to her front and took out her own pack of cigarettes from the small pocket. She lit her private peace and exhaled in his face.

"Didn't you just say you were pregnant?" he asked, eyes wide and brows raised.

"What do you care? You just told me you wasn't gon' be around for your baby, so why you care if I smoke?"

Roman nodded. Dragged to the end of his cigarette then threw it down, where he stamped it underfoot. "We good?" he asked.

Nadia took a drag. Blue smoke curled out of her mouth. She asked if he wanted to know anything.

He shrugged. "Keep it. Get rid of it. Whatever you do, that's on you."

She watched Roman stride to the parking lot, get into his car, and pull out. She watched until the car she'd known so well merged into traffic on Halsted then turned left on Ninety-Fifth Street. He was headed back to Beverly. Back to his family. Nadia smoked as she walked to the bus stop. She smoked another while she waited for it to arrive. And another as she walked from Crandon and Eighty-Seventh to Toya's building on Eighty-Third.

The music was loud when Nadia pushed into the apartment. Teena Marie's "Deja Vu" pumped from the bedroom. Nadia covered herself on the sofa even though she smelled of outside. Bus fumes and exhaust. Ash and smoke. Old books and papers. Hair color and relaxer.

Her stomach flipped, and she ran for the bathroom. One hand over her mouth, the other a fist pressed against her belly, she held it down until she could release it all in the commode. Smoke-tinged throw-up gushed from her mouth as snot ran from her nose and tears flowed from her eyes. She flushed it all to the city.

Day eight.

The smell of coffee roused Nadia from where she laid on the cold tile of the bathroom floor. On shaky hands and knees, she peeled herself off the ground, rinsed out her mouth, and splashed her face with water. It was of no use. Her puffy, red eyes and ashen skin told the story she wouldn't. Even her hair was soggy and damp from where it had gotten stuck with sweat and grime against her neck. She knew she didn't look like herself, but she couldn't help but wonder when she would.

"It's just us," Toya called from the kitchen.

Nadia stepped out of the bathroom to see Toya, in her robe, waiting for her at the table. A mug waited for her as well. The bedroom door was open. The bed made.

"I sent him home after he saw you passed out in the bathroom."

"Sorry."

"Don't worry about it. How'd it go with . . ."

Nadia held up a hand before Toya could say his name. "I told him," she said. "He doesn't care."

"What do you mean he doesn't care?"

Mimicking his caustic delivery, Nadia repeated, "'Keep it. Get rid of it. Whatever you do, that's on you.'"

"He said that shit to you?"

"Yeah." Nadia sipped from her mug.

"Oh, uh-uh," Toya said, getting up from the table. "Hell nah. You need to cuss him the fuck out." She snatched the phone from the cradle and shoved it into Nadia's face. "You need to call his ass, now!"

"It's only his pager number. He's not going to respond."

"Girl, you betta blow that motherfucker up."

Setting her mug on the table, Nadia grabbed the phone, dialed the number, and waited.

It didn't ring.

The three-tone dial resounded, followed by a staticky, computerized message. "I'm sorry, the number you have reached has been disconnected."

13.

When word reached Sampson, he had already considered going back to Land's End. In Mobile he had no job and barely anything to eat. His clothes were threadbare, and his shoes had holes in the soles. Even though he had a degree and certification from the training school, it was of no use. With white men outta work, there wasn't nary a job for him. Four years of education didn't mean nothing if you had no food and only a little bit of water. Who had time to think about books when your stomach growled and there was only cornmeal mush to salve it?

In Land's End, he walked heavy. He had never seen so much food cover tables as they had in the fellowship hall for his grandmother's repast and then again on Sundays after service. Sunday meals he skipped out on to be with Ruby at the Dupree beach. When he received her letter about a baby on the way that belonged to him, it was all the convincing he needed. Sampson packed his sack, put on his best suit, and shined his shoes for one last trek. He was a man in need of his own house. Down in Land's End, he believed he could be as his father was to him, his mother, and three siblings.

Only he didn't own anything. When he left, Claudette's house—a falling-down quarter shack from the days of Zephaniah Foster Dupree—had been closed. He thought he would open it again and build it up for Ruby like George had done for Emma, but upon his arrival he noticed the plot where the wood-frame house had stood was bare. Knocked down and picked clean for firewood by the workers and field hands living in the neat blocks behind, where they worked the Dupree land.

They saw him coming and felt no ways sorry for him. When his mother and father first left Land's End, years ago, it was goodbye and good riddance. Folks figured if leaving to beg for a boot and a hand in Mobile was considered better living, then go find it. Most everyone else had learned to be content. To be satisfied with the routine of the days and the roles and positions they played. The Duprees had the farm. The Danubes, the general store. And each had their own beach. This was the balance that kept Land's End from being like the other cities they heard about. The ones where the Black people were bombed and burned out for living better than some of the white folk. While there were all manner of businesses on the Dupree side of the tracks—tailors, seamstresses, barbers, and more—no one owned a general store. It was an unspoken agreement that preserved life in more ways than one.

When they saw Sampson cross the tracks and walk to where they'd been all their life assuming he was going to take up where Claudette had left off—though she'd been in the ground for six months—they could only come out to their porches and laugh amongst themselves. Not one to suffer needlessly, Sampson passed the empty plot as if he'd never meant to stop. He kept straight toward the house with the women who ran things on this side of the tracks.

If he thought his new destination would wipe away the smug smiles and bemused smirks launched at him amid the evening gossip, he was wrong. When everyone realized where he was going, they monitored his movements more out of curiosity than mirth. Though they'd never admit to being meddlesome, they were certainly intrigued by what they might see once Sampson reached the door of Emma and the one who no longer liked to be called Jubilee. His arrival made them remember that not only had Jubi been shut in since her return, but they hadn't seen her girl in a while either.

"Ruby Ann is that child's name," they said amongst themselves as Sampson walked toward his intended.

"Truth be told, I ain't seen that child since that boy's grandmama passed."

"She ain't been to church or school, and she ain't been in the storehouse with Emma helping her with the figurin' either."

"Then you know that's why he back, don't you? What else could it be?"

Humphs and harrumphs of speculation echoed each one of Sampson's footfalls. By the time he reached the Dupree door, folks had gathered in the middle of the road for what they called their weekly walkabout, knowing good and well they had started it right then. An idea spread by osmosis due to their need for knowing. Word this hot couldn't be kept going porch to porch. They needed confirmation. Someone to see and substantiate what they believed to be true and then run back and tell word that they'd been right all along.

Sampson knocked. Jubi answered. She ushered him across the salt line at the threshold, bookended by a bowl of water and the bucket of goofer dust. Once he was inside, she didn't close it right away. She heard the humming of voices in her bones and felt the sear of stares on her skin. Light skin, light eyes, light hair unwrapped and flowing about her head, held high, she absorbed their shock and imbibed their drunken wonder. Standing in the doorway, she let them lay eyes on her. Gave them something altogether different to whisper about as they roamed back home. Ruby they couldn't have.

Cured of their captivation, they headed back to their porches. Though they didn't get the answers they'd come for, they were all in agreement that they'd lucked up on something even better.

"Did you see Jubilee?"

The murmurs went around once more fixated on the woman they'd known as a girl. The rare sight led them all to surmise, "Something's got to be going on with Sampson and her girl."

"I heard the girl is pregnant with twins."

"Why else would she stand outside like that?"

"It makes sense and explains why she ain't been to school either, even though this would've been her last year."

Word traveled well for weeks as the stories grew more fantastical by the month, until screams pierced the night coming from inside the Dupree door. It had to be that somebody walked by when Ruby let out her first yelp from the inside. The unmistakable cry of a woman in transition, caught between life and death. The delicate balance from which babies come forth. It had to be a woman who walked by too, because who else could hear a scream and immediately know the cause of the agony? Only someone who had been through it, who'd seen the other side while nudging life along centimeter by centimeter.

The news of what was happening inside the Dupree house spread faster than when Sampson first returned. It passed from porch to porch, and instead of sitting in their rockers and kicking back with one foot caught between their chairs and their banisters, nearly the whole of Land's End on their side of the tracks got up and called forth.

"You think Jubilee in there helping Emma deliver the baby?"

"She should be."

"How could she? You know she ain't trained in the way."

"Emma learned from Evangeline. Between the two of 'em, they birthed us all."

Head nods of agreement swept through the crowd as another scream pierced the night. Outside they kept watch. Held vigil. Praying for the girl to only peek around on the other side but to come back to them with her new baby in arms.

That was the prayer of the women. The ones who had peeked themselves. The men could only stand solemn-faced, gritting their teeth, waiting on word—good or bad—the same way they had waited when their own wives disrupted the night with screams that shot vertically through the air. They never bought into the newfangled talk of "*We* had a baby." They knew they'd never had a damn thing. No screams had ever left their lips. No contractions had ever erupted from the centers of their sacrums and radiated outward with the pain of forced opening. From where they stood, they could only remember what it looked like to see someone, two someones, splayed before God, their bodies an exhortation to give them breath or give them rest.

They'd stood in the same spot Sampson was standing in now: in another room, away from the women, hands shoved in his pockets, his top teeth grinding against the bottom. He'd long been put out of the room he shared with Ruby. When she felt the first pang that wasn't practice, a belly tightening different than before, she reached for him. Woke him up out of a sound, snoring slumber with the kind of grip he knew was the clench of life. As Ruby's heavy breaths turned to moans, and her moans to screams heard by a woman walking outside, her mothers came rushing, their bodies wrapped in white and ready to work.

"Spread another line of salt at the door, change the water, and put some more mixture in the bucket. Fill that one to the brim."

"Boil some water for me on the fire."

"Get me some towels."

"Sampson, go'n out the way."

"C'mon, baby girl, it's time now."

Emma barked orders and Sampson, Ruby, and Jubi all followed what she said. They had no other choice. She was the only one with the knowledge. The only one who had been present on the occasion of all three of their births. Sampson's was ordinary, while Ruby's was not. And when Emma delivered Jubilee, Evangeline had been coaching her the way she'd coached Jubi, the way she was coaching Ruby now.

Birthing babies is women's work if there was ever any real division of such things. Men may get all the glory for it with their hospitals, tools, and book learning, but some things can't be taught. They have to be learned through experience. Felt on their own time, spontaneous and unscheduled, and ushered with gentle firmness. A coaxing, not a blitz.

Standing between Ruby's open legs, Emma coaxed forth. From her position at the head, Jubi ushered her girls in from the other side.

She said, "Bear down. Take my hand."

Even halfway between heaven and earth, Ruby felt the fullness of the moment. Her mother offering her hand. Giving her permission to touch. It was all she had ever wanted. What she'd first found in Sampson finally came back around between her and Jubi. Ruby placed their palms together and intertwined their fingers. She pushed her body into the bed, gritted her teeth, and let a screaming moan tear through her torso as her daughter was shoved into the world into Emma's warm rag waiting hands.

"She's here," the old woman grunted.

Emma cleaned the baby's nose and throat until the lungs cleared and a different kind of cry pierced the night. The sound sent Sampson scrambling into the room.

"How do?" he asked.

"Right fine," Emma answered. "Now go'n back out. We gotta clean them up."

Ruby gave a small nod that sent him shuffling outside. On the porch, where the last stragglers were gathered around waiting for word, Sampson gave a nod that sent the women on their way. They already knew all was fine inside the Dupree house, for they had heard the baby cry. Thrust into the world, kicking and greedy, baby squeals were piercing yet proud. The women knew Ruby had tasted death but pulled through and chosen life. Only the men were left. They approached the Dupree porch and shook Sampson's hand. No matter what they'd thought of him before, he was one of them now. A son of Land's End with a baby of his own and a need to take care of it lest he live off his women.

One man, called June, on account of him being Jeremiah Job Erickson Jr., said as much.

"We ain't seen you 'round much since you been back."

"I thought it best if I be 'round for Ruby," Sampson said.

He was too ashamed to admit he'd returned without a plan. While he had no prospects in Mobile, he didn't know where to begin to look for work in Land's End. It was one thing to know there were jobs available but you couldn't get them because you didn't fit the description. It was also fine to know that there were simply no jobs. But Land's End presented its own conundrum. It required creation. The community, insular and needing nothing outside of itself, except groceries, was a mystery to him. A code of work he could not crack. Everything he could do, anything he could offer, Land's End already had. Emma had offered him work around the farm helping her and Jubi with the facts and figures, but he knew that was only because they had put Ruby on bed rest. He had her job. A position she'd been born into on account of her name. Whether he was there or not, he knew Ruby could always be employed in the work of the farm, but Sampson wasn't that kind of man. He did what he was told, biding his time, waiting for the day he could decline.

June said, "With more children running around, we need more teachers at the schools."

Sampson nodded, trying to follow where June was going.

"We heard you had some college schoolin'. Is that right?"

"Yeah, that's right," Sampson said.

"We was thinking maybe you would be fit to teach a class at the high school."

Sampson nodded. "Sounds like a good idea to me."

"Most of us 'round here ain't ever left out of Land's End, let alone went to no training college in the city. If teaching is all right with you, it's all right with us."

"That's all right with me."

Sampson sighed, relieved. He looked at June, who would one day inherit his father's church, the same as Ruby would inherit the farm, the same as all the other sons and daughters of Land's End would inherit whatever work or business that employed their parents, be it field hand or fixer, barber or baker. He shook June's hand and watched him walk off. No *thank you*, or *you're welcome*, or *congratulations* uttered between them.

Back inside, Ruby cooed to the baby as Sampson entered the room. "Look at your daddy, right on time."

"How's our girl doing?" he asked.

"Eating," Ruby said.

"That means she's fine," Emma answered.

"Can I hold her?"

Ruby nodded her head and slowly unlatched the nursing baby from her breast. She tightened the swaddle blanket around the baby girl who kicked at the air as she was passed to Sampson. He looked down on the little one who looked nothing like him. Looked nothing like Ruby either. Their daughter took after Jubi and Emma. A bundle of light called forth from the caverns of the deep.

"You name her yet?" Sampson asked.

"Not yet," Ruby said.

"How about Gladys," he offered. "Because that's how I feel looking down at her now. Just mighty glad."

Ruby nodded. "Hello, Gladys," she said, when Sampson passed the baby back to her.

There were no objections. Not even from Jubi, who still stood in the corner beside Ruby's head. She reached for the baby's little hand with one finger. Waves of words unspoken washed over her. Ruby noticed. The delicacy. The tenderness of touch. She watched as the sternness she associated with her mother's face melted without a disappearance into the distance or a head shake to rid it away. Twin arrows of grief and love shot through Ruby. Emma called them closing contractions on account of her nursing, but Jubi and Ruby knew the truth. Looking down on the baby, they both swallowed bitter pills of resentment.

Ruby focused on baby Gladys's face, though she struggled getting her latched to the other breast. She wanted to ask for help, to reach for Jubi's hand, but she didn't. It was just as well. It took every inch of Jubi to keep her hands to herself, though her face told it all, shining like it did with tears that looked like love. She gazed at Gladys with only one thought. She knew that was the baby who was supposed to be hers.

14.

It was upon the occasion of Gladys's birth when Jubi began to feel like her old, created self again. Whenever she looked at the bright-skinned babe she had wanted for her own, she'd snatch her grandgirl from Ruby and Sampson and carry the girl to her room, only taking her back to her parents when the child's acute cries for milk overwhelmed all who could hear.

With Gladys she could pretend like she did when she first met, courted with, and eventually married Logan because he had assumed she was like him despite Emma's warnings it couldn't be done.

"You think you gon' marry that white man and make a happy life forever?" Emma had asked, when Jubi announced she was moving into the rooming house on the other side of the tracks.

Jubi had answered flippantly, "Maybe so."

"And whatchu gon' do when he find out who you really is?"

"He ain't gon' find out."

Emma had humphed at her daughter's confidence, Jubi's certainty in who she was becoming. She and George didn't understand the jumps Jubi's mind made to get her to believe she was someone other than herself, light skin be damned. Emma and George were just as bright, if not more so, on account of both of their fathers being white. But they knew better. That looking similar was not the same as being. They didn't believe people could hide their whole selves, put on someone else as a costume, and disappear. But that is exactly what

Jubi did. Her vanishing act was so complete that Emma and George had to hear about their daughter's pending nuptials to one Logan Jefferson Danube III from the staring, murmuring, whispering folks who worked for them.

No, they weren't invited. Jubi was lost to them. That is, until she dragged herself back, bloody and dirty, behind her mother. Emma and Ruby were all she had left, with George dead and in the ground the year before her unceremonious return. Everybody said his heart gave out while he was working. He'd gone to swing the ax but never got it off the ground, the attack sudden and swift, but Emma knew the real reason. Her George had grieved himself to death. He never got over the loss of their boys, and Jubi leaving was too much to bear.

Jubi didn't know what was worse. The fact she was back or back with a baby and no daddy, not even her own. She shut herself inside out of both fear and shame and did the very least for the girl who'd outed her and forced her back into her old life. Not that it wasn't a comfortable life, but for Jubi it would always be less than the life she'd created with Logan.

It wasn't so much that she was covetous of what someone else had. She had learned, first from Emma and then from Logan, that if you think you're lacking you'll never have enough. Because really, what is enough? Jubi didn't long for more things, but she knew she could never be too white. She had tried it on and worn it for as long as she could, even though it was a dress that was forever two sizes too big, no matter the amount of alteration.

Even when she was found out and had been forced to take it off, Jubi knew deep down that her covetousness wasn't about color. It was about access, ease. Land's End may have been an outlier, but no matter how unique, how idyllic or utopic, it was still the South. It was still Alabama. Maybe the Klan didn't ride across the tracks, bomb homes and churches, and set fire to the fields, but the lynching letters from other parts of the state filled with pictures and postcards of mangled, mutilated bodies were still left in strategic places as a reminder of who they were. Where they were. Who they used to belong to, even if all of that now belonged to them uppity-ass Dupree women, including Jubilee.

The night she returned, dragging ass and shuffling feet after having a black baby, was a night their side of the tracks wouldn't soon forget. They speculated for years about where Ruby's color had come from since she looked in no way similar to her mother and Emma.

"What about Evangeline?" some would wonder. "Maybe Ruby's color came from her."

Most would nod, satisfied that they'd figured out the conundrum, until an elder on another porch, hearing the lukewarm gossip, would throw gas on the fire with a casual reminder.

"You gotta remember, Evangeline weren't Emma's real mama. She raised her, but she didn't birth her."

The admission would make most wonder because there weren't but a handful left living who could remember the one who had actually given birth to Emma, and they had been children then. They didn't speak of such things. The pain they'd endured and the pain they'd witnessed was tucked away tight in the vaults of their minds. They didn't visit those memories to make sure they were there. They held no value. Only a reminder of what was. Of what had been. Which is what most people did with their pasts, their history. Dimmed the details so dull that even when they added a little color to an old story they were hardly believed. The ones who remembered those details, even if only on semi-lucid days on their deathbeds, could only shake their heads and mutter to themselves about that damn Jubilee carrying on the way that she was.

They didn't expect Jubi to slip back into her old ways so easily. But she did when Gladys arrived. How could she not? Gladys's skin never changed. She remained the color of tinted clabber. Only her thick hair with the rough roots could give her away. Nothing a hat couldn't fix.

In matching hats, favoring dresses and little lace gloves, fashionable replicas Jubi made from fabric Ruby fetched from Danube General, grandmother and granddaughter made their first venture together across the tracks. Jubi took Gladys because she was young. Just barely walking. She had not been seen on this side of town. She was not known the way Jubi once was.

With their hats angled to hide their faces, eyes lowered demurelike, and chins pointed toward the ground, Jubi and Gladys walked through the front door of the store hand in hand. Gladys's long, sandy hair had been curled with rags and pulled together into two bunches of ringlets flowing down her back. Jubi's was twisted, wound around itself, and held with a pin at the nape of her neck. She made sure none of their coloredness could give them away. Neither hair nor knuckles. Jubi put on her old drag and forced Gladys into it too, praying, as she stood in line, that it would finally fit.

There weren't too many people in the store. Just enough that Jubi had to wait in line behind a woman she wasn't sure she recognized, with a baby boy about the same age as Gladys. The two little ones entertained themselves with games of peekaboo and keep-away from the comfortable distance of the grown-ups' legs, exploring the newness of their environs as toddlers are wont to do. The cans stacked neatly on the shelves begged to be pulled, tugged, thrown, and jostled in a game only babies could play. So much so that Gladys's hat came off and Jubi had to bend low to the ground and quickly replace it lest the top of the girl's head be exposed, with its unruly roots that didn't gather as good as the curly ends.

"I'm so sorry, they're just making a mess, aren't they?" said the woman in front of Jubi.

"They sure are," Jubi answered, sharpening her shape to hide her face.

"But you can't blame the babies, can you?"

"You sure can't," she said. "Come on up here with me."

Jubi scooped Gladys from the ground and held her against her left hip, further hiding her features with the little girl's body. The line moved. Jubi was next. She listened in as the woman behind the merchant counter exclaimed a greeting to the woman and little boy standing in front of her.

"What are y'all doing here! I thought you were heading back to Birmingham to be with your sister?"

"Mama, Delilah can wait. We wanted to surprise you before we left," the woman in front of Jubi said. "Had to let Carl Darren see his grandma before we got out of here."

"Karen, I told you about that word. I am nobody's grandma. I can be a nana, though."

"Oh, Mama, you are what you are, no matter what name you give yourself. Grandma Adilene or Nana Adilene, it's all the same."

"Not to me," Adilene said.

"Where's Uncle Logan?" Karen asked. "Doesn't he usually help you in the store? I don't see him."

"He's around here somewhere."

Gladys squirmed in Jubi's arms, working to wrestle herself away so she could go back to playing on the ground with Carl Darren, who had found his own fun in kicking the counter. Jubi held her tighter. Shifted the girl even more in front of her after realizing she was in line behind her niece, waiting to be rung up by her sister-in-law. Hidden beneath her hat, she tried not to let her sharp intake of breath blow her cover. Even if Adilene didn't recognize her, Logan would know his wife. His lying, deceitful, colored wife.

"You don't belong here, and you know it," Logan whispered in Jubi's ear.

She hadn't seen him come from around the back of the store,

where the colored customers waited. Hadn't expected that he'd clocked her before she'd had a chance to realize he was there.

He said, "Do us all a favor and leave. Take that little one with you 'fore you make any more trouble for yourself."

Jubi opened her mouth to speak, but Logan held up his hand. He stepped in front of her and blocked her from moving any farther forward in line. With Adilene, Karen, and Carl Darren hidden from view, Jubi finally slid Gladys to the side of her body to meet his gaze. In it she saw nothing of the Logan she remembered. The one who'd brought her flowers and opened his arms, his life, to her. The green-eyed, mischievous charmer who had bumped into her and assumed she too was like him. That man was long gone. In his stead was a grim, stone-faced man whose rage seethed pink beneath his skin. The man who'd cussed her out of his house when she was torn from tip to tail and dripping blood and water with each unassisted drag step she took toward home.

"Logan, move out the way so I can help the next customer," Adilene yelled from behind the counter.

Logan glared at Jubi. Heightening her voice, she said, "Silly me, I left my change purse at home," and retreated from the store.

Like the summer she first became acquainted with Logan and didn't want him to find out where she was really from, Jubi marched for half an hour with Gladys in her arms, all on the wrong side of the tracks, to minimize her own embarrassment. She ignored the burning sensation of tired muscles seizing up from the weight of a fifteen-month-old continuously against them. But no matter how long she delayed her return home, the whispers and murmurs were already waiting.

In her effort to slip into Danube General Store unnoticed by the other white customers, Jubi had forgotten to attend her attention toward the colored customers who'd crossed the tracks with her on their own errands. The ones who knew she'd left the porch after all these years. The ones who, when they finally saw Gladys, remarked with smirking mirth about how much she favored Jubilee. They knew it was the two of them marching in Jubi's own madness toward the front door. In line at the back, they snickered amongst themselves about how the new baby had brought her back to the scene of her old shenanigans. *What stories did she tell herself to give her so much gumption?*

It was these out loud wonderings that Logan listened to as he helped the negro customers while his sister helped the whites. When he realized who was in the store and then saw her for himself helping the little girl, he refused to let history repeat itself. He would not stand for being made the fool twice. No matter how many hats she wore, gloves she covered herself with, and ways she hid her muddy accent, Logan would forever know Jubi Etienne neé Jubilee Dupree. The woman he'd held, the woman he'd loved, the woman whose body he'd clutched close to his own. That woman who'd left his home smelling of lavender. A scent that surrounded him in springtime when it bloomed wild and fresh and drove him mad with memory.

It was her deceit that had broken him. Her lie that had killed her and the baby they'd made together. The Black girl and her white-presenting mother had been banished across the tracks until she thought she could pass again with a grandbaby who'd grabbed another color. Logan wouldn't stand for it, and neither would the neighbors who were watching and waiting when Jubi and Gladys finally returned.

By then, Ruby and Sampson had already heard. He was busy building their house to get out from under the Dupree women when he was first told of the whereabouts of his daughter, a message he passed to Ruby, who passed it to Emma. The three were outside waiting when Jubi walked up with Gladys. They were her buffer from the wild words and mocking *mmph*s that were ready to fly had the main employers for this side of the tracks not stood as her protection from scorn.

Jubi kept her eyes on them as she moved. Arms tired, lace gloves ripped across the knuckles from weight strain, and Gladys sleeping on her shoulder, their hats askew. Jubi walked with what little pride she had left, chin high and nose toward heaven. She would not be pitied for wanting more. Desiring better. Even if that meant she was the talk of the tracks from those who could never pass. For she had tried, and for a time she had succeeded. For a time she had been one of them. Had tried them on despite the ill fit and partied and danced and laughed and had family. Community. Shorn hers for theirs and was loved. Accepted.

For a time.

Facing Ruby as she made her way to the porch, Jubi couldn't hide her contempt. She handed off the baby that should've been hers to the black girl who'd ruined her and the baby's brown-skinned father, who shouldn't have made any offspring that close to white. But they had. And so she had tried again. Refusing to face her own mother, Emma, who never maximized her color for conceit, Jubi walked past them all into the house, stirring the water, mussing the salt, and leaving a cloud of goofer dust in her wake.

Emma said behind her, "You should've known it weren't gon' last."

Part 3

Aftermath

15.

What doesn't last is lies.

It had been four years since Tati had learned her daddy's name, and she was no closer to knowing anything more about Roman Brown than she'd been that Sunday in the salon. The only thing that had changed between her, Nadia, and Mimi was the date. Home from her freshman year of college on Thanksgiving break, Tati was lounging on the futon in the salon reading a copy of *Vibe* when Nadia gave her a direction that would finally yield some answers.

"Tati, go upstairs in my room, and in my closet on the side by my shoeboxes get that new pack of plastic rollers so I can set Mrs. Loretha's hair."

"What color?" Tati asked.

"The aqua ones."

Tati left the basement and bounded up the stairs to her mother's bedroom closet. It had an earthy smell from the new products she'd ordered from some woman in Brooklyn who was making hair cream in her kitchen. Between the products and the new computer Nadia had bought to keep better track of her books, it was almost like going to a real salon. Tati found the rollers easily enough. She snatched them from a plastic bag on the floor between the chest of drawers and shoeboxes, but when she turned to leave she kicked one of the boxes open. Instead of shoes tumbling out, there was nothing but junk. Sewing needles and thread even though Nadia couldn't do more than patch a hole and maybe hem a pant leg.

Tati put the box back together and stacked it on top of another shoebox when she noticed a piece of paper sticking out of the side. She grabbed it to throw it away, but the paper was wider than she expected. A folded piece of notebook paper that had yellowed around the edges. The blue lines were faded like the paper had been dropped in a puddle. Tati opened the letter and the first lines, written in Nadia's own hand, jumped at her.

> *How do you carry a child in fear?*
> *Step 1. It starts with him not being here*

"TATI, HURRY UP!" NADIA YELLED THROUGH THE HEATING VENT IN the basement. "It don't take that long to find them damn rollers. They right there."

Tati folded the paper, shoved it in her pocket, and ran back to the basement.

"It's about time," Nadia said as Tati handed over the rollers.

She didn't respond. On the futon, across from Nadia and Mrs. Loretha, Tati placed the note inside her magazine and read to the end.

> *How do you carry a child in fear?*
> *Step 1. It starts with him not being here*
> *Step 2. Forget the fairy tales*
> *Step 3. Remember the lies*
> *I'm going to leave my wife.*
> *I don't want to live my life without you.*
> *Step 4. Replay the reaction when you told him the news*
>   *What the hell you want me to do?*

You know, I already got a ball and three chains!

Step 5. Sing to yourself, "Is my living in vain?"

Step 6. Pray

Step 7. Break the news to mama

Step 8. Go to church with her

Step 9. Be mortified by her testimony filled with your shame

Step 10. Explore ALL options

> *Keep it?*
>
> *Adoption?*
>
> *Abortion?*

Step 11. Make a decision

Step 12. Doubt decision

Step 13. Repeat steps 10, 11 & 12 until you're three months
out from your due date

Step 14. Realize it's too late

Step 15. Try to tell him again

Step 16. Find out he's moved

Step 17. Make a plan

Step 18. Doubt the plan

Step 19. Cry uncontrollably, inconsolably until you're out of
tears

Step 20. Remember Step 1, He's not here

TATI KNEW THE NOTE WAS ABOUT ROMAN. LOOKING OVER THE TOP
of the magazine, Tati stared at Nadia as she clipped Mrs. Loretha's
ends. They talked about movies. What was better between *The Wood*
and *The Best Man*. Nadia wasn't particular about either, only that she
couldn't stand Morris Chestnut's hypocritical character Lance.

"That's men." Mrs. Loretha chuckled. Her butter-rich voice was
full with an inside joke that was as good to her as scratch-made

pound cake. "You can't understand their madness. You just gotta love 'em through it."

"Guess that's why I ain't never been in love."

Tati raised the magazine as the women went through plot points of both films, loud-talking over the new Mary CD. She read the note again. The handwriting was rushed, in splotchy blue ink, as if the pen had burst from writing too hard, too fast. The words *wife*, *abortion*, and *adoption* levitated from the page. Tati read it again, each step a new revelation.

Step 16. Find out he's moved.

Tati read the line over and over. Anger rose with each word. *She's known where he is this whole time*, she thought to herself. Tati closed the letter in the magazine. For most of her life she'd wondered about Roman. His whereabouts. A question to which Nadia would only answer, "Not here." When Tati asked, "Do you know where he is?" Nadia said, "No." Tati had always thought it was a lie, but to confirm it hurt worse. The difference between knowing the truth and assuming the truth was slight but mattered. With an assumption there was chance for error. The possibility of being wrong. Tati had always wanted to be wrong.

She looked at Nadia, who wore her smock over black leggings, and a Whitney Houston in *The Bodyguard* T-shirt. Her hair was dyed so jet black it shined blue. She had it secured in a low ponytail, having finally let her French roll go only a year before. Tati searched Nadia's face for answers as she put end papers and rollers to graying hair. Her blank gaze was gone. Her eyes were engaged, intense, in the conversation with Mrs. Loretha.

What happened? Where is Roman?

Tati wanted to know the real story and not the twenty-step guide

Nadia had written to help her cope. She rolled up the magazine and stood from the futon.

"I'll be back," Tati said.

"Where you going?" Nadia asked. "To see that boy?"

"Xay and I broke up before we even left for school."

"I bet you still wanna see him, though. Y'all was together all four years of high school."

Tati huffed. "I'm going to see Desi."

"You know they moved."

"I know."

Tati rolled her eyes and shook her head as she grabbed her coat, scarf, and purse and headed for the bus stop.

THE SMELL OF FOOD HIT TATI AS SOON AS SHE STEPPED OUT OF THE eighth-floor elevator. Cinnamon and nutmeg were in the air for either candied yams, sweet potato pie, or both. Tati knocked against the Christmas music playing loudly from the other side of the door. The full falsetto from the Temptations' "Silent Night" blared out once it swung open wide. Desirée's father opened the door holding a drink in one hand and the knob with the other. He was light-skinned and curly-haired like the timeless R&B icons of the '80s, his thin, rimless glasses sitting square on his face the only tell of his older age.

"Hey, Mr. Cortez. I'm Tatiana, Desirée's friend."

"I know who you are," he said forcefully. "C'mon in." He closed the door and yelled for Desirée.

She and Toya burst into the combination living and dining room and smothered her in hugs. "Tati, whatchu doin' here today?" Toya asked.

"Yeah, girl, I thought you were coming tomorrow?" Desirée added.

"I thought I'd surprise y'all today. I hope you don't mind."

"Not at all, Tati," Toya said. "You're family."

"Thanks," Tati said hesitantly.

"We're prepping in the kitchen for tomorrow, I'll leave you and Desi to it."

"Mama, you mean *you're* prepping," Desirée jabbed. "Daddy, you know you can't cook."

Tati smiled at the singsong voice Desirée used to taunt her father. She'd only ever heard her cousin Alexis use the tone with her uncle Terry. She thought it must've been something particular daughters did with fathers. Though Tati didn't know much about Mr. Cortez. She hadn't met him until she and Desirée graduated high school, but he teased her like he'd been in her life all along and not just during spring and summer break.

"Girl, I've been cooking longer than you've been on this earth." He grinned.

"Ordering takeout," Toya said.

Desirée rolled her eyes, grabbed Tati by the hand, and pulled her into her bedroom. Its stark white walls were plastered with photographs. Four-by-six-inch photos, in cheap five-by-seven-inch black frames with white paper matting. Desirée's walls were a shrine to her young life. There were pictures in the park, at school, in the hall, in class, and some Tati didn't recognize. They were recent, many snapped downtown, where Desirée attended the Art Institute. A last-minute decision she'd made after her parents reconnected and started dating again, even though she'd gotten into Savannah College of Art and Design.

"What I'm leavin' home for?" Desirée had asked seriously when she looked over all her acceptances.

It was a question Tati couldn't answer. Desirée had good memories and more to make. She was living her dream, photographing city life and trying to intern at *Ebony*, *Jet*, or one of the papers.

"Where's your brother?" Tati asked, looking at the photos.

"With his dad."

"So, your mom and dad are really back together, huh?"

"Yeah. It's been nice. And we finally moved out of Englewood, so that's definitely a plus." Desirée gestured around her bedroom, which was twice the size of the one she'd had when she and Toya lived on the second floor of a two-flat on Sixty-Fifth and Green.

"I wish I could say the same," Tati muttered.

"Whatchu mean?" Desirée asked.

"I'll show you."

Tati fished Nadia's note out of her bag and handed it to Desirée to read while Tati unraveled from her winter wear.

"Damn!" Desirée yelped from the first line. She pulled the paper back and looked at Tati before she continued reading, her excited utterances peppered throughout.

"Oh, shit."

"Well, damn."

"Oh, shit!"

"Gaaaaaahtttttttdamn!" she said in final exclamation, dragging out the syllables. She folded the paper and handed it back to Tati. "I guess that's where you got the writing from."

"Doubt it." Tati lay back on Desirée's bed. "I ain't never found nothing else she wrote."

"Seeing as how that's the first thing you found, you don't know what else your mama got. When'd you find it, anyway?"

"A couple hours ago."

"Oh."

Side by side, Desirée and Tati stared at the popcorn ceiling and fan. Tati couldn't help but wonder even more about Roman. Roman and Nadia together. What they were. When they weren't. Who'd been the first to realize they couldn't.

"You think they know?" Tati asked, sitting up on the bed.

"They who?"

"Your parents?"

"Know about what?"

"About my mama and Roman?"

Desirée sat up on the bed. The weight of what Tati asked was wedged between them. They'd grown up as close as sisters, though their mothers were barely friends. They only really spoke when it was about their girls. Sure, they'd make plans to get together, but they were never kept. And Tati and Desi both had been witnesses to the half smiles and rolled eyes Nadia and Toya traded.

"It can't hurt to ask," Desirée suggested.

Tati waited until Desirée stood first. She knew Nadia's note was fire and what she wanted to ask was liable to burn everyone connected to it. When Desirée opened the door and headed to find her parents, Tati followed behind her, resolved to get the answers she'd always wanted.

In the kitchen, Desirée's parents waltzed around each other like two partners anticipating each other's moves. They passed pots and pans, and placed platters of prepped food in the refrigerator nearly wordlessly. Both in sweatpants, they looked like a young couple, so in love they'd begun to dress alike.

"Y'all are just in time to do these dishes," Toya said when she noticed Tati and Desirée.

"Ugh, of course we are," Desirée said.

She moved to the sink on the far wall of the kitchen and began running water. Tati stood beside her. She said, "Why don't I wash and you dry, since I don't know where anything goes in here."

"Fine with me," Desirée said, switching places.

With her back to everyone and her hands plunged into hot water Tati washed the few forks and cups in the sink before moving on to the dirty pots. Desirée bumped her elbow and shot her side glances, but it did nothing to encourage Tati to ask the question she'd long wanted the answer to. How could she even bring herself to form the words? It wasn't anyone's responsibility but Nadia's, and Nadia had made it clear she didn't want Tati to know. And what if Desirée's parents did know? What if they told her what they knew? What would she do then? Knowing instead of just assuming like she'd done all these years, these last few hours.

"Tati has something she wants to ask you," Desirée blurted.

"Really, Desi!" Tati shrieked.

"Yes, really, because I wanna know too."

"Know what?" Toya asked.

Tati turned around and dried her hands against her jeans. She looked from Toya to Mr. Cortez. He leaned forward against the granite counter. She leaned back against the refrigerator. They were comfortable in either their oblivion or their lie. *Too comfortable*, Tati thought. She exhaled. "Do you know where Roman is?"

"Roman!" Toya exclaimed.

"Yeah. My father."

"Tati, I . . ." Toya started and stopped herself three more times before she gave up trying to form words and hung her head.

"He's in Indianapolis."

"Lou!" Toya exclaimed again.

"It's time she knows. I mean, for God's sake, she looks just like him."

"Now you wanna say something," Toya accused. "She needs to talk to Nadia."

"For what?" Tati asked. "It ain't like she gon' tell me anything. I might as well find out about Roman from y'all."

"Roman and I go way back." Lou turned and began making himself a drink from the egg nog in the refrigerator. "Me and Toya and your mom and dad used to kick it real heavy back in the day."

"Really?!" Desirée and Tati exclaimed.

"Really," Lou answered as he poured.

"Then what happened that y'all can't stand each other now?" Tati asked.

"We don't see eye to eye on some things," Toya answered.

"Those things have to do with me and Roman."

"You need to talk to Nadia, Tati. We don't agree. And we're not as close as we used to be, but—"

"But you're still keeping her secrets for her," Tati finished.

"The same way you would for Desi even if y'all fell out," Toya said.

"You know I've been lookin' for him all this time and you've never said a thing."

"Wasn't for me to tell."

"Desi, did you know too?"

"No! I'm just finding this shit out right here with you."

"Watch your mouth in my house!"

"What happened?" Tati asked. "Between my mom and Roman?"

"He was—"

Toya held her arm in front of Lou. "Talk. To. Nadia."

"I already know he was married," Tati said.

"Then you know why he's not around."

Tati's eyes widened at Toya's response. It sounded so much like Nadia. Too much for her to accept. She screamed, "I don't know shit but the lies y'all tell me. Y'all may not be friends no more but y'all just alike. Always 'Do what I say, not what I do.' Fuck y'all. You and my mama."

"Tati," Desirée pleaded as she stormed out of the kitchen and back to the bedroom. Tati shoved herself into her coat and scarf and snatched up her purse as tears fell from her eyes. She couldn't help it. She'd been holding back the stings for years. She'd been holding out hope for the truth for just as long, and yet every adult in her life was lying dead to her face. Toya. Nadia. Mimi.

"Tati, what are you doing?" Desirée asked, coming into the bedroom.

"I'm going home. This is some bullshit. You know they lying."

"I know, but what can you do about it?"

"Fuck them," Tati raged. "I'll find him my damn self."

"How?" Desirée yelled as Tati burst through the door.

"I don't know, but it's time to shake shit up."

"Okay, Tati, but there's a difference between shaking shit up and burning shit down," Toya said, meeting Tati and Desirée at the condo door.

"The fuck you know?" Tati yelled, incredulous. "You don't want to tell me anything, but you don't want me to find out on my own. You keep telling me to ask my mom, and you know she ain't gon' say shit. So tell me, Miss Grant, what do you want me to do?"

"Tati, stop cursing."

"Get the fuck outta here."

"I know you're mad, but cussing everybody out ain't gon' make you feel no better."

"And you think lying to me does?"

Toya didn't have an answer. The answers she did have, she couldn't give. She'd lied to Tati for Nadia, just like she and Lou had lied to Nadia for Roman. She'd lied for so long she didn't know what to do with the truth.

"That's what I thought," Tati said as she swung the door open.

It closed heavy behind her just as Desirée managed to eke out, "Happy Thanksgiving." It wouldn't be a happy one if Tati had anything to do with it. She stomped back to the bus stop, ignoring the grown men who looked her way every time she passed. They had been giving her looks and licking their lips and tongues at her since she was twelve and ran laps around Jesse Owens Park to improve her track times. They were always there. A part of every neighborhood. The *damn, girl, you fine* men. The *can I run witchu?* men. And eventually, the *fuck you, then, bitch* men when she didn't respond to their advances. She didn't care if they cursed her today as she tried to understand Lou's willingness against Toya's refusal to answer her questions. She couldn't be sure—all she had were more half-formed assumptions—but Tati believed whatever it was had fucked them all up. Her and Desirée. Toya and Lou. Nadia and Roman.

By the time Tati returned home, her tears had dried. She went down to the basement, ready to listen if Nadia was ready to talk. On the futon she watched Nadia sweep and sing "Your Child" along with Mary. She bobbed her head, rolled her neck, stamped her feet, and added her own emphasis to parts where Mary had none. Nadia even jabbed the air with two fingers like she was muffing a man in the middle of his forehead. Roman, Tati suspected. She wondered what he looked like through her mother's eyes. Which moments in their relationship did she revisit over and over? The beginning, the end, or somewhere in the middle? As Tati watched Nadia, her face smooth, clear, and contorted in pain, she realized the nearly two-decade-old affair was as raw as it was when she wrote the letter. That her mood, calm yet angry, was always simmering just beneath the surface. A tectonic plate on an active fault line, ready to rub Earth the wrong way.

"Jesus, Tati!" Nadia yelped as she brushed up against her feet. "How long you been sittin' there?"

"Since the song came on."

Nadia crossed over to the stereo and turned the volume down. "You must think I'm crazy," she mumbled.

"No, I don't think you're crazy," Tati said softly. "Just makes me wonder—"

"Wonder what?" Nadia's defenses emerged like lawn sprinklers out of the ground with just the inflection of her voice. A warning to tread light. Tati flanked her suspicion. Asked instead whether Nadia had ever been in love before. The question gave her pause.

"I heard you and Mrs. Loretha talking earlier," Tati explained.

Nadia nodded. She understood the curiosity. It was in the basement, when her music was on, and her hands were in a client's head as they talked about life, experiences, movies, music, celebrities, and whatever may have been on TV, that she spoke freely. Unguarded and unfiltered, her conversations with customers were propulsive. Fed by honesty, no matter if it was joyful or bitter, sweet or sour. The salon was sanctuary and safe space for wearied women who would always look their best, no matter if they were at their worst.

"Can't say that I have," Nadia said.

"Not even with my—"

The cold look that crossed Nadia's face silenced Tati. Her eyes sliced the boldness right out of her body. Nadia exhaled through her nose but didn't speak. Instead, she bit the inside of her cheek until she tasted blood. They were in new terrain. Nadia exhaled again and released her cheek from between her teeth.

"Like I said," she began again, "can't say that I have."

Tati nodded her acceptance and lounged back on the futon.

"How was everything by Desi and Toya?" Nadia asked.

"Fine," Tati answered curtly. "They were just getting ready for tomorrow."

"You going back over there?"

"Nah. I think I'll spend the day with family."

She grabbed her purse, pulled out her magazine, and opened to the page with the note. Tati read the words as she simmered in the truth Nadia wouldn't give her. She didn't know whether to marvel at her mother's self-control or pity the tight grip that let nothing she didn't want out escape. Nadia was gas in a jar, unstable, potent, and invisible. Tati the match.

Time to shake shit up, Tati thought, not knowing that cornering Nadia into answering her questions was to make her relive what she never wanted to remember.

16.

The sound of the dial tone hollowed Nadia in half. There were no more numbers to dial. No one else left to tell except the family she'd been avoiding. She couldn't tiptoe around Gladys any longer. She placed Toya's phone back in the cradle, walked into the living room, and packed a bag.

"Where are you going?" Toya asked.

"Home," Nadia answered.

"You know you can stay here as long as you like."

Nadia lifted her head. She choked back tears. Her face a dissertation of bad decisions, she patted the stings at the corner of her eyes, shook her head no.

"I can't," she said.

"Why not?"

Nadia held her bag so tight her knuckles turned colors. Eyes hardened and glazed over like acrylic on nails, she said, "Honestly, staying here with you . . . It'll just remind me of how I got myself into this situation in the first place."

"What?" Toya asked, her voice tinged with hurt.

"I met Roman because of you and Lou."

"Wait," Toya said, cocking one hand on her hip. "You blame *us* . . . for what happened between you and Roman?"

"Who else is there to blame?"

"You can't be serious," she said. "When we introduced you to

Roman, all we said was talk to him. Ain't nobody said fuck him. You did that dumb shit all on your own, knowing he was married, so try again, sis."

"Like I said, I'm going home."

Toya nodded. "Maybe you should."

Nadia slung her bag across her shoulder and headed for the door. Toya cleared her throat. "My key."

Nadia fished it out of her pocket and tossed it across the room.

Home was not a trip she wanted to make, but she couldn't think of anywhere else to go. Though she'd saved enough for her own place, she hadn't decided what to do yet. She wasn't ready to pay a security deposit and first and last month's rent, when she might need the money for something, or someone, else.

NADIA SIGHED AS SHE TURNED HER KEY INTO HER PARENTS' LOCK. While she knew Bryan and Terry were at school, she wasn't ready to face Gladys. She walked through the dining room and into the kitchen. The house was criminal quiet, but Gladys was right there waiting for her as if she knew who to expect. Sitting in her corner chair at the table, another Jackie Collins novel open in front of her, she looked up at first with a surprised smile until she seemed to remember the last time they'd seen or spoken to one another.

"Well, the prodigal daughter has returned," she said, looking down at her book.

"Hey, Mama." Nadia kept walking toward the basement steps.

"What brings you around these parts in the middle of the week and"—she looked out the window beside her—"damn near the middle of the day?"

"I can't come home?"

"Nobody said that." Gladys turned a page. "Just surprised to see you."

Her nonchalance threatened to topple Nadia down the basement steps. Words all canines and incisors, she asked, "What are *you* doing here?"

"Since you not here and your brothers are older, I went back to working nights so I can spend my days with your father."

"Where is he?"

"Upstairs taking a nap."

"Must be nice."

It wasn't lost on Nadia that Gladys's ever-changing schedule was only to her benefit and no one else's. She hurried down the stairs, irritation mixing with confusion, and unpacked. She put away clothes that had been shoved in her bag with haste and cleaned up the dusty space that was exactly as she left it. Clothes strewn all over the unmade bed, wardrobe doors open, hangers on the ground, shoes picked over for the practical. That it was left untouched said something. About who—Gladys or herself—she wasn't sure.

Nadia showered when she finished cleaning. Beneath the hot water, she fingered the flat terrain around her navel and imagined it distended, the linea nigra copper against her caramel skin. Her mind filled with questions she couldn't answer. *Do I want this? It? You?* She pushed them away and thought of everything else. The best techniques for hair coloring. How to handle a client who wanted color and a relaxer. The best ways to cleanse a scalp without scratching it raw, no matter how good it felt. She focused on the technical, the chemical, ionic bonds and what breaks them. Anything but what was bonded inside her.

Fuck.

She had nowhere left to run.

Bathed and dressed, she went back upstairs and found Eugene had joined Gladys at the table. In his white T-shirt, pea-green slacks, suspenders, and slippers, he poured himself the last of the morning's coffee. Nadia put one hand over her stomach and the other over her mouth as she tried not to retch right in front of them.

"What's wrong with you?" Gladys asked.

"I'm fine," Nadia mumbled. "Hey, Daddy."

"What happened that you walked home and ain't get a ride with your friend in the car?" Eugene asked, running his hand over his silver-gray hair.

Nadia gritted her teeth. "He hasn't given me a ride in a long time."

"Oh, y'all ain't friends no more?" Gladys asked, looking up from her book. "That's why you come home?"

"No!"

"You sho'?"

Gladys studied Nadia for a sign. Eugene stifled a yawn and sipped his coffee.

"You can come in the kitchen," Gladys said. "We don't bite. You hungry?"

"Nah, I'm all right," Nadia lied. She surveyed the table. With Gladys in the corner by the window, and Eugene opposite her by the stove, there was only one seat left for her to take. The head of the table. It was as if they had choreographed the conversation they would have upon her return. A verbal dance they'd practiced many a time without her, so second nature that all they were doing now was running the routine.

Nadia went to the refrigerator and pulled out a bag of green seedless grapes. She set them on the table in front of the seat reserved for her and worked her way through the fruited vines. She tried to remember the last time she ate and couldn't. The amount of time between meals seemed infinite. Focused on the sticky, sweet fruit she tried to get full.

"How's school going?" Eugene asked.

"Good." She swallowed. "I have about six more months before I get my license. I have a lab today."

"That's what you call practicing doing hair?" Gladys asked, incredulous. "A lab."

Nadia nodded her answer as she shoved more grapes in her mouth. Gladys grunted.

"You stayin' long?" Eugene asked.

"I have class in a little bit, and then I'll be back."

"That's not what he meant!"

"Gladys," Eugene admonished.

"It's all right, Daddy." Nadia swallowed. "I'm back, but just 'til I get my license."

"Mm-hmm," Gladys humphed. "You couldn't find your way in the world as good as you thought you could. Ain't no more man, so you gotta come home."

"Roman and I broke up the day I left," Nadia said icily.

"So where you been?"

"Stayin' with Toya."

"Well, I coulda told you that was a bad idea. You gotta stay close to your own kind."

"Gladys, let the girl be." Eugene treaded the churning waters between them. He said, "You wanted her home. Be glad she here."

"But it's a reason why she home, and I bet you any money I got that it's got somethin' to do with that man. Don't it?"

Nadia rolled her eyes and grabbed a bunch of grapes. *Isn't this what I came back for?* she asked herself. After all, she had come home for a reason. Packed her things and picked a fight because she needed what? Wisdom? A mother's touch? Understanding? All of the attributes Gladys didn't possess. Characteristics she hadn't had since before Nadia's own birth. Gladys went on, nagging to know what happened. Certain that something had in fact transpired. Something big. Why else would Nadia go from sneaking in and out on the weekends to coming through the front door in the middle of the day contrite for nothing?

Nadia sighed. Chewed. Began slowly, "I just nee . . . wanted to come home."

"*Wanted* to come home or *needed* to come home?" Gladys demanded, noticing Nadia's slip.

"Gladys, it don't matter," Eugene said. "I'm going upstairs. You didn't need to wake me up for this."

"Uh-uh, Eugene. We gettin' to the bottom of this right now. Somethin's going on, and I ain't lettin' your daughter play nann one of us for a fool we ain't."

"Gladys!"

"It's all right, Daddy. I knew she was gon' be like this."

"Oh, well, now you got me believin' ya mama might be onto somethin', 'cause you ain't never excused her mouth before. Not even when you was a little girl and had to take it."

"I told you," Gladys said, pushing up from her seat. She crossed her arms over her housecoat with a self-satisfied smile. She asked, "Was it Roman? Or Toya?"

Nadia shoved more grapes in her mouth. She chomped through the skin and pulp until the corners of her mouth bubbled with juice.

"Both, huh?" Gladys deduced.

"Let her alone, Gladys," Eugene said. "If she don't wanna talk about it, she ain't got to."

"Even when she don't wanna talk about what's going on, she ain't never been mute like she is now. Only reason she got to be this quiet is if somebody is pregnant."

Nadia felt her throat constrict. She coughed.

Gladys continued, "You caught your so-called friend sleeping with your so-called boyfriend and she popped up pregnant?"

"No."

"So what is it? Who is it? Is it you?"

"Yes," Nadia mumbled.

"Nadia! Nadia."

Eugene stopped himself from saying anything else. The anger he may have had with Gladys for whipping up the hurricane of chaos gave way to disappointment. The sentimental kind, full with pity more than anything else. He sat beside Nadia at the table, his arms an isosceles triangle covering his face, while Gladys paced, demanded to know everything. Nadia had no choice but to start from the beginning. How they'd met, his marriage, his separation, his pending divorce, and the day it all changed, when Deborah had news of her own.

"What you say?" Gladys's question was rhetorical. High in inflection and intonation, she paced some more. "So it's two of y'all pregnant for the same triflin'-ass man."

"Seems that way," Nadia answered.

"What're you gon' do?" Eugene asked softly.

"I don't know." Nadia shrugged. "Keep it, get rid of it, whatever I do is my choice."

Gladys grabbed the back of a chair and shook her head. Muttered to herself, "All my running from them people and their ways and you want to do this to yourself."

"It's not the same, cher," Eugene said to Gladys.

"What's not the same?" Nadia asked.

"It don't matter," Gladys yelled. "Cain't nobody help you but Jesus."

"And what *he* gon' do?" Nadia demanded. She stood from the table and headed toward the door.

Eugene called behind her, "What about the baby?"

"What about it?" she yelled back.

The door slammed as Gladys cried out in prayer. Prayers she would say for months before Nadia gave in and agreed to attend church with her.

December 1980

Pastor T. G. Longfellow's voice boomed from the pulpit despite his small five-foot-five stature. For two and a half hours, Nadia had sat through singing, announcements, more singing, visitor welcome, and the sermon, before they reached the benediction. In a suit and tie, Pastor Longfellow mopped his brow with the handkerchief from his breast pocket as he ran through the last announcements regarding the church's upcoming fashion show fundraiser, an awards luncheon for members of distinction, and the members of the congregation who were on the sick-and-shut-in list and in need of visitation.

"Someone to sit with 'em for a while," he said, pausing a moment for his volunteer request to sink in.

"Well, now, church," he resumed. "We've come to the end of our time together today. But before we go, we need to close out in a final prayer."

"Pastor, if I may." Gladys stood with one finger in the air.

"Sister Washington, go right ahead."

"Church, I don't mean to hold you . . ." she began, "but I just want to ask for your prayers for my daughter."

Nadia looked up to see Gladys's face pointed heavenward in supplication. Her hands were raised, palms to the sky as if she expected the windows of heaven to open and pour out a bounty of blessing. The surrendered serenity ignited anxiety in Nadia's belly. She tugged her arm, but Gladys only shook her away.

"You see, my daughter, Nadia, is here with me today, and she's in a bit of trouble."

"Mama," Nadia said through clenched teeth.

"Trouble not unlike that of David and Bathsheba. Only the man in her story is no king. Certainly not a man after God's own heart."

"Mama, what are you doing?"

"You see, Nadia is with child."

An audible gasp flew through the church.

"Out of wedlock. And the man involved, well . . . let's just say he's in wedlock with someone else. A wife also with child."

"Mama!" Nadia yelped, shrinking low in her seat.

"So I would just like your prayers for Nadia. For her to have wisdom and discernment about the future of the child she's carrying. She's indicated that she may not want to keep the child. And I'd just like y'all to pray for her that she finds it in her own heart to consider other alternatives. Can you do that for me, church?"

Gladys lowered her head from its tilt toward the sky and opened her eyes to survey the room. The congregation, a harem of women, nodded their heads in agreement, *amen*ed and *mm-hmm*ed to the prayer request for the sinful daughter defiled by a married man.

"Church, let us stand to our feet and oblige Sister Washington's request."

Everyone in the congregation stood except Nadia. She ducked down in the pew as if she were hiding from masked men come to rob the church of its tithes. Pastor Longfellow cleared his throat. Gladys reached for Nadia, she tugged what loose hair she could grasp to get her to stand up and not embarrass her before the Lord, but she didn't budge.

"Sister Nadia, would you please stand so that we may pray for you," Pastor Longfellow commanded from the altar.

Nadia slowly rose to her feet, though she never raised her head. Never looked to the pastor for prayers or penance.

"Thank you so much, Sister Nadia," Pastor Longfellow said. "Church, would you stretch your hands toward this troubled soul."

He prayed, "Dear heavenly father. Be with your daughter in her time of need. Show her that despite her condition this moment doesn't have to define her. Like it didn't define David. Like it didn't define Bathsheba. Nadia too can overcome. Oh my my my . . ."

*Amen*s and *mm-hmm*s burst from the mouths of the congregation like fireworks on the Fourth of July. Their chorus added to the litany of voices playing in her head.

Keep it. Get rid of it. Whatever you do, that's on you.
All we said was talk to him. Ain't nobody said fuck him.

She heard everyone's condemnation as her tears fell fat and juicy. They pooled in the grooves between her fingers. With heavy shoulders, Nadia's body heaved under the weight of the invisible pressure pouring from the hands of the parishioners, who thought their outstretched arms equated the reach of God. Despite the fervor led by Pastor Longfellow, who prayed in a language all his own, their earnest words fell on deaf ears. The cacophony of voices inside her own head was as suffocating as a sarcophagus against the storm of pleading. As the congregants invoked the assistance of the heavenly hosts and implored the angels on her behalf, Nadia begged a request of her own.

She prayed for an end, or at the very least an answer.

One didn't come until three weeks later, when she rolled over in her basement bed and reached for the phone. All compulsion, her heart rate spiked, and skin warmed despite the crisp air. She acted on instinct and dialed his number, which had been disconnected for months. She waited for the three tones she'd heard the last time she called, but they never came. Instead of a computerized voice, the call went through. It rang and rang and rang until it clicked and a maternal voice, syrupy and decidedly Southern, began speaking.

"Hi, you've reached the Darlings, home of Hill, Lyana, Heidi, and Liam. We're not in right now, but please leave a message, and we'll get back to you as soon as we can. Bye bye now."

The line beeped. Nadia hung up. Fueled by her own despondence, she got out of bed as best she could and donned the all-black clothing she'd taken to wearing to fit in with the rest of the stylists at the department-store salon, where she had a day of washing heads to look forward to. The clothing also helped her hide, especially from herself, since she thought more about what hadn't happened—the six hundred dollars she hadn't spent and the time off work she hadn't taken—than she did what was happening. What had yet to happen.

At twenty-six weeks, the navel of her gravid stomach protruded from her skin because of the force behind it. She no more wanted to see the distention of her body, which carried a baby girl who kicked and rolled on her own time and schedule, than she wanted to see the grayscale photo Gladys had framed and placed on the nightstand beside her bed. The sonogram showed a head, belly, legs, and arms, enough of a baby but not enough of a reality. Nadia didn't know whose eyes or hair color her girl would inherit, let alone whose complexion she'd take: hers or Roman's.

She headed up the stairs and toward the door, not stopping for the country breakfast Gladys had insisted on cooking because Nadia was eating for two.

"You leaving a lil' early, don't you think?" Gladys said, following behind her.

"I got some things to do before work."

"I hope one of them things is tending to your head." Gladys snarked. She wasn't above picking a fight, miffed as she was at Nadia not eating after she'd gone through the trouble of making breakfast. "How you gon' be a hairdresser with nappy hair?" she asked.

"It's not nappy. It's natural. And if you knew what was in relaxer, you'd stop getting it too."

"No, the hell I wouldn't."

"I gotta go."

"On the bus?" Gladys asked. "Why don't you let me or your daddy take you?"

"I'm good. I got some things to take care of."

Nadia opened and closed the front door before Gladys could protest any further or she lost her own nerve. Maybe it was the Darlings, the woman's voice on the answering machine, that insisted she move on. Roman had, and so had the phone company. Wasn't it time she do the same?

That's what she reasoned when she rang the bell for Toya's apartment and waited on the porch step for her to answer.

"Who is it?" The intercom crackled with static.

"It's me." She paused before saying more, searching for words that would have erased the months of time. She had none. "It's Nadia."

The building door buzzed, and she walked through, but the door to Toya's apartment was still closed. She knocked lightly. The lock clicked, the dead bolt slid, and the chain was removed. Toya cracked the door open and stood, arms crossed in front of her robe.

"Wassup," she said icily.

"I needed to ask you something."

"You could've called."

"Yeah . . . but—"

"But what?"

"I also needed to apologize," Nadia said. "You were trying to get me out of the house for one night, and I made it into more."

"Mm-hmm," Toya said. Her eyes traveled from Nadia's face to her belly protruding beneath her black T-shirt. "How've you been?"

"Tired."

Toya stepped back and opened the door wide. "You wanna come in?"

"If it's all right with you?"

"Baby, who's at the door?" Lou asked, stepping up behind Toya.

Toya stepped back into his bare chest. "It's Nadia."

"My bad," Nadia said. "I didn't know you had company."

"It's just Lou. You can still come in."

Toya stepped back farther, forcing Lou to move out of the way, but Nadia didn't move. Instead, her mind overflowed with questions and assumptions. She figured Lou had to know where Roman had run off to, his new number, at the very least the club he would be promoting for the weekend. But knowing those things and telling her the answers were two entirely different endeavors.

Noticing Nadia's hesitancy, Toya asked, "Did you still want to ask me something?"

"I . . . I . . . I did," Nadia stuttered.

"Well, what is it?"

"I just, um, I just wanted to know if you knew where Roman was."

"He moved," Lou answered. "About a month ago."

"You know where?" Nadia asked.

Lou didn't answer. Toya looked from her man to her friend, caught in the middle, with an answer she was unwilling to give. Nadia watched them communicate with their eyes, neither of them wanting to break a confidence on her behalf.

"He told y'all not to tell me, huh?" Nadia said, ending the silence between them.

"He's having a baby with his wife," Lou began. "They're starting over. This gives them the best chance."

"And what about *my* baby?" Nadia demanded.

"What about it?" Lou asked. "He don't know that's his baby."

"He don't know that Deborah's baby is his baby either, but that didn't stop his ass from running behind her."

Lou shrugged. "That's his wife."

"Toya, get ya man," Nadia snapped.

"C'mon, y'all, that's enough," Toya said, straddling the threshold between them. "Nadia, please don't put us in the middle of this."

"Y'all been in the middle the whole fucking time. What do you mean don't put you there? That's where you started."

"Maybe so, but now we're staying out of it," Lou said. "We got our own family to worry about."

"Are you pregnant?" Nadia asked, wide-eyed and incredulous.

"She is," Lou answered. "We were actually celebrating before you knocked on the door, and we'd like to get back to it."

"Asshole, I believe I was talking to Toya."

"Hold up!" Toya raised a hand between them. "I know you mad and all, but Lou didn't do anything to you."

"And you taking up for this nigga tells me everything I need to know about where I stand with you."

"So much for that sorry-ass apology you came over here with."

"You right. It was sorry, because I'm not. When Lou leaves you just like the others, don't come crying to me because you knocked up and don't know what to do."

"You mean the way you crying to us right now? Get the hell on, Nadia. Roman's gone. It's time for you to be gone too."

Nadia turned away from Toya and Lou without another word. The slam of the door pronounced the end of their friendship. Lines had been drawn. Sides had been taken. Lou and Toya versus Nadia and no one else. She was alone. Roman was gone. Gladys was playing pretend at being a doting grandmother, and Eugene, though he cared, was too old to concern himself with the goings-on of young people. He'd lived long enough to know that relationships changed, alliances forged could be broken, and sworn enemies could become something close to friends if enough time had passed.

For Nadia and Toya, that time would be more than three years. In the fall of 1984, Nadia walked into the tiny lobby of South Harper Montessori School, a storefront day-care center on Stony Island, with a three-year-old Tati holding on to her fingers ready to enroll her for school. She nearly bumped into Toya, who was walking out of the school with a three-year-old Desirée in her arms. After awkward *hellos* and *how are yous*, they parted without an acknowledgment of what had happened before. Where and how they'd left their friendship.

Their reacquaintance began with little updates shared nonchalantly between the curb and the girls' day-care classroom. Lou and Toya breaking up shortly after Desirée's birth. His move across the country to take an accounting job for NBC in Burbank. Toya moving from South Chicago to Englewood. Nadia getting a house through a rent-to-own plan. Her opening her own salon in her basement.

By the time the girls were going to kindergarten two years later, there was a friendship that had progressed to taking turns at daycare pickup, happy hour meetups when they were able to get a sitter, Nadia doing Toya's and Desirée's hair, and the girls having sleepovers at least once a month. But they didn't look back. They tried once as they filled out forms to enroll Tati and Desirée into the same magnet elementary school, which would funnel them into one of the city's prestigious high school gifted centers.

"Who else did you put down for next of kin, besides me and your mom?" Toya had asked, sitting in the basement salon.

"No one," Nadia had answered. "Is there someone else I should put down?"

"I always add Lou."

"I don't have that option. Remember."

"Are you ever going to tell Tati about him? About Roman?"

"Why would I do that?"

"That's her father. She's gonna ask."

"I'll tell her the truth. He's gone. I don't know where he is. I'm enough."

"And what if she asks me?" Toya asked.

"What do you mean, what if she asks you?"

"It's just, sometimes Desi talks about Lou, and Tati will ask her questions about having a daddy. One day she might not just ask Desi. She might ask me."

"Then you'll tell her the same thing you told me," Nadia said, no longer making perfect capital letters to fit in the square boxes of the enrollment application. "He's gone and you don't know where he is."

With her eyes, Nadia dared Toya to say different. To offer a different story. The one she should have given the first time Nadia asked, Lou be damned. She didn't. They finished filling out their forms, and then Toya retrieved Desirée from where she played in Tati's room. No, Desirée could not spend the night. Toya offered to drop off Nadia's form at the school along with her own; Nadia declined. Toya left out the front door. Whenever Nadia offered to do her hair, she declined. Their boundary lines were redrawn and reinforced by the lies they chose to live with.

They were each other's emergency contact, a family of sorts. And just like family, they didn't always like each other, but they were there for each other due to necessity and proximity as well as their history. A past that looked at them daily in the present. Never buried. Never settled. Always waiting for an opportune time to get loud.

17.

Mimi's dining room table was covered with food. Macaroni and cheese, collard greens, perloo rice, brown gravy, candied yams, corn bread, sweet potato pone, cranberry sauce from the can with the pre-indented ridges for slicing, and a fried turkey still dripping with peanut oil. Eleven people were gathered, holding hands, with their heads bowed, shifting from foot to foot, waiting for Bryan to finish praying. Before he said "Amen," he asked everyone to say what they were thankful for. Bryan and Terry's broods began with the speeches they'd prepared at home with their parents. Their thanks were robotic and rehearsed; it was evident they didn't know the meaning of the words coming out of their mouths as they looked toward either Lorraine or Chloe for approval. They in turn looked to Mimi for affirmation.

Tati gritted her teeth. She released Mimi's hand for a moment and rubbed her palms against the thighs of her mustard sweater dress. The thankful train was ping-ponging its way toward her and she had yet to think of something to say. Not with Nadia's note still tucked in the magazine inside her purse hanging from the back of her chair. Gratefulness was not the emotion she connected with, but she had to pretend since she was next after Nadia, who gave thanks for her being home from college.

"Tati." Terry squeezed her hand. "It's your turn."

"Umm . . . I'm thankful for . . . I'm thankful for . . ."

Nadia lifted her head and narrowed her eyes. A demand to hurry up. But Tati was still pulling for words. She couldn't answer that she had nothing to be thankful for. She had to invent. Find a sliver of truth in a lie. Mimi helped her stall. Bobbed her head back and forth like she was in church and told her to take her time.

"I'm thankful that everyone is here together as a family to talk to one another," Tati finally mustered.

"Mm-hmm. Amen," Mimi moaned. She opened her eyes and looked around the table. "I'm thankful to see all my children are doin' all right. Bryan and Lorraine, Terry and Chloe, Nadia, y'all doin' all right. And y'all kids are doin' all right. We got us a college girl with four more comin' behind her. Amen."

"Amen," Uncle Bryan parroted.

"I wish Eugene could've seen it," Mimi continued. "He'd've been peacock proud at how good y'all doin'. Thank you, Jesus."

"Amen."

The final agreement was the loudest. Everyone pulled their chairs and made their plates. Tati pushed the holiday staples around and around until they became soggy from sitting in a pool of their own juices.

"Dang, Tati, you been away at school so long with that dorm food you forgot what to do," Terry joked beside her.

Tati laughed as he wiped stains from his charcoal slacks with the orange linen napkins Mimi had folded like candlesticks.

Bryan asked, "How's school goin'? What you studyin' in addition to runnin' track?"

"Tati's an English major," Nadia answered.

Tati swore she saw Nadia's chest and chin lift two inches from her body, pride obvious, as if accomplishments were transferable. Then again, if burdens could be passed down, surely blessings could move up.

"Whatchu gon' do with an English degree?" Bryan asked.

"Write. Teach. Law school. I'm still figurin' it out."

"That's all right, Tati," Terry said. "You figure it out as long as you need to, because you goin' to the Olympics first. Ain't that right?"

He held his hand up and she slapped him five.

"You that fast?" Mimi asked, her forkful of food poised in the air.

"I do all right."

Mimi shoveled food in her mouth and the conversation lulled. There was no music on in the background. Mimi forbade devilment on a day the Lord had made. Which was every day, especially man-made holidays. Without the filler, the quiet of the dining room overwhelmed. The only sound was the steady clinking of polished silver against china, which begged for interruption. The raucous kind.

"Anybody else got news to share?" Mimi asked. "It ain't like we get together this often with y'all being so busy. With everybody here—"

"Not everybody," Tati mumbled.

"Tati, what you say?"

Voice stronger, she answered, "Not everybody in the family is here . . . Not for me, at least."

Nadia dropped her fork on her plate. Mimi set hers down on the napkin. Tati felt the eyes of her aunts and uncles shine toward her as they waited to understand what she meant.

Mimi said, "Papa Eugene been on the other side a long time now. Everybody else that's *meant* to be here is here."

Mimi's eyes implored her to agree and drop whatever burning bush singed her tongue. Nadia, on the other hand, cut her cold. Her glare was a dare for Tati to disrespect her space and violate her boundaries.

Tati continued, "I'm not talkin' about Papa Eugene."

"Then who you talkin' 'bout?" Mimi asked.

"Roman."

"Really, Tati," Nadia scoffed. She balled up the napkin in her lap and threw it onto her plate of half-eaten food. "You want to do this now?"

"When else I'ma do it? You never wanna talk about him. You never wanna tell me nothin'. I'm tired of not knowin' when everybody sittin' here got all the answers."

"Baby, your uncles were kids themselves," Mimi said.

"Thanks, Mama." Nadia rolled her eyes. "Tati, the reason he ain't here is because he didn't want to be."

"Does he even know about me?"

"I told him I was pregnant."

"Did you know he's been living in Indianapolis all this time?"

"Who told you that?"

"Miss Grant and Mr. Cortez."

"That's new information to me. When I asked Toya and Lou about Roman a few months before you were born, *those two* refused to tell me. They protected him. I protected you."

"Did you ever try to ask about him again?" Tati asked softly. "For me?"

"Toya tried to tell me some things once. But I didn't wanna know. Didn't wanna remember. Everything ain't meant to be remembered, right, Mama?" Nadia swung her head and glared at Gladys.

"I always told you to do better by Tati than I did by you."

"It don't matter now, Mimi," Tati said. "I know enough."

"You don't know what you think you know," Nadia said.

"I know you didn't want me!"

"Tati, it's not that simple."

"Then explain it to me," she demanded, pulling the note from her purse.

"Where'd you get that from?" Nadia asked, her voice steely and calm despite the rage turning her cheeks golden red.

"It was stickin' out of one of the shoeboxes in your room when you sent me to get the rollers for Mrs. Loretha."

"You had no right to go through my things."

"Well, when else was she gon' learn?" Mimi instigated.

"She supposed to learn the same lesson I learned from you," Nadia sneered. "Stop asking questions you ain't never gon' get the answers to."

"Whatchu talkin' about?"

"You dote on Bryan and Terry like they're your pets. Like they can do no wrong. You so proud of them, and for me . . ." Nadia stuttered. " . . . for me . . . you just can't stand me."

"Is that what you think?"

"You ain't never showed me nothin' different."

Mimi grabbed her napkin, cleaned her fingers, and threw it onto her own half-eaten plate. With both fists on the table she hunched over until her shoulders met her ears and then dropped them down again. A heavy sigh escaped her lips. Tati stared at Mimi's face and swore she saw her age ten years in ten seconds, like time-lapse photography. Her body seemed heavier, as if she were carrying weights.

"You don't know what you think you know," Mimi warned.

"Then tell me," Nadia pleaded. "Tell me why you ain't never been able to stand my ass all these years? Why you were always so hard on me when I got my life together without your help or her damn daddy?"

"If I tell you, are you gon' tell Tati what she wanna know?"

Nadia didn't answer. She refused to make any promises she knew her obstinance would force her to break.

"Mm-hmm." Mimi rocked her body from side to side with her eyes closed. "You think I came running up here behind your daddy and got pregnant right away, don't you?"

"I thought you were pregnant before you got here," Nadia said.

"I was. But not with you."

"You never told me that."

"Wasn't for you to know." The skin of Mimi's face sagged as she swallowed a lump of spit.

"So, what happened?"

"What happens to light-skinned women in the South assumed to be uppity because you walk with your head high down a dirt road on Sunday morning to get the word. What happens when white men in a pickup truck drive past you high off shine and drunk out of their minds, huh? What happens?"

No one answered. Dinner was over. Bryan suggested Lorraine and Chloe take the whiny, antsy children away from the table. "They don't need to be here for this," he said.

Mimi waited for them to clear before she continued. Alone with her children and Tati, she told them she'd had no choice but to follow Eugene. "Place like Land's End, wasn't gon' be long before everybody knew. Small-town folk like to gossip."

"Mama, you don't have to do this," Bryan said.

"Yes, she does." Nadia's voice was cold and caustic. She asked, "So you trapped my daddy?"

"I did no such a thing. He *asked* me to make a life with him. I did."

"So what happened when you got here?" Terry asked.

"I lost the baby I was carryin'. The South takes from you, and the North can't save you."

"Did he know?" Nadia asked. "Did he know what happened in Alabama?"

"News like that travels just like the train. Fast, far, loud, and in a hurry."

"But you didn't have that baby, so why did you hate me so much?"

Mimi looked long at Nadia. Her face, near the color of her own father's, was racked with the same kind of pain that had consumed Sampson in the days after. It was the kind that ate from the inside like a tapeworm and left nothing but a hollowed frame subsumed by sickness. With as much love as she could muster, Mimi said, "I didn't hate you." She looked Nadia directly in the eye but couldn't hold it. She couldn't keep the gaze of glares that reminded her of all she'd left. The women she'd left. Mimi looked to the empty chair. The one set for her husband.

She said, "Even though I loved Eugene, wanted to be a family for him, I lost the longing for myself."

"So you had me because Daddy wanted me?"

"He was so much older than me, I didn't want to deprive him any longer."

"But you didn't want me?"

"Nadia, it's not that simple."

"Same thing I told Tati."

"What happened to me and what you did to yourself is two different thangs."

Nadia rolled her eyes and crossed her arms. She refused to be set apart. Set aside like she'd done something wrong,

"I tried with you as best I could—"

"You ain't have to try that hard with Bryan and Terry!"

"Because I know what happens to girl children in our family. My mama, my grandmama, even my great-grandmama. We're different, but we all carry her scar. I knew what could happen to you, and . . ." Mimi trailed off. She shook her head as if she'd meant to close her mouth before her mind took control, but it was too late. The sentence had begun. Nadia pressed.

"And what?"

"Mama, what are you talking about?" Bryan asked.

"Whose scar?" Terry asked.

"And what?" Nadia repeated.

Mimi hesitated. Sighed. "And enough time had passed to give me a scab. To try again. I thought I'd get another girl to do over with. Never expected boys. Not in a million years. Not from my line.

Nobody else had more than one child that lived. And never any boys. My grandmama and great-grandmama said we was cursed. When Bryan and Terry came along, they were such a blessing—"

"Then what was I?"

"Stop making this about you. You s'posed to be talkin' to Tati."

"You want me to talk to Tati. I want you to talk to me."

"I just told you everything,"

"No, you didn't. And you know it."

"Nadia, we all got our own crosses to carry." Mimi's shoulders slumped and rounded. "You got yours, and I got mine."

"And what about me?" Tati interrupted. "Did you ever think that y'all's crosses became mine?"

"Roman is gone," Nadia said. "He left before you were born. That should be enough for you to know what kind of man he is."

"It's not. Just like you messing with him when he was married doesn't say what kind of woman you are."

Tati stood from the table and grabbed the note that had landed between the half-eaten plates of food. The corner had gotten sucked into brown gravy. Tati wiped it off with a napkin, making sure not to rip or ruin the old loose leaf further. She placed it back in the magazine and then rolled them both safely into her purse.

"I'll find him myself." Tati marched out of the room, unmoved by Nadia's constant questioning of "Where are you going?" and her demands for Tati to come back to the table.

"Let her go," Mimi said as Tati grabbed her coat, gloves, and scarf. "Just let her go. Some things she has to figure out on her own."

18.

April 1953

It was a Sunday morning, when Gladys walked down the road kicking up swirls of red clay dust. It whirled around the backs of her bare legs, dirtying the slipped hem of her white cotton dress. Old white shoes, the soles nearly separated from the gums, dangled from the fingertips of one hand. The other was thrown across her brow, trying in earnest to hold on to her floppy hat that blocked her face from the sun. Hips swinging, loose hair flipping, high-yellow skin browning, Gladys marched toward the sounds calling to her soul.

It was a clarion call most folk in Land's End answered when they passed by the Dupree house. It sat in the middle of a fork in the road. To the left, on the other side of the fence post—land that used to belong to the Duprees—was Ms. Teena's, the tin-roofed juke joint where blues was blasted by singers belting their pain, lest they be consumed by their own piddly sadness. On a small stage elevated just a few inches over the packed-earth floor, folks sang, played, banjoed, drummed, and tambourined themselves out of their sorrows. The next morning, they made a right at the fork and headed to church to ask forgiveness for Saturday night's sins and mercy for Monday morning's troubles.

All except those from the Dupree household. They didn't so much as swivel their heads, shimmy their shoulders, or even put a bounce in their steps when Ms. Teena's got to jumping. They never looked to the left. It was as if the world ended at their fence. They didn't acknowledge what was next door, any more than they questioned the peculiarity of their place at the fork in the road. The Duprees lived for Sundays, when the song from St. Joseph's AME was more reliable than the old rooster that crowed whenever it felt like it.

The voices of the choir were always louder than the pianist providing accompaniment. Gladys sang as she walked about how her mind stayed on Jesus.

She belted her part as she made her way closer to the white clapboard church. She was late as it was, having spent the morning talking with Jubi, who hadn't set foot in St. Joseph's all of Gladys's eighteen years. Not even for her baptism. Ruby and Sampson left figuring their girl would make her way when she was done being doted on. On account of their positions in the church, they had to be at service early and had no time to tangle and tussle with Jubi, still color-struck after all these years.

With her eyes near to the heavens, Gladys marveled at how the church steeple poked away the clouds in the clear sky. Her focus was so fixed on her destination, she didn't listen for any differences in the sounds she'd grown accustomed to, not even the grumble of the slow-moving pickup truck behind her. Inside, cousins Carl Darren Danube and JB Springer watched her form swish as their lips drooled beer from breath that still reeked of last night's whiskey.

"That gal, there, think she better than the rest of 'em," JB said.

He wiped his leaky lips with the back of his hand and passed a paper-bag-sheathed beer bottle to Carl Darren, who nodded in agreement.

"She probably think she better than us," Carl Darren said. "My granddaddy told me don't trust none of them Duprees. He say they act the way they do on account of their color. All except that gal's mama. She 'bout the only one, I reckon, who know her place."

"Why don't we have us some fun," JB sneered from the driver's seat.

If Carl Darren had wanted to disagree, he didn't. JB crept closer to Gladys, who never once looked over her shoulder. Nearing the house of worship, she picked up her part with the altos as the choir wrapped up its final song before the sermon.

Her own voice reverberated so much in her ears as she sang "The Lord is Blessing Me Right Now" that it wasn't until the extra heat from the engine warmed her legs and bounced gravel nicked her calves that she knew she was not alone. Holding tight to her shoes, Gladys stepped off the road and into the fields to let whoever was behind her pass. Instead, they slowed. She dropped her arm from her hat and gazed at the ground. Carl Darren, with his arm hanging out of the window, seemed to press his back into the leather seat of the truck. JB leaned across him.

"Whatchu doin' out here on the road all alone?"

His lips turned to reveal a pernicious smile Gladys tried not to see. She didn't know whether to raise her head and respond or keep her head down and pray for them to pass.

"I asked you a question," JB demanded.

She raised her eyes, then answered, "Just headed to church."

"You think the good Lord save souls like yours?"

"I don't know." Gladys stared back down at the ground. "I reckon we won't know 'til judgment day."

"We can be the judge of that."

JB snickered and patted Carl Darren on the chest. He cut the engine to the truck, opened the door, and hopped down. As he made his way around to Carl Darren's side, Gladys stepped back onto the road and continued her walk. She wanted the music to overtake her mind but couldn't afford the oblivion of distraction. She had to pay attention. Hadn't her mama always told her to be aware of her surroundings? Hadn't Jubi told her to never trust white folks, no matter how nice or well-meaning they were? Hadn't Mama Em told her to never get close enough to be needing their niceness?

All her life she'd heard the whisperings of the women in her family about the ways of white folks. Whisperings that ceased when they realized she was in the room. But even in the snatches of conversation she caught from the hidden corners of the two-room house she shared with Ruby and Sampson, the lesson was always the same. As her daddy said, "Don't trust 'em. Don't put nothing past 'em."

What would he say if he knew she was in a position of needing their niceness now? Specifically from JB and Carl Darren. The worst ones to need well intentions from.

She'd seen how Carl Darren, his daddy, and even his granddaddy, if he happened to be around, treated her when she went with Ruby into town. She always felt an extra chill as soon as she crossed the threshold. It pulled up her back like a fingernail tracing from the base of her spine to the middle of her neck. Facing the Danubes unnerved Gladys, but not Ruby. Rendered immobile and useless, Gladys would wait for her mama at the door of the store under the watchful eyes of the Danube men, who counted every dollar down to the penny before they let Ruby leave, lest they be cheated out of what they'd never miss.

Gladys knew slinking away from Carl Darren and JB would be much more difficult now. She had no cover to cling to, no person to protect her, and God himself was a mile away if he was an inch.

"Where you runnin' off to so fast?" JB asked.

"My mama and daddy waiting for me at church," Gladys said.

"They shouldn't have left you behind. A pretty little thing like you. Anything could happen."

JB and Carl Darren fell in line behind Gladys's purposed and intentioned steps. JB walked with a hitch, hard and wanting, as Carl Darren shuffled to keep up. Gladys mumbled her song; hymns trembled on her lips as she clutched her shoes and held her hat even tighter. All her limbs had a job to do. One in opposition to the boys behind her.

JB reached for her shoulder and pulled her backward until he could throw his full arm around her body. He maneuvered her neck toward one of his stinking pits as he whispered that it wasn't right for her to ignore them.

"God say you're supposed to love your neighbor," he espoused. "Ain't that right, Carl Darren?"

"It sound like the good book to me."

Gladys tried to pull away, but JB clutched her close.

"So tell me something, Gladys Dupree . . ."

She looked up, shocked he knew her name. A smile played across his face. A grin so wide and devious she could make out the devil in his dimples. He had sandy hair, greasy and stringy, stubbly shadow, and gray eyes. Gladys knew JB could be handsome, charming, and unassuming when he wanted. She knew there were girls in Land's End who would have welcomed the attention she was so easily receiving. But those girls were nothing like her. And with them, JB and Carl Darren would behave nothing like this.

" . . . Do you love me and my cousin the way God says you s'posed to?"

"I reckon," Gladys answered, looking down toward the ground.

"How can you say that and you ain't never showed us? Has she, Carl?"

"'Fraid not."

JB pulled a fistful of Gladys's dress as he squeezed her neck and shoulders.

"Don't run, now," he mused, adjusting his belted pants. "Carl Darren, get her."

From behind, Carl Darren grabbed Gladys and covered her mouth. She could neither get out of his grasp nor run around JB, who blocked her path. Off the road and into the fields, Carl Darren pulled Gladys by the arms while JB shoved her torso. Deeper and deeper they went, into the cotton that was no taller than their waist. Not yet in full bloom, the field was more green leaves and yellow flowers than the white bolls that wouldn't show until September.

"Grab her feet," JB huffed, out of breath. "It'll be easier that way."

Drunk as they were, they stumbled under the sun beaming on their heads as they hauled her deadweight. Even Gladys closed her eyes against the bright rays that promised of the oppressive summer to come. Not that she knew anything about working in the field. Perhaps it's the reason they chose her. Like Carl Darren and JB, Gladys had gone to school. She'd graduated. She'd planned to go to college. They assumed she thought herself better. They mistook her fear for arrogance, but to them it was all the same. Uppity was uppity.

"This good enough right here," JB said, dropping Gladys's feet.

Steady, she bit the fingers of Carl Darren's free hand and ran.

"The bitch bit me," he yelped.

JB tackled her. She thudded to the soft earth, skin scraped on the way down by the spurs of plants that had yet to open. Her hat shifted forward on her head and covered her eyes. The shoes she had casually dangled by her fingertips, she gripped like a barrier that could keep them from her. In the end it wasn't to be so. Gruff hands tore at her dress. Mouths whispered filthy words against her ears. Belts jangled loose, followed by the unmistakable zip of pants coming undone and the shuffle of limbs detangling themselves from clothing.

Gladys bucked her legs and hips, but they pounced upon her body, one forced to hold her still while the other thrusted. She did not plead. Gladys did not beg. She froze. And even this they took for insolence. Her fear mistaken for hubris. JB was insulted at the nerve of her pride. As if it alone would keep her from ruin. In his blinding anger, he wound his belt around his hand and whipped Gladys's hat-covered face with the wide gold buckle until the straw tore, her yellow skin bled, and her mind went blank in blackness.

WHEN GLADYS AWOKE, IT WAS TO BIRDS CIRCLING THE AIR ABOVE her. They hovered low, ready to peck her clean. Separate skin from bone. She felt around her body. Legs, arms, face. Blood coated her fingers, thick and goopy. It didn't pour from the wound. It coagulated in the cut, clotting for the preservation of skin. Between the absence of voices in the distance and the position of the sun in the sky, Gladys figured it was late evening, almost supper time.

They gon' be looking for me, she thought to herself as she tried to stand. Her feet barely held her, even though it had been more than four hours since she was attacked. When she was finally upright, she noticed the stickiness and throbbing pain between her legs. The pulsing from her face. Her dress was tattered, but she was still alive. Gladys left the shoes but grabbed her hat. She smashed it onto her head and held it there as she stumbled out of the cotton fields.

On the road, she could see her home. Sampson's truck wasn't in front. No doubt he was looking for her. It was just as well anyway. Gladys didn't want to walk in the front door. Didn't want her shame to even darken Deacon Sampson's doorstep. Instead, she cut through the fields on the other side of the road until she came to the clearing between the new house and the old.

The new house was the one Sampson had built on Emma's land. The one that sat in front of the fork, judging everybody who made a left. The old house was the one Emma had grown up in, raised by Evangeline.

Approaching the house, Gladys smelled supper cooking from the pots inside. She let herself in and welcomed the shadows of the dim room.

"Ruby, that you?" Jubi called from a corner Gladys couldn't determine. "You find her?"

Gladys opened her mouth, but no sound escaped. She had none to give. Neither reason nor explanation. She thought it best if she was found, even if she had to do the legwork of her own rescue.

"Chile . . . Gladys, is that you?" Jubi came closer to the door and saw Gladys standing stock-still just inside it. "What happened?" she asked.

Gladys opened her lips but said nothing.

"Jubilee, who is it?" Emma called from deep within the old house. Her voice, though hoarse, pronounced her full name, as Emma had intended her to be called.

"Gladys, Mama," Jubi answered.

The irritation in her reply was as evident as the skin she could not shed and the heritage she failed to hide. Turning back to Gladys, Jubi closed her eyes and took a deep breath.

"Looking the way you do, it was bound to happen." She shook her head. "C'mon in here and let us get you cleaned up."

Jubi took Gladys by the arm and walked her slowly through the house until they were in the living space. What used to be the only space. There she left Gladys standing alone as she busied herself dragging out a massive tin washtub and a small cauldron.

"What's going on in here?" Emma asked.

She emerged from the bedroom she at one time shared with George; a shawl draped around her shoulders and wool socks covered her shuffling feet. Gladys turned her head slightly. It was enough for acknowledgment but not enough to see, hoping she wouldn't be seen in return.

"I'm gettin' Gladys cleaned up. That's what's going on," Jubi answered.

"What happened?" Emma croaked.

She cleared her throat as Jubi kissed her teeth. "Can't you see what happened?"

In the dim light, Emma had to strain her bluing eyes to see Gladys clearly. It wasn't until she was beside her, lifting the strips of the ripped dress, gently pressing the gash across her cheek, and eyeing her bare legs streaked with dirt and blood, that she understood her own daughter's contempt. Gladys, the baby of the family, could no longer be treated as such. She had encountered the ways of the wicked in Land's End. The ones who'd run Jubi back across the tracks. Those who'd hated Evangeline's and later Emma's midwifery work, but called on them in the dead of night when one of their own was losing too much blood during a hospital birth. Those same ones who'd taken her mother from her before she'd even opened her eyes. Emma saw their handiwork as Gladys stood waiting for a way forward. Or better yet, a way out. But all she could be offered was a ticket through.

"Take them clothes off," Jubi instructed.

She poured hot water from the cauldron she filled from one of the pots on the stove and then headed outside to the garden. Mama Em put her own hands to work, taking her great-grand girl apart bit by bit. The raggedy dress slipped from her shoulders and the tattered slip fell from her hips. Torn underclothes were pulled down and away until Gladys could do nothing more but hold on to her hat. It was all she had then. It was all she had now. But Emma knew better. Her gentle fingers grazed across Gladys's back and pulled her in close. She removed the straw from her hands and dropped it on the pile.

Emma's embrace was the only salve for what Gladys braced herself through. The old woman let her feel all of her until her shoulders dropped, her back slumped, and her head drooped into the crook of Emma's shoulder. The thick blood from the gash on her cheek began to loosen and run with the wetness of her salty tears. Gladys wept the way she wouldn't with Carl Darren and JB until her cries turned to sobs, her sobs to wails, and her wails to convulsions, rocking both her and Emma's frail body.

"C'mon now," Jubi said, coming in with a bundle of herbs. "Ain't no use carrying on like this. What's done is done."

"Give her time, Jubilee. She ain't got what you made of."

"I'm sure it's making in her now. C'mon, baby, get in."

Jubi gently pulled Gladys from Emma's bosom and helped her settle in the tub. Gladys didn't even wince from the heat. Steam swirled as she lowered herself down. Despite the length of the trough, Gladys drew her knees to her chest, circled her arms around herself, and buried her head. In her own cocoon, she sat in the water unmoving, not at rest.

"Jubilee, you gon' need some more herbs in that water—"

"I already got 'em, just trying to get her settled."

"Well, you better get to it. I hear the truck pulling up outside."

Emma shuffled to the door. It slammed as she and Jubi stepped onto the rickety porch, leaving Gladys in the tub of steaming water and leafy herbs: mugwort and rosemary, dandelion and lavender, chamomile and sage, and a heavy hand of cotton root just to be safe.

On the porch, Emma took to the rocking chair her George had carved and whittled while Jubi stood behind the rail. With the truck parked in front of the new house, it was only a moment before Ruby and Sampson burst through their back door. Surprise etched across their faces to see Emma and Jubi waiting for them.

"Where's my baby?" Ruby asked, breathless.

"Inside," Jubi answered.

"We need to see her. There's talk in town and across the tracks?"

"Go'n inside."

Ruby and Sampson moved as one, but Emma held up her hand. "Just Ruby," she said.

Sampson looked from his love, the color of the universe before God called for light, to her mothers twice over. Their white-oak faces studied his cinnamon with stern warning. One he ignored. He said, "She's my daughter too."

"Some things men ain't meant to see," Emma added.

"I'll holler if we need you," Ruby said.

She moved forward toward her mother and grandmother, never once looking back. They had decided that she must see Gladys alone. Sampson watched Ruby clear the few yards between the back porch of the new house and the front porch of the old. He fixed his eyes on the locks of her thick brown hair braided tight to her scalp, until she was gone. Until all that was left to look at were her mothers, who bore screws through his skin, so much darker than theirs, until he had no duty but to retreat. Their hard faces repeated what Emma had already made clear. *Some things men ain't meant to see.*

They had never shown weakness in front of anyone before, and they weren't about to start now, even if he was kind of their own. Jubi waited until Sampson's door slammed shut before she helped Emma out of the rocker. They walked inside the old house, hand in hand, to see Ruby kneeling beside Gladys in the tub.

"Who did this?" she asked.

Gladys didn't say. She didn't lift her head to address her mother. She didn't turn around to see Jubi and Emma. Hugged to herself, Gladys wished to abandon her body the way she had lost her mind when she had the audacity to stroll on to church as if she owed neither taxes nor tithe.

"What you heard in town?"

Emma asked the question Jubi was too afraid to give voice. She knew how gossip swirled. Truth and lies digested like soup all in one swallow.

"Heard something about some boys bragging across the tracks?" Ruby answered.

"'Some boys' got a name?" Emma asked.

"JB for sure," Ruby answered. "Maybe Carl Darren."

Jubi inhaled the wisps of her wraiths.

"I'm glad you know your mess when you hear it," Emma chided.

"It ain't wrong wantin' a better life," Jubi said.

They carried on conversation as if Gladys and Ruby weren't sitting amongst them. Not that they were listening. Jubi and Emma spoke freely, taking up sides in their same fight. Ruby reached into the water, not bothering to unbutton her blouse sleeves, searching for a towel.

"Your clothes getting soaked," Gladys said, as she felt her mother's fingers move around her body.

"They ain't more important than you. Besides, this shirt gotta be cleaned anyhow. All the sweating I did in service trying to praise my way away from worryin' 'bout you, it's some funky."

Ruby laughed, trying to inspire her daughter to do the same, but she was met with a portent of silence. Towel in hand, she squeezed water on Gladys's back, leaving a trail of herbs sticking to her skin.

"You gon' have to wash her hair too," Emma said. "Can't leave that devilment lingering on her head."

"I will," Ruby answered.

"I'll help you," Jubi said, coming over to the washtub.

"I'll make the tea," Emma said.

"What for?" Jubi questioned.

Emma gave her a hard stare, willing words to stay on the right side of her mouth. Though the sentiment was the same, as old as they were, it no longer had the effect it once did. Jubi rolled her eyes and ignored the warning. She humphed then sneered, "If'n she anything like us, it's a boy, and she won't need no tea."

"Remember, I wasn't like y'all," Ruby said softly to Jubi beside her.

"Jubilee!" Emma sang, her tone another test. "We don't leave these things to chance."

Emma shuffled into the kitchen to prepare the tea beside the fires simmering the long-forgotten supper. On either side of the washtub, Jubi and Ruby, mother and daughter, scrubbed Gladys until her skin was smooth and tender to the touch. Squeezing the towel over her head, Ruby washed her daughter's hair last. With care, she scratched and massaged her scalp the same as she had her body.

"Mama, you'll get me a comb, please," Ruby asked, raking her fingers through Gladys's lush, sandy-brown tendrils.

Her hair curled at the roots and waved at the ends, nearly straight, like Jubi's and Mama Em's. She was more their daughter than Ruby's. Favored them in what Jubi would say were all the right ways. Now she was bound to them by burden. Connected through a cautionary tale.

"Here you go," Jubi said, handing over a fine-toothed comb.

"Thank you." Ruby studied it for a moment, knowing she had never used such a comb for herself. It would have snapped in half before it ever pulled through her tight coils with ease. Shaking her head, Ruby released the old indignity. She raked her fingers through Gladys's hair and chased it with the comb, detangling the strands and making sections. When she was done, she dropped it on the floor and let her hands do the rest. They pulled together Gladys's hair into a neat braid that stopped well below the nape of her neck. Length was all they had in common.

Jubi braced her body against the braid. An affront to all she'd become. "I wish you wouldn't do that."

"Why not?" Ruby asked.

"You know why, and ain't no need in getting Mama started today. Old as she is, it'll put her in the ground."

"It won't, and you know it." Ruby smirked.

"You don't know what'll do what. We've been killed for less."

"Gladys didn't die today."

"Maybe she did, maybe she didn't. Who's to say?"

"She is," Ruby said. "Lean back for me, baby."

Jubi marched away from the tub and joined Emma outside as Gladys reclined like she was told. Under her mother's touch, she tolerated the cooling water floating with conjure potions a mite longer. Ruby worked her arms and shoulders, humming hymns, until Gladys let her head fall into her hands, giving up more of what she'd tried to hold tight. Of what she'd wanted to brace alone.

"You gon' be all right, you know that, baby," Ruby said gently.

"You sure?" Gladys asked.

"I am. This don't change nothing. Nothing at all."

"You sure?"

"Only if you let it. That's the only way this can have power. Is if you let it."

"What about Eugene?" Gladys whispered.

Ruby stilled her hands from their work on her daughter's body. She was intentional about not letting the end of her healing be abrupt, but this question was one she hadn't planned for. In her own worry with Sampson, she hadn't considered that there could be someone else with as much care or concern. Yes, she knew Eugene Washington was courting her daughter, but she'd never imagined it to be serious. Not since he was fourteen years older and Gladys was dead set on going to Tougaloo to become a nurse and not some man's wife. She assumed on account of the age difference alone it was only kind words they were keeping due to the distance, not a serious relationship with the prospect of marriage.

Ruby asked, "When does he come back?"

"Saturday."

Ruby detected the desperate hope in Gladys's voice and let her lead. "Well," she began, "if that's what you want—"

"It is, Mama." Gladys sat up in the tub and turned her head to face Ruby. Whispering, she added, "In case trouble comes."

Ruby nodded, thankful her complexion didn't give away the blood draining from her countenance. In their family, trouble always came. She thought that by now the curse had been broken.

Taken a season off like the fallow land on the farm. But now she saw it persisted just like the generations. Returning stronger and with vengeance.

In half a day, Gladys had reorganized her future on account of what was done to her. She swapped school for security, education for Eugene. Playing with all the permutations, Ruby stroked Gladys's braid and nodded her head. She accepted the rash hoping it was wise.

"You ought not put him off . . ."

She couldn't bring herself to add the fear Gladys had already aired.

In case trouble comes.

Ruby knew it had already arrived.

19.

It wasn't until Gladys was gone for good that Jubi crossed the
tracks for the last time in her life to put all trouble to bed. She set
out for Danube General Store. Sure, she could have asked Sampson to carry her in his truck, but she wanted people to see her
walk. She wanted the nosy neighbors, church ladies, and anyone
else who'd come to get their fill of the latest Dupree family fall to
know, which was grounded in incontrovertible fact, instead of just
hearing about it.

In a white skirt suit she'd made for herself, plus matching gloves,
pantyhose, short heels, and no hat, Jubi walked unhidden with her
long, now-gray hair, loose about her shoulders, swinging across her
back. She may have been dressed like one of St. Joseph's ushers, but
her mission was nothing close to biblical. But it was of God. If necessary, vengeance would be hers. And who could blame her? Carl
Darren and JB going after Gladys was certainly a sin and a shame.
At least that was the consensus from the porch-watching neighbors
who had nothing better to do after a day of work than to talk about
the goings-on at the Dupree house. They'd been shut out and ranks
had closed against them from even asking *How do?* when passing
the porch or borrowing a cup of sugar ever since Jubi came back
bloody from across the tracks.

Seeing her in all her white—for she was still in ritual with
Emma—walking with no hat, not even trying to keep her precious

skin from turning color, they could do nothing but be gobsmacked by their own speechlessness. Their general pitiable condescension turned over into muted pride.

They let her pass them by before they began a new line of peppery prate.

"Did y'all see Jubilee walking into town?"

"She looked some good, huh?"

"You know she goin' to talk to old man Danube 'bout what happened to her grandgirl."

"You think he know?"

"If he don't, he sho' 'bout to find out."

Jubi didn't care for the whispers, but she smiled to herself anyway, giving the people something more to talk about. She'd been whispered about for thirty-six years; at least this time she knew all the talk would be in her favor. The gossip bolstered her step, pushed her farther and faster across the tracks until she was standing on a road familiar and unfamiliar all the same.

Paved over to better handle the car traffic, with a few stop signs and a traffic signal, the road, now known as Main Street, looked much different from when Jubi was there last. Then it was still a dirt road and mostly everyone still walked to get what they needed. But concrete hadn't changed much else. In addition to the colored folk automatically knowing to go to the back door to receive any type of service, there was now a sign proclaiming their entryway separate and apart from the whites'. As if they needed a billboard to announce their supposed humiliation.

No one likes to admit that shame is an internal type of feeling, something you perceive within yourself. Can't nobody give you shame to feel. They can't pile it on a platter and hand it to you, telling you this is what your insides are supposed to contort around. There was no shame amongst the negroes of Land's End, who didn't need a sign showing them they weren't welcome. That they already knew, but some of the younger Danubes had insisted. They had learned a different way where they were raised.

Jubi saw the sign for the first time with its narrow arrow pointing toward the back of the store. Colored Entrance. She shook her head, rolled her eyes, and kept on her way to the front. She hadn't entered through the back door of Danube's since she was Gladys's age, and she for damn sure wasn't about to start now.

As soon as she crossed the threshold, Jubi paused. Her eyes roamed as she took in the fresh coat of white paint and the shelves packed with cans and jars of packaged food that hadn't been there the last time. The last time she'd visited, she had been run out. Refused service. The memory inched its way up her throat so far that she had to cough it back down. She wouldn't be turned away this time.

"I'll be right with you," yelled a young boy from the front counter.

"No need," Jubi yelled back. "Where's Logan?"

She used her full voice and not the one she played pretend with when she was married. If Logan was around, which she knew he was, he'd hear the familiar tone and timbre and make himself known. Just like last time.

"Granddaddy will be right back," the boy said. "He just went across the way to get a haircut over by Mr. Jacob. You know he don't like his hair getting too long nowadays. He say it's bad enough the cataracts getting the best of him, he don't need his hair trying to blind him too."

The boy laughed. Jubi only nodded.

"Anything I can help you with, before I help them?"

Jubi looked up to see the line of folks she knew waiting for service. Their dark eyes shined from brown faces knowing exactly what she was up to. She looked back toward the boy. *He can't tell either.* Hmphing to herself, Jubi said, "Only Logan can help me with what I need."

"If there's anything I can do for you, ma'am, just let me know, and I'll stop and get it."

Jubi knew his delays had more to do with him than whether she wanted packaged chips, a chocolate bar, or soda. She shook her head as she moved down the aisles. Her gloved hands swiped across shelves in need of both a dusting and a polishing. She walked the creaky floor, which hadn't been mopped in what looked like ages and suppressed the memories of when she used to burst through the front door and be swept up in a hug and twirled off her feet. The days when she was so sick from carrying babies that couldn't live that she sat at the counter sipping a soda, hoping to make her flip-flopping stomach feel better. Listening to the young boy, no more than fifteen, speak to the other customers, calling them *boy* and *gal* when he was still scrawny enough to go over their knee, filled Jubi with some kind of sadness.

She had wanted better, yes, but his behavior was hardly her desire. *Maybe everything happened the way it was supposed to.*

Jubi released the thought as soon as it tried to settle in her mind. She shook her head to remove the cloud covering her face and continued her stroll down one aisle and up another until she was facing the door as heavy steps, assisted by a cane, announced his presence.

Logan stopped when he saw her. He ran his hand over the little hair he had left as if he was sprucing himself up for some long-lost lover. In a tan seersucker suit, Logan crossed one foot in front of the other and rested his weight on his wooden walking stick. Memories returned to him darkened his features and set his mouth in a thin line.

"You still coming through the front door? After all these years?"

"Why would I stop?" Jubi asked. "Especially today?"

"What are you doing here, Jubilee?"

She didn't react to the spit that flew from his mouth when he enunciated every syllable of her given name. Steeling her eyes and planting her feet, she said, "You know exactly why I'm here, and don't pretend you don't."

"If my recollection serves me correctly, you're the one who likes to pretend."

"I didn't pretend nothing. You never asked. I never told. And we were happy."

Jubi couldn't prevent the crack in her voice. She couldn't prevent the wave of emotion that rolled down from the top of her body to the soles of her feet. Grabbing hold of one of the shelves, she anchored herself as the feelings she'd fought away daily for decades rushed at her from every imaginable angle. Eight years she'd spent married to Logan. Eight years they were together, the perfect couple. She'd kept on his side of the tracks in Land's End and was never suspected when they traveled to Mobile or Birmingham. She'd shopped in boutiques and been serviced by young white girls eager to help the wife of Mr. Logan Jefferson Danube III.

But it wasn't the access she longed for. Not the things. Not any longer. It was those moments that couldn't be accounted for she missed the most. The way his hands felt when they massaged her scalp and dragged through her hair. When she would wipe smudges of preserves from the corners of his mouth after breakfast in the morning. The way they'd dance around the parlor, swaying to music playing soft and scratchy from the gramophone. He indulged her when she asked him to buy the record of the Fisk Jubilee Singers and even admitted that they'd sounded good for "colored gals."

Those moments of her youth, of their youth together, became cold air in her bones. Her ankles and knees swelled with ache. Jubi knew it was due to the lies they'd told. Her lie to escape and his to save face. Both rotten at the root and souring everything connected to them.

Logan wanted to respond with what was in his heart. He wanted to say he hadn't been happy since she'd left.

Since *she'd* left.

As if he hadn't forced her out, threatened her life, then called her dead. But that's the way he chose to remember it. He couldn't bring himself to say that he had spent many a night of his own sitting in a car parked far off to the left of the fork in the road staring at the Dupree houses. It was the only way he could see behind the new house to the old. To the home where his wife lived with her mother and his daughter he didn't know, who was raised to believe her daddy was a war hero who became victim of his own pride. He made a point to never harass her when she came through the back door of the store, doing Jubi's bidding. To him Ruby seemed a sad, lonely girl—now woman—by herself all the time. She stayed close to her own kind, never having any friends outside of the Dupree line. He watched her every movement when she came for fabric and little foodstuffs they couldn't grow on their own, looking for traces of himself. For traces of Jubi. Of Jubilee. But found none.

For years he'd tried to figure out to whom she really belonged. What Black man had Jubi run around on him with and why he hadn't known. Why he hadn't been told. But in all these years the rumors from across the tracks had never reached his ear. Not like they had when Jubi went back home. That he'd heard about.

"Well, you know, she was over there passing for white."

The whisperings ran through the line of colored customers waiting for service for nearly three years after her return. And though Logan listened to it all, he never heard tell that she wasn't telling the truth about the dark girl she called his own. Too stubborn to stomach his own nostalgia, to allow the cold air breaking through Jubi's bones to get into his, he did what she would have done: shook his head and sucked his teeth, kissing away the clouds.

"What's done is done," he said.

"And what's that supposed to mean?" Jubi asked. "She's your granddaughter, Logan. Your own grandgirl."

"She ain't none of my kin."

"Carl Darren is."

"You don't know that it was him."

"If this tea don't take, we'll find out in forty weeks whether she in Chicago or not. Especially if she carrying . . ."

Jubi's voice trailed before she could finish her sentence. As much as she didn't want to believe in Evangeline's curse, her body was a living witness to what could not be continued. The baby boys that had to die.

Logan closed the gap between him and Jubi. Bending his head toward her ear, he said, "You lucky it wasn't you."

"I know you don't expect me to say thank you."

"You're welcome anyhow."

He stepped back. Smile twisted with derision, Logan seemed satisfied with his empty threat. As if he'd considered then to dole out punishment of his own. To take advantage and steal the night from his wife because of a lie. An omission. Justice, Southern-fried, was of course justice all the same. It needed not sheriff or record of arrest, neither judge nor jury. Only the scent of injury. The wounded party allowed to reap and repair by issuing a sentence to assuage their own perceived suffering. Never willing to believe that the anguish had been equal. That there was parity in the internal torment. Those thoughts, those feelings, stayed tucked tight. Carapaces always covering the tender emotions and raw wounds they rarely returned to.

Jubi neither swayed nor took a step back away from Logan's wistful words. They were hollow. Carved out and whittled through until all that was left was old bark begging to fall. They were stumps of their former selves. Their lives the sum of their lies.

I'm glad you know your mess when you hear it.

Jubi heard Emma's voice from when Gladys first staggered home. Her mess stood right in front of her, smug in his delusion that their brief union hadn't caused all this. What Carl Darren and his mother,

Karen, Gladys, and Ruby didn't know, they did. Jubi knew she was alive and well just as Logan knew the box buried six feet under in the white cemetery reserved for the Danube family plot was empty as could be.

She approached him gently and laid her gloved hand on his chest. Patting the same point below his heart that she used to when they'd lain in bed, she said, "It's time to tell the truth."

Jubi pushed past Logan to walk out the way she'd come. He caught her hand. Held the tips of her fingers with all the familiarity of consummated man and wife. After all, it's what they were. It no longer mattered who saw them. Who in the store was looking. Not the customers at the back door, not the white women perusing the shop windows of Main Street, not the boy behind the counter, a distant relation of them both. He held her fingers and for a moment his gaze softened so that his green eyes glowed. He would take to his own grave the truth. Buried above an empty box that couldn't contain his wife.

He let go.

Jubi left.

Again.

It would be the last time she saw Logan. The last time she would greet the past versions of her fractured self with the clarity of age. Head high, gray hair swinging, buried secrets begging her for freedom, Jubi crossed the tracks, knowing the last folks left to confront were the ones at home.

20.

When Tati returned home for winter break, she arrived with a plan to meet Roman. Between final papers and final exams, her last three weeks in North Carolina A&T's library had been productive. The bank of computers useful. She searched through Yahoo!, Google, LexisNexis, and even Ancestry, a new website, though that didn't lead her to Roman Bishop Brown. According to his white pages entry, he was a club owner in Indianapolis. He had a website and email to boot.

Tati had wanted to show Nadia the correspondence she had printed and shoved in her purse as soon as she got in the car at Midway, but instead, they argued most of the ride home. It had been three weeks since they'd spoken. Tati had tried to get Nadia to understand it was strange to go back to the way things were without acknowledging all that had transpired, but Nadia just shook her head at the thought that she was somehow supposed to excavate the things she wanted to keep from her own self for the sake of her daughter's healing.

"It's always been you and me," Nadia reasoned. "I don't know what else you expect."

"It don't have to be," Tati had said. And that was all she needed to say. Nadia knew Tati had finally found the daddy she'd been looking for since she was four, when she realized there was another kind of parent picking up kids from the preschool.

She asked, "When you supposed to meet him?"

"New Year's Eve," Tati answered. "I'm going to his new club, Worship Haus, down the street from the Clique. He's opening early *for me*. Before the crowd gets there for the countdown."

Nadia heard the pride in Tati's voice and didn't have the heart to tell her not to get her hopes up.

But she tried.

"I hope you know what the hell you're doing," she said. "You can't always put the jack back in the box."

BUT WHO WAS THE JACK?

That's what Tati wondered as she stood inside the warehouse of Roman's club. They'd shaken hands and exchanged names and that was it. There was no *nice to meet you*, or *I hope you found the place okay*, just the awkward quiet wrought by a lifetime of curiosity. Tati could hear the low rumble of the furnace gently heating the space as she took in her surroundings. Two bars butted up against the long horizontal walls, and a singular staircase gave access to the VIP balcony levels.

"Would you like a tour?" Roman asked.

Tati nodded as she turned around in the room beneath the buzzing fluorescent lights. They had yet to be switched out for the track theater lights in blues and reds that would create the ambiance for guests who arrived at ten thirty, trying to get in free before eleven.

Roman narrated all she saw. "This is the main floor of worship, like an outer court," he said, his deep voice sentient and excited. "All the dancing will take place down here. Up there is where the DJ will set up."

He pointed to a corner on the third level where turntables were encased in glass. Tati had heard on the radio that the Bad Boys from WGCI would host a live show until the countdown and midnight.

In the fishbowl Roman had created for them, they'd be able to see everything happening in the club while also immersing themselves in the music, without being distracted by drunk patrons wanting to put in their requests.

"Nice," Tati said. "What's on the upper levels besides the DJ?"

"The second floor is the sanctuary," he said, walking toward the staircase. "It's like a lounge. Plush couches, tables, things like that."

"How much does it cost to get up there?" Tati followed behind him.

"Preordered tickets only."

"And what about the third level? Is that preorder too?"

"The confessional? Not quite."

"Then who's up there?"

"Special guests. Personally invited."

He stopped on the second floor in front of a velvet rope and sign that read, WE WORSHIP IN THE SANCTUARY.

"Would you like to talk out here or go in my office?" Roman asked.

"You have an office?"

"I do. Right this way."

Roman led her behind the velvet rope, past the mirrored wall the couches were pushed up against, to a storage area that held extra barstools, chairs, and crates of liquor. Just beyond the pallets of extras, there was a small door, inconspicuous in its matte gray paint. There was no door handle, and Tati barely noticed the lock before Roman seemingly parted the wall.

The floor inside the office was thinly carpeted. A heavy desk sat in the center of the windowless room. It was topped with a new, fat-backed iMac and piles of papers. Sleek oak filing cabinets, made to look like furniture, lined the walls on either side of the desk. Atop them were statues, trophies, and even a few framed photographs.

Tati gravitated toward a small silver frame where Roman stood beside a woman, three children in front of them, two boys and a girl.

"This your wife? Family?" she asked, picking it up.

He hesitated. "Yeah."

Tati replaced the picture then sat in one of the dark oak, ladder-backed chairs facing the desk. Roman scrambled to the other side, tripping over his Stacy Adams wingtips, and took his seat in his large leather chair. They looked as if they were going to have a con-versation about business and not talk around the reason her picture wasn't amongst his mantel display.

"How old are you?" Roman asked.

"Eighteen. I'll be nineteen in March."

"Is that right?"

"How old are your kids? My brothers and sister."

Roman turned his head away from Tati toward the picture she picked up. Tilting his head and squinting his eyes, he tried to deci-pher what had emboldened her to possess his paternity, his family, his children, as if they were hers to claim. She followed his gaze. Lingered on the image of his wife. His type apparent. She was the same complexion as Nadia, her hair a reddish brown, probably from a bottle of Bigen. But where Nadia's eyes photographed hard and stale like week-old bread, Roman's wife glowed with light. She radi-ated in a way Tati had never seen before.

Roman cleared his throat. Told her about his boys first. Roman Jr. and Daniel. They were twenty-seven and twenty-three. He paused before he mentioned his daughter. Faith. "She's eighteen."

"Like me," Tati said.

"Like you." Roman grimaced.

"When is her birthday?"

"February eleventh. When is yours?"

"March twenty-sixth."

"Is that right?" Roman mumbled to himself. With his elbows on the arms of his chair, he steepled his fingers in front of his face as he ran the math. Calculations crisscrossed the smooth terrain of his face like quadratic equations, but all he came up with were probabilities. The possibility that he could in fact have fathered two children, two daughters, with two different women at once.

"What's your wife's name?" Tati asked.

"Deborah."

"Y'all all got names out the Bible?"

"God is the head of our house."

"Then isn't it blasphemy to name your club Worship Haus? This is the furthest place from church as people can get."

"Let's just say I'm a different kind of Bishop." He smirked. "God has his ministry, and I have mine."

"Hmph," Tati grunted, understanding why Mimi didn't like him. She held her chuckle and asked where he and Nadia had met.

"In a club on the South Side," he answered. "I was promoting parties back then."

"Were you married back then too?"

"Deborah and I were separated when I met your mom."

"Did you like her?"

"She was cool. Hard. But cool."

"What does that mean? Hard?"

"I don't know. Just . . . hard. A ballbuster. She ain't take no shit and didn't let people in easily."

"People or just you, a married man?"

"I see you're just like her."

"Is that right?" Tati mocked.

"She used to do that too."

"Because you say it a lot. Even in your emails. It's patronizing."

"Is that right?"

Tati sighed. Silence covered them. Roman didn't offer anything more than the answers to what she asked. He outlined but added no color. Tati gazed back around the room, trying to learn something, anything, but there was no art on his office walls to indicate taste. His space was refined but sparse. The awards and trophies monuments to his ego, the image of his family a testament to his legacy. Tati looked back to the family photo and wondered what it would have been like to visit for weekends and on long school breaks, like Desirée did with Lou, had she not been a secret. Would she have been photographed, smiling in the light, with her father and half siblings, while his wife tried to hide her contempt? Would Deborah's eyes have resembled Nadia's if she'd known?

Tati shook her head and asked after the one answer she'd come for. "Why'd you leave?"

"I'm married. My wife . . . We were going through a rough patch—"

"Couldn't have been that rough."

"She was pregnant—"

"So was my mom."

"I don't know what you want me to do." Roman sighed. "When your mom told me, I hadn't seen her in months. I didn't know if you were really mine."

"Are you trying to say my mama was loose?"

"No." He hesitated.

A pause Tati assumed concealed his real answer. She said, "You were separated from your wife, but you didn't question if Faith was yours?"

"She's my wife."

"And what was my mother?"

Roman paused again.

"She was a friend," he said finally. "Your mother and I were friends."

Tati nodded. Stood. On her side of the office between the door and the chairs, she rubbed her hands against her thighs in an effort to bring life back into them after they'd hung limp along the chair. She looked at everything but Roman. Which wasn't much. She couldn't take how relaxed he appeared. So in control of his comportment despite the flurry of anxiety that whirred through her body, charging every node and neuron in her nervous system.

He said, "So tell me something about yourself."

"I run track." She paused, tried to think of more. "Oh, and my middle name is Merét."

"Your middle name is my mother's name," Roman said quietly.

"I didn't know."

"But she did."

It was Roman's turn to stand. To pace. Tati had finally made him uncomfortable in his own space, his Worship Haus changed from heaven to hell. Tati sat back down and watched him walk. She watched as memories flooded his mind the same way they did Nadia's. On good days, she allowed her mind to go off into a distance to retrieve a smile and a burnished glow flecked with red and gold of a bittersweet happiness she only deigned to taste. Tati watched as Roman's eyes opened wider. He faced the filing cabinets and stared at the family picture. He looked between it and Tati before he turned the frame photo-side down.

"I always knew this day would come," he said.

"So you always knew I was yours?"

His back still turned, he bobbed his head yes.

"Then why'd you leave? Why didn't you claim me?"

"I was married. I *am* married. What was I supposed to do?"

"Stay!"

Tati stood and leaned against the filing cabinets on the opposite wall. A face-off of familial proportions, but she couldn't help but notice their similarities. Both of them dressed in black and red. Both of them brown-skinned. Both of them tall. Height and color she got from him, as neither Mimi nor Nadia surpassed five five, and Nadia was only as brown as a paper bag. She chewed her cheek. He bit down on the inside of his lip until it bled.

"I don't know what you want from me." He paused. "I mean . . . it seems like you turned out all right."

"No thanks to you."

"Like I said, I don't know what you want from me. Just because your mama gave you my mother's name doesn't mean anything. It's not like we've had a test done."

"Really?" Tati was incredulous. She felt the stings but blinked them back.

Roman continued, "All I know is what you've said. What she said. That don't mean anything. Women lie all the time."

"Now my mother's a liar?"

"I'm not saying that—"

"Then what are you saying?"

"I'm saying you too old to be barking up the daddy tree. You grown. Live your life. Forget about me. I . . ."

He didn't finish his sentence. He didn't have to, but Tati still didn't understand. How could he not wonder, not dream, about her the same way she did him? For someone who said he'd known the day would come for his bastard baby to return kicking and scream- ing like the brat she was, he surely didn't act like it.

"So that's it?" she asked. "That's all I get?"

"What else were you looking for?"

"An explanation. An apology. For you to blame my mom and say she kept you away from me. Something."

He shrugged with both shoulders and both hands. An *I'm sorry for being a disappointment* stance. All Tati recognized was the *sorry.* The word, not the regret or grief behind it. She finally un- derstood why on Saturdays in the shop, most of the women, while under Nadia's hands, went on about sorry-ass, triflin'-ass, good-for- nothin'-ass men—when they were being kind. Niggas when they'd been done cruel. Tati had been hearing all her life about men like Roman, thinking he'd be the exception to the rule of lived experience. She should've listened more to the women when they asked amongst themselves, *Who hasn't loved a sorry man?* If she had, she would have known that every woman had loved at least one in her lifetime: husband, fiancé, boyfriend, brother, or daddy, it was all the same and she was no exception.

"I'm married," Roman said again.

It was in answer to her question, yes, but also an excuse for his sorriness. His triflinity. As if matrimony were a bandage for his ways outside of wedlock. Sutures that never showed the gaps in his story.

"Where's your wife now?" Tati asked. "Shouldn't she be here?"

"My God, you sound just like your mother."

"Oh, so you do remember her."

"I never said I forgot."

"How could you when she and your wife look alike? Is that why you fucked my mom? Because she reminded you of Deborah?"

Roman walked to the door as Tati seethed in her own anger. It caught her off guard. Leapt before she ever felt it rise.

"Like I said"—Roman turned the handle—"I don't know what you expect."

"I want to know why you left me."

"I didn't leave you. I left your mother."

"I wasn't born."

He smirked. "You weren't born and I didn't want you. She did! *That's* why you're here."

"And is that why you weren't?"

"Tatiana, whatever it is you're looking for, it ain't here."

She walked through the open door. Between the pallets of items shrink-wrapped for storage, she stopped. "Does your wife know about me?" Tati asked. "About me and Mama?"

"No," Roman answered.

"You've been keeping us a secret for eighteen years."

"And you'll be a secret for eighteen more if I have anything to do with it."

His honesty gave Tati in one bowl what Nadia had been trying to spoon-feed her for years. Roman wasn't shit, and therefore Nadia was enough. It was the only thought Tati could hold on to. What she'd thought she had to know for herself, she didn't need after all. After all this time she finally understood Nadia's demand for validation. She too had been rejected. She too had made a choice in spite of her circumstances, and she hadn't run when she'd had the opportunity to do so.

"So that's it?" Tati asked.

"What else did you expect?"

"Not this," she answered. She walked to the stairwell and down to the main floor of the empty club. "There's just one thing I don't understand," she said, stopping in the middle.

"What's that?"

"Why'd you say you knew this day would come if you don't even believe me or Mama that I'm yours?"

"Who said I didn't believe you?"

"You never said you did."

Roman, again, ran his hand from the back of his head over his hair and face like he was changing theater masks. His sleepy, squinting eyes opened wider and hardened, as did all the muscles in his face.

He said, "Just because life-changing shit happens doesn't mean you have to change your life. Your mama knew where I stood. She let that shit happen to her. I ain't lettin' it happen to me."

"By 'that shit,' you mean me?"

"If that's how you take it, then that's how you take it. You've seen my priorities. It's time you and your mama go find your own."

Tati let the echo of her footfalls in her boots answer for her. She crossed the club to the door and pushed into the cold. It dried the stings in her eyes. The ones she didn't let fall in front of him. The ones he was never worthy of to begin with. Inside Nadia's car, Tati drove away from the club as the Worship Haus sign illuminated the darkness. The red neon letters took up two stories, covering the sanctuary and the confessional, blaspheming for blocks the ways of the false bishop inside.

21.

The smell of pressed hair hit Tati as soon as she opened the back door. Nadia had taken clients for most of the day, getting their hair together to ring in the new year. She'd even offered to do Tati's. An offer Tati had declined. She hadn't wanted Nadia to try to talk her out of going to meet Roman. A decision she had to add to her regret of having met him at all.

"Tati, that you?" Nadia called from the basement.

"Yeah."

"You comin' down?"

"Gimme a minute."

Tati crept upstairs to her room and pulled out the notebook she still kept tucked between the mattress and box spring. Inside, all her old words jumped out at her. All her *Dear Daddy* and *Dear Roman* entries from when she didn't know any better. She ripped them out one by one until the metal spirals that kept the notebook together were bent out of shape and all that remained were blanks.

Dear Mama,

> *You were right.*
> *He beat me with his words*
> *And they hurt worse than the sting of any belt.*
> *The crack of any whip.*

The cut of any cane.
The welt
Bubbled with blood
Pooled with pus
Was invisible to every eye but my own
I was thrown
For a loop by his audacity
I was his shame
But for me you became
Everything I needed
And even things I didn't
Overbearing, overprotective, and distant
I don't understand why you guard your heart from me
But I know there's a reason
Even if I can't see it in this season
I know now there's always a need for secrets

Love Tati
December 31, 1999

On her way downstairs, Tati tossed the sheets of paper she'd ripped from her notebook into the burning fireplace. The radio announcer's voice greeted her as she entered the basement.

It's eleven o'clock, and we are live from Chicago's hottest, newest nightclub, Worship Haus Chicago. It's crazy out here. If you ain't left the house yet, you can forget about it, because the line is thiccckkk. Mike Love and the Diz will join us soon to get this party started as we bring in the new year. You're listening to Chicago's number one station for hip-hop and R&B. Live from Worship Haus Chicago for the ninety-nine and the two thousands.

"Please turn that off?" Tati collapsed on the futon as the chords of Juvenile's "Back That Thang Up" came through the speaker.

"What's wrong with you?" Nadia asked.

She turned around to face Tati. A flat iron in one hand, her hair sectioned and parted, she began straightening the strands at the nape of her neck.

"They're live from Roman's club."

"I know. How'd it go?"

"It went."

Nadia grunted. "You've had us worked up over this mess since Thanksgiving, and now you can't bear to hear the radio broadcasting from his club? You might as well tell me what happened."

"He basically said you made your choices and he made his."

"That's it?" Nadia asked, standing up straight. She held the flat iron less than an inch from the skin of her neck.

Tati shrugged. "He said I was too old to be barking up the daddy tree."

"Shit!" Nadia released the flat iron and set it to the side. "I'm sorry, Tati." Her knees cracked as she sat in her chair. "I know this is not the way you wanted things to go."

"I didn't have any expectations."

"Yes, you did. You always have."

Under the recessed lights of the basement, Tati watched as Nadia's blank gaze softened. Everything that she'd kept to herself was out in the open. The hardness she'd held was broken apart. The entombed tumor of her past removed. Nadia met Tati's gaze with her own knowing look. They were women, together, not just mother and daughter, parent and child.

"We weren't together very long. Only a few months. I met him when I was still trying to figure out what I wanted to do with my life after I dropped out of school."

"I didn't know that."

"There's a lot of things you don't know, Tati, but that's another conversation. Anyway, he and his wife weren't together at the time. I knew better. But . . ."

Nadia shrugged. Tati nodded. There was nothing left to explain. Nothing to apologize for. Nothing that could be changed. What happened, happened.

"He had a way of making me feel like I knew him. He was good at making me feel like I was wanted when he didn't wanna have shit to do with me. Not in the end."

Tati recognized the pattern. The emails, the willingness to meet, the direct answers to her questions followed by the rejection. His rebuke had been on replay in her mind.

You've seen my priorities. It's time you and your mama find your own.

Nadia stood from her chair.

"You goin' outside?" Tati asked.

"Nah," she said, sitting back down. "Not tonight. It's past time I start tryna quit."

"Never thought I'd hear you say that."

"I didn't start smoking 'til I was pregnant with you," she said, looking down at her hands.

"Mama!"

"What? I'm being honest. Isn't that what you lookin' for?" She shrugged. "It reminded me of him . . . Later . . . it helped me forget about how hard it was being a young single mother. Whether I was raising you right. Whether I made the right decision."

Nadia didn't specify the decision but Tati knew. Her birth was less than ideal. It was a choice that she was alive. Nadia's choice to birth, to raise, to love. Active in every step. A daily acceptance. She met Tati's gaze, eyes wet but full with life and not a hint of regret. She said, "It's time to put that cross down. For good. Like I should have a long time ago."

Nadia pressed the sides of her face with her fingers to dry the eye stings that had escaped. Standing, she returned to her station and picked up the flat iron from the burgundy towel where it rested.

"Whatchu 'bout to do?" Tati asked.

Nadia clicked the plates. "What it look like? You see my head is a mess."

"I didn't notice."

Tati smirked as she stood up from the futon. She approached Nadia and took the flat iron from her.

"Tati, what the hell! What are you doin'?"

"I'm about to do your hair."

"Is that right?"

They both laughed. The sound twinkled around them, joyous in their relief, boisterous with freedom. Each of them liberated in their own way.

"C'mon, Mama, sit down," Tati said.

She bumped Nadia's hip with her own to get her to move out of the way and sit in the chair, then followed the steps she'd seen Nadia do for years. She tied the barber paper around Nadia's neck and whipped the cape over her body.

"Oh, you for real?" Nadia said.

"I told you, I got you."

Tati took over the station. She checked the temperature of the flat iron and placed the hot comb in the electric stove to heat up to hit Nadia's edges when it was time. Tati pulled the rattail comb from where it was stuck in Nadia's head and let her blow-dried pouf of a mane fall down to her shoulders.

"You ready?" Tati asked.

"I should be asking you the same thing," Nadia said. "Make sure you got that oil for my scalp."

"I got it."

Nadia released herself to the salon experience. She closed her eyes and relaxed her neck, a rag doll as Tati's hands plunged into her hair and massaged her scalp. Tati's fingers raked through the locks from roots to ends before she began to part rows and sections for straightening. Without music, the basement had never been so quiet. Aside from the fireworks going off outside in the neighborhood, the only sounds were their breathing and the sizzling of the irons until they heard a click at the door and a turn of the lock.

"Who is that?" Tati asked.

"Probably your mimi. I gave her a key when you left for school."

"You told her, didn't you?"

"Told me what?" Gladys asked as her short heels clopped on the concrete floor.

"Mama, what're you doing here?" Nadia asked.

"Yeah, I thought you were going to Watch Night at church to wait for the Rapture." Tati smirked.

"If the Lord is coming, I'm sure he'll know where to find me," Gladys said. She set the book she was carrying down on the futon as she took off her coat and gently removed her scarf from where it covered her hair. "Besides," she continued, "if I do go, I wanna go free."

"What do you mean?" Tati and Nadia asked together.

Gladys grabbed the book. "Tati, here, once asked me about the names in this Bible."

"I used to ask you about the names in that Bible," Nadia reminded.

"Okay. Well, y'all both asked me. Do you wanna know about 'em or not?"

"New Year's Eve is the day you wanna tell us about our family tree?" Tati rolled her eyes.

"You already found one good-for-nothing branch that needs to be sheared, might as well find the vine that's fruitful," Gladys said.

"Mama, not tonight," Nadia said.

"I ain't here to talk about him." Gladys looked from Tati to

Nadia, her eyes warm and face soft. They had never heard Gladys sound so gentle. As if she remembered the moment she too needed tenderness. Despite their differences and all their bickering in this moment, they were on one accord. Agreed in the ways of women with experience. She continued, "What's going on with Tati made me remember some of the stories I've heard."

"Like what?" Tati asked.

Gladys closed the distance between the three of them. She set the Bible with the cracked spine and fragile, gold-rimmed pages in Nadia's lap and opened it slowly to the page of names. Nadia and Tati both pored closely over the names, written in a thick black ink they knew hadn't come from a regular pen.

"Why's that one scratched out?" Tati pointed to a space that had been struck through and blotted. As if whoever's name had been written was never supposed to be known.

"I don't know. This Bible belonged to my great-grandmother, Emma. You see her name there." Gladys pointed to the top of the page, where the names began. "I called her Mama Em. She was born enslaved. Daughter of the owner."

"Really?!" Tati exclaimed.

"Mama, you wanna talk about slavery now?" Nadia asked. "On New Year's Eve?"

"If I don't tell you, you ain't never gon' know. And if the Y2K coming for us—"

Gladys sighed and shook her head. She left them with the Bible and crossed back over to the futon. Rocking on the cushion, she stared past Tati and Nadia to the steam rising from the hair stove as if she were trying to decipher code. "They cut off her head because she ran," Gladys said. "That's what Mama Em used to mutter."

Nadia looked up from the Bible. "What does that mean?"

"It's why I never took you back to Land's End. Only once when you were a little girl. It's the reason you don't remember."

"What are you talking about?"

"Whose head?"

"When you find all this out?"

"Why you telling us now?"

Tati and Nadia peppered her with questions, but Gladys didn't answer. She stared at the steam and watched the girl dance in the smoke, legs and feet lifted from the ground and hands spread, arms akimbo in the air. She watched her with joy before she recounted the pain. Like Ruby, Jubi, and Emma before her, Gladys was overcome by the spirit. She'd have sworn on the Bible that belonged to her mothers that she'd heard a voice say, clear as day, *Go*, while she was standing in the church pew, singing from the hymnal, waiting to see what the end was gon' be. Without thought she'd followed the instructions that burned on her heart. She'd gone home, gotten her Bible, then driven to Nadia's to give them the truth. They had thirty minutes until midnight. She figured that was enough time to give them the gospel. A testament of their own family. But she had not the voice for the words. All she could do was rock and stare as the girl danced in the steam. All she could do was repeat the legend she didn't even know herself to be true while Tati and Nadia asked for answers.

When Gladys finally found her voice, dry and gravelly, it was two minutes after midnight. With her soul still sound in her body, she told Tati and Nadia the story that had been told to her.

Not that it was much, for she'd heard it secondhand from Jubi, who'd heard it secondhand from Emma, who'd never gotten it straight from Evangeline.

Part 4

The Beginning

22.

If you must know . . . it began in the barracoon.

That's what she would have said if she could have told her own story.

It began in the barracoon and continued on the ship. Plucked as she was away from the pack of captives marched for miles over a month or more across the continent to the coast. Instead of staying in the bottom, she was pulled away, prodded with the butt of a gun out of the dungeon and up to a room where a white man waited. Though the air was clearer, not as thick with the stench of shit and blood or filled with the mourning wails of women and children, it still trembled with its own kind of terror. To stand as one before a pale face without the comfort of closeness to others of her kind instilled in her a fright she couldn't name. The scream she felt climb from the turmoil tossing her belly caught in her throat. So she stood by the closed door, unmoving, watching the candlelight flicker. She wished the fire were closer, bigger, big enough to consume her on the spot and take her away from this hell she'd been forced to enter.

He sat on the small bed in the spacious room. The captain's quarters. It had a window looking out over the coast. The salty air blew in on a breeze, but all was black. The ocean, the sky, the room, her skin. She was the oldest of the young ones. Her hips were still narrow and stomach taut. Supple breasts stood instead of hung. But she'd had more than one blood. He could tell from the streaks he saw crusted and dried on her legs when she was brought in. She was old enough to bed, but young enough not to know better. He'd chosen her because he believed she would be compliant on the first try. But even if she wasn't, he knew how to make her malleable. The cat was wound on a wooden chair near the window, its barbed, biting tails sleeping like a rattlesnake turned in on itself.

Sitting on the bed in his full shirt, which doubled as a dressing gown, his trousers with suspenders and boots cast off to the side, he held out his hand. The gesture did not inspire forward motion. She recoiled farther into the corner. Wedged herself between the door and the bureau.

"You don't have to be afraid of me," he said.

His voice was flat and nasal. It held none of the musicality she was used to hearing when people spoke. No clicks or intonations. Everything even and without distinction of place. The adapted cadence of a man with no home. She had heard tell of the white man before. The pale-faced people who'd come first with gifts, then their God, and finally their guns. In the village where she'd lived, the first daughter of a second wife, she had listened to the stories while braiding baskets as her mother braided her hair with seeds and shells. She knew the pale faces supplied the raiders from rival tribes and kingdoms with weapons. Enabled them to capture and conquer as they rode through the night, setting fire to everything, taking until their coffers were full of yam and their coffles of connected people sold into horrors unknown. Now she was amongst them. A prisoner of the pale-faced man who held out his hand.

He brought it to his chest and laid it flat against his skin. "Master Z.F.," he said slowly.

He punctuated each word by slapping his hand against his chest, overenunciating and exaggerating the shape of his mouth.

She heard the screams from the levels below. They were not muted or muffled. The voices weren't tired of begging. Yet here he was pretending as if he did not hear. Or maybe he was merely used to the cacophony of captives clamoring against their gates for attention. For favor. For a chance at a way out. Standing, listening, she knew she preferred being where she was than amongst the many, but that didn't mean she too didn't crave escape.

He repeated himself with his slow, thick tongue she knew was for her benefit. He thought her dense, if he thought anything at all, patting his chest as he repeated the same sounds, "Z.F., Z.F., Z.F."

She repeated the chant back to him, and he smiled, wide and garish, revealing teeth rotten at the root. With his large hands, he patted his chest again and said, "Master Z.F.," then pointed to her. Understanding he wanted her name, she answered. All he heard was a mumble. He tried twice more, and each time she mimicked his tone and copied the exaggeration of his facial muscles to make her enunciation. But in his mouth, he garbled her mother tongue, jumbling the sounds.

Zephaniah Foster pursed his lips and glared with cold eyes. She registered the resignation in his countenance. The give-up in trying to be hospitable. In keeping up the charade that he was courting and not keeping.

He said, "Sarah," with renewed confidence. "I'm going to call you Sarah. It's easier for me than the bush babble you were born with."

Named anew, she remained rooted where she was listening to the screams below. Zephaniah Foster stood from the bed and closed the distance between them. Taking her by the hand, he pulled her to him, covering her face with his lips. Sarah(?) pushed against him, scratching at his skin, and tugged his ears away from her own. He smelled heavily of his own musk and tasted of bitter ale and the decay coming from his mouth. She broke free of his embrace but had nowhere to run.

Zephaniah Foster recognized the wild look in her eyes. The flight response triggered by fear. He'd seen it in every captive he'd ever carried on any ship he captained, but eventually it was extinguished. Lights behind the eyes dimmed and eyelids hooded dark pupils with despair. Very few kept their feral ways after weeks or months in the dungeons and even more months in the hold of the ship. *She's just a girl*, he thought to himself, knowing he would break her, spirit and body; it didn't matter which came first.

He touched the spot on his cheek where she'd dug her nails and felt the damp from droplets of blood. The realization brought a twisted smile to his face. She thought he looked like a gnarled and mangled tree, one that had shrunken in on itself, close to the ground, all angles and elbows instead of long-limbed branches that reached for the sky and beyond. As she studied his face in the moment, she didn't see his hand rise, only felt the sting of the slap and the flow of blood from her nose. The blow sent her backward into the bed behind her.

Zephaniah Foster let no time pass taking advantage of her downed defenses. He grabbed her legs and dragged her to him. Turning her over on the bed, he gathered her mid-back-length braids where they hung free at the base of her neck. She struggled until he held her in a headlock and with one free hand roamed her body, taking from her what he wanted for himself. He grunted and pounded; he the pestle, her body the plantain smashed in the mortar. Torn through and snapped in two, she shrieked and screamed on the bed, became one of the wailing. She bit his thumb when he tried to cover her mouth. Gagged for air when he choked her. She clawed at the sheets, kicked her feet against his thighs, thrashed and bucked her body, made every attempt to fight him off. But he held until he was breathless and she was still. Then he pushed her from the bed to the floor, where she collapsed in a heap of herself.

Sarah(?) rolled so that she was closer to the bureau, away from the bed, and folded into the fetal position. She tried to hide herself but could barely move. Her body held the memory of his hands pulling, grabbing, tugging, choking, slapping, beating. Somehow sleep found her, but she lived her own nightmares. Endless days, endless nights, of the same. In the room, on the ship, until finally there was land.

THE OTHERS WERE PULLED OUT OF THE HOLD FIRST. MARCHED into daylight, a bucket of cold seawater thrown across their dirty, ashen, and gaunt bodies. Some screamed from the shock, others from the sting, salt in the wounds of the sores that had been ripped into their skin, either from the cat or the creeping of disease they'd been festering in during the voyage.

They were barely able to walk under their own weight, but cries of relief erupted from them all the same as they set foot on the sugar-sand shore, where more pale faces waited. Bound together, arms and feet, they shuffled up the bank through the sand and into the marsh, tripping over roots and felled swamp trees. Tall grass hid their bodies, but nothing could cover the sound of their voices. Timbres and trebles of rejoicing song devolved into wearied weeps with the understanding that, no, they had not returned home.

Sarah(?) was the last to leave the ship. Naked, she followed behind Zephaniah Foster. He carried her long, loose leash in one hand and the cat in the other. He figured there was a difference in walking out under your own power and of your own volition or being marched out, chained and coffered, with a whip at your back. There was no whip at his back. It was in his hand, and he hoped she felt it just the same. The menacing threat to stamp out the wildness that still lived within her. It lived in them all. Especially on land. He'd seen it before: a whole shipment turn back toward the sea, running into the surf, openly inviting death. Bodies that didn't drown bloated, floated, and beached themselves along the sand. That's when he'd had the job of hiding the evidence. He'd burned the bodies and he'd burned the ships to keep from getting caught by the maritime patrols appointed in the North and sent south, as if they knew the cost to keep the country afloat. Breeding couldn't replace the import business, ban be damned.

No longer a burn boy, but a captain, Zephaniah Foster walked with the prize he kept for himself, all the way to his land, where his wife, Elizabeth, waited, mistress in his stead.

"This the new negress who's going to tend to our house?" she asked.

Zephaniah Foster nodded his head. "Yes."

"What's her name?"

"I called her Sarah."

"Well, send her over to Evangeline to get cleaned and clothed before she sets foot in my house."

Elizabeth walked back toward the house made of white paneled wood. Her long dress, the color of a wilted rose, flowed about her despite the heat. Sarah(?), still loosely leashed to Zephaniah Foster, looked around the expanse of the land. The rows and rows of crops being tended; cotton bolls in full bloom. The scores of bodies that looked like her own dotted across the rows with rucksacks across their backs.

Zephaniah Foster gave a tug and Sarah(?) followed. They walked toward the house and then behind it, where the shanties were erected, all wood-roofed and -sided, with dirt for floors. In front of the first one, he stopped and hollered inside.

"Evangeline!" he called, gruff and insistent. "Evangeline! The new negress is here and needs cleaning before she tends to the missus."

Evangeline, round and wide, emerged from the interior, a naked baby bouncing in each arm. She shifted their weight as she assessed the girl before her.

"What's her name, sir?"

"Sarah." He spat, dropped the leash, and walked away.

Evangeline and Sarah(?) stood still as Zephaniah Foster made his way back toward his house, the cat coiled in his grip. It wasn't until he'd gone up the back steps, leaving his dirty, mucky boots on the porch, and the screen door clanged behind him that either one of them seemed to breathe. Even the babies had switched to shallow inhales in his presence.

"C'mon in here, chile," Evangeline said, once he was gone.

Evangeline turned on her heels and disappeared into the dark. Sarah(?) had no choice but to follow. Bound as she was, she shuffled her feet through the tangle of rope left on the ground in front of her until she crossed the threshold into the shanty. She blinked rapidly, her eyes adjusting to the lack of light. As they did, her nose picked up the smell of herbs and flowers. Sarah(?) looked around the room to the pallet where Evangeline laid the two babies.

"I takes care of the babies and the mammies when they birthing," Evangeline began. "It's been that way since me and my husband's own babies never did live."

Evangeline talked as she maneuvered around the shanty, grabbing a pail and filling it with two cups of fresh water from a larger bucket.

"I either started bleeding early or they born too early and couldn't make it past a few breaths. It was all I wanted to give Henry chillun. He had plenty on the plantation, but I was his only wife. We jumped de broom one Sunday right in front of that door you came through, and then Henry turn around Monday morning and used that same broom to sweep the stables. Massa used his youth up good with the bucking. Was his own personal stud horse, until he sent him to the stables to break actual horses, but his real love was carving. He could make anything outta wood. Would whittle away in the dark and leave me something nice in the morning like this here table and chair. It didn't last long, tho'. My Henry went on over to the other side last year. He took a kick to the head from one of the mares and then the illness. Nothing I made for him could help him. Truth is he ain't wanna be helped. All his children sold or dead, it's enough to make anybody wanna meet 'em in the ground. Massa doctor blamed the 'sumption. But I knows it was the grief."

Evangeline set a corner of soap and a rag with frayed edges on the small round table beside the water bowl and a smattering of different leaves and buds.

"Let's get you washed up," she said.

Sarah(?) held up her hands, which were still bound together. Evangeline untied the knots until she was free. "I'll let you do your bidness."

She gathered the ropes that held Sarah(?) captive and took them outside. Sarah(?) followed the sound of her voice from the entrance of the shanty to directly behind it, where she heard singing that nearly covered the sound of the ropes being beaten against the ground. When the thrashing stopped, Evangeline's song changed and got louder, as smoke crept from behind the house into its interior.

Sarah(?) recognized something familiar in Evangeline's voice. It held the melodic notes she was used to and contained none of the flat, nasal dialect the pale-faced man used. Briefly comforted, Sarah(?) grabbed the soap and rag from the table where Evangeline left it, dipped it in the shallow water, and soaped herself until her own skin was raw from the rough material.

When Evangeline reappeared, she was carrying a dress. She said, "This here from the big house. From Missus Elizabeth. Her old maid gone on over to the other side and she ain't wanna wait for none of the young girl chillun to grow up. Had Master Foster go and find you special. Said she figured waiting a few months better than waiting a few years."

Evangeline laid the burgundy dress with its white apron on the table in front of Sarah(?). "Go'n get dressed now."

Sarah(?) registered the urgency in her voice despite the warmth of her tone and stepped tentatively toward the dress. She traced the fabric with her fingers, palming the lace appliqués on the apron and thumbing the soft material that looked nothing like the rough-hewn garments she'd seen the people outside draped in.

"You need help puttin' it on?" Evangeline asked.

Sarah(?) stared with the full moons of her eyes blank and nearly black. Evangeline slowly closed the distance between them, approached with her hands up, the same way people instinctively back away from threats. With no common tongue between them, Evangeline could only act on instinct and what she knew the outcome was supposed to be. She held the dress open for Sarah(?) to step into the bloomers sewn inside. One foot at a time, Sarah(?) put on her new identity. No longer the first daughter of a second wife in her village, she was now Sarah(?).

"Sah-rah," she mumbled to herself.

She tried to make her mouth fit around the syllables. To imitate Zephaniah Foster's speech and inflection when he'd kept calling the word and looking in her direction every time he said it.

"Sah-rah," she said again.

"Yes, chile," Evangeline answered. "Yo' name Sarah now."

She stepped away from her, smiling slightly. "You look fine," she said. "The blackest thing to enter the big house this side the 'lantic Ocean, but missus wanted a new girl and here you is. Now what we gon' do 'bout this head?"

Evangeline reached for her hair, but Sarah(?) recoiled from her touch. Evangeline reached again. Sarah(?) backed away until she was flush against the opposite wall.

"Mm-hmm," Evangeline humphed. "You one of them believe in superstitions. In haints and higes, duppies and the dead come back to life. I can always tell when Massa Foster come back with one o' you from across the water. Y'all believe the haunt starts on the head. I ain't gon' hurt it or trouble you none. Just wanna take it down."

Evangeline held up her hands and turned them back and forth.

Seeing her hands empty and uncoated, Sarah(?) slowly stepped forward. Ambling over to the pallet where the babes lay, Evangeline lowered herself onto the covered thatch and opened her knees for Sarah(?) to sit between.

"I'se just gon' take it down," she said.

Sarah(?), towering over Evangeline's seated frame, slowly lowered herself to the ground. Evangeline grabbed the tail of one braid and used her broken nails to unravel the matted hair. As she did, the seeds and shells braided between strands fell in her own aproned lap.

"I reckon we got to see what you done brought us here," Evangeline said, a chuckle undisguised in her throat.

Sarah(?) leaned against the fat of Evangeline's belly as she worked her way through her head, unraveling braids, collecting carry-ons, and cleansing the strands. Using the same soap and water, Evangeline scrubbed the girl's scalp, sullying her new dress only a little, until her hair, springy, thick, and long, stood all over her head.

"I can do it for you," Evangeline said, using her hands to brush Sarah(?)'s hair together.

Sarah(?) pushed away until she sat face-to-face with the woman. She opened her eyes to their full height and width to keep Evangeline's attention. The older woman nodded her understanding. Sarah(?) lifted her hands as she tilted her head and closed her eyes. She parted her hair with her own chipped and ragged nails and began to braid a section as she imagined her own mother doing before the battle in the village and the raid they were captured in. Part for part, she imagined it was straw grass or the hair of one of her sisters she was braiding instead of her own, until she reached the end. No more hair to grab, Sarah(?) set her working hands in her lap and opened her eyes.

"It's some beautiful," Evangeline said, "but we can't let the missus sees you like that."

She planted her feet and hands on the ground and hoisted herself upright. Evangeline untied the white rag fastened on her own head and let it unfurl to the floor. Holding it in the middle, she ripped it in half and gave a strip to Sarah(?). As Evangeline retied her scarf, covering her own plaited hair, Sarah(?) wrapped the strip around her head until all her braids were covered and her ends were tucked beneath the cloth.

"You'll do right fine," Evangeline said when she was done. "C'mon, let's get you over to the big house. The missus don't like waiting for nothing. She gon' call on you day and night, and you got to answer her. Especially once Massa make you big."

Evangeline prattled on with instructions Sarah(?) didn't understand as they walked from the shack into the bright sun of the day up to the back porch of the white house, where Zephaniah Foster had gone inside.

"One more thing," she said, giving Sarah(?)'s shoulder a squeeze. "No matter what happens in there"—she pointed—"you come back here wit' us at night. Ya hear me? Us." Evangeline motioned between their bodies. "We belongs to each other now."

23.

War.

    Run.

Those were the two words Sarah(?) knew best. She had counted five full moons since she had arrived. Which meant it had been at least eight or nine since the raid. In all that time away from home, her village, her family, her land, she had begun to pick up on the ways and words of the people around her. In the house, where she worked cleaning and tending to Missus Elizabeth in the day and being broken open by Zephaniah Foster at night, the word *war* was present all the time. It was loud, said proudly, spoken with a certainty, especially after the secession. For the pale faces who lived in and those who visited the house, war was a foregone conclusion. A matter of when, not if.

But it was the other word that intrigued Sarah(?) most.

    Run.

In the evening, when the work was done and she was able to lie down for a mite in her own shanty, before Zephaniah came sweaty and searching though she was getting big with his child, she heard the whispers rolling through the quarters like a wave of fire.

    Run.

The word burned every tongue. Singed the inside of the mouths of those who held it and ran laps around the minds of those who'd dare think it. It too was loud, but in a quiet way.

When Sarah(?) first heard it, it had to have been a Sunday evening. The one day when they were not bound to the barriers of the fields, and she to the house, from cain't see to cain't see. It was the only time they were allowed to gather together near the marsh—on the side that butted up to the plantation, not the ocean—and hear tell from Gordon, the designated preacher, the word of God; Father, Son, and Holy Spirit.

Sarah(?) had heard of the pale-faced people's three-faced God before. Those stories too had floated around her village, but they'd not been as fiery as they were here. They hadn't held the people rapt in attention and sent them to dancing and shaking and running though there was no drum. But in one of those gatherings, Gordon the Preacher kept repeating, "Whom the son sets free is free indeed." Then the women would sing, not a whole song, but one with the same line repeated over and over. "Steal away, steal away." Sarah(?) learned those words too. Learned to hum the melody while she worked, though she had yet to learn what it meant.

Until one day down by the marsh, where she sat upon a wet log, resting from the baby thumping her skin from the inside, and saw Gordon the Preacher and some others huddled together, tracing their fingers in the dirt. By that time, the people around her were waiting for her weight to drop. Those who'd been around long enough knew it was Zephaniah's custom to make big the nigras he brought back from across the water. It was his way of breaking. How he anchored them in place and removed the wildness all at once.

Even Missus Elizabeth didn't mind the handful of half-breeds running around with features like their father, long as she didn't have to worry about waking up one morning on her own because her maid or the boy who emptied her chamber pot had run. It was brutal business to try and find and bring them back. Zephaniah Foster and the brood of bounty hunters he kept on call employed the dogs, the guns, the whips, the chains, and sometimes a brand, an ax, or even a saw, all in an effort to keep them in place. He learned early to stop bringing nigra boys and men from the ship. It didn't matter how often their bodies were broken open, red and pulpy, or stretched from hanging by hands or feet, their spirits never ceased.

He figured Sarah(?) would be like the other mothers bought and brought over time. Resigned to stay because of the first babe and then bred to have as many as she could carry. One a year if they timed it right; one every other if the seasons were off. But those other mothers hadn't come when Sarah(?) came. They hadn't heard the words Sarah(?) learned.

War.

Run.

So as the sun set, and the men who milled around in the dirt began to disperse, Sarah(?) hoisted herself from where she rested and followed them at a distance back to the quarter. They didn't disappear, each into their own shanty, where sometimes women and children were waiting for their return, but they went into a shack that had been left empty after old man Joseph had died.

Approaching the door, Sarah(?) reached down, grabbed some of the thin gray dirt, and tossed it over her shoulder before she crept across the threshold. Gordon the Preacher and the other men were bent down, huddled in a semicircle marking on the ground. A stubby candle provided the only light. She watched from behind as they drew the same set of lines and circles over and over. One would draw and then another would kick it over with his foot and then the other would draw and another would kick it over with his foot or mess it with his hand and that one would draw. Silent, intent, Sarah(?) watched each man commit the image to memory until their hands could maneuver while their eyes were closed and their mind could see their destination.

"We got it," Gordon the Preacher said, standing.

Upright the six men stood, shifting more than just their stature.

At their full height, Sarah(?) sensed something else lift with them. She'd sensed it before. Before the water, before the ship, before the barracoon. It was the air of the men in her village before the raid. Before their capture. When they wore confidence. Now it wore these men despite their lack of weapons or training. The confidence was in their hands, in their eyes, in what they could remember to write upon the ground to right their way.

"After work, on the equal night, we run."

Sarah(?) said, "I go too."

The men turned around. They hadn't felt her presence in the door or even noticed her at the marsh. Twelve eyes fell to her belly poking through her dress.

Gordon the Preacher said, "No."

"Women only slow us down."

"Woman big as you is get us caught."

"Massa and Missus be looking for you early. Be on our trail befo' they s'posed to know we gone."

"No."

"No."

They gave her rejections. Reasons why she was not invited. But Sarah(?) persisted.

"I go too," she said, pushing through their huddle. In the center of the semicircle where they'd been drawing on the ground, Sarah(?) reached her hands up to her rag-covered head and removed the wrap. Her hair fell loose about her shoulders, fresh from the washing Evangeline had given it earlier in the day. Closing her eyes, she hummed the melody of the song the women sang, the refrain that told the men it was time to go.

They watched as her fingers moved furiously through the humidity-tangled tresses, crudely creating the course she remembered. Through her bush of curls she braided into order the same lines and circles they had spent months learning to draw upon the ground. There on her head she connected the straight and narrow paths with the roundabouts and the zigzag trail to the rivers they'd follow until they were forced to stay on land, going from house to house, looking for a friend of a friend.

What should have taken hours took minutes, but even in her rough iteration she was sure of its truth. When she finished and dropped her hands, the men gathered behind her and looked at her head. One even reached his finger and traced the path she'd plotted upon her scalp. Sarah(?) didn't flinch. She didn't shy away from the strange hand as she should have. As she had always been warned and wont to do. The desire beating within her was too strong. It called forth the same as the djembe. It was greater even than the kicks of the baby burrowing its head down beneath her belly.

"She got one," Clarence said.

Gordon the Preacher pushed past them all and examined her hair himself. He followed the plaited paths distinguishing south from north, all they were leaving behind and all they were hurrying toward. Reaching for her shoulder, he turned her around to face him eye to eye. Sarah(?) sensed his defeat just as she sensed their collective confidence. They thought she was broken because she was big. They didn't understand that she had been born free. There was no anchor or attachment, at least not yet, and before it dropped, she planned to be free again. She knew the word *run*. She knew what it meant. Even spoken in a different language, its brevity and urgency conveyed the same meaning. She had heard it the night of the raid. She had heard it whispered on the march. She had heard it screamed from the bottom of the barracoon. She had seen it in the dash of those who leapt from the ship to the ocean floor. And she had heard it whispered in the rows, in the hushed tones in the house, and muttered over in the marsh. Even when it was different, it was the same in every language.

Run.

Staring at Gordon the Preacher, Sarah(?) nodded her head further, getting him to agreement.

She said, "I go too."

24.

As it would happen, the men couldn't stop Sarah(?) from leaving with them. But that didn't mean they were going to concern themselves with her keeping up. It's something some selfish set down in a man with his mind made up about a plan, and damnit to hell if they let a woman, any woman, even one who could help, get in the way.

The night they were to leave, Sarah(?) met Gordon the Preacher, Clarence, and the other men at the designated spot on the line between the Dupree land and the Lawsons'. Sarah(?) was the second to arrive, her steps slow but methodical. When the others made it to the meetup location shortly after her, their bodies coursed with sweat even as they stood still. Under a moon not stretching to its full potential, the men shifted from foot to foot. They shoved their fists in their pockets and beat their thighs. No one knew the protocol for running. Especially not in a group as big as theirs: seven people—six field hands and a house girl in the family way. Unsure of what to do next, Sarah(?) reached her hand to her head, pulled off the rag covering the map she'd braided into her scalp, and tucked it in her skirt. Gordon the Preacher stepped behind her, looked at the fresh map in her hair, and leapt away.

The others followed, galloping through the thin tree line that separated the Dupree property from the Lawsons' beside them. They stuck to the stands, knowing the rollers would patrol the land with clear-cut paths from carriage wheels. Besides the song of crickets and frogs, the only other sound was their breath and feet. Heart-beats, loud to their own ears, were completely undetectable to the others.

At eight moons, and nearing nine, Sarah(?) trotted as quickly as she could to keep up. Her small feet and round size kept her a yard behind the men, but she kept going, one hand holding underneath her belly to encourage the child to stay awhile. Their steps were her guide, the breaking of branches underfoot, the heaves of air they inhaled to expand their chests and keep going despite the burn they felt from overtaxing their lungs. All they carried were themselves and the few rations they squirreled away in their pockets, while Sarah(?) was saddled with not only supplies but her unborn. The expected anchor she was determined to buoy to freedom. They had a long journey. That she knew. *Canada* was the word they'd said her hair-braided map would take them to. She wasn't sure if it would be farther than when she was marched to the coast, but she had to try, even as big as she was.

Everything hurt. Her ankles and knees were swollen beyond their regular size. Her fingers, also swollen, pulled at the air as she propelled herself forward. They had to get to the water, the bank of the bay, where they would wade until they reached the mouth where the rivers split.

Had this been years earlier, they might've found assistance deep around the river lands from one of the five tribes, the nations, that had lived there long before the pale faces arrived. But they were gone. Remnants of what had been of them were buried in the blood-soaked ground, turned over, mowed down, and planted with cotton.

They ran, she trotted, until the bottoms of their feet burned with each step. Only Sarah(?) had worn shoes around Zephaniah Foster's place, and she had discarded those at the outset of their journey for pinching her already-hurting feet. Feeling the mud between her toes and the sticky sand spurs biting her heels motivated her to keep moving. To keep listening. It was one thing if she pushed her own body to breaking. It was altogether different done at the will and whim of Zephaniah Foster. She ruminated over his taking and the seed he'd sown into her and picked up her pace. Managed for a moment to catch up with Gordon the Preacher, who nodded his own grimaced face.

They were pushing against the darkness, running to beat back the light. Hedging that on the equal night they'd have hours before any cocks crowed or overseers blew the horn for work. The farther north they went, the harder it would be to stave off the day, because the men had heard through whispers and word wanderings that the sun rose on the free people first. The Southern-born and bred in bondage received the last light of the sun's rays and all of its wrath.

But in the midst of running, some longed for what they'd left. The pallets on the dirt floors of their shanties and a guaranteed meal in the morning. The faces of the people they knew, the ones they called kin. It wasn't enough to make them stop, or make them turn, only slow because anything was better than ragged breath, cut feet and arms, and feeling like your heart was about to jump out of your chest. In those slowing steps of doubt, they had to name their goal.

Freedom.

Reinforce for their own sanity what it was that they were doing.

Running for freedom.

The song, "Don't Let Nobody Turn You 'Round," began as a mumble in their mouths.

Though they couldn't sing and refrained from humming, they chanted in time and tune beneath their breath. Their bodies moved to the rhythm of their words. Fourteen feet and fourteen arms stepped and pumped and beat as one until at last they'd reached the water. Sarah(?), Gordon the Preacher, Clarence, and the rest threw themselves into the cool and sank to the bottom. They doused their scent, calmed their bodies, slowed their hearts, tended to their cuts, and baptized themselves anew all in one dunk.

Slowed down for the moment, Sarah(?) felt the full weight of her body as she walked through the shallow water. Her joints screamed for rest, but she chanted on.

She popped and cracked the knuckles of her fingers beneath the surface of the water to bring back to them a normal feeling despite the swelling. But it wasn't her fingers or her feet she had to worry with. She felt the shift as soon as she was submerged but kept going anyway. The lowering of the baby in her womb. The first pain shot through her like an arrowhead to the inside of her leg. A warning. One she would have to ignore if she wanted to keep up. If she wanted to make it until they stopped, just before morning.

She kept on walking some, swimming most, following the men in front of her. Every now and again, one would hang back to glance at the map in her hair or draw it out again in the air. They studied the bends and curves she carved with her own fingers before they pushed past her, sloshing water and creating waves as they went.

They ate nothing of the few vittles they'd brought before entering the water, knowing it would need to last them at least a week, maybe more. Spurred on by the adrenaline coursing through their bodies, they at last reached the mouths of the many narrow rivers that fed the bay. As Sarah(?) trudged on, she noticed the men splitting off two by two. Joshua and Clyde went left. Amos and Clarence to the right. Gordon the Preacher and Jedidiah stayed straight. It was then she realized why they'd each had to make their own marks on the ground. Why Clarence had said, "She got one." Each man had his own map. They were to leave as six but end up as one, each man breaking off at different points in the journey together, hoping the many different trails would throw off the dogs and get at least one of them all the way to freedom.

So whose map did Sarah(?) have? Which path had she braided? She tried to catch their eyes, but none looked back, not even Gordon the Preacher. She felt in her hair, wet but still tight to her scalp, and found the starting point of the braids. Where she began marked the Dupree land. She followed the path she'd crossed in her strands until she got to the spot that marked the open mouth of the bay and the straight braid that indicated the way.

Sarah(?) followed behind Gordon the Preacher and Jedidiah, waiting to see which of the two would take her all the way. Whose course had she copied? As they moved into the river, the tree-lined banks rose up beside them. Tall and thin, eerie and ominous, Sarah(?) looked up toward the heavens as another pain in her pelvis gave her pause in the murky brown water. It sent her pitching forward, splashing as she flailed and failed to find her footing.

"She gon' get us caught and killed fa sho'," Jedidiah muttered.

"We ain't long together here," Gordon the Preacher whispered in a gruff voice. "After tonight you'll be off on your own."

"Not if she don't stop with all that ruckus 'lertin' the rollers like she doing."

"You just keep on going your way. We'll go ours."

Jedidiah trudged away from Gordon and Sarah(?), placing distance between him and the ones who could keep him bound. In the middle of the river he walked, only his head and shoulders above the water as Sarah(?) kept in step with Gordon the Preacher in the shallows.

In quiet, anger-stabbed silence they walked until day began to break and they had no choice but to leave the scent-cloaking safety of the water for the inconspicuous obscurity of the trees. Back on land, Sarah(?) followed Gordon the Preacher and Jedidiah away from the water's edge to where the trees nearly touched, roots overlapped, and branches created a shady canopy cover to disappear into.

There is where they began their climb. Jedidiah scaled the thick bark of one of the trunks until he reached a pair of limbs that would hold his weight.

"You gotta go your own way," Gordon the Preacher said before he did the same.

Shooting pains came from every which way now that she was back on dry land. Sarah(?) knew she was in no condition to climb. She wouldn't even be able to get her swollen feet to grip, let alone her swelled hands to brace her weight as she tried to move up. Understanding the plan more fully, she walked away from Gordon the Preacher and Jedidiah resting in the treetops. Limping and waddling, hands in her hair, she made her way through the trees, tracing the straight path she knew was hers, and maybe someone else's, until she found a dip in the dirt carved out by tangled tree roots and filled in with a felled trunk. Sarah(?) pushed her way into the knuckle in the ground and huddled her body in a ball, hoping to calm the waving pains in her womb and put both her and her baby at rest. With her hands knotted together beneath her belly, she held them both firm, humming "Don't Let Nobody Turn You 'Round," and "Follow the Drinking Gourd," mixing melodies on her way to dream.

SARAH(?) HEARD THE HOOVES BEFORE SHE EVER FELT THE HANDS. Their rumble trembled the ground and rent her away from slumber. Caught in her cove, she knew she had but two choices. She could stay crouched and covered and wait to be cornered by the horses and the dogs, or she could run. Her eyes blinked wild and rapid, adjusting to the broad sun as she inched away from her crawl space. Though she heard the coming commotion, they still seemed to be behind her. Padding gently but quickly, Sarah(?) tipped on her toes, watching every step to neither break a branch nor trip over a root or rock as she made her way back to the river. Down the bank and into the water she went as the waves in her womb started up again.

Pains, sharp and deep, forced sounds from her mouth she tried to drown in the water. She submerged herself fully every time she felt them coming. Still the screams wrenched her mouth open, forcing her reflexes to swallow, choke, and gag for air. She tried to measure her movements to the surface. To only allow her nose to break for breath until she could get to the other side. The other bank. But the dogs were in the water, paddling with their paws toward her floundering form.

They latched on once they reached her. One on each arm, biting down with their canines and incisors, forcing her to yelp from the penetrating pain. Sarah(?) tried to wrestle herself away from the pair of hounds. When that didn't work, she tried pulling them in deeper to drown them. But it was too late; Zephaniah Foster had already caught up to where they were. Sitting atop his freshly groomed white racing horse, he looked down on the struggle in the water as he waved a rag in his hand. Sarah(?) recognized the covering she pulled from her head and tucked in her dress, knowing it had fallen in the running and given them away. Their eyes connected, and victory glowered over defeat. A smirk that started at the corner of Zephaniah Foster's mouth spread across his face into an ugly sneer as he swung his legs and dismounted the horse. He trudged down the bank and whistled for the dogs to return to his side as he entered the water in his high boots.

The dogs released Sarah(?), and she sighed momentarily, relieved of the sharp pain. Until the wrenching in her womb started up again. The kicks and punches mixed with the deep waves of contractions sent her pitching forward into the water, doubling over at the waist, begging to the spirits that enchanted the river for relief or death.

Neither arrived.

Only Zephaniah Foster.

His hand seized Sarah(?) by her uncovered head. He dragged her backward through the water and up the bank, where he dropped her in a pile of her own writhing, blubbering bigness.

"I got her," he hollered.

Soon more hooves came galloping to where Zephaniah Foster stood with his catch. His sons, identical twins, Alexander and Antony, sat high upon their horses while Gordon the Preacher and Jedidiah cried from behind after being dragged the distance from their treetop hideouts to Sarah(?)'s cove. She chanced a look at the two men who'd meant to leave her, the ones who blamed her for their capture, and saw blood running from their legs. They'd been hamstrung in haste and dragged yards behind running horses; their cries were the song of pain and anger. Hurt and hatred. The mixed bag of hard emotions that produced the sorrowful soulfulness of the blues and generational trauma. Whomever came after in the lines of these three captives would be cursed with the blood memory of their torture.

"Ooooooowwwwwwww," Sarah(?) cried out from where she cowered.

The baby she carried worked its way down, teasing and testing to prepare her for the pain to come.

"Nigra thought she'd abscond with my property like I wouldn't come after it," Zephaniah Foster spat. "All you niggers belong to me. We'll make sure you don't need any more reminders."

"Father, how would you like to get them back?" Antony asked.

The spitting image of their mother, from their comely faces to their swirling red curls, the twins, only five years older than Sarah(?), waited for their father's word.

"Those two you can drag all the way back to Land's End. This one here"—Zephaniah Foster kicked Sarah(?) in the back with his sopping boot—"needs to go on the flatbed behind the carriage."

He kicked her again, and she splayed on the ground, collapsing over her own distended belly as she cried out in pain. More concerned with what she carried, Zephaniah Foster quickly snatched her up and locked the heavy iron shackles around her wrists.

"Father, have you seen this?" Alexander asked.

"Seen what?"

"Has this wench ever worked for Mother without her head covered?"

"Alexander, what does that have to do with anything? You know your mother won't dare have her back. It was a chance as it was, having her tending in the house, as dark as she is."

"What I mean, Father, is there's something in her hair. Something Mother surely would have caught if she ever had her hair uncovered."

Zephaniah Foster yanked Sarah(?)'s chain, turning her around to see what Alexander referred to. Though dripping wet, tangled with leaves and mud, the map to freedom was unmistakable. With heavy hands he tossed her head back and forth like a ball, assessing the path plotted in the overlapping plaits. Using a finger, he found their position and pressed into her head.

"Two hundred and twenty-two miles you made it with my property." Zephaniah Foster yanked Sarah(?) back by her braids. "That's the number of lashes waiting for you when we get back."

He struck her across the face. The force from his arm and open hand clotheslined her when the blow connected and knocked her back to the ground.

FOR TWO HUNDRED AND TWENTY-TWO MILES, SARAH(?) RODE hog-tied in her chains, lying on her side, on the flatbed behind the carriage driven by Zephaniah Foster. Antony and Alexander had galloped ahead, with Gordon the Preacher and Jedidiah being dragged behind them. Their bodies bounced against the ground in the race to return with hands, feet, legs, and other limbs occasionally tramped by a hoof. In the beginning of the journey, Sarah(?) could count on their consistent screams to keep her company as she howled through the agony of birthing pains. But somewhere along the way, their cries died down to trembled whimpers, and then even those she ceased to hear. By the time they approached the peak of the bay, Gordon the Preacher and Jedidiah were death quiet. Alexander and Antony cut their bodies loose and tossed them in the water.

"It's a shame too," Alexander said. "I was looking forward to delivering their lashes."

"We still have that one." Antony nodded toward where Sarah(?) lay in the flatbed.

"Yes, but Father said he wanted to see to her personally."

Perhaps it was the personal insult that she'd tried to run off with *his* child, though he didn't think of the child as a person to raise but as another thing to have. Whatever the injury, the journey warped Zephaniah Foster's wrath. Once they reached Land's End, they trotted past the quarter shacks, paraded in front of the big house where Missus Elizabeth sat in her rocker sipping sweet tea.

"Who knew the women could be afflicted with the drapetomania as much as the men," she said as the carriage made its way toward the whipping tree, a large oak that stood between the stable and the shanties.

Zephaniah Foster disembarked from the carriage in an even greater rage than when he'd plodded through the river and pulled Sarah(?) backward up the bank. Marching toward the house, he hollered orders.

"Barnabas, dig a hole to protect my property. Make haste or you'll be lashed too.

"Evangeline, I want my property out today. You understand.

"Antony, take my blades to Thomas and have him sharpen them enough to slice ice.

"Alexander, fetch my cats out the house."

"But, Father, we don't have cats," Alexander protested.

"We don't have pets, but we have two cats coiled in the corner of my study. Fetch them for me. It's time to make them sing."

Zephaniah Foster opened the back of the flatbed as *Yas, Suh* and *Yes, Father* rang from the lips of all who were commanded. Sarah(?) locked eyes with him and saw only the frigid stare of a man disconnected from all feeling. He dragged her chain across the flatbed and then carried her bound body to where Barnabas had dug the hole for her stomach so she could lie on her belly.

Prone on the ground, prostrate before the whipping tree, Sarah(?) whimpered and writhed in the dirt as the pains started up again. Her movements muted as Zephaniah Foster released her legs, granting himself full access to her back. He ran the chain still connected to the cuffs on her arms around the base of the tree, the chain around the shackles on her feet he secured to one of the wheels of the carriage. Sarah(?) was pulled taut, unable to roll, shrivel, or wiggle away from the pain coming from inside her own body, let alone the crack of the lash once Zephaniah Foster started swinging.

Alexander returned with the cats, which had spiky barbs on their tips.

"Thank you, now gather everyone around. I want them to see what happens when you get a notion toward freedom and the audacity to chase it."

"With a map no less," Alexander added.

"With a map no less," Zephaniah repeated.

Alexander met Antony by the blacksmith's workshop and passed the word to gather everyone around the whipping tree. It was a message that didn't take long to spread and a task that needed no hurry to complete. Everyone in the quarters had heard them arrive. Those who hadn't been directly employed to assist in what was sure to be a spectacle already crept around the edges, curious about the cruelty that was going to be administered.

Standing above Sarah(?), a cat in each hand, Zephaniah Foster bellowed to his progeny and property.

"They say a war's coming," he began. "I say let it come. It's time these Northern-born Yankees understand that everything they have comes from us. The cotton of their clothes and the crops that make up the food on their tables. It all comes from right here. Without it, without men like me, they'd have nothing."

As Zephaniah Foster spoke, the audience watched his face contort and change colors. The red deepened beneath his skin as his cheeks blew out words and sweat dripped from his brows, nose, and lips, matting his hair to his scalp. In the same shirt, work pants, and high boots from the journey to retrieve Sarah(?), he marched amongst the crowd, dragging the cats and jerking them for emphasis.

"Slavery now, slavery tomorrow, slavery forever," he screamed. "We had to go two hundred and twenty-two miles to Tuscaloosa to bring her back. For every mile it's a lash. And if one of you looks away, there's two hundred and twenty-two lashes for you too."

Zephaniah Foster turned away from the crowd of somber brown faces to where Sarah(?) lay on the ground. She rattled her chains and whimpered from the dull ache of built-up pressure and the sharp shooting pains of her coming babe.

The cats cracked.

Nine knotted tails ripped open what was left of the material clothing her body. Nine more followed, tearing into her skin. Sarah(?) howled as Zephaniah Foster worked the whips in continuous circles. Antony and Alexander kept count. A strike from each cat, a couplet, counted as one complete whip.

Sarah(?) was beaten until red blood ran from her body and colored the brown dirt beneath her with rivulets of her life. By the last set of lashes, she no longer shrieked in pain. Her body no longer jerked between the chains. Not even the worming down of the babe in her belly, ready to open her up, brought a sound from Sarah(?)'s lips. She dangled near death, wishing it would kiss her good night.

"Antony! Bring me my blades," Zephaniah Foster hollered when he had finished the flogging.

The twin ran from where he stood to his father's side with the satchel of sharpened knives.

"This is what happens when you chase after what you were never meant to have," Zephaniah Foster yelled, selecting the longest razor. "You niggers have got to understand that this is the only life you'll have. Forget freedom. It's not coming for you. And if the Yankees have a notion to take it for you, we'll fight 'em until every last one of 'em is dead."

Zephaniah Foster walked toward where Sarah(?)'s head rested on the ground. Her breath was shallow, barely blowing at the dirt. He lifted her by the tails of her braids, holding them tight at the base of her neck. Sarah(?)'s eyes didn't even flutter from being pulled against her wounds. No sounds came from her mouth. Her back, a mangle of mush, contracted in on itself, congealing the blood as he used one hand to hold up her head. With the other he placed the razor to Sarah(?)'s scalp and dragged it back against the grain of her hair. He worked methodically, following the twists and bends of the plotted paths to a freedom she would never have, until her long locks were shorn and fell into the cracks of her opened skin.

"Alexander! Unchain her. Antony, get my brine."

Antony ran quickly for the barrel kept filled to the brim beside the whipping tree. He pushed it slowly toward where Sarah(?)'s body lay on the ground, lining it up so that when he tipped it over all contents would fall in her cuts.

"I'm done, Father," Alexander said once he'd released her.

"Pour," Zephaniah Foster yelled.

Antony kicked over the barrel. The sting of the solution made of vinegar, turpentine, salt, and red pepper brought Sarah(?) back from the brink of wherever she had been. She emitted a shriek so piercing and loud, the flocks beating their wings in the sky changed direction. But no one noticed the birds. No one looked up. No one looked away. They watched her pain, were witness to her torture.

"Evangeline! Deliver my property."

"Massa, let me take her in the—"

"Right here!" he demanded. "You do it right here."

Evangeline scurried over to Sarah(?)'s side and tried to gently turn her over onto her raw back. Sarah(?) kicked and twisted away, trying to find a salve, a balm for her body, but there was only dirt, only hair, only brine. She shook in pain as Evangeline pushed her legs open.

"I sees the head," she said aloud. "Push for me, and it'll be over soon."

She coached Sarah(?) in a gentle voice. Sweet and full of song. "Push for me and your babe'll be here and you'll be on the other side of it all."

With an unknown source of strength, Sarah(?) wrestled herself up to her elbows, bared her teeth and body, and gave a good push. And then another. And another. And another . . .

"Wh-aaaaaaahhhh," the baby wailed.

"Issa girl," Evangeline said, pride pronounced in her voice.

Zephaniah Foster marched over and with the same blade he'd used to cut Sarah(?)'s hair he cut the cord.

"Take her back with you," he said.

Evangeline didn't even protest about how she still needed to deliver the afterbirth. She wrapped the baby in her apron, clutched her to her chest, and pushed through the crowd of people standing shoulder to shoulder, stiff with the images of what they'd witnessed. Brown eyes dead, muscles flexed and tensed, they'd never forget what they'd seen. What they were about to see.

Allowed to turn her back, Evangeline was walking away when she heard the first of Sarah(?)'s new screams. Piercing as it was, it curdled her blood and even quieted her baby. She turned around and from the middle of the crowd she saw Antony and Alexander standing where they had rechained Sarah(?)'s body to the wheel and whipping tree. Zephaniah Foster stood over her with his blade in hand, cutting each one of Sarah(?)'s fingers below the knuckle until she had nothing but nubs.

"This is what happens when you run," Zephaniah Foster yelled to the hushed crowd.

He snatched Sarah(?) by the collar of her shredded dress and swiped the blade once across her neck. The baby kicked and shrieked against Evangeline as if she too felt what her ma'am was feeling. The little bundle wailed with wanton abandon, crying all the tears Sarah(?) never would.

No one looked away. No one blinked. Not even Sarah(?).

Separated from her body, she still wasn't dead. They didn't know that while bodies could be kidnapped and used, bought, sold, and bruised, seasoned until broken . . . minds could never be tamed.

OOH, THE YAM SMELLS SO GOOD. MAMA AND THE OTHER WIVES HAVE BEEN *preparing the continuation day celebration for Baba for many moons and now it's finally here. Pounded yam and plantain, a whole roasted goat, fish, and a new drum for Baba as a gift. I helped Mama fit the skin tight so it would talk.*

Ba–ta–ta. Ba–ta–ta.

She won't mind if I play a few taps.

Ba–ta–ta. Ba–ta–ta.

Wait! What's that?

Ba–ta–ta. Ba–ta–ta.

Why is it so warm? So bright?
Ba-ta-ta. Ba-ta-ta.
I can't see.
Mama, is that you?
It's me—

Epilogue

When Gladys told Tati and Nadia all she knew just minutes into the new millennium, she began with her return to Land's End in 1960 with Eugene and four-year-old Nadia, just five days before Jubi was put in the ground. Emma followed shortly thereafter. They were eighty and ninety-nine then. Laid side by side in a bed of the old house, in the room that had once belonged to Emma, George, and Jeremiah, they mustered an unknown strength to speak what they had never spoken before.

Jubi's marriage to Logan. Their bloodline connections on both sides of the tracks. The admission punched Gladys in the gut and hollowed Ruby right where she stood. But there was more. Emma told all who gathered the truth about a grief-stricken George and the boys she couldn't keep. When Gladys walked Tati and Nadia through the Bible of names, she told them the same and about the curse that, maybe, broke with her. For she was the first one to keep all the babies she'd wanted. The first one to have boys. The first to be released from the blood. A mercy from the one no one knew. Gladys told them her legend, and by the time she left she had but one request.

"When I go to the other side, take me home."

It was on the trip to honor Gladys's final wishes in 2019 that Tati first felt the pull of the land. While the Dupree beach had long been taken by the local government through eminent domain, the farm was still in the family. The old house, like Ms. Teena's next door, was beyond disrepair, and the house Sampson had built was a cottage for a caretaker. Tati walked the grounds, through the dirt patch where nothing grew and between the graves. The three crosses for the boys tucked in the fence. The headstones for Emma, Jubi, and Ruby and the new plot where Gladys had just been laid.

By the time she'd made it to the cottage and walked the rooms where Gladys grew up, she was convinced of but one thing.

"Mama, let's stay," she'd said.

"Tati, I can't just pick up and leave. I have a life."

"Ask Mr. Curtis to come too," Tati suggested.

Nadia had met Curtis Knight when Tati was still in college. Curly salt-and-pepper hair, mustached and goateed, he was attractive in the way of a shorter Rick Fox. At the time they were both in their midforties and had children from previous relationships and a want to be in something real without a whole lot of drama. Over the years they'd dated, gone on vacations, and created a life together even though they maintained separate homes. Nothing that couldn't be overcome by an overnight bag and making space in drawers when they wanted to be closer. Which they often did.

Nadia looked at Tati curiously. "I guess," she said, for she felt the pull too. The needling to find a reason to prolong leaving the Southern land.

How? was the only question left to answer. They returned to Chicago after Gladys's service as planned, but they knew the trip would be temporary. They gave themselves a year to close down their lives in the city and begin again in Land's End.

For Nadia, that included selling the salon she had opened after

Tati graduated undergrad. The storefront on Seventy-Ninth Street between Yale and Princeton Avenues had been home to Nadia's Nubian Salon for sixteen years. It featured all the fixtures and comforts she had first procured for the salon in her basement, multiplied by eight stations: large burgundy chairs, silk capes, and the latest R&B, especially Mary, played from speakers mounted conspicuously throughout the space. She had also brought in two nail techs. When people came through her doors, she wanted them to stay awhile, to fellowship in the ways that only women can when, for a few hours, their heads were in someone else's hands and their hearts were free from the stress and burdens of kith, kin, or some man they loved, sometimes more than they loved themselves.

Selling what she had worked so hard to build over thirty-five years gave Nadia both grief and gumption. Doing hair, owning her own business, had been the backup. Something she had never planned for but believed the one Gladys had told her about, whose name no one knew, had destined for her all along. What else could it be? It was as if she was marked from birth. Selling it off felt like both betrayal and freedom. The ending of one legacy and the beginning of another.

As for their homes, Curtis sold his house on 125th and Longwood, while Nadia decided to rent hers out.

"It's time to make a commitment we can't easily walk away from," he'd told her one night as they lay in his bed.

"And you wanna prove that by moving with me and Tati to Land's End?"

"Nadia, we've been committed to each other for years. There's nothing left to prove. You know where I stand."

And she did. He'd been kind and patient with her. Given her space to soften and room to rely on someone else. He'd made her feel safe and opened himself so that there were no secrets between them, not even closed doors when they went to the bathroom. He'd loved her with all of himself and in turn she couldn't help but do the same.

Together they packed his home and then hers from top to bottom, along with help from her brothers and their wives and children, and finally with Toya, Tati, and even Desirée, who was home between photo shoots in her busy career as a photographer that took her all over the world. The grievances and grudges between the women had dissolved with the truth.

"I can't believe y'all leaving for the country," Toya said, sitting on the futon in the basement. Nadia had kept her original salon intact despite expanding to the storefront. She still preferred to do her hair at home, along with Tati, who'd started coming to get her hair done on Sunday mornings in Mimi's stead.

"It's time to do something new," Nadia answered.

She couldn't explain what she felt in Alabama. The urge to set roots on land that, even though it was rightfully hers, she never knew. It's a trying thing to get people in the North to understand why, as a Black person, you choose to live in the South. A land of terror and terrible memory, yes, but also of such beauty and rich history, despite the blood.

But Tati knew the reason. The real answer. She said, "It's the right thing to do."

Once Curtis's and Nadia's homes were emptied and loaded onto trucks to drive south, Tati's condo in the South Loop was next. A junior partner for Sidley Austin specializing in labor and employment, Tati had wanted for years to do something different. Coaching track at her old high school and sometimes reading her poetry at open mic nights in the city gave her moments of joy and snatches of satisfaction, but what she was looking for was peace and maybe a partner. It was something about Land's End that said it was there she could have both. And she was determined to get it.

She sold her two-bedroom, two-and-a-half-bath place on South Wabash, not caring, wanting, or needing the security that could have come from renting or subletting. While Nadia felt the call in Land's End, she wasn't as convinced as Tati or even Curtis about it being something they could do forever, somewhere they would live forever. If she had learned anything in her sixty-three years, it was that plans change, sometimes by mistake, sometimes on purpose, even if you don't know it at the time. She kept her house because it was both an investment and a testament to all she'd come through. The same reason Gladys had kept up the property in Land's End.

When Tati, Nadia, and Curtis arrived at their new home in January of 2020, it was eleven months after Gladys had been put in the ground beside her beloveds. They greeted the caretaker, Ethan Danube, who had expected their arrival from the correspondence Tati kept up after Gladys died. In the warm, dry air of a Southern winter, Ethan handed over the keys to the cottage and Tati paid him his severance out of the proceeds from the sale of her condo. He then got in his pickup truck and headed across the tracks to where he lived with his own wife and children. In all her emails to Ethan, Tati never did inquire after his family. She didn't want to stir up trouble before she had gotten settled, but the nagging of knowing a Danube man never left her.

"What do you want to do first?" Tati asked Nadia and Curtis once Ethan was gone.

Holding on to Curtis's hand, Nadia looked over the land, the cottage in front of them, and the fence to the left, where she could just make out the crosses of Emma's lost boys.

"I don't know," Nadia answered. "We can do whatever we wanna do, right, Miss Moneybags?"

"Mama, it's not even like that," Tati deflected. "I got enough to get us through a year, maybe two, between my savings and the condo sale, but maybe you should open a shop. Collect some booth rent along with the rent money from the house."

"Won't be no need for that," Curtis said. "I got us."

"We are retired and plan to act like it," Nadia added.

"Mmmm." Tati scrunched up her face. "Y'all nasty."

"Old ain't dead." Nadia squeezed Curtis's hand.

He kissed her temple. Tati rolled her eyes and headed toward the door. Nadia joined her while Curtis hung back. They walked into the cottage together, the house of Gladys's youth, through the rooms and out the back door. On the porch, where Sampson had once been barred from entering the built-upon shanty, they looked out over the burial space and paid silent respect to the loved ones lost, known and unknown.

As they went about the business of moving in, Tati's first step was getting the land listed on the National Register of Historic Places, the old house preserved, and the cottage equipped with a salon space for Nadia. One she insisted on.

"I still gotta do my hair. Besides, it's memories."

"You still gon' do my hair, right?" Tati had asked.

"Yours and mine," Nadia had said. "Yours and mine . . . especially since I don't have no grandbabies."

Curtis and a contractor built a screened-in carport with a walled-off room where Nadia set up her salon chair from the basement along with her hair stove and hung her neon sign. It was in that space that Nadia, again, broached the subject of babies with Tati.

"It's too quiet around here," she said, standing behind the chair, preparing to do Tati's hair.

"We live in the country. What else did you expect?" Tati answered, flipping through an issue of *Rolling Stone* where Desirée had shot the cover star.

"I expected it to hopefully be more than just us," Nadia said. "All them stories your mimi told us, it don't seem right for us to be the last two."

"Gotta have a man to have a baby," Tati lamented.

With all that had happened with Roman and all she knew from

Nadia and Gladys, she had been wary about babies ever since. It
was a dealbreaker for the men she'd dated seriously. Her hesitancy
to start a family. Her lack of desire to carry. Her diligence in sticking to a prescribed method of birth control. But as fate would have
it, there's not much to do when the world shuts down and you've
moved a thousand miles away from home besides surf the internet
and scroll through apps.

She changed her location from Chicago to Land's End, expanded the radius of which she was willing to travel for a date, and
scrolled and swiped until she'd made a match.

His name was Joshua Freeman IV. Born in Toronto, he'd moved
to the States as an adult and made Mobile home. A professor in the
sociology department at Talladega College, he kept a small apartment near the campus during the semester but preferred to spend
his time near water. Never married, no children, Tati and Joshua
were the forty-year-old unicorns they didn't know they had been
looking for.

Dates on Zoom, with dinner delivered via Uber Eats, turned into
face-to-face meetups at beaches and parks. When Joshua came to call
on Tati in Land's End he too felt the call gurgling from the ground,
though he couldn't name it. He thought the eerie feeling was due to
the graves behind the cottage and not his own blood alighting with
familiarity. Chasing after ghosts had never been his thing, despite his
profession. He knew his family started from somewhere in Alabama,
but where exactly, he couldn't call. Those stories had stopped being
passed down by the time he came along, but he indulged Tati on
trips to the courthouse and the archives all over the state in search of
a name. With enough money in the bank, and a lower cost of living,
instead of jumping back into law, Tati gave herself fully to writing,
penning the stories of her family and the land completely in verse.

She and Joshua spent their days wearing white gloves, elbows-
deep in dusty record rooms searching manifestos, captain's logs,

and personal diaries, delicately photocopying what they could, and taking notes of what they could not. Her only lead had been Mimi's Bible and the 1870 census, where she saw with her own eyes Evangeline's mark and Emma recorded on her own, with Zephaniah Foster Dupree mistakenly listed as her child and not her father. As for his last will and testament, given to Emma with the Bible after his death, and the records Evangeline pulled from the big house, they were lost to time, all unbeknownst to Tati.

With the information she did gather, Tati would write for a few hours in the evening while Joshua prepared syllabi and assignments for his online classes, before they found themselves in bed, sometimes their own, sometimes a hotel if they were too far to return. They'd make a night of conversation and questions, the mental stimulation increasing sexual appetite, which they indulged with reckless abandon.

Naked, minds full, and bodies spent, they clung to one another as if they had found every answer they'd been looking for, though they had none. Only with Joshua was Tati not so hesitant, did her desire shift and her diligence wane.

It was summer, a Sunday, two years after the shutdown, when she realized she was carrying. Or, more specifically, that Nadia pointed it out to her.

"When you plan to tell me you pregnant?" she asked casually.

"Tell you I'm what?" Tati asked, incredulous.

Nadia continued maneuvering around the kitchen, washing rice and chopping okra. She'd taken to cooking after discovering a tin of Gladys's recipes written in her own hand when they cleaned out her house after she died. Amongst them sweet potato pone, a pan of which she had in the oven beside the corn bread. Nadia shook her hands dry in the sink and stared out the window that looked over the fork in the land.

"You glowing, your face is round, and your breasts are bigger than they've ever been."

Tati paused, touched her body. "I thought it was just getting older."

"Girl, you know gravity don't work that way." Nadia turned around, a smile dancing across her lips. "When the last time you had a period?"

Tati paused again. Thought. Counted. Couldn't remember. A sheepish grin spread across her face.

"You better tell him," Nadia advised.

Neither of them acknowledged the slight crack in her voice. The wounds from Roman they both bore but they didn't speak of. He was as much on the other side as the ones laid out back. Instead, Tati invited Joshua for dinner. Over smothered okra and fried catfish, corn bread, sweet potato pone, and sweet tea, Tati broke the news. The expectation she'd confirmed with a test from the pharmacy.

"Are you serious?" Joshua asked, pushing long locks away from his face.

"I wouldn't play about something like this, sugah," Tati said.

"Well, shit, let's get married!" Joshua jumped out of his seat and pulled Tati out of hers. Though she was glad for his excitement, his jubilance didn't carry.

"For what?" she asked as he rocked her side to side.

Joshua pulled back and looked at her squarely. "If we're having a boy, I want him to have my name. It's tradition."

"Most folks in our family have girls first," Nadia said, from where she sat beside Curtis at the table.

"And she can still have your name, even if we're not married," Tati added.

"They're still yours," Curtis said, trying to soften the sting. "Both of them."

"Is it because *you* don't want my name?" Joshua asked Tati, his hurt unmistakable.

Tati didn't answer. Not right away. In the moment she didn't quite know what she wanted. She had told Joshua about Roman. About growing up without him, writing poems dedicated to his absence, and what happened when she found him. He understood why she had avoided children, and in a way, also marriage. But here were both offered on the same day. A baby she hadn't planned for but hadn't prevented, which she planned to keep, and a man who wanted them both. Over time she said yes. And though they didn't have a big production of a wedding to entice Instagram envy, the small ceremony at St. Joseph's just up the road from the farm where only their immediate families were in attendance was enough for them both.

In a loose white dress that gave room for her growing belly to breathe, Tatiana Merét Washington exchanged vows with Joshua Daryl Freeman IV. She stood in the same place where Gladys had stood with Eugene, the circumstances similar but different. And when it came time for the birth, she opted to stay home and have a midwife come to her. In a new house she and Joshua had built behind George's addition, she sat in a birthing pool erected in her living room and ushered forth life from her womb.

A girl of medium brown with a head of jet-black curls. Their small family complete and full. They walked with her, at first strapped to Tati's chest, and then in a stroller, from their door to the shack, where they ran her small fingers over the plaque affixed to the cured wood that established part of her family line. They walked her through the graves and grass to Nadia's cottage, naming all that they knew. They gave her a litany, a liturgy, a history to hold on to and recall at will.

At the cottage, Tati and Joshua found Nadia in the carport salon. Emma's mirror stood in the corner. Nadia faced away from it, her head down as she worked a flat iron roots to ends in her graying hair.

"What y'all doing?" Nadia asked.

"Taking a break from writing," Tati said.

"Thought we'd walk with the baby for a while," Joshua answered.

Nadia turned to look at Tati as she held the baby. "When you gon' start doing this child's hair?" she asked. "She's eight months. You need to start her in a routine now or she gon' be tender-headed."

"I do it," Tati said.

"Not enough."

"I told Tati to let me cut it off," Joshua joked from his seat at the dryer.

Both Nadia and Tati stared at him as he chuckled to himself, a blank gaze laid over both their countenances.

"It was just a joke, geez."

"You know some things we don't joke about," Nadia said. "Why don't you go on in the house with Curtis. I think he's watching the game or something."

"I know when I'm not wanted," Joshua said, feigning hurt, as he retreated from the salon.

Once he left, Nadia clipped her half-done hair out of the way and then grabbed the baby from Tati's arms.

"C'mon, let your nana do your hair," she said.

Nadia sat in the seat of the washbowl with the baby clutched between her thighs. The little girl pointed at Emma's mirror. Babbled. "Ma, ma, ma, ma."

"Yes, baby, that's your mama right there," Nadia said, parting her granddaughter's hair with ease. "So how's the writing going?"

"I finished the dedication," Tati answered.

"The dedication?" Nadia repeated, still focused on parting the baby's hair. "Ain't that only a name?" she said, as she tried to coax the little girl away from the mirror, but she was stubborn. She kept looking at herself. Kept saying, "Ma, ma, ma."

"Yes, I'm mama," Tati said, standing in front of the mirror. To Nadia she said, "The dedication is more than just one name."

"Well, let me hear it," Nadia said.

Tati pulled her cell phone out of her pocket, opened the file with her manuscript, and read:

Dear Sa'rah,

> *Who celebrates the dead?*
> *Who claps for the decapitated?*
> *The discarded*
> *The forgotten*
> *The answer is*
> *We do*
> *We speak*
> *Her*
> *And Emma*
> *And Jubilee, who preferred Jubi*
> *And Ruby*
> *And Gladys, who I called Mimi*
> *And Nadia, who you call Nana*
> *And me, Tatiana, who you call Mama*
> *And you*
>
> *Who takes pride in legend?*
> *Who boasts about the beheaded?*
> *The cursed*
> *The christened*
> *The crowned*
> *The answer is we do*
> *We speak*
> *To the land where she came in chains*
> *Soil made rich and fertile by our blood*

Connected in our bones
Bound through time like the sinews and tissues
She was here
As you are now

Who sings a mother's song
Who finds joy in the souls on the other side
The angels
The ancestors
The ascendant architects of our purpose
The answer is we do
Because we remember

Acknowledgments

Dear God, where do I begin? With you. Lord, thank you for giving me this story, and to all the angels and ancestors who've whispered to me in the writing, thank you.

This novel came together through a myriad of inspirations. Ashanti Anderson, your poem "Busts of the Beheaded" in *Black Under* and our conversation about it never left me and told me what Sarah(?)'s ending would be when I unlocked the first line. Deesha Philyaw, thank you for EVERYTHING. I've told you in person and in writing (several times now) that you talking about how you wrote "Peach Cobbler" and the workshop you teach because of it, took my "simple" family story about a teenaged girl who didn't know her father and expanded it into a generational family epic, with my own chilling first line. Ms. Honorée Fannone Jeffers, your encouragement to get an agent confirmed for me that I was ready to try again for big publishing after years self-publishing. You and the rainstorm during the Miami Book Fair in 2022, but that's another story for another day.

To Celestial "Mbinguni" Holmes, who was with me during that rainstorm and for all of my personal storms while writing this book, thank you. Thank you for reading the raw pages as I sent them to you and believing in Tati and all the daughters. You know you got next.

Jenn Baker and Andrea Pura, thank you for taking the time to talk and strategize with me while we were at Blue Mountain Center.

Danielle Chiotti, thank you for keeping your inbox open to me as I revised that original "simple" story. Thank you, Adiba Nelson, for seeing me when you didn't even know me and for connecting me to Jess Regel. And Jess, thank you for referring me to Peter, my agent.

Peter, I knew your name before I knew you. Your reputation precedes you and it is a good one. Thank you for opening your DMs after seeing my laments about querying on Twitter, responding to me when I got saucy, and offering to represent me the same day I finalized my divorce. One door closed and another burst wide open. I will never forget that day. You changed my life on a day my life changed, and I am so grateful.

To my editor, Alison Callahan, unbeknownst to me you've loved Tati since 2021 when I submitted for the Gallery Books contest. Thank you for championing her story once she crossed your desk two years later in her mostly final form, for loving all the daughters (I know Gladys is your favorite), and for the thoughtful care you took in editing my work. This experience has been beyond what I ever imagined or even dreamed of and it's because of you.

Deep thanks and gratitude go to Jen Bergstrom and the entire Scout Press/Gallery Books/S&S team. I'd also like to thank every guest who has come on *Black & Published*. Your journeys inspired me to keep going when I wanted to give up.

To my roommates, the Fly Duval Chicks, and my crazy Carrageous friend, thank you for doing life with me.

And finally, to my family, especially my children, thank you for loving me.

Love always,
Nikesha